The sky was suddenly full of large black ships, braking hard with their forward engines as they moved in rapidly to surround the three carriers. Each ship was long, wide and flat of hull, in many ways very much like the Starwolf Carriers in form but only a third as large. Unlike nearly all union ships, they were as black as space, without windows or running lights. The similarities between the two types of ships were so pronounced that they looked more like companions from the same fleet than well-matched opponents.

At least the mock Starwolf cruisers had not yet launched their fighters, and that gave Velmeran a chance to strike first. The Starwolves were outnumbered five to one, but their carriers were still faster, better shielded and better armed. Velmeran was about to order the carriers to fire their conversion cannons when he realized the mock Starwolves were holding their positions.

"Message coming in," Korlaran reported.

Velmeran nodded. "Let me hear it."

"Commander, this is Captain Jaeryn of the *Avenger*," the young male voice declared boldly. "I ask you to surrender."

STARWOLVES
TACTICAL ERROR

Also by Thorarinn Gunnarsson

STARWOLVES

STARWOLVES:
BATTLE OF THE RING

STARWOLVES TACTICAL ERROR

THORARINN GUNNARSSON

WARNER BOOKS

A Time Warner Company

WARNER BOOKS EDITION

Copyright © 1991 by Thorarinn Gunnarsson
All rights reserved.

Questar® is a registered trademark of Warner Books, Inc.

Cover design by Don Puckey
Cover illustration by John Harris

Warner Books, Inc.
666 Fifth Avenue
New York, NY 10103

 A Time Warner Company

Printed in the United States of America

First Printing: April, 1991

10 9 8 7 6 5 4 3 2 1

THE CREW OF
THE **METHRYN**

Velmeran: The Methryn's captain, although called by the Starwolf title of Commander. (Captain is the formal title for a pack leader.)

Valthyrra: The persona of the Methryn's sentient computer system. Although the ship itself is simply the Methryn, she is often referred to as Valthyrra Methryn.

Consherra: The Methryn's first officer and Helm, she is the ship's second in command. She is older than Velmeran by several years, and served in the same position before he became Commander.

Venn Keflyn: A non-humanoid alien, a Valtrytian of Altrys, who has been an advisor aboard the Methryn for the past two decades.

Keflyn: The daughter of Velmeran and Consherra, and named after Venn Keflyn. She is young, twenty years of age, and a very capable pilot in Baressa's pack.

Baressa: A senior pack leader, she was a teacher and supporter of Velmeran's when he was younger.

Baress: A member (male) of Velmeran's special tactics team.

Tresha: The Methryn's (female) chief engineer.

Dyenlayk: The Methryn's (female) chief medic.

Cargin: The Methryn's Weapons Officer, his main weapon console is adjacent to Consherra's helm station.

Larenta: The Officer (female) at the Methryn's scanner station.

Korlaran: The Methryn's (female) Communications Officer.

OTHER STARWOLVES

Tregloran: The Commander of the Vardon, and a former student of Velmeran's.

Theralda Vardon: The sentient computer system of the Vardon.

Maeken Kea: A Starwolf spy, although she is not herself a Kelvessan but the sterile offspring of the mating of a true human and a female of Trader stock, now a separate species adapted for the stresses of spaceflight. She has been with the Starwolves for twenty years, having come aboard the Methryn as a stowaway. She has lately been aboard the Vardon with her Starwolf mate Tregloran.

Bill: A sentry automation of Union construction and 're-formed' by Velmeran for Lenna Makayen's use as a spy. In form he is white and heavily armored, with a large main hull on four long legs, no arms, and a small head. He seems to possess a crude personality, although his actual sentience is limited.

Quendari Valcyr: One of the first Starwolf carriers, she was lost testing an experimental jump drive, and has been locked within a continental glacier on Terra for thousands of years.

Denna: The Vardon's First Officer (female).

Daelyn: Commander of the Karvand, and Velmeran's older half-sister.

THE REPUBLIC

Admiral Laroose: The elder commander of the Republic's military concerns, he is in theory Velmeran's superior but has deferred to the Starwolf's leadership for twenty years. His former title (in the previous story) was that of Fleet Commander, a title that Velmeran now holds.

THE TRAITORS

Alac Delike: The President of the Republic, a weak and fearful man.

Arlon Saith: First Senator, therefore the elected leader for the Republic Senate.

Marten Alberes: Party Chairman, leader of the political party that now controls the Republic Senate.

THE UNION

Donalt Trace: Sector Commander of the Rane Sector and now High Commander of the Combined Union Fleet, his specific duty is to destroy the Starwolves.

Maeken Kea: A shrewd Union Captain (female) and now Trace's assistant.

Richart Lake: Councilor (political leader) of the Rane Sector, and Donalt Trace's cousin.

Barg: A security guard on the ice planet.

Salgey: A security guard on the ice planet.

OTHERS

Iyan Makayen: Lenna's full-human half-brother, he is a constable on the independent colony of Kanis.

Jon Addesin: Captain of the Free Trader tramp freighter Thermopylae; which serves the Feldenneh colony on Alzmedz.

Derrighan: A Feldennye of a feral, vaguely humanoid race. The shipping master of the Feldenneh colony, and a secret representative of his government.

Kalmedhae: The elder leader of the Feldenneh colony.

- 1 -

The freighter slipped smoothly out of starflight well short of its target, coasting into system at high speed. It was small for an interstellar cargo craft, well under a hundred meters in length, looking more like a large tender used to offload the immense bulk freighters than a starship in its own right. Four main drives were tucked tightly within the fixed inner portion of its variable-geometry wings, now swept full back for flight, while a deceptively small but powerful stardrive was fitted neatly between the twin stabilizers of its tail.

Swift and powerful, the ship was in fact the commercial variant of a successful but antiquated missile carrier. And as such, it was the first cousin of the freighter that Lenna Makayen had flown before she had left Kalennes to join the Starwolves, the major difference being that her ship had not been fitted with a stardrive. Sitting in the jump seat behind the pilot, she found everything about this little ship refreshingly familiar. Perhaps surprisingly familiar might have been a better phrase, since she had not seen that freighter of her's in twenty years.

The years had passed swiftly; they had been so busy, but it had still been a long time. Starwolves never seemed to age, but she knew that she had. She was a long way from being old, still in her mid-forties, but she was no longer young. The crushing G's that were an unavoidable part of their environment were no longer

1

quite so easy to take, and it was sometimes a little hard to get out of bed in a ship where the temperature was kept as brisk as an autumn morning for the comfort of its rightful inhabitant. Her remaining years with the Starwolves were already numbered, so it was not too soon to think about what she would do with herself after her retirement. She had been with them two decades, and no one had said a word about pensions.

Lenna was herself the sterile offspring of a Terran descendant and a Trader, a separate species that had evolved slowly from human stock during their long adaptation to the crushing stresses of spaceflight. But as quick and strong as she was, she could not begin to match the tremendous power and durability of the Kelvessan, that space-faring race known as the Starwolves. Theirs was an entirely artificial biochemistry, able to endure the flesh-ripping accelerations of their swift fighters and carriers, possessing speed-of-light reflexes and the strength to function under crushing G's. Hers was only nature's best mimicry of their artificial perfection.

The Starwolves had been created in the depths of time five hundred centuries before, as the last, desperate attempt of the fading Terran Republic to resist the tyrannical conquests of the Union. And after all that time, both they and their ancient war still existed, the Starwolves winning every battle, but lacking the independent initiative to pursue the war to its conclusion. The Starwolves had themselves been evolving with time, only now achieving the self-possession to determine their own future plans, and the first thing they desired was an end to this long, pointless war.

It seemed that both sides were equally determined to have a final end to this long conflict. The Union was dying, ravaged from within by genetic deterioration. It had its own brutal plan to save themselves, but they first had to be rid of the distraction of the Starwolves. The last battle had begun, and Lenna had been a part of it from the first when she had been a stowaway on the carrier Methryn. She had stayed on as their expert spy, able to go places where their elfin faces and double sets of arms would betray them immediately for what they were.

But now times had changed, and the old days were gone forever. She had left the Methryn over a year earlier, having decided to stay with her mate Tregloran when he had gone over to be the captain of the newly-built Vardon, leaving Velmeran and Consherra and all of her old friends. She thought that she would still be seeing enough of them, considering how closely the two ships would surely be working together. Tregloran was himself no longer the eager, awkward boy she had first met, but the calm, rational leader he had been trained to become, in most ways a lesser copy of Velmeran himself. It was hard enough to have a relationship with someone of a completely different species, although people in every sense of the word had been doing that for a very long time. Part of the problem was in having a mate who was still very young, while she watched her comparatively short time slipping by.

Lenna looked up, checking their approach on the scan monitor. The ship was making a secret approach, dropping out of starflight well short of its destination, then coasting in at high speed, braking gradually only near the end of its run. As an atmospheric-capable missile carrier, the aging ship did possess rather antiquated stealth capabilities, at least as far as Union technology had been capable of achieving. Certainly it lacked the ability to cloak like the big Starwolf carriers. They could not hope to remain undetected all the way in, but this tactic might allow them to get fairly close. Then they would break for a rapid dash in, accomplish their mission, and retreat as fast as that small but spirited stardrive would carry them.

"There's a lot of natural debris in this system," the captain offered, glancing at her over the back of his seat. "We could still swing back out and hide ourselves, in case you need us."

Lenna shook her head firmly. "They would know that you hadn't left and that would put them on their guard. Besides, they're subtle, I can tell you, waiting to pounce on you when you least suspect."

He shrugged. "I just want it understood that we're willing to do that for you, if it would help. You're a long way from home, and no one has told me how you plan to get out again."

"No?" Lenna was surprised; security dictated that outsiders, even these allies, should know as little as possible of secret missions. But things had gone a little too far. "Bill has an achronic transceiver all his own. Once we discover what we're after, we'll call in the Starwolves to take care of things."

Lenna did not really care to talk about a coming mission this late in the game. She knew the plan already, but even after all these years she was still subject to stage fright. Things had been much easier when she had only worked alone or with Starwolves, but that had not lasted long.

The Union was losing its internal battle of control; it's bold but wholly unnecessary program of mass sterilization had been predictably very unpopular. More and more colonies and impoverished fringe worlds were turning to the Starwolves to support their dangerous bids for independence. In the past ten years, a broad underground network of rebellious spies and quiet saboteurs had extended deeply into even the inner worlds.

This little freighter had been called up just for her use from the underground; she had been working with their people quite a lot over the past few years. Most often she pretended to be one of them, hiding her association with the Starwolves. Rebels were occasionally caught, and she did not want the Union to learn that the Starwolves were using a spy who actually lived and worked with them. A large part of her unique advantage was that no one had ever expected her existence, more than human but less than Kelvessan and well able to live with either race. Even the two crewmembers of this little ship had no idea of her name or past, just as she knew nothing about them.

As often as she had been through this before, she still worried about these two. While she might be going into a secret enemy stronghold, it was possible they had the more dangerous part. They had to get in close enough to put her and Bill overboard and then disguise that landing by drawing attention to themselves, leading the inevitable attack away by staying out of starflight until the last possible moment. Only a stingship could follow this swift freighter into starflight; at least they did not have to worry about those vicious ships, which lacked the support of a local orbital base.

Of course, the Union was far from defeated, having made strong gains of its own. The worlds it had lost were not missed, for the most part. It had been more a case of trimming the fat, minor distractions that had been turned into major liabilities for the Starwolves to protect. The consolidation of their military command under Donalt Trace had been tremendously beneficial to their defensive efficiency, and the new fleet of Fortresses was a threat even the Starwolves had to consider. There were now twenty-five of the immense ships, two more than the current number of operational Starwolf carriers, and Trace was bringing them into the fleet at the rate of just over one a year.

And now what? There was a secret Union base on this glacier-locked world, but the Starwolves had known that for decades and, seeing no danger in it, had politely pretended ignorance. Lately there had been rumors of an inordinate amount of activity at this supposedly small and remote base, that had been going on for years. There were rumors of a new super-weapon developed by the Union to defeat Starwolves, one that Commander Trace felt would end the war in a matter of weeks. There were even rumors, which had since been confirmed, that Donalt Trace came here as often as he could manage. A Starwolf drone had tracked his ship to this world, and every indication was that he was still here.

"You worked with the Starwolves before?" the captain asked, realizing too late that he had been indiscreet. "No, forget I said that. Starwolves make good allies, but it's dangerous to be involved in their business. But I suppose that I don't have to tell you that."

Lenna shrugged. "With what I've been involved in, I don't see how I could be in any more trouble, if the Union ever did catch me. I've been into quite a lot of mischief over the years, which they probably put down to quite a few very different people. I try never to show them the same face twice."

"Sorry?"

Lenna shrugged again, disinterested in this subject. "You'd never recognize me yourself, if you did happen to see me again."

That was true enough. The Starwolf medics she had worked with over the years had learned a thing or two about humans, or at least about Traders, a related but radically different sub-species, to which she belonged. She was no longer completely dependent upon unreliable cosmetics. At that moment she was several shades darker than her usual self, and the light-sensitive contact lenses meant to protect her eyes from snow blindness had also changed their color to black.

The main scanner made a small but insistent beep, demanding attention. Lenna glanced over the back of the captain's seat. A small ship was closing quickly from behind, still moving in from one side.

"That's it," he said, indicating the ghostly image. "I don't yet know what, but something is definitely after us. Do we go ahead and attempt our run?"

"How far do we have to go?" Lenna asked, seeing only one ship about the size of their own freighter on the scan.

"Not that far, but it will take some smart flying or they'll have us for sure."

Lenna considered that briefly, and waved the pilot out of his seat. "Let me take over—I'm of Trader stock. As long as this ship can take it, I can out-fly anyone they could be sending against us."

"This old bird can take it," the captain agreed as he turned over his place to her without question, moving into the copilot's seat. Then he leaned closer to the scan monitor. "Confirmation is coming through. That's a stingship."

"Bless us!" Lenna exclaimed under her breath, staring at the monitor for a moment. Then she set to work on the ship's master computer. "I wonder where they were keeping that? Must have a stingship carrier in orbit. We'll have to settle our affairs and get you boys out of here before they can get any more of those monsters into space."

"We can't outrun a stingship, not sublight," the captain reminded her. "Our engines are actually a little small for a ship this size, to fit inside their aerodymanic housings."

"I can do something about that," Lenna said absently as she continued her hurried work at the keyboard. "It's a little-known trick, but I've learned a thing or two from tricky people. It will be an uncomfortable ride for the two of you. . . ."

"Better than being shot out of space," the copilot remarked.

"Just strap yourselves in tight and don't think about how much it's going to hurt when you wake up again. I just hope that you can recover quickly enough from high G's to fly yourselves back out." She glanced at the monitor briefly. "Yes, here we go."

The stingship was circling well around to come up behind the freighter, her crew no doubt assuming that they were pursuing a slow, aging ship that would be easy prey. Indeed, the complete lack of response on their own part suggested that they were actually unaware that a hostile ship was closing with them. Lenna waited, leading them in. It was an old game for her, and one that she had learned very well. Anyone who was good enough to fly with the Starwolves could handle a stingship, although she would have been happier with her converted fighter than this ancient freighter.

Lenna waited patiently until the stingship turned in to begin its next run, then gave full power to the freighter's main drives and pulled up tight. Although the two human crewmembers made small sounds of protest against the fierce G's, it was actually a fairly easy turn compared to what she intended to do. She was saving her tricks for later on in the game.

"Go ahead and extend the missile cradle," she instructed the captain. "I'll have to take him out, or he will never give us the chance to make our run on their secret base."

He activated the freighter's improvised defense system. The doors of the forward cargo bay, built into the bottom of the hull to facilitate loading, swung open and the rotating cradle with its six large missiles was extended just outside the hull.

"You want me to take weapon systems control?" the captain asked.

Lenna shook her head firmly, watching the scan monitor as the stingship swung around for another run. She was keeping her distance, but deliberately setting herself up to put her enemy on her tail. "You'll not stay conscious through the little surprise I have for our friends. Just be ready."

Lenna rolled the freighter through a long evasive turn, knowing when she started that she would end up with the stingship still squarely on her tail. This part was the window dressing, building false confidence in an opponent who was obviously not particularly experienced. Under other circumstances, her evasive tactics would have been the best that anyone could have done. This freighter did not have the high-intensity acceleration dampers of a stingship, nor did she have the special acceleration suits or padded flight cradle the enemy pilots enjoyed. But the Union pilot would not suspect that she was a Trader, able to take harder turns than he could despite all of his protections.

She continued to lead the stingship in, feigning just enough helplessness to lure the enemy close before he fired, sure of his kill. She waited as long as she dared, then activated her program modifications to the control system and gave the main drives full power. Following the automatic commands she had set, the computer control also engaged the stardrive at very low power, just enough to give their thrust a firm boost.

The freighter catapulted forward, and Lenna lead the ship through a torturing 60-G turn. Its spaceframe groaned aloud as the ship bucked and shook, protesting the sharp change of direction. Lenna had to fight the pain and crushing forces herself, without the aid of the armored suit that usually supported her through harsh accelerations in her own fighter. She could only hope that her two companions had survived, facing G's that humans never should have taken unprotected. Even stingships did not attempt this.

She looped the freighter completely over, coming up behind the stingship and catching the enemy pilot by surprise just long enough for Lenna to lock the missile tracking system on target. Perhaps the stingship's pilot never thought he should have anything to fear from a freighter, even after that last surprising move. He had only just begun to accelerate away almost casually when Lenna released her first missile. Carried by a small drive that would quickly burn itself out with its own power, the missile found its target in a matter of seconds.

Sure of her prey, Lenna did not even wait to see. She had to get the freighter within the planetary atmosphere before they were intercepted by another stingship. She brought the ship back on course, keeping their speed as high as she dared until she was forced to decelerate rapidly. With no time to spare to orbit in, she guided the ship straight in at a sharp angle as she continued to cut their speed, retracting the missile carriage and bringing the atmospheric shields to full. It was only when the freighter entered the atmosphere, wrapped in a shell of thin flame, that she finally leveled off to an acceptable attitude for entry.

By that time, the two regular crewmembers were beginning to recover from their rough handling. Lenna glanced at the captain quickly. "Do you think that you can take over? I need to get Bill and myself packed away."

"Yes. Right." He released his straps and pulled himself from the copilot's seat, moving with exaggerated care. Lenna knew that he would be regretting it far more tomorrow. She just hoped that he would be doing better by the time they began their attack run.

Lenna relinquished her seat and hurried to the rear cargo hold, cramped with the heavy, white form of the ejection module. Bill, the sentry, was already inside, securely strapped down in his own impact cradle. He was in fact an armored security automaton of Union construction, commandeered for her use by the Starwolves during her first mission and later modified to suit her more demanding needs. In form he was a great, white, armored bulk standing on four solid legs, now retracted beneath him, his small head dominated by a battery of guns and a pair of small camera pods behind protective flanges. Loyalty and firepower were his strong points, but he was still an exceedingly stupid machine compared to the sentient Starwolf carriers. Lenna climbed inside the module and secured the hatch, then strapped herself into the single acceleration couch. Then she settled in to wait.

The little freighter had continued its approach unopposed, having dropped down to within a hundred meters of the surface and holding at twice the speed of sound. According to the original plan, she was to hold a much greater speed at an even lower altitude, but her captain was still reeling under the effects of Lenna's evasive tactics and he did not trust his ability to fly this ship, and it had not had a functional low-level attack guidance system in years. The extra altitude would also give Lenna and Bill a better chance of surviving when they went overboard.

Just as the freighter was coming up on a hundred kilometers short of her target, the missile cradle was extended again. This time, however, both the forward and rear cargo bays were opened. The ship had been transversing a desolate world, a rocky, mountainous land cut by vast glaciers and immense plains of ice and snow.

Coming up behind one high, narrow ridge, the freighter dropped down as low as her captain dared to take her behind that wall of rock, hidden from radar and quite possibly from scan as well. The small white and gray shape of the ejection module popped out of the rear cargo hold. A tiny drogue chute, white as snow, snapped out almost immediately. Too small to break its fall, it was meant only to keep the module upright and to control its descent at a rate meant to get it grounded as quickly as possible.

It hit the ground like a meteor, nearly burying itself in the snow and ice. The freighter had already disappeared over the horizon, continuing its run. Just as the sprawling surface portions of the secret base became visible twenty kilometers ahead, it released three of its remaining missiles in rapid succession, too far short of its destination for the weapons to have locked on target. The freighter turned immediately and shot away, climbing back out of the atmosphere and the safety of open space. It was meant to seem an act of cowardice and desperation, a rebel attack run aborted because of fear and bad judgment. Such things happened from time to time, sometimes successfully but most often not. But the real goal of that feign had been accomplished. Two passengers had been safely delivered.

At that moment, Lenna knew that she had been delivered but

she would have debated any mention of the word safely. She was beginning to have some understanding for the two circumspect pilots she had tried to assassinate with a good, tight turn. The ejection module, adapted from a small escape pod, had been built with its two unusual passengers in mind. Lenna could walk away from impacts that would have left ordinary humans dead or badly injured. Bill had, of course, been built to very demanding specifications, at least by Union standards. The replacement of many of his vital components, especially his brain and other electronics, with constructed parts had made him especially durable.

Lenna glanced about. The lights were still on and there were no icy drafts at her back, so it seemed that the module had survived the one brief, dramatic journey of its career. Bill was still folded away in his own shock-absorbing cradle, his armored head and camera pods rotated around to watch her. He said nothing. He was obviously his usual charming self; Lenna saw no reason to be worried about him.

"You want to go for a walk?" she asked.

"Baby, it's cold outside," Bill answered obliquely; heaven alone knew what he had in mind by that response.

"Why don't we find out how cold," she said as she began unstrapping from her seat.

At least she maintained the good sense to get everything ready before she opened the hatch. As a part of her usual procedure, she was dressed in a Union officer's uniform complete with arctic survival gear, weapons, and forged identities that were good enough to survive even a computer check. Starwolves knew quite a lot of interesting tricks, including magnetic strips on identity cards that told the computer reading the card that it knew her.

Ready at last, she released the hatch and threw her packs outside before following herself. Getting Bill out of a hatch that was three sizes too small was quite another matter, especially now that the module was no longer resting completely level. The sentry was in fact surprisingly agile, his reflexes faster even than her own, but he always moved with exaggerated slowness and deliberation in enclosed spaces. Lenna had never figured out whether that was a function programmed into him or an acquired idiosyncrasy. He had collected a few in the course of his existence.

"You know, that was an exceedingly stupid idea," Lenna remarked as she stretched. All of her bones felt as if they had been rammed together.

"It was your exceedingly stupid idea," Bill reminded her with the perfect honesty that came from perfect innocence.

Lenna frowned as she began tossing her packs over his back. "You never have learned the meaning of discretion."

"It is hard to be discreet when you weigh the better part of a ton."

Sometimes, when they were alone for days or weeks on end, Lenna wished more than anything that Bill possessed the spontaneity to engage in real conversation. Then, on some rare occasion such as this, Bill would do his best, and Lenna was reminded that she was probably better off with a reticent robot.

She turned to survey the horizon to the west, knowing that the approach path of the freighter was to have left her due east of the base. She had no idea of the distance. The drop was to have been where some landform, such as the ridge several kilometers to the west, offered protection from scan and radar. Without any good maps of the planet, finding such a place as that had been entirely a matter of chance. They could be ten kilometers short of their target, or a thousand. If they could make their way to higher ground, then she could put Bill's optical scanners and sensors to the task.

"Let's be on with it, then," she said, rapping affectionately on the sentry's hull. "I've got to keep moving before I freeze."

"I contain no material which could freeze at the predicted temperatures for this environment," Bill offered for reasons that no one could begin to guess.

"Bully for you."

Leading the way, Lenna started out across the ice field. This was going to be hard walking. She was really not cold because of the self-warming arctic gear; she never had to worry about freezing, as long as she had a spare set of fresh batteries to charge from Bill's generator. But the loose snow and broken rock and ice would make for very rough going. She had grown up in a world that was as mountainous as it was wintry, although she had been an artist and a part-time pilot rather than a ranger in the wild. She was most worried about Bill, and what might happen if he fell over into a tight place. He was so heavily armored that he weighed quite a lot, and he had two sets of legs but no hands.

"It was a better plan than your first one," Bill proffered after more than a minute of walking.

Lenna turned to stare at him. It took her a moment to realize just what he was talking about, their discussion of the stupidity of her plan for getting them down having been brief and some time past.

She shrugged, resuming their march. "I don't see how it could have been worse. Riding in to our destination inside a missile and then parachuting down would hardly have been a rougher ride, as long as the parachute opened at the end. It would have saved us this long walk in."

"I would not have fit inside a missile," Bill explained in a voice that conveyed simple, patient logic.

"Oh, excuse me!"

"Would you like for me to shut up?"

"No, not at all. Who else would I have to talk to, out here in the middle of nowhere? I am at your mercy." She paused, having seen a small movement in the snowfield just ahead. "What was that?"

"What was what?" Bill asked.

Lenna saw something move again, and pointed. "Look!"

"*Look*!" An entire course of small, high-pitched voices echoed her.

Lenna could have tripped over her own face, she was so surprised. She looked around, finding herself in the middle of a vast complex of small holes skillfully hidden in the ice. A considerable number of the holes held small, white-furred animals standing upright just above their burrows, peering at her with bright eyes and perked ears. They were about the size of a very small dog, certainly nothing for her to worry about. At least not as long as she had that walking battleship staring over her shoulder.

"What are those things?" Lenna asked quietly. All the information there was to be had on this planet had been downloaded into Bill's secondary memory storage.

"Ice gophers," the sentry explained simply, then seemed to shift gears. "Extensive colonies of ice gophers, numbering anywhere from less than a dozen to several hundred, are borrowed into the ice of glaciers and ice fields. The small but hardy pseudo-mammals are intelligent and gregarious, and are noted to be very curious and fearless. The members of the colony are in continual and apparently extensive vocal communication, defending their colonies through the diligence of constant sentries. Their most remarkable trait is their ability to mimic the sound of other animals, even complex speech, with truly amazing clarity."

"Thus spake Zarathustra," Lenna said under her breath. "Knowing our friends, they probably have an entire colony of vast proportions surrounding their damned base. Hello!"

"*Hello!*" several dozen ice gophers obligingly called back.

"Heigh-dee heigh-dee ho!"

"*Heigh-dee heigh-dee ho!*"

"Heigh-dee heigh-dee hay!"

"*Heigh-dee heigh-dee hay!*"

"By the gods, what a feeling of power!" Lenna said to herself, then started forward again through the middle of the colony. "Take it, maestro!"

"Hey heigh-dee heigh-dee, heigh-dee hay a gopher hole!" Bill roared in a deep, gravelly voice as he followed, his massive hull seeming to sway in time with the rhythm. He was a machine of many unique talents, but music was not one of them.

The first hint Lenna had that they were anywhere near the base was when the small patrol ship came over the top of the hill to their left, moving quickly to intercept them. She recognized the ship immediately as a hover tank, a fairly standard type used by the Union in rugged terrain, part attack craft with powerful weapons and part transport. It could fly like a real aircraft for covering rough ground, although it usually hovered just over the surface on a form of field drive to save power. It could even float, although such a function was of little use in this place.

The tank settled to the ice a short distance away and the main hatch opened, dropping down to form a boarding ramp. Lenna waited patiently while a pair of soldiers in environmental suits like her own stepped out.

"What are you doing out here?" the apparent leader of the pair asked. At least he asked in the calm, almost bored voice of someone who expected a perfectly reasonable answer. After all, Lenna was dressed as one of their own and walking about this disgruntled countryside with a sentry. She relaxed.

"Performing cold-weather exercises on this experimental model," she explained, indicating Bill. He bent one foreleg and nodded. "We were flying along when something came up behind us in a hurry and blasted us good."

"Must have been that rebel freighter that made that laughable pass at the base three days ago," the second of the two offered.

"I imagine so, considering the fact that you've been walking due west along its approach," the first one agreed. "Why don't we give you a ride in, as much as that might seem like better late than never."

"How far are we from the base?" Lenna asked as she directed Bill into the rear portion of the tank.

"Oh, it's just over that next hill, not more than a kilometer away."

There was certainly something to be said about being delivered to the front door, although she was just as glad that they had not found her before this. As it was, it seemed likely that she would be allowed to simply disappear inside the base as soon as they arrived. Otherwise, after finding her in the middle of the frozen nowhere, there would have been too much time to wonder about her, perhaps even to test her identity to greater depth than her forged idents could endure.

The base was sprawled across the icefield that filled the wide, circular depression of a valley that appeared to be the better part of fifty kilometers across, although only the tops of a few mostly-buried buildings broke through the surface of the snow in widely-scattered clumps. Very little information existed about this base, and no photographs. Lenna was not surprised to find that the largest part of the complex was actually deep underground, in the zone of constant temperatures and therefore sheltered from the deadly cold of the winter storms.

The tank cut a straight path across the ice to the nearest of many long, featureless buildings. The massive metal door opened at their approach, revealing a long, steep ramp descending into the depths. Lenna watched with interest as they descended beneath the relatively thin lens of ice that filled the shallow, valley floor, down within the rock itself. Even the Union knew better than to build something that might be expected to last for centuries in the ice itself, which had a disconcerting habit of moving and cracking, as well as simply accumulating and then disappearing altogether over long periods of time.

They arrived at last in a type of underground garage, where some two dozen hover tanks were parked, with empty stalls for several more. The ceiling seemed a little low, at least to Lenna. She thought that she would have felt just a little nervous in trying to guide a tank through this enclosed space, since the machines had no wheels and were obliged to float about a meter off the ground. There seemed to be about three meters of clearance over the roofs of the parked tanks. Considering how massive they were, that was cutting it just a little close.

Her own tank settled to the floor and the main hatch began to fold down, although the two soldiers remained seated in the forward cabin. The leader turned to look at her.

"This is patrol depot three," he explained briefly. "We have to go back out on duty, so we'll just let you out here. The tram station is through that passage on the far side of the chamber."

"We're on the eastern perimeter?" Lenna asked, sending Bill on through the narrow hatch.

He nodded. "This is the main complex, of course. Hangars for the supply ships and the mock wolves are on the far side of the western ridge."

Lenna was so surprised by that unexpected lead that she almost forgot to tender the appropriate thanks and farewells as she followed Bill out the hatch. The tank rose and moved away, accelerating up the long ramp back to the surface. Lenna hardly even noticed as she walked absently across the garage toward the tram station, while Bill followed loyally behind.

Things seemed to be going about as well as she had any right to expect. First she was delivered right inside the base itself, without the need to bluff her way through security, and then she was given the lead she needed to begin her search. Apparently the vague hints were perfectly true. The Union was developing a new form of missile or automated fighter that employed high-speed artificial intelligence to out-fly the Starwolves, a highly advanced variant of the old Wolfhound missiles that had been used to limited effect in the past.

"Get a move on," Bill told her softly. "You might attract attention to yourself, shuffling about like that."

"All right. You just keep your shell on," Lenna answered softly. "What's your problem? You have a short in your patience chip?"

"What do we do now?" he asked, his usual practical and unperturbed self.

"Now we establish our cover," she said, directing Bill into the first of the two compartments of the tram. "First we turn up the personnel sections and requisition ourselves an apartment where I can leave this arctic gear, and then we begin having a look about. If things continue to . . . Hello!"

"Hello," Bill answered pleasantly.

"Oh, debug yourself!" Lenna snapped, waving him away impatiently. She had been bent over the control panel in the front of the compartment, where the operator could select from between some three dozen tram routes. There was a very extensive map of both the passenger and heavier cargo tram routes. "Why, just look at this map. This place must be as large as a city. And a fairly large city, at that."

"Many places to look," Bill remarked innocently.

Maeken Kea stood at the window of the observation deck, watching the loading of the cutter that would take her back to Vannkarn. The ship looked small and lonely in the immense, underground bay now that the fleet was under way, just as this entire complex seemed silent and empty now that its primary function was done. She wanted out of here, but she did not want to go home. She wanted to be out with her fleet, at the command of a swift, powerful ship. Even a Fortress would do, for all that she seemed to have bad luck with the monsters.

Donalt Trace stood a short distance behind her, leaning back with crossed arms against the table that rested against the inner wall. He was a towering man, as big as she was small, a stately, ruggedly handsome man with streaks of white in his hair and a regal face lined by years of care and reconstructive surgery. They were both growing old in the pursuit of his schemes.

"It's just not fair," she insisted, turning to face him. "We've worked on this for years. Twenty years of planning all coming together at the same time, hitting the Starwolves in more ways than they can possibly handle. Next to you, I've done more than anyone else to make this happen. I want to be a part of it."

Trace shook his head slowly, perhaps even sadly. Maeken expected no concessions from this man, not even for her. Obsessed men were supposed to be cold and uncaring, to use others as they used themselves. Most people assumed that Donalt Trace was a man obsessed with the destruction of the Starwolves, a certain Starwolf named Velmeran in particular. But Maeken thought that she knew him better. Fighting Starwolves was simply his job, and he took it very seriously.

Trace's task was simple in definition, but seemingly impossible in actual implementation. He had to find a way to destroy the Starwolves so that the Union would be free to turn its military might inward to enforce the sterilization of complete segments of its own population. Genetic drift was slowly degenerating the human species; the essential rule of nature that only the strong should survive had not been in effect in hundreds of centuries, and the Union wished to impose its own standards of just who should survive and reproduce. The Starwolves were enough of a distraction that the Union's ability to police and control its own was beginning to slip, with elements of internal rebellion growing rapidly for the first time in thousands of years.

Fighting the Starwolves meant fighting Velmeran, their tactical leader, a Starwolf of tremendous cunning and initiative. Twenty years and more had passed since Donalt Trace's last meeting with Velmeran, and he had, in a strange way, benefited from that meeting. He had been matured by what had happened to him that last time. He had shed his blind loyalties, beliefs, and prejudices, his foolish self-limitations that had made him the simple, shallow man he had been. He had learned wisdom the hard way, through defeat and the cynicism born of his failures. He had become a serene, calculating man of tremendous depth, a man qualified at last for defeating the ultimate weapon of war, the sentient fighting machine of artificial design known as the Starwolf.

He had learned to defeat them in the only way he could. He knew now that he could never build better ships or weapons than they possessed. He had come to realize that he could never build better pilots, living or mechanical. The only way to defeat Starwolves was to be more creative than they were. The only weapon that would work against the Starwolves was themselves. Twenty years of careful planning had gone into a relentless series of attacks designed to make the Starwolves outsmart themselves.

He pushed himself away from the table, his biomechanical arms moving with their typical hesitation. "Every part of my plan is ready except for the contingency clause. That's the part that only you can do for me. If we win, we win everything, perhaps even an immediate end to this ancient war. We certainly make our victory inevitable. If we lose, we lose everything. That means that someone I can trust has to be there to pick up the pieces."

"No, don't say that," Maeken protested. "There's no way that we can fail now."

He stepped up close behind her, placing his hands on her shoulders. She almost could not stop herself from flinching under that touch, knowing the incredible strength contained in those hands. Stronger even than the hands of Starwolves, although he had only the two. "Just keep in mind who it is we're fighting, and never underestimate them. They are very, very good. Their only weakness is that the only way they know how to think is like themselves. My only remaining concern is how much Velmeran might have learned from fighting us."

Maeken glanced out the window, seeing that the cutter was being sealed for flight. She bent to collect her bags. "Well, I suppose that I should be on my way. They seem to be ready."

"They have to wait for you," Trace pointed out as he took one of her bags for her. "It's your ship."

Maeken laughed, giving him the benefit of the doubt. He joked so seldom, but he was often funny without intending to be. "So, what will you do when it's all over? Retire?"

"If I can," he said as they walked over to take the lift down to the main level of the bay. "It's hardly going to be that simple, as if the war will just end. I don't know how many of their carriers we can catch all at once. We might be hunting down Starwolves for some time yet to come. But it *is* good to know that we can finally defeat them."

"If you are so sure of that, then why do I have to stay behind to pick up the pieces if something goes wrong?" Maeken said softly, mostly to herself. Trace did not seem to hear as he pressed the call button for the lift. Maeken frowned. "What will happen, when the war is over? I mean, everything about our military, our government, even our economy, is designed to run on this war. We build a massive amount of ships, weapons and equipment each year, and the Starwolves oblige us by destroying a large part of it all so that we can build some more. I had always assumed that we would have done something to end this war one way or another a long time ago, if we really wanted."

"That might have been true, in the past," Trace answered. "The war was a ready-made justification for limitless spending on construction and research, for tight control on trade and interplanetary travel. But then this business of genetic deterioration became an inescapable fact, and the war has turned from an asset to a liability."

"But what do we do now?" Maeken insisted. "If the basic economic structure of our civilization is about to come to an end, what do we put in its place? What can we do?"

"What can't we do?" Trace asked in return, then stepped out of the lift when the doors snapped open. "Don't you understand?

The Union wants to take itself apart. A war economy is a system that belongs to a forgotten age. I like to think that we have outgrown that, that perhaps we outgrew such things a long time ago and just never realized it. I would like to see my fleet become something very different than it is now, perhaps a body of explorers and peacetime troubleshooters, and I don't mean anything military or clandestine by that, but an organization of scientists and diplomats and teachers.''

"In all the years that I've known you, I never suspected that you were secretly a starry-eyed optimist," Maeken remarked as she hurried to keep pace with him. "So with everything else in the known universe about to change, what is to become of you? Time at last to be yourself? Maybe settle down and have children?''

Trace considered that, his face making no less than two almost comical contortions. "If I had children now, I would be just old enough to settle down and have grandchildren.''

Maeken frowned to herself. She could see that she would get nowhere along that line, at least not until the war was over. "Well, if those are your objectives, why not just make peace with the Starwolves? I've always found them a very reasonable and honorable people.''

"That is the contingency plan," Trace said in a cold, tight voice. "But not now, not when we finally have them trapped. If we make peace with them, we're stuck with them, and there is no place for Starwolves in our future. It's their fault that this damned, ridiculous war has gone on so long. They would never leave us alone and give us a chance to go our own way, and I should hope that we have too much human pride to let a pack of glorified laboratory animals dictate our future to us. Right now, we're fighting to stay alive as a race. If we have to turn ourselves over to the Starwolves to guard our collective conscience and police our every move, then we might just as well die.''

Trace walked in a rather angry silence, leaving Maeken Kea almost running to keep up with him. They crossed the twenty or so meters of the bay floor to the boarding ramp of the cutter. Trace passed her bags into the hands of a junior crewmember who was making final preparations for getting the little ship under way, indicating for another to take the bags she carried. They hurried into the ship with their burdens, and Trace turned to leave just as abruptly.

"Good luck, Commander," Maeken called after him, determined that he would not simply disappear without a word. Once he developed a case of Starwolves on the mind, he forgot all else.

He paused only long enough to nod once, looking over his shoulder.

"Commander Trace!" she insisted, running after him a few paces. "You can surely spare me a moment more of your time. You're on your way to your carefully contrived meeting with Velmeran, and if that goes the way it has in the past, then I may never see you again. There are a lot of things that I've never said, out of respect for military necessity, but you can damned well do better than that."

Donalt Trace just stood where he was for a long moment, looking startled and slightly confused, before he turned and walked slowly back to stand before her. He towered over her, remote and silent, and Maeken wondered almost fearfully if her quiet hopes had only earned her his wrath. Then, to her great surprise, he bent to take her hand, and kissed it gently. From anyone else, that would have seemed a contrived and ridiculous gesture. Donalt Trace was, if nothing else, a man of quiet majesty and gallantry, and he had meant that gesture in perfect sincerity.

"To a future of many hopes, my little lady," he said, then turned to walk away.

Maeken Kea wept silently, knowing that she had forced the question and wondering if she would have been better for never having known the truth in matters that she could never have the way she wanted.

- 2 -

Vast and dark, the Starwolf carrier moved quietly through the shadow of the ring, the black arrowhead shape of her armored hull almost invisible against the bands of bright colors of the immense gas giant. She stayed close to the underside of the ring, hiding in its pale shadow and the sensor distortion from the haze of fine particles of ice surrounding the ring, ready to run into the planet's own deep shadow if unwanted visitors were to arrive in the system. No small, black fighters moved through her closed bays. Her few windows were sealed, and her running lights were dark.

On the Methryn's bridge, Velmeran paced with pent-up energy before the central bridge. Seated at the helm station, Consherra watched him quietly. She was reminded of Mayelna, his mother and predecessor, gone now these past twenty years. She had always been content to remain inconspicuously in the quiet recesses of the commander's station of the upper bridge, while Velmeran would more often descend to the main bridge where he could move about, watching the various stations. He was a very capable commander, but he would never be completely at home on the bridge. He missed being a pilot more than he would ever admit, and Consherra would always regret the necessity that had taken him away from the one real delight in his life. He had been a legendary pilot, but he was needed too much on the bridge of this ship.

At least they would be meeting old friends this day. Tregloran had left the Methryn over a year before to prepare his own ship, the Vardon, for her launch and initial tour of duty. With him had gone Lenna, perhaps the most unusual crewmember ever to walk the corridors of a Starwolf carrier, as well as most of the rest of Velmeran's old pack. Only the core of Velmeran's special tactics team remained: Baress and the two transport pilots, Trel and Marlena. Baressa's pack now served Velmeran for the remainder of his special tactics team.

Of course, Velmeran was anxious to see the newest ship in the Starwolf fleet. Valthyrra was a little anxious about that herself. Consherra had been quietly amused by watching the ship's camera pod, which had been engaged in its own form of nervous pacing, looking over the shoulder of every bridge officer in an erratic cycle. Occasionally Commander and camera would fall in beside each other as they conversed privately. That was occasionally a bit of a trick for Valthyrra, who had to choreograph the movements of her camera boom.

"Have you heard any gossip?" Velmeran asked the ship as they both stopped just before Consherra at the helm station. "Has there been any hint that Theralda remembers anything important?"

"There has been precious little gossip on the subject of Theralda

Vardon, beyond the fact that she is up and running," Valthyrra explained. "It has been a closed subject, considering the importance of the information she may be carrying. Why did you never take me to look for Terra while you were still in the business of predicting the future?"

Velmeran did not answer, knowing when he was being teased and not necessarily too kindly. As it had turned out, the almost god-like psychic abilities of the High Kelvessan were limited to only a few months of hyper-sensitivity at the time when those talents were coming to their full maturity. Velmeran and several other of the Kelvessan aboard the Methryn were still remarkable telepaths, even by the standards of his own kind, but his apparent ability to predict the future had long since been severely diminished.

The Aldessan had been so disappointed, they had refused to have anything to do with him for a year.

Velmeran was still young for a Kelvessan—very young to command a ship of his own, young even for a pack leader. He was tall for one of his kind, although the Kelvessan did not vary greatly in most physical characteristics, and he was still smaller than most humans, even at the height of their genetic decline. Like all Kelvessan, he had large, dark eyes and long, thick hair of chestnut brown, but he was of mutant stock, the reason for his unusual height as well as the fact that he was somewhat less human in appearance than most of his kind, his long skull and hint of a short muzzle making him almost feral in appearance. Consherra, who shared his mutant features, had finally figured out that the High Kelvessan were beginning to resemble the Aldessan of Valthrys, their creators.

"Here they come," Valthyrra announced, with an almost predatory eagerness that made Consherra look up. The ship dropped her voice in a conspiratorial manner. "They came out of jump exactly five light-minutes from the planet. I never had that kind of control from my jump drive."

"Your frame could never take it," Velmeran reminded her. That was a very sore point with Valthyrra. She damaged herself just a little more every time she jumped, so she was obliged to save it for emergencies. "I would like to take a short ride in that ship, all the same, if you would not consider it too disloyal."

"Just a moment, you two," Consherra interrupted, sitting back in her seat with both pairs of her arms folded. "That is the Vardon, and Tregloran is the commander of that ship. She is not the property of either one of you."

Both Velmeran and Valthyrra stared at her, looking too surprised to be hurt.

"I know you both," she continued sternly, glaring at Velmeran. "You get so caught up in your schemes that you begin to give orders as if you were in command of the entire Wolf fleet. While that ship of yours always has been willing to try anything she can get away with, she has also acquired some of your bad habits."

Velmeran shrugged helplessly with both sets of arms. "I *am* in command of the entire Wolf Fleet."

"You can still be polite."

Valthyrra had tracked the main viewscreen around to observe the approach of the other ship, and they looked up in time to see the almost breathless approach of the Vardon, appearing suddenly under the ring and braking sharply with her forward engines to pull to a sudden halt barely twice her own length away. There was a certain amount of blatant showing off in such a maneuver, although Valthyrra had to think that fifteen million tons of ship was a lot of weight to throw around so casually for a machine that was still making her trial flight.

The Vardon advertised herself willingly as the new Starwolf supership. Her hull employed a new type of armor, a silver-titanium fusion that could disperse most direct cannon strikes in itself, but which could be infused with a structural shield to become harder even than the heavy quartzite used by the Union on their Fortresses. Because the ship was still under her trials, the black polymer impact layer that gave other Starwolf ships their distinctive appearance had not yet been installed. Her hull was still the bright silver of the original metal, except for a wide border of black impact shielding around the edges where her upper and lower hulls met along her lateral groove. There had been some discussion of leaving her in that form, a clear warning of the special threat she represented. She hardly needed that complete coat of impact polymer.

Although the Vardon was still the same size and shape as her older sisters, she did possess some other subtle differences. She had six main drives in a slightly larger housing under each of her short, slightly downswept wings rather than the usual four. Her stardrives were the same size as previous ships, since she depended more upon her jump drive for interstellar distances, and she was the first carrier to have twin conversion cannons, a pair of the large muzzles protruding just slightly from beneath her nose.

"She is a pretty thing," Velmeran commented softly. He still regretted the fact that other business had caused him to miss her launch.

"Everything a ship could ever want to be," Valthyrra agreed wistfully.

Velmeran glanced at her. "They have one just like that with your name on it, waiting for you. It should be ready soon now."

"It would be nice, just to feel young again," she replied vaguely.

Velmeran did not answer, knowing that she was tearing herself apart in the duty he required of her, using the jump drive that was destroying her to keep his schedule. He had wanted for her to transfer into this ship, let Theralda wait for the one that would soon be coming out of her construction dock, but the time for going home had never been convenient, and it had seemed more important to have that twenty-third carrier in operation as soon as possible.

"Could you find out if Tregloran wants to talk to me?" Velmeran asked.

"He is standing by already," Valthyrra reported; she had already been in private communication with the other ship. She moved her camera boom closer. "I will put you through on my own pick-up."

"Treg?" he asked, addressing the camera pod.

"Tregloran here. We are ready to go to work, Commander."

Velmeran glanced at Consherra. "He still knows his master's voice. Treg, we will be coming over for a little talk."

"Do not trouble yourself, Commander. Theralda and I will come over to the Methryn."

"Not on your life!" Valthyrra interceded. "We will be over in a few minutes."

"You want to see how a new ship works?" Theralda asked.

"This from a ship whose claim to fame was her ability to get herself blown out of space?" Valthyrra responded even more sharply. "I can still take you in a fight, sister. I just wanted to see if you were keeping yourself in any sort of order."

"You just bet. Come on over, and I'll show you how it's done."

"Just clear a path," Valthyrra said, and cut the channel. She turned her camera pod to look at Velmeran. "You know, I think I like her."

When Velmeran and Consherra reached the transport bay, they found that Valthyrra was already waiting for them. The small wedge-shaped hull of the probe was hovering near the door of their transport, the shielded camera pod at the end of its long, flexible neck bent around to regard them.

"You have elected to join us?" Velmeran asked. The probe was perfectly capable of independent space flight, as small as it was. It was essentially just a field drive system and a transceiver for Valthyrra's use inside an armored shell.

"I might as well take it easy on myself," she replied. "All of my remaining probes are getting a little shabby, and we are sitting in a very cold and uncomfortable section of space just now."

The probe turned and drifted inside the open hatch of the transport, and the two Starwolves followed, but they paused in mild surprise as soon as they stepped inside. Venn Keflyn stood in the aisle between the transport's rows of seats. The Aldessan was not as massive a creature as she seemed but exceptionally rangy, a dragon's body in long, chestnut-colored fur, both sets of long, triple-jointed legs braced wide as she held to the back of the seats with all four arms. Her head was bent low to avoid the rather low ceiling, her large cat's eyes glittering at them through the fringe of her mane.

"Glad that you could make it," Velmeran commented.

"You people seem to think this business quite important," Venn Keflyn replied. "There is a reason why I should be there."

That was certainly vague enough. Velmeran had met several Venn warriors from her ancient and mysterious race, but she remained his idea of the archetype. The Venn were the members of the elite group of warrior-scholars of the Aldessan—an admittedly strange combination of professions for anyone. They had created his own race, the Kelvessan, some fifty thousand years before, supposedly as the ultimate peacekeeping weapon —a function that they had not fulfilled especially well—but apparently also for the excuse for having the company of another race that was in most ways like themselves. Velmeran was even less certain that that had worked out quite as well as intended.

They were still taking their seats when the small ship came to life, rising a short distance from the deck. A moment later the deck itself dropped away as the massive doors of the cargo bay opened, the interior atmosphere held in by a containment field. The transport moved down through the containment field and out between the parting halves of the bay doors.

Velmeran looked into the control cabin, curious about their impatient pilot. He and Consherra were still taking their seats in the front of the main compartment. The pilot glanced at him rather guiltily, and Velmeran was surprised to see his own daughter.

"Keflyn, what are you doing here?" he exclaimed, then regarded her shrewdly. "You expect an invitation to this meeting."

"Oh, sure, since I am already going in that direction, I mean," she agreed innocently, as if accepting that as an invitation in itself.

Keflyn had of course been named after that same Aldessan standing behind them in the cabin, at a time when Velmeran had felt far more impressed with the mysterious Venn Keflyn. She was in most ways like her father, although she was always eager and ready for anything while Velmeran had accepted greatness reluctantly. In her younger years, the only way they had found to keep her out of trouble was to constantly move her ahead in her training, until she had gone to the packs at the very early age of fifteen. Now twenty, she had nearly five years of experience with Baressa, the best pack leader in the ship, and was ready for a pack of her own.

But Keflyn differed from Velmeran in one very important respect: both her interest and her real talent lay in command. She would be a pack leader because it was a necessary step to becoming the commander of her own ship, as well as the best use of her talents until Velmeran could find a ship for her. Perhaps in that respect she was more like her mother, Consherra, who had given up the packs and the possibility of command because she had always felt that her place was on the bridge.

Velmeran sat back in his seat, folding his arms. "Just why is this so important to you? Is there a purpose at work here, or are you consumed with overwhelming curiosity?"

"No, I have to go to this meeting," she said, her voice becoming soft and serious. She did that rarely, and everyone had learned that it meant for them to pay attention. "I have this premonition that I have some important task to perform."

"Oh, my!" Consherra muttered, rolling her head back on the top of the seat cushion. "What do you think?"

"She is about the right age for that to begin," Velmeran admitted. That was a bit of an exaggeration; he had actually been twenty-seven at the time when he had begun such tricks in earnest, although he had not enjoyed the benefit of Aldessan training. That brought something else to mind and he glanced over his shoulder at Keflyn's alien namesake, standing quietly in the back of the cabin. "Is this why you came along?"

"Perhaps."

Twenty years he had had this fox-faced, snake-bodied wiseacre on his ship, and he was still occasionally tempted to slap the mystic pretentiousness right out of her.

"Can I come?" the younger Keflyn asked, unable to contain her suspense any longer.

Velmeran thought about it a long moment. "You can come along, then, but you will abide by our decisions."

"When did you train to fly a transport?" Consherra had to ask.

"Oh, well, I really never had," Keflyn admitted hesitantly. "It just never seemed to me that it should be so difficult."

Velmeran looked rather uncertain. "Was it?"

The transport bay doors on the Vardon closed, and Keflyn brought the little ship down on the deck. This bay was in most ways identical to the one they had just left, except that something about it just looked new. For one thing, the machinery did not seem to rattle and clang so much, and the paint on the bulkheads and beams did not have the blurred, lumpy look of several centuries of coats. Perhaps it had just been the sight of that sleek, silver and black ship that they were now inside that made the difference.

Like a dutiful son, Tregloran was there as soon as they stepped from the transport. Like both Velmeran and Consherra, he was dressed in the white tunic, pants, and short cape that were the unofficial dress uniform of a Kelvessan bridge officer. Keflyn wore her full armored suit, with a black cape attached at the shoulder clips, in a less subtle effort than she might have wished to emphasize her own rank and experience. Venn Keflyn wore only her belt and harness, with its small arsenal of knives, guns, and small explosive devices.

"Venn Keflyn, this is an honor," Tregloran exclaimed, honestly surprised when the Aldessan appeared at the hatch of the transport.

"Stuff it, Treg," she told him bluntly. "Did you think that I would not be involved in this?"

"I hear that you are doing well with this ship," Velmeran commented. "No problem with the adaptations?"

"None at all," Tregloran insisted. "She really had handled perfectly, perhaps even better than the older carriers handled even when they were new. After fifty thousand years of exactly the same design, it was time for a change or two."

They stepped to one side as manipulator arms locked onto the transport and lifted it away for storage. It was an old habit on board starships to never leave anything with mass of any consequence setting about unsecured. As soon as the little ship was well clear of the deck, the small group of visitors followed Tregloran to the nearest lift.

"It is good to see you again, Consherra," he said. "I never realized just how much you really do as second-in-command until I had one who was new to the task, and who never wanted the job in the first place."

"Who do you suppose does all of the real work?" Consherra asked. "I suppose that you knew all there was to know about commanding a ship?"

"Actually, Velmeran was a very good teacher."

Escaping the wrath of a first officer, he dropped back close beside Velmeran. "Have you heard anything from Lenna?"

"Only that the crew of the freighter that had carried her in released her and Bill on the surface, they think safely and undetected," Velmeran answered. "I do not expect to hear from her until she is ready for us."

Tregloran stood aside as they stopped before the doors of the lift, waiting for the others to proceed him.

"I worry about her," he admitted after the lift had started. "Not so much because of what she does, but because she will soon be too old to do it. I was watching her during our trial runs, and I could see that the accelerations are beginning to hurt her quite a lot. I have to wonder how much longer she can take it. As hard as it is to think about it, I suppose that she is starting to get old."

"Lenna?" Velmeran was frankly surprised. He remembered the girl Lenna who had followed him home twenty years earlier. She was older than he was. Was that old for a human, even of

Trader stock? He frankly had no idea. "Well, when it comes time to put her off the ship, there are just two things that you should remember."

"What is that?"

"First, it is now your responsibility to tell her."

"Oh, nice!" Tregloran complained. "What is the second thing?"

"When you do put her out, be sure to lock all the doors."

Consherra turned to afford him a medium-range dirty look. "I think that what troubles him most is that he does not want to have to put her off the ship in the first place."

"Oh, I know that," Velmeran agreed. "I indicated that I am sympathetic with the problem, but that I have no better answer except to say that it is his own fault for getting involved with someone from a different species."

Tregloran looked puzzled. "Yes, that is exactly what I thought you were telling me."

The discussion was mercifully concluded by the arrival of the lift at the bridge, and they arrived sooner than the visitors from the Methryn would have anticipated. Valthyrra, who had been conspicuous in her remarkable silence, bent her camera pod around to peer at the lift. Her own had not run so smoothly and swiftly even after her last overhaul. A moment later she happened to glance outside the lift into the bridge just beyond, and she was captivated. She drifted along, heedless of her companions, staring in rapt fascination. It was just like her own, but it was so new and bright and . . . neat. Really neat.

Tregloran made quick introductions all around. Curiously enough, this was the first meeting between Velmeran and Theralda Vardon. He had rescued her from the museum in the port of Vannkarn more than two decades earlier. She had at the time been dormant, only a single memory cell remaining from the vast network of memory storage units and processors that formed the sentient computer systems of the Starwolf carriers. This was actually the second ship to carry the name and personality of the Vardon, the original having been destroyed over sixteen thousand years before.

Velmeran was curious to discover just how much of the original Theralda Vardon actually remained, and whether or not she still remembered one very important piece of information. Legend, or rumor, had always insisted that she had been the last ship to know the location of lost Terra. Valthyrra, who was old enough to have known the first Vardon, thought it likely, although not even Theralda was old enough to have been there herself.

Tregloran completed the introductions with his first officer Denna, a tall, rather dark Kelvessan with a surprisingly shy, even self-effacing smile; commanding a completely new ship had taught both her and her young commander a lot about being humble. Theralda had her camera pod bent completely around, staring at the captivated Valthyrra.

"She will probably refuse to leave until you show her engineering and the main fighter bays," Velmeran said softly. "I suppose that we should get on with this little meeting. Perhaps one of the smaller conference rooms . . ."

"Yes, or we could just hang curtains from her and use her for a hatstand," Tregloran added, just to see if she was listening.

"Oh, certainly," Valthyrra agreed, returning—with some effort—to the here and now. "We might just as well retire to one of the conference rooms and get started."

"An excellent suggestion," Velmeran agreed, amused.

Such meetings in the conference rooms located behind the bridge of the Starwolf carriers were a common occupation for most of those present, meetings that would often lead to major defeats for the Union. Keflyn had contrived to sit in on a few of the most recent meetings on the Methryn, following along as the second to her pack leader, Baressa. The group from the Methryn sat on one side of the oval with Tregloran and his first officer on the other. Denna looked rather lost and intimidated by such exalted company, and frankly fearful of the Aldessa.

"Well, I know what the question is," Theralda began. Her presence was through the camera pod at the end of the sort boom hung over the center of the table, currently rotated around to watch her visitors. "I have some good news and some bad news. No, I do not know the location of Terra, at least not accurately. I have a lead. Not a conscious lead, but the location of a world that is very important to finding Earth, in some way a stepping stone on the way."

"But you do not recall the specific importance of this world?" Velmeran assumed.

"No, not specifically, although I do think that it was an important base to the early Starwolves. I remember being given the coordinates of this world from Meykenna Haldayn and she told me that she had been refitted here, but the conversation exists in my current memory only as a fragment. I think that this world may have been Alameda, the original location of Home Base before it was removed to Alkayja in the heart of the Republic, and was abandoned at the same time that Terra was lost.''

"I hope that there is something there now," Velmeran prompted. He and Consherra both noted some vagueness to Theralda's personality, a small lack of spontaneity and a sense almost as if her mind had a tendency to wander. Her personality programming had obviously not survived intact in that one memory cell, and she was still filling in the missing pieces. After a year's time, she seemed to be doing very well for herself. Once she was speaking, she seemed normal enough. Her tendency toward the melodramatic was a trait she shared with all her sister ships. Velmeran found it refreshing to note that some things had never changed.

"Even allowing for five hundred centuries of planetary drift, there is only one planet it could be," she explained, turning her camera pod to the large viewscreen on the wall to one side of the table. A simple schematic of the Union and Republic space came up. "It is located here, in territory held by the Republic but near to Union space. This was once quite near a fairly active region of human space, near the center of that one cone of human expansion that led into what was to become Union space. But those were ancient colonies, dating well before the Act of Unification, and they were all destroyed in the early years of the war. It has always been a remote region of the Republic."

"Remote?" Consherra asked. "It is almost off the chart."

"That is hardly surprising," Valthyrra commented. "We know that the Republic was struggling to survive in those days. When Terra was lost, they withdrew to their major colonies that had not been ravaged by the war, those most remote from Union space. I would guess that Terra herself would lie somewhat nearer to the heart of the present Republic, and deeper in from the regions of Union space."

"My thoughts exactly," Theralda agreed, continuing this duel of the data processors. "Of course, Home Base was later severely damaged in an attack by a Union assault force that had wandered upon its secret location entirely by chance. That led to the destruction of the computer libraries that held a considerable amount of this old but no longer important information, such as the location of former major worlds like Terra and Alameda. And yet, while those worlds were abandoned for reasons that even I cannot guess, I *do* know that the evacuation was sudden and quick, and that the Union never completely destroyed them or attempted to hold or plunder them.''

"They were unlivable," Keflyn reminded them needlessly.

"Exactly," Theralda agreed. "But we now know the probable location of the planet Alameda, and somewhere on that world may still exist important clues for finding Terra herself.''

''Yes, a brilliant deduction,'' Valthyrra approved.

''Thank you very much,'' she responded amiably, turning her camera pod toward the Methryn's probe and dipping her lenses as if taking a bow. ''Now I do not expect such clues to be obvious, unfortunately. I recall no record of the climate of Alameda before it was abandoned, but it is now a mountainous, heavily forested world just recovering from a long, hard ice age, with great sheets of continental glaciers still in retreat. It is really too cold for human habitation, but has since been settled as a Feldenneh colony.''

''Feldenneh?'' Velmeran asked, surprised. The Feldenneh was a race feral in appearance, long-lived, and intelligent, but not very populous, quiet and very peaceful in nature. They had no sympathies for the Union, but their home world and colonies were within Union space and so subject to its dictates. ''That makes this a Union-held colony by default.''

''Yes, but there is no Union representation, diplomatic or military, on the planet,'' Theralda explained. ''The colony was only settled in the past decade, and there is still only the one, main settlement. The Feldenneh are not great explorers, which would explain why they have not found traces of any previous settlement.''

''That and the effects of heavy glaciation,'' Valthyrra added. ''Continental glaciers can sweep away the ruins of even extensive modern civilizations in a relatively short amount of geologic time.''

''A most astute observation,'' Theralda approved.

''You are most gracious,'' Valthyrra purred with delight, dipping her own armored camera pod.

''Oh, enough!'' Velmeran exclaimed, smiling. ''You two are incorrigible. It seems to me that we have discovered this lead only just in time. If there are any remaining ruins, the Union would know about it soon enough. I suppose that you have not been there yourself.''

"No, we dare not," Theralda agreed. "The presence of a Starwolf carrier, or Starwolves in general, would call undue attention to this planet. I would not care to have to fight the Union for possession of this world, once they learn of its importance. And above all else, I would not have them discover the location of Terra before us.''

"Yes, that is what I have to do!" Keflyn declared suddenly.

When everyone turned to stare at her in mystification, she made a vague shrugging gesture and sat down self-consciously.

Velmeran thought he understood what she was talking about. "Yes, your premonition that you have some important task to perform. You assume that I should send you to this colony, to find out what you can.''

She nodded thoughtfully. "Yes, that does sound like a good idea.''

Velmeran turned to Venn Keflyn, sitting back on her tail to one side of the table. "Have you had anything to do with this?''

"We had discussed the nature of premonitions earlier," she agreed. "Since my people are not subject to such admonitions, it is not my problem.''

That left Velmeran to contemplate what he had accomplished by having this Valtrytian on his ship for the past twenty years. They were full of advice, but they never seemed to give any of it.

He glanced at his daughter. "Could you give me one good reason why I should agree to such a thing?''

"I can give you five," Keflyn answered. "First, you have a ship to care for and cannot go yourself. The same is true for Consherra, and for Commander Tregloran. And Lenna Makayen is previously occupied. And it was my idea in the first place.''

"And give me one good reason why I should send you instead of one of the experienced members of my special tactics team like Baress?''

"Because I want to go?''

Velmeran considered that for a moment, watching her closely. "I suppose you can go, if you are smart enough to figure out a way to get yourself on that planet undetected.''

Keflyn thought about that for a long moment. "Well, there is a colony on that planet, and that means a supply ship of some type. The Feldenneh have always been supportive of the Star-wolves. A colony that small might not be served by a regular freight line or a company ship, and that would mean a small, independent freighter. The independents have always been on our side as well, since we protect their shipping from Union monopolies. I suppose that we could work something out.''

"Now that is an interesting suggestion," Tregloran remarked. "Theralda, would you happen to know anything about that?"

"Oh, I just might," the ship replied, as pleased with herself as her Commander was that they had anticipated this. "The ship that services the colony is the Thermopylae, a small, very old, and slightly impoverished Free Trader under the command of a Jon Addesin. She makes this run every six weeks, since the Feldenneh colony is presently exporting a fair amount of specialty wood products back to their own worlds. If arrangements can be made quickly, you can be on that next run."

"Are you still interested in going?" Velmeran asked.

"Oh, certainly," Keflyn insisted. "I mean, it could hardly be dangerous, compared to Lenna's expeditions. And it would be nice to see other worlds outside the Methryn for once."

— 3 —

Kanis was a neutral world, at least in theory. A cold, mountainous planet of dark forests, it supported only a small population that thrived on the export of one luxury item, the immense, soft pelts and downy wool of the native langies, beasts of small wits and large tempers. Being independent of Union rule, there was no trade monopoly for that one product, and Free Traders shared the market with smaller Company ships. Since it was now late summer in the north and late winter in the south, the second of the biannual export of wool and pelts was still weeks away. There would be no Company ships down in the port of Kalennes or orbiting the planet itself, nor had there been in several months.

Kanis was a favorite world of the Starwolves, both because of its cool climate and its relative unimportance to the Union. It was one of the rare worlds where they could come for port leave and not have to wear their heavy armor, or fear attack from fanatics and assassins. Of course, the benefits were mutual. The constant presence of Starwolf carriers in the skies above this world helped to insure that the Union maintained an attitude of polite indifference. And with every ship in the Wolf fleet calling here for brief vacations, as well as the regular patrols of the Methryn, Kanis was the best protected independent world in Union space.

It seemed like a good place for Keflyn to find a Free Trader that would take her to Vannkarn for her meeting with the Thermopylae. It seemed unlikely that Union spies would observe her transfer from the Methryn, at least as long as they were discreet. Kanis was by no means immune to Union spies. Velmeran had once faced both a Union operative and an assassin in the port of Kalennes, on the same day.

In order to maintain the necessary discretion, the Methryn had settled quietly into orbit and immediately began putting packs and transports down to the surface as she would during any other port leave. Keflyn followed several hours later, after nearly half of the Methryn's crew had already been down and spread out through the town for some time.

Keflyn had to wonder if she was doing the right thing. A large part of the strength of the Starwolves lay in their numbers and organization. A Starwolf was never alone, yet she would be completely alone for several weeks. If she got into trouble, she would be on her own. She would be without the defense of her armor, or the very important cooling it provided to protect her from the oppressive heat of human environments. Above all else, her safety would be completely dependent upon the trust she had to give to a great many people who would help her along the way, aliens all.

"Your contact on the surface will be Iyan Makayen, Lenna's older half-brother," Velmeran told her as he helped to carry her bags to the transport that would take her down. She was dressed in human manner, in clothes of dark, heavy cloth, and a cape to hide her Kelvessan form and lower set of arms; her hair was worn in two loose braids to hide her pointed ears.

"Is he anything like Lenna?" Keflyn asked as she began tossing her bags into the open hatch of the transport.

"I have not seen him in over twenty years," Velmeran said. "He is not of Trader stock, as Lenna's mother was. I remember that he was a quiet, practical man, more cautious than Lenna, but one to be trusted. He has made arrangements for you to travel on the Free Trader Karabyn, which will take you through two scheduled stops before she leaves you in Vannkarn. The Karabyn's captain will put you in touch with the underground in Vannkarn, and they should be able to get you on the Thermopylae."

On the way down, Keflyn had a few minutes to think hard about her own future. She looked upon the role of a pilot, even a pack leader, as dull and repetitive. She certainly did not want to give up her command status as a pilot to become an officer like her mother, but centuries could pass before she might have a ship of her own. The only answer for her seemed to be special tactics, and she was contemplating stepping into the role that Lenna Makayen would be forced to vacate in only a few years. Although Keflyn did not know it, she was cursed with her father's leadership abilities. She possessed a quick wit and insatiable curiosity that could never be satisfied in any role short of the one making the rules, and if she could not be the leader then she was much better off working on her own. She did not know that Velmeran had himself nearly left the Methryn for special tactics, only that he had acquired such a team in addition to his own pack in some manner that she had never considered.

She knew only that things had apparently been handed to Velmeran to comfortably fill up the limits of his considerable abilities, not that he had sometimes paid a bitter price for his accomplishments.

The transport landed in the small port field outside the town of Kalennes. It was night, and they planned to use the darkness combined with the dark clothes that Keflyn wore to cover her departure from the transport. As soon as the hatch opened, she grabbed her things and made a rush for the concealment of the shadows at the edge of the port buildings.

"Miss Keflyn?"

The voice had come out of the shadows of one dark corner, a rich, warm baritone that was deeper than any male Kelvessan voice could ever be, and holding a curious accent that she recognized instantly as being the same as Lenna's. She ducked into that same dark corner, her large, sensitive eyes able to pierce the shadows and see the tall, broad-shouldered man who waited for her.

"You are?" she asked cautiously.

"Iyan Makayen," he answered briskly. He was wearing the uniform of the local police; Keflyn remembered Lenna saying that he was a port constable.

"You look like Velmeran, for all that you're a girl," he observed, peering at her closely.

She nodded. "He is my father."

That seemed to startle this tall man, but he made no comment of it. He reached to take a couple of her bags. "I should think that we would be well advised to get you under cover as soon as possible. It's a slow time in the season here in town, with the rangers still in the wild and only the one ship in port."

He turned and backed his way through a wide, double door into the hallway beyond, gallantly holding the door for her. He had by chance taken the heaviest of the bags, and he was having some trouble with their weight. She could have carried all of the bags easier than he carried the two, but they had to maintain appearances. He was a head taller than her and weighed more than half again as much.

The main, commercial district of Kalennes was enclosed into a single structure known as the Mall, although the heavy, timber-supported roof was meant more to keep out wind and weather than the cold itself. As her companion had said, there were few people about even though the hour was still early. These people were of a purer Terran stock than most humans, tall, light of skin and hair, and heavy of build. Small and dark, Lenna was plainly of a very different racial stock from these people. She was obviously an outworlder, in spite of her disguise.

"Is Lenna still on the Methryn?" Iyan asked quietly as they walked quickly through the nearly deserted corridor, most of the shops already closed.

"No, she went over to the Vardon a year ago," Keflyn replied, wondering how much she should say. No one had told her anything about this. "She is on an important mission of her own just now, or she would be here instead of me."

"I always thought that she would come to a bad end, running

off with Starwolves like she did," he remarked, mostly to himself. "It seems that she had been much better at delaying that bad end than I would have thought."

Out on the port field, a small, dark form skittered on spider's legs through the night. It was no living creature but an automaton, a small mechanical device with a simple, box-like body and a single optical sensor for an eye, carried on six long, multi-jointed legs. It scurried rapidly from one patch of darkness to the next until it eventually disappeared into the blackness beneath the transport that had just brought Keflyn to the surface. It was still there when the transport lifted from the field a short time later.

The transport moved back into its bay, hovering in place while the manipulator arms moved in to capture it, lifting the small ship directly to its berth in the racks so that the bay doors could remain open. Velmeran waited outside while the transport was locked down and secured for flight. After a long moment, the main hatch opened and Trel stepped out.

"All set?" Velmeran asked.

"I think so," the special tactics pilot answered. "Everything went according to plan, and I could not see that we were observed."

"Well, we've done the best we can," Velmeran remarked. "That freighter is due to leave port early tomorrow morning. We will have to wait a few more hours after that for the sake of discretion, and then we will be on our own way."

"Commander Velmeran, please come to the bridge," Valthyrra's voice echoed through the bay.

"She said please," Velmeran remarked. "It must be serious."

It apparently *was* serious, since Consherra hurried to meet him as soon as he stepped out of the lift onto the bridge. "We have just received an achronic message from Home Base. They have called us in, as soon as we can get there."

"What?" Velmeran could not have been more surprised, or confused. "Did they give any reason why? Is there some emergency, or have they just missed our charming presence?"

"No explanation," Valthyrra reported as they came to the center of the bridge. "We have simply been ordered to return. Ordered, I might add, in a very abrupt, even curt manner, that I for one found quite insulting."

Velmeran leaned back against the console of the central bridge, his arms crossed, obviously deep in thought. "We can hardly leave Union space at this time. Lenna will be signaling for us to come for her as soon as she finds what she is looking for, and now we have Keflyn off the ship as well. Two of the most critical missions that we have ever had running at the same time, and they expect us to drop everything and run home."

"Do we ignore the order?" Consherra asked. "You are the Fleet Commander. In theory, only you can give such orders."

"There is one higher authority," Valthyrra reminded them. "This order has come directly from the Republican Senate."

"Oh, my!" Velmeran muttered thoughtfully. "Well, I have to assume that such an august body has a very good reason for doing this, although I would never bet money on it. Valthyrra, call up the Vardon and have her assume our patrol. Treg and Theralda are going to have to watch things here. If Lenna's call comes in, we will just have to drop whatever we are doing. We will get under way as soon as the Karabyn leaves port tomorrow morning."

"Oh, mercy!" Valthyrra exclaimed. "The powers that be will have to wait a few hours more."

"They will have to wait a few days," he told her. "I refuse to wreck this ship rushing home for some unexplained summons. No jumps, and no excessively high speeds. We will hurry, but we refuse to hustle."

Hours later, after the transport bay had been secured for flight, a small, dark shape dropped down from beneath one of the little ships. It crouched low to the deck for a long moment, using its single optical sensor to probe the immediate environment. It was not a particularly intelligent machine, less so even than a sentry. It had only one purpose, to make its way into the heart of a Starwolf carrier. It had no clear idea of its goal or how to get there, nor even what it was looking for. Its primary logic function was to compare what it saw with its internal records of starship design, and to keep moving until it found what it sought. It was also programmed to keep itself under cover and avoid discovery.

The spider drone's first task was to scurry down to the bare deck formed by the sealed bay doors. It sat down tight against the deck, and a small cutting beam within its body began to bore a tiny, almost microscopic hole all the way through the door into the cold space beyond. Into this it inserted the lead of a tiny antenna, sealing the hole against air loss, then the drone spun a minute spider's web of an antenna across the bay to the tiny receiver it hid in the shadows along one wall. Now that it could receive orders, it hurried to complete its task.

A combination of data—or rather the lack of it—from both its optic and sonic sensors led it to infer that it was relative night on board the Methryn, the corridor lights turned down combined with a general lack of activity. The deck below was down, analogous to the ship, and it knew how far forward it was in the carrier measured from the nose, since it had to have been brought on board through one of the transport bays. Those were simple bits of logical deduction, but by constructing a memory map of its turns and straight runs as it moved through the ship, the drone was able to always have a fair idea of where it was. Sonic data allowed it to guess when it was entering inhabited regions, and visual references permitted it to guess whether it was in a major corridor or a small, unimportant passage.

By keeping to the shadows and jumping into any available cover at the slightest sound, the spider drone was finally able to work its way to the core of the ship between her broad, thick wings, and into the maze of main engineering. Once there, its most difficult task began. The machinery it observed was beyond its experience, both because of the complexity of Starwolf technology and the tremendous size of these generators and power grids. But by a careful comparison of what it saw with what it knew, it was finally able to trace the main power linkages to the main switching core on the outside, a single piece of metal pipe two meters wide by twelve meters long.

The spider drone scrambled up the machinery and scurried along the main switching core to its very center, then settled itself tight against the pipe and held on firmly with all six legs. There it awaited its orders.

Although Velmeran made a joke of pretending impatience and suspicion for his summons back to Alkayja Base, he still believed that it must be important. Starwolf carriers traditionally returned to Home Base only at need, perhaps once every hundred years for overhaul. A direct summons was almost unknown, although far less unusual than it had once been. As soon as the Free Trader Karabyn was safely away, he ordered the Methryn out of orbit as well.

"I may have missed something," Valthyrra remarked, her camera pod watching the main viewscreen over Velmeran's shoulder. "How are we supposed to get Keflyn back?"

Velmeran glanced at her. "Back? Who said anything about getting her back? I was just hoping to get her off this ship before she realized the flaw in her little plan."

The camera pod afforded him an impatient stare.

"She has a small achronic transmitter in one of her bags," he explained.

"If the mission had been less important, I might have believed you." The ship paused, and her camera pod shot up in a habitual gesture of surprise or alarm. "Incoming ships. Three of the beggars, and by their size they can only be Fortresses."

Velmeran's first thought was that the Union had finally decided to bring Kanis in line. The colony and its flaunted independence had been a very sore point with the Union for centuries. But why Fortresses? The immense warships now only traveled it groups of three, too tall a task for any one Starwolf carrier even with the new missiles that cracked their quartzite armor. The Fortresses were not especially useful in planetary invasions in themselves, but they could keep a lone Starwolf carrier from breaking up an invasion.

"Move to intercept," Velmeran ordered. "Buzz past them just out of range. We want to lure them away. How soon can the Vardon be here?"

"Five hours, even if they covered the entire distance in a series of long jumps," Valthyrra answered. "Is there any chance that we can chase them away?"

"The idea is to delay them for now," he answered. "If we can harass them in a series of hits and runs, we might be able to keep their attention on us long enough for the Vardon to get here."

The Methryn rushed directly at the trio of Fortresses, still moving very quickly into system at more than half of light speed, flying in very close formation of barely fifty kilometers apart. Since the vast ships were themselves twenty-five kilometers in length and wider than a Starwolf carrier was long, they made a very impressive sight indeed. Only the development of the energy-plasma missile that could peel the quartzite shell right off of these invincible monsters, together with the incredible destructive power of the Starwolves' conversion cannons, had made it possible for the Kelvessan to fight these immense engines of war.

Even so, carriers and Fortresses had fought only five times in the past twenty years, to the destruction of two of the larger ships. The Fortresses had countered the Starwolf advances by flying and fighting only in groups of at least three. The Starwolves could have pressed the issue by attacking the Union ships in their own battle groups, and Velmeran had sometimes thought that he should. But the Fortresses were a force to be considered even for the Wolf fleet, and he had no wish to engage these ships except under circumstances entirely of his own choosing, when he could press every advantage. At the same time, the Union was very reluctant to press these very expensive machines into battle situations where they could be destroyed, and they could usually be bluffed into withdrawing by a Starwolf carrier taking a determined posture. But once a trio of these ships were entrenched in close orbit, a lone Starwolf carrier was usually the one to retreat.

The Methryn continued her determined rush at the enemy ships, a swift run that Velmeran hoped would be taken as a prelude to the launch of the missiles that would crack the quartzite shields of the Fortresses. She would have made a very inviting target, except that she was still well out of range. At the very last moment, just before she would have come under fire of hundreds, if not thousands, of powerful cannons, she turned sharply and shot away at an angle. The Fortresses turned as one to follow.

As the Methryn retreated, a simple, brief signal was broadcast from the Fortresses, intercepted by the slender antenna that the spider drone had put through the door of the transport bay. The signal was received by the small transceiver that had been left in the shadows of the bay, relaying to the little automaton a message that would not have otherwise penetrated the ship's shielded hull. Deep within the interior of the carrier, the drone responded to that message in an abrupt and violent manner, exploding with tremendous force, taking out a length of the main switching core, the one vulnerable link in the Methryn's power grid.

The entire ship was plunged into a moment of darkness as the entire main power network failed. The Methryn's engines and defensive shields powered down, and even the ship's atmosphere and gravity were lost. On the bridge, Valthyrra's camera pod sank slowly to the deck as her entire computer network went down. After a moment the ship's emergency backup systems came on line, restoring a minimal environment control and lights. A few seconds later, backup generators powered up to restore Valthyrra's main functions. She at least was self-contained, but even she could do nothing with a dead ship.

"Valthyrra, what hit us?" Velmeran asked. He watched as Consherra abandoned her station without a word, hurrying to main engineering.

"Nothing hit us," she replied absently. Her camera pod was returning slowly to position as her primary attention remained elsewhere, exploring her self-diagnostic network. "Something internal failed. My main switching core seems to be down. That is damned peculiar."

"Why?"

"Because it is a relatively new unit," she explained. "That unit is not prone to sudden failure, and it was inspected recently with no sign of any problem. Chief Engineer Tresha is inspecting the damage now."

"An explosion has shattered the main link of the switching core," Tresha herself reported immediately. "The explosion has every appearance of having occurred externally, although there is nothing anywhere near that could have caused such an explosion. I would say that it looks very much like sabotage, if I thought that anyone could get on board this ship."

It had happened before, although certain measures had been taken on board all Starwolf ships since Lenna Makayen's successful penetration of the Methryn twenty years before. Velmeran frowned. "I would not rule it out. The main question I have now is, how soon can you have main power up and running?"

"We are already clearing out this unit," Tresha responded. "We have no ready replacement for the unit, but we can rig a makeshift connection that would give us at least three-quarters full power without certain redundant safeguards. No less than twenty minutes."

"Get to it. I will find you that time," Velmeran ordered, nodding to Valthyrra to close the line. "Sweep out this ship with your sensors for intruders, although I am sure that you will find none. Nothing biological could have sneaked past your routine sweeps, but a small automaton is something we never considered before now. Right now, we have another problem."

"Afraid so," she agreed. "Should I prepare the packs?"

"Would twelve packs do a damned thing to stop three Fortresses?" he asked in return. "How long before those ships intercept us?"

"About ten minutes, allowing for their present determination. They will be close enough to open fire in only five minutes."

"I do not think that they will," Velmeran said. "Keep one thing in mind. All Fortresses have a receiving slot in their lower hull the right size for a Starwolf carrier, with grappling arms and docking probes. For the first time in history, the Union has a disabled carrier within reach, and they will not refuse the prize. We cannot stop a capture, but we might be able to prevent a boarding long enough to get power back. They will be able to attempt boarding at any one of six airlocks along our lateral groove. That means two packs with heavy guns each, ready to move into the docking probes as soon as the seals are made. Other crewmembers will have to go secretly out onto the hull, to plant explosives that will free us from the grapples."

"Will that work?" Consherra asked, returning from the engineering station. "We could put all of our transports out and have them tow us long enough to get power back up."

"It would take at least ten minutes to set that up, and then they would begin shooting at us to prevent our escape. We have to entice them to capture us."

"Tresha says that she has found the remains of some type of small probe in the debris," Valthyrra reported. "It seems that you guessed right."

Velmeran had apparently guessed right about something else, for the long minutes passed and the three Fortresses held their fire even after they were well within range. Then, as it began to move up close behind the Methryn, the lead ship began to rise slowly until it was slightly above its prey.

"They definitely are moving to intercept," Valthyrra announced. Since the main viewscreen was still down, the bridge crew was dependent upon her reports of everything that happened outside the ship. "I anticipate that they will move in to begin grappling procedures in the next minute."

Outside, the massive Fortress began to settle slowly over the top of the Methryn's broad, flat, upper hull. Although the Fortress' own hull was a maze of angled plates designed to deflect enemy fire, one large section under its nose was essentially flat, with an impression designed to fit perfectly over the armored upper hull of a Starwolf carrier. Maneuvering in careful, precise movements, under the control of her own sentient computer system guided by her sensors, the Fortress aligned herself perfectly over her prey and settled in until the two hulls met with an echoing impact. The grappling arms moved in quickly, catching the carrier in the deep indentation of the lateral groove that ran completely around her hull, locking the two ships together.

"That does it," Velmeran remarked as the rumbling echoes of contact died away. He turned to Valthyrra. "Are you able to see those grappling and docking probes?"

"I can get external cameras on some of the grapples and all six of the docking probes."

"Warn our people at the airlocks when they seem about to open up and come through," he told her. "Do not allow them to destroy your airlocks. Open up first. How much longer on those repairs?"

"Less than ten minutes now," she reported. "I am sending the crews out now to begin planting the explosives on those grappling probes."

Smaller airlocks along the Methryn's lateral groove opened, and crewmembers began to move outside cautiously. Wearing the solid black armored suits of the pilots, they stayed under cover of the deeper shadows as they moved secretively along the hull to the grappling probes. The probes themselves were massive rectangular blocks which locked tightly into the carrier's lateral groove, hinged at the top where they swung in against the captive ship and completely retractable into the Fortress itself. They were to plant their explosives on the back sides of each probe's hinge, its single point of vulnerability and, fortunately, well away from the Methryn's own hull.

Within the Methryn, Pack Leader Baressa readied her two packs for the assault on the airlock they had been set to guard. She could well guess that, once a Fortress had a carrier captive, actually boarding it would be a very difficult task indeed. The trick was to get a boarding party through a single, relatively small series of doorways at the airlock itself, where the attackers could be easy targets as they came through at defenders who might not have to show themselves. She knew her advantages and meant to make the most of them.

She also knew that the airlock design was by necessity not the best for bringing an overwhelming press of attackers to bear quickly. Valthyrra reported that the shape of the airlock probes suggested a fairly large lift dropping down into a huge, staging area, where the attackers could assemble under cover before charging the airlock itself. The only thing she could not know was what to expect when those doors opened. She could be facing human soldiers, massive, armored sentries, or the giant Kalfethki warriors that Velmeran had found on board the Challenger years before.

"The docking probe is moving in," Valthyrra reported through the communication system built into Baressa's helmet. "Stand by."

"Acknowledged," she responded, stepping aside from the airlock doors so that she could wave her defenders forward. "Move those beasts into position and power up. Everyone else move to cover."

Several of the pilots under her command brought forward a pair of massive cannons, each one bearing four barrels designed to fire rapidly in pairs, and protected by its own heavy, armored flaring. These guns could make short work even of Union sentries, but were protected against almost any weapon that was likely to be brought against them through that airlock. Set to fire straight through the tube of the airlock, they could be operated remotely through their own sensors by operators who never had to show themselves. Baressa hoped that these two guns would be enough to hold this airlock for the few minutes they would need.

She did not need to be told when the docking probe made contact; she could hear the impact of the structure against the Methryn's hull even through her suit. She waved the remainder of her pilots to cover, within either the main corridor directly opposite the lock or the two side corridors. The Starwolves were themselves armed with powerful rifles, the only weapons that would stop both armored sentries or Kalfethki warriors.

"Stand by. I will open the doors on my count," Valthyrra reported to her defenders throughout the ship. "Three. Two. One."

The doors snapped open, revealing a group of sentries standing near the airlock and, at least to the few Starwolves who saw them, seeming to wear the most startled expressions. The pair in the very front were just preparing to bring their powerful cannons to bear on the airlock doors, a task that would have probably taken several moments of concentrated effort. The sentries just stood there for a couple of tense seconds as their simple brains adjusted to the unexpected. Then they attacked.

Baressa waited as they charged forward, until they were well within the airlock, before she had her main cannons open fire. The searing bolts from the powerful weapons cut effortlessly into their armor, discharging in violent explosions that ripped the automatons apart. Baressa was actually relieved to see that it was sentries that they faced, and not living opponents, for all that they were walking arsenals. Massive sentries continued to press forward as rapidly as they could, to be destroyed by bolts from the cannons and rifles of the Starwolves as they pressed through the narrow tube of the airlock. Within a minute, the tight passage was blocked with the shattered hulls of fallen sentries, too heavy for the automatons on the other side to force their way through, and they were too heavy and awkward to climb over the top. Those which did attempt the passage only presented themselves as easy targets.

"We are holding our own against the boarding parties at all six of the targeted airlocks," Valthyrra reported. "We have the time we need. Our people on the outside have planted their explosives and are coming in."

"Keep an eye on them," Velmeran said. "I would not want to leave anyone outside when we make our break. How much longer?"

The main viewscreen remained obstinately blank, although Velmeran found himself staring at it out of old habit. He was not used to having the fighting at such close quarters that he could not watch its progress either visually or through the scanner's schematic presentations.

"The repairs should be done any time now, certainly no more than another two minutes," the ship answered.

Velmeran frowned. What did he do now? This attack had obviously been aimed at capturing the Methryn, taking advantage of the admittedly ingenious abilities of the little automaton that had been used to rob the carrier of her main power. He doubted that the Methryn was in any shape to fight these three Fortresses even when she did break free, yet he could not leave Kanis at the mercy of this attack force.

"Do not bring main power up until we need it," he directed at last. "When we break free, we will accelerate straight ahead at high speed. Have two quartzite detonator missiles ready for launch."

"Understood," Valthyrra agreed. "Main power will be ready when you need it. Our people are now all inside and accounted for."

Velmeran nodded. "Secure the airlocks as soon as the packs can have them clear, even if you can close only one set of doors."

He turned to Consherra, who had stepped up behind him. "Well, this has been a close one. They catch us by surprise every now and then, but it only works once."

"From now on, we have to scan all boarding ships for hitch-hikers," she agreed. "I hope that we do not have to fight. I have a very good idea what they must be doing to replace that main switching core, and it might not hold under any real stress."

"The airlocks are all secure," Valthyrra announced. "We can get out of here any time you want. Main power is definitely available."

"No matter what, do not stress yourself beyond three-quarters of your normal full capacity," Velmeran told her. "Go ahead and power up for flight. Turn over the main generators."

The entire ship shifted back from emergency support to main power, her environmental systems returning to normal levels and her full interior lighting coming back up. On the bridge, banks of consoles that had been sitting idle returned to life. The main viewscreen came up last of all, showing an unmagnified forward view. The bulk of the Fortress loomed vast and threatening over-head.

"Blow the grapples," he ordered.

Valthyrra triggered the explosive devices that had been planted on the joints of the grappling probes. A series of powerful blasts shook both ships as the Methryn all but disappeared within a cloud of flames and debris. Only three of the grapples were ripped away by the explosions themselves, but the rest were all so weakened that they failed immediately when the carrier began to pull away, dropping down away from the Fortress to clear the depression in the underside of her hull.

The Methryn engaged her main drives an instant later. Riding the double glare of her flaring engines, she shot out from beneath the vast nose of the Fortress and away into open space. She accelerated rapidly, putting distance between herself and the three Union ships before they could recover from this unexpected move and open fire. Then, even as she ran, the Methryn fired both of her missiles simultaneously, emerging from the small, hidden bays under her nose.

Propelled by powerful drives, the missiles were visible only by the fierce glare of their engines. They hurtled ahead of the Methryn until they were well clear of the carrier, then looped around tightly, each one turning across the path of the Methryn, reversing their course completely to pass just to either side of the ship. As massive as they were, the Fortresses could not begin to evade impact in time. They were committed to a collision course at more than half the speed of light.

Unshielded, that impact alone would have probably vaporized a sizeable portion of one of the Fortresses. Even so, quartzite shielding at full power could have survived even that with only minor damage. The missiles struck the middle Fortress with the force of small nuclear explosions, shattering the quartzite shielding over an area of little more than a square meter. But that was all that was needed for the wave of plasma energy created by the detonation of the missile to penetrate those cracks and begin spreading like a circular wave over the hull of the ship just under the surface of the shielding, shattering the quartzite and lifting it away from the skin of the ship like the shell of an egg.

By that time, the Methryn was already circling back well out of range of the thousands of powerful cannons of the three Fortresses, the middle one still losing it's quartzite shielding. The Starwolves had never had a chance to use this weapon before, or even to test it on a large subject. They had no idea just how much of the ship would be stripped by the plasma wave, and they were interested in finding out. The Fortress was not being damaged in any other way, but she was suddenly very vulnerable to attack. The other two Fortresses were already moving to position themselves between their stricken sister ship and the carrier, but they had not changed course or opened fire. The Methryn's rather aggressive response, circling around as if ready to attack again, no doubt left their captains wondering if there were missiles ready for launch at their own vessels.

The answer was a definite yes, although Velmeran did not care to continue this battle except in defense of Kanis. He had to chase these three ships out of system before the Methryn could respond to her own summons home. He was saving that second set of missiles to accomplish that goal. He certainly did not expect this group to try to take the planet now, and he doubted very much that that had ever been their intent. Considering the planning that must have gone into getting that automaton on board, the capture or destruction of the Methryn had been their primary ambition. Hard work, fast action, and a certain amount of quick thinking had saved his ship this time.

"What did this cost us?" he asked, turning to Valthyrra's camera pod.

"No losses or severe injuries," she reported. Her continual contact with the suits of her pilots allowed her to keep easy track of such things. "Very little damage to the ship itself, except for the main switching core. Should I begin to synthesize a new unit, or do we wait until we get home?"

"Get to work on it right away. We have a long journey home ahead of us, and that patch could fail at any time." He turned to lean on the console of the central bridge, where Consherra remained at the helm station. "What are they doing?"

"They seem to be waiting, no change in course or speed," she answered. "They probably want to see what our little weapons are doing to their ship. If the process continues to completion, it could take half an hour to strip that ship."

He nodded. "We will continue to circle like a scavenger until they decide what to do. I do expect that they have had quite enough and are entirely on the defensive just now, but we have to watch them until we know that they have had enough."

– 4 –

The Vinthra Commercial Complex was surely the largest, most sprawling orbital station Keflyn had ever seen. Since she had visited here on several occasions in the past, she was not particularly impressed. Under the present circumstances, she was far from thrilled to be here. This place represented the lion's mouth, and she was about to stick her head in all the way up to her shapely Starwolf derriere.

Following the orders of station control, the Karabyn had spent the better part of an hour working her way into system as a part of the small fleet of in-coming and departing ships with the precision of a stately dance. After having done it the hard way, she was beginning to have some understanding of the havoc that the sudden, menacing arrival of a Starwolf carrier must have upon a station like this. Keflyn had been taking advantage of her esteemed reputation with the crew of this ship to observe the docking from the small and rather crowded bridge, hiding her alarm at watching two-handed humans trying to dock a ship that was not smart enough to begin to dock itself.

Since the Karabyn was a regular courier for the Union rebels, she had been scrupulous in following the protocol of asking no one their names and they did not ask for hers. She knew the name of the ship itself only because it was listed, along with her recognition code, on either side of the hull. She had been told that the crew was changed every few weeks, and that the ship herself was given a new name, code, and registration papers twice a year.

An aging independent freighter of less than 140 meters, the Karabyn obviously did not rate very highly with the port authorities. She was nuzzling into a simple docking sleeve in one very remote corner of the station, hardly more than a large cargo airlock for her nose and a pair of braces that was ready to catch her. Even if it had been allowed for such a humble ship, they had no interest in bringing the Karabyn down to the surface as she had at Kanis. Although she had no atmospheric control or lift surfaces at all, the Karabyn was perfectly capable of landing.

The ship shuddered slightly as she slipped her docking probe into the main airlock. The braces closed against the hull a moment later, locking her in. The bridge crew hurried to secure the ship, powering down all systems except environmental and maintenance.

"Well, here we are," the captain said, turning to her. "I'll go find out if the Thermopylae is in port and where she is located. You won't have to leave the ship until everything is ready."

"Will she be on schedule?" Keflyn asked, knowing that their arrival had been timed perfectly.

"She's a ship hired out for a regular run," he explained. "They have to keep their schedule within a reasonable tolerance or they risk losing their contract. Barring accident or major emergency, they'll be here."

The captain left in the company of a junior officer, leaving the ship's regular business in the hands of the first officer and cargo

master. Keflyn spent the time as best she could, getting herself
into costume and preparing her bags for travel. As far as she was
concerned, this was the most dangerous part of the operation. The
captain of the Thermopylae could turn them all in for a very
sizeable reward, if it included her as the main prize, and she would
never know until they came to take her away. And even if that
part went well, she still had to reach the other ship, which could
be kilometers away through a very crowded station. Although she
knew to look for the tell-tale signs that gave her away, she still
thought that she looked very much like a Starwolf pretending to
be human. She was never entirely sure if she had been teased
when she recalled her father's story of how he had once fooled
all of Port Kallenes for a couple of days, including the redoubtable
Lenna Makayen.

The junior officer came to collect her several hours later, helping
her to place her bags into a shipping container that would be
transferred over to the Thermopylae. One of her bags contained
an achronic transceiver that weighed half as much as herself. It
seemed that the negotiations with the captain of the Thermopylae
had gone extremely well, and that he was completely willing to
accept the risk of transporting her to the colony on Alameda, which
the Union called Charadal. But they would have to hurry, since
the Thermopylae was on the Port Schedule to depart in only a few
hours.

The shipping crate was put on a cart which the officer from the
Karabyn proceeded to navigate through the crowd. Keflyn was
obliged to follow him at a discreet distance, with just one of her
bags over her shoulder, playing the part of a passenger looking
for her ship. She had to wear the cape to hide her lower set of
arms, and that prevented her from wearing a uniform that would
have allowed her to pretend to be the member of a ship's crew.

Having lived all her life in the monotonous uniformity of the
same ship, she was in fact too busy enjoying herself during her
walk through the station to be frightened. The corridors of the
station were nearly overflowing with the press of aliens of every
type, mostly human. She was so busy looking about, in fact, that
she had a hard time keeping within sight of her guide. They arrived
in time at an airlock essentially identical to the one they had just
left. Following the instructions she had been given, she loitered
at the observation port while her crate was loaded onto the ship.

That gave her a chance for her first look at the ship that would take her to her destination. The Thermopylae was a moderately large ship by Free Trader standards, some 300 meters or more in length, but old and generally decrepit. On the whole—and largely because of Starwolf intervention—the Free Traders led a fairly profitable existence. For one to be in this state meant that they had been down on their luck for some time, perhaps impoverished from the debt of unexpected repairs. She had heard tales of Traders reduced to smuggling or other illicit schemes in their desperation to pay their port fees and keep their ships in space. This lot had apparently swallowed their pride and accepted a long-term contract for a run that would not have paid for the larger ships of the Companies.

"We should get you on board."

She turned quickly to the man who had suddenly stepped up beside her. She had never met a Free Trader before. But remembering Lenna and how she could pass for Kelvessan, Keflyn was not entirely surprised at how much he looked like one of her own kind. He was too tall for a Starwolf, but he did have the same tan skin, dark brown hair and dark eyes, and the same smooth, almost child-like features, perhaps more so because he was obviously still quite young. The Free Traders were nature's answer to the Kelvessan, the very best that natural selection could do to adapt a living creature to the same high-stress environment of space flight that the Starwolves had been designed to conquer. The outward resemblances between the two races were, as far as anyone knew, entirely a matter of coincidence.

He did not, of course, possess a second set of arms, nor could he take more than just a fraction of the crushing accelerations that Starwolves could endure. He could not endure even an instant of the vacuum or the super-cold temperatures of open space. He could not lift thirty times his weight, nor did he face a life expectancy of centuries.

He was sort of cute, all the same.

"We will be leaving in less than three hours," he said as he escorted her to the airlock. "The sooner we get out of here, the better I'll feel about it, I do admit."

They were both happier once they stepped through the airlock and entered the ship itself, moving quickly through the wide tube of the docking probe and into the cargo hold. The Thermopylae was essentially just a single, long storage bay, with her engineering section in back and the crew quarters in a single deck above.

Her companion indicated a set of stairs leading up with a gallant wave of his hand. "She's not much, but she always gets there on time. So far, at least. I'm Jon Addesin, Captain of the Thermopylae."

"Keflyn, no last name, lately of the Methryn, Starwolf extraordinaire."

"I've never met a Starwolf before," Addesin said as he boldly lifted her cape to look at her second set of arms. Most humans would not dare to touch a Starwolf, which they considered a quick way to certain death. Perhaps she just looked small and defenseless without her armor; humans were also not used to seeing Starwolves in such an advanced state of undress.

"You might find something in there you do not expect," she said, trying to sound stern and threatening, although she was more amused than anything.

"I doubt that," Addesin remarked. He stepped off the stairs and paused almost immediately before the door of a cabin. "I thought that we might put you here on the nearest end of the passenger section, right up against the crew quarters. Being a colony supply ship, the Thermopylae has to carry a fair amount of passenger space, although we have nobody but yourself on this trip. Since most of our passengers are Feldenneh, the environmental system has been converted over to their tastes. Tell me if it runs a little cold."

"I am not likely to complain," she said. "Starwolves were meant for cold climates, like the Feldenneh."

"Is that so?" He stared at her closely. "Where's your fur?"

"You seem to be very interested in what I have inside my clothes," she said, deciding to tease him hard in return. She was young enough to be quite flattered by the attention, but old enough to know better. "Do you have a thing about Starwolves? That is about as weird as it is dangerous."

"Just polite interest in something new and different."

"Different? I should introduce you to one of my Valtrytian friends, if extra limbs excite you."

Addesin seemed to be at a loss for an answer to that one; Keflyn wondered if he was not used to young, innocent prey that knew how to fight back. She had learned to bluff from the best, having watched her father for years. And Lenna Makayen had told her a few things that Starwolves hardly ever knew.

"Why don't you stay under cover until we leave the station," he said as he turned to leave. "The port authorities sometimes come on board to inspect the cargo before we go, but they never come into the passenger area."

A few short hours later, the Thermopylae backed away from her place at the Vinthra Commercial Complex and accelerated in a slow loop that carried her out of system. Eventually, as she pushed laboriously toward the speed of light, she engaged her stardrive and slipped away into the endless night between the stars. Unseen, a small, dark ship followed closely.

Almost immediately, eight vast ships left their place of hiding in close orbit over a remote planet of that system. Seven of those ships, moving in a wide arrowhead formation, were standard Union Fortresses. The last was a ship the Starwolves had heard about in rumor but never seen. The SuperFortress, vast almost beyond belief, was nearly fifty kilometers in length, twice the size of any other Fortress. Larger even than any mobile station ever built in Union space, an armored monster vast, dark, and threatening. Slow and awkward, the strike force took the better part of a full day to accelerate to light speed, and even then they lumbered through the stars like a pack of large predators on the hunt. Indeed they were already on the scent, following the Thermopylae's trail at a discreet distance.

Thermopylae was a fitful, temperamental little ship. Her stardrive phased in an endless repetition of surges and stalls. The relentless pulsing was enough to drive Keflyn to distraction, for Kelvessan had been bred with the ability to sense stardrives as an alternative to having to rely upon scanner images when pursuing their prey. She went at last to the main engineering compartment in the back of the ship and began the subtle task of recalibrating the drive to phase smoothly.

No race in all of space understood drives better than Kelvessan, and she soon had the aging freighter purring contently. That brought about certain very noticeable changes on the displays on the bridge, most importantly an increase in speed of almost one-fifth. That, along with the nervous complaints of the chief engineer who had been chased out of his domain by a determined Starwolf, brought Captain Addesin to investigate.

He found Keflyn well in the back of the engineering compartment, closing access panels on the main power coupling feeding into the stardrive. That frightened him just a little; with the drive powered up, a mistake here could have vaporized the ship. He stood where he was, leaning against a post as he watched her.

"I know you are there," Keflyn said at last.

Addesin shrugged and sauntered over to join her. "The position of chief engineer was not open, but you can have it if you want it. Do people come on board the Methryn and start taking her apart?"

"The Methryn has never been in such bad shape," Keflyn said, tightening the final bolts on the panel. "That rough phasing was giving me fits."

"You're some kind of strange perfectionist?"

"Starwolves can hear drives phasing," she said, tapping her head. "That is no secret to the Union, although it is not common knowledge. That is why we are such good fighter pilots. We can track drives more accurately than any scanner."

"That's a neat trick," he commented, surprised and obviously skeptical. "I've never believed in magic."

"Starwolves have nothing to do with the supernatural." Keflyn teleported the wrench that she had left beside the access panel into her hand; she had inherited her father's remarkable abilities, although simple teleportation was actually the limit of her powers. "What we can do with the natural is something altogether different."

You are showing off, she told herself. Starwolves were not supposed to do things like that in front of humans, not even their friends. Of course, most Starwolves could not begin to do that. Then again, who was he going to tell? No one would believe him.

Addesin thought about it for a moment, and decided to change the subject. "Ah, if you are quite finished tinkering with my ship, would you like to see the rest of it? Or would that just tempt you?"

"I might as well," Keflyn agreed as they walked slowly back to the main corridor. "I mean, we really need to get down to business."

Addesin looked startled. "I thought so, too, but I never expected it so soon."

Keflyn looked profoundly embarrassed. "I . . . really need to know about the Feldenneh colony. I mean, how long have they been there, how large is the colony now, and how much have they explored?"

"In other words, do they possibly know anything so important that it would attract the attention of Starwolves?" Addesin elected to attack the matter boldly. "Say, why don't we get just one matter of business over with early and be done with it. I know that colony fairly well; I helped to set it up. If I knew what you were looking for, I could possibly help to steer you in that direction. If I can't know, then I'll keep quiet on the subject from now on."

"Well, I wish you had not asked that," Keflyn declared with exaggerated regret. "Now I have to throw you out the airlock and commandeer your ship."

"What?"

"Why are you not afraid of Starwolves?" she asked with equal bluntness. "Humans are all supposed to be afraid of Starwolves, as if maybe we all run around poking people's eyes out, or something."

"Kill you as soon as look at you is the proper expression," he told her. "I don't know. You see, I've lived my entire life without ever seeing a real, live Starwolf in person, and then you walked onto my ship."

"You went outside and got me."

"You know what I mean," Addesin exclaimed. "That was a line, a come-on—flattery. You speak the language reasonably well, well enough to change the subject."

"You changed the subject. I asked why you were not afraid of me."

Addesin paused a moment, then indicated for her to proceed him up the ladder to the crew deck. "I don't have an answer. You simply do not frighten me. I've seen things in my life that have frightened me a whole lot more than you. Now, do I get an answer to my question, or do you even remember what it was?"

Keflyn frowned as she considered how much to tell him. "We think that your colony used to be a major world of the Terran Republic nearly fifty thousand years ago."

"A major world?" Addesin asked. He looked both directions along the wide corridor that ran most of the length of the ship, choosing to go toward the back. "We've found some ruins, but nothing to suggest a major world."

"You have found a few glaciers as well, I imagine," she said, and he nodded. "Those glaciers have been at work for five hundred centuries."

He nodded thoughtfully. "I can tell you now that there are some buried ruins, but quite extensive and well-preserved ruins all the same."

"Does the Union know about these ruins?"

"No, I don't think so. The Feldenneh consider this world to be their own, and they can be very secretive about anything that they consider to be their business. I've always respected their privacy, since I work for them. At the same time, they seem to trust me."

They entered the large galley and lounge at the end of the corridor, with its wide bank of windows overlooking the ship's rear drive section. Keflyn flipped the switch that opened the metal shields of the windows, looking out into the blaze of colors of the Thermopylae's passage. Jon Addesin stepped back from the window. Few humans, even Free Traders, could endure the vertigo of looking directly into the glaring visual distortion of starflight. It was a Starwolf's native element.

"How long?" she asked.

"It's a long way," Addesin explained. "It's way on the outside, even from the Rane Sector. New territory for the Union. The schedule calls for three and a half weeks."

"And how long before you have to go on?" she asked.

"Only a week. I hope that gives you all the time you need to do whatever you have to do."

"I will not be leaving with you," Keflyn explained.

"Oh, I see." Addesin was obviously surprised and dismayed to hear that.

"Could we get there ahead of schedule?" she asked, turning to look at him with a Kelvessan's big, innocent eyes. She was no fool; he would know that every day they arrived early was another day he had with her. "I mean, surely you can get just a little more speed out of this ship."

It was rather bad acting. Keflyn was new at this; she knew the theory, but she had never practiced the technique. All the same, young Captain Jon Addesin swallowed it whole.

"Well, I suppose that we could step it up just a little," he agreed reluctantly; something about this made him very nervous. "Especially after what you've done to our stardrive, we could probably step up the speed as much as one-third without stressing the engines much more than we were. There's just one thing that I have to ask."

"And what is that?"

"Can you work on my generator also?"

The Thermopylae arrived in orbit above the world that the Feldenneh natives called Charadal a full week ahead of schedule. It was a cool, green world of two wide seas between two large, continental regions, mountainous and forested between massive poles and vast plains of glacial ice. It was the type of world only a Feldhennye could love, and a world that the Kelvessan could learn to love.

As soon as the Thermopylae had settled comfortably into orbit, the crew began the process of unloading their cargo into shuttles. The two atmospheric shuttles were kept in their bays in the underside of the freighter, where they could be loaded directly from the main cargo bay. The Feldenneh colony was receiving so little cargo on that particular journey that the whole shipment was easily loaded onto the two shuttles in only one trip. Depending upon the type of shipment the colony had for export, loading their cargo could be as easy or it could take the better part of a week. Jon Addesin never knew what he would be carrying out until he got there, but he was expecting a fairly large shipment of cured wood.

When Keflyn followed Captain Addesin into the shuttle bay for the ride down, she had immediate reservations—the two aging transports were even more decrepit than the freighter herself, worn out from uncounted circuits into and back out of planetary atmospheres. The shuttles were an ancient and simple design, intended for slow, rough, atmospheric entries with low-powered shields that allowed a great deal of heat to leak through, deflected by the shuttle's own ceramic composite hull. The low-powered design was slow and awkward, but it allowed for more of the shuttle's interior room to be given over to cargo and less to massive generators.

Keflyn was even more alarmed when she entered the forward cabin of the first shuttle to find Jon Addesin at the controls. She was not particularly surprised; the Thermopylae was flying under a minimal crew, with just about everyone taking multiple duties. Jon Addesin was not only captain but helm and navigator, and it seemed that he fancied himself a pilot as well.

"Away we go!" Addesin declared as the shuttle fell away from its cradle out the bottom of the bay. "Have you ever ridden in one of these before?"

Keflyn shook her head. "I usually have more sense."

The shuttles had no reverse-thrust engines, another weight-saving peculiarity of these machines. Addesin simply rotated the ship over on its back and engaged the main engines enough to brake their speed before rotating back to a nose-first position, letting gravity draw the shuttle down toward the planet. After a while the shields began to burn against the outer edges of the atmosphere, and from that point they were going down in a hurry.

Keflyn had never before ridden a ship down from orbit to landing entirely by gliding unpowered. The main thing that impressed her was how long it took, nearly an hour-and-a-half after leaving the Thermopylae's bay, a leisurely trip of about fifteen minutes in her own fighter. Unlike most transports, which would stay at speeds of two thousand kilometers or more except at landing and take-offs, this lazy shuttle spent nearly half of its glide down drifting at subsonic speeds.

It did give her time for a good, long look at the Feldenneh colony. It was located well inland in the north of the smaller continental area, at the eastern base of the mid-continental range of mountains. Like Kanis, this was a heavily forested world, the inherent imbalance of the cold continental and polar areas and the warm equatorial seas driving a weather system that distributed a fairly even amount of precipitation year-round over almost the entire land areas. Keflyn had her closest look at the continental glaciers while they were still very far up, several hundred kilometers away.

The colony itself was not that large, it's single impressive feature being the three-kilometer runway for the shuttles. Some distance away, tucked back under the edges of the forest, was the colony itself, some five dozen simple wooden houses and a few larger buildings. The Feldenneh were not farmers, their diet limited to nuts, bread, and meat, and they certainly had not come to this world to farm.

It occurred to Keflyn then that Jon Addesin was looping the shuttle around to align it with the runway, and that he intended to bring the little ship down in a rolling stop. She realized for the first time that this aging shuttle had not even been designed for field drive vertical landings. She had never made a rolling landing before. For that matter, she had never even been in a ship that had wheels, much less used them.

Fortunately the shuttle had been designed with large wheels and rugged landing gear for high-speed landings on unimproved runways. Addesin rotated the wings forward and dropped the flaps, and the ship shook and rattled as it protested the slower speeds. Moments later it bumped hard against the runway, and Keflyn was certain that the landing gear must have collapsed to leave the shuttle sliding in on its belly, the ship shook and vibrated so violently. She was contemplating abandoning ship when the machine suddenly lurched almost to a complete stop and rolled off the runway onto the cramped parking apron.

"There, that was something of an adventure even for a Starwolf, I'll bet," Addesin remarked happily as he began shutting down the little ship.

"Flying a Starwolf fighter is an adventure," Keflyn remarked as she removed her belts, intent upon finding an open outer door. "That was a very inefficient attempt at self-destruction."

"Inefficient?" Addesin was too surprised to be annoyed.

"We are still alive." She stared at him. "I cannot imagine that space flight was ever that primitive."

The nose of the shuttle split vertically just under the cockpit and opened to either side, and a ramp rolled down. By the time Keflyn reached the cargo deck, a cool, fresh breeze was stirring through the wide hatch. She stepped out onto the ramp, looking across a long, narrow meadow of deep, dense grass surrounded by forests and low mountains. It was a perfect day. The sun was bright but not hot or intense, and a gentle wind stirred through the grass in green waves.

A flatbed land transport, loaded with crates ready for shipment, rolled along the road from the settlement to the base of the ramp, and a pair of male Feldenneh stepped out of its front cabin. Vaguely wolf-like in appearance, with slender, thickly-furred bodies and long, narrow heads, they were both nearly a head taller than Keflyn, no doubt chosen for their tasks as loaders because of their considerable size for their kind. They were about to board the ramp when they saw her standing at the top and stopped short, staring. Nothing betrayed the Starwolves more for what they were than their second set of arms. Keflyn was dressed in a conventional manner for a Kelvessan civilian, in burgundy pants and tunic with a black vest, all of heavy material, but with no cape to hide her lower arms.

The smaller of the two relatively husky Feldenneh seemed to consider the meaning of this unexpected appearance of a Starwolf for a moment, then stepped quickly up the ramp to meet her. It had never occurred to Keflyn to wonder if Jon Addesin would have warned the Feldenneh what he was bringing them. It seemed that he had not.

"I am Derrighan, shipping master," he introduced himself simply, his voice the soft, rich purr of his kind. "How may the people of Denneshyann serve you, warrior?"

"I am Keflyn of the Methryn," she answered, a little disconcerted by his intent and slightly bewildered stare. "I have been sent to seek the answers to a very ancient riddle. We believe that this may have once been a major world of the Republic."

"You will have to ask our Speaker, Kalmedhae, for any answers to your questions that we may have," Derrighan said guardedly, "but I think that you will not be disappointed."

Keflyn helped to unload the shuttles, since she could lift so much more than anyone else, before she rode the last transport into the settlement. She thought that she should do these people a favor or two before she came asking for hand-outs and hospitality . . . not that the congenial Feldenneh where likely to refuse her. More than anything, she was busy reviewing her strategy, because nothing in the greater universe outside the Methryn's hull had gone at all the way she had expected.

She had been watching her father's techniques for years, and that had let her down from the start. Velmeran's method of operation had always been quite simple; everyone he had ever met had been frightened to death of him. His reputation alone made his enemies afraid to cross him, while he would approach a would-be friend with that spontaneous innocence and understanding of his and win loyal supporters. That system adamantly refused to work for Keflyn. The Feldenneh found her cute and charming, and perhaps even a little lost. Jon Addesin fancied himself in love. The Feldennye shipping master Derrighan was in love, and too polite to let on. But no one was in the least bit frightened except Keflyn herself, who needed a bit more cooperation and a few less alien admirers.

Her meeting with Kalmedhae was to take place that night over dinner in the Speaker's own house. Kalmedhae was an older Feldenneh who served the colony as Speaker, as far as Keflyn understood a combination of mayor, judge, and social councilor. Aside from Kalmedhae's own household, the other guests at dinner were Jon Addesin and the shipping master Derrighan. She could imagine why Derrighan had wrangled himself an invitation to dinner; he stayed close to Keflyn's side to insure his place beside her at the table. Addesin was, at least at first, too annoyed to notice that he had competition. He was forever trying to raise extra money for his ship by selling goods on speculation to the colonists he supplied. Because of a mistake in labeling the shipping crates, something he had bought to sell to the fur-bearing Feldenneh had turned out to be five thousand bottles of suntan lotion.

So there Keflyn sat, trapped at the table between her pair of strange suitors, knowing that there might be trouble as soon as Jon Addesin recovered from his mood of annoyance enough to notice. Keflyn entertained some hope that Addesin might never know. Despite his occasional obvious and very self-conscious attempts at acting the part of the daring young pirate captain, he was too absorbed in nursing his shaky business and ailing ship to be aware of anything that did not present itself as a profitable venture. The possible romance of a Starwolf and a Feldenneh would not interest him beyond its threat to his own plans . . . unless he could figure out some way to sell tickets.

Leave them both alone, Keflyn told herself. *You will soon be going back to your own ship and your own kind. One is furry, and the other is descended of baboons. Why would you want to become involved with either one?*

It would be different?

She told Kalmedhae everything about her mission that she had been willing to tell Addesin, not daring to allow even the Feldenneh to know the greater scope of her search. The Feldenneh gave their wholehearted support to the Starwolves, who protected them from slavery under Union control. At the same time, they were a part of the Union and often found themselves forced to fill the roles of non-combat technicians in the Union military, and they seemed to feel that that did not compromise their loyalty. Unlike Addesin, however, Kalmedhae was honestly interested in her quest, and shrewd enough to realize its implications.

"This was once Republic space," he observed, watching her closely with his large, solid black eyes. "Do the Starwolves consider that it still is?"

"That depends upon the level of ownership you wish to define," Keflyn answered carefully. She was well aware of all the members of Kalmedhae's household seated about the table, watching her expectantly. "At this time, the only people living on this world are your own. If your loyalties are to the Union, then the Starwolves will respect that. If you wish to sever your ties to the Union and be independent, then the Starwolves will defend your decision to do so. If you wish to open this world for Republic expansion, we would be grateful."

Kalmedhae considered that carefully. "What would the Republic find of interest in this world?"

"Essentially nothing," she admitted freely. "The export of wood or other materials, or your own products. But the Kelvessan, my own people, would find it very interesting. This is one of the few worlds cool enough for us to live comfortably. Our metabolisms are so high-powered that they produce excessive heat, and we must be artificially cooled to tolerate human environments. Here, we can live very comfortably."

She glanced at Jon Addesin, who was wearing a lined jacket even indoors. He did not notice, still distracted with thoughts of suntan lotion.

Kalmedhae considered that, and nodded. "That is well. Kelvessan would make very good neighbors. I had not known that there were those of your kind who do not lead the lives of Starwolves."

She shook her head. "There are now several million Kelvessan, but only a few thousand Starwolves."

"There are secrets in this world that you should see," the older Feldenneh announced suddenly, as if coming to some important decision. "But it has a price. The Union must not know these things. Once the Starwolves know the secrets of this world, then they will have the responsibility of defending those secrets. You will agree, when you see for yourself and understand."

"You have had that promise already," Keflyn assured him. "What are those secrets?"

"Perhaps it would be better for you to see those things for yourself."

Jon Addesin looked up suddenly, like a startled animal. He apparently had not been in a world completely of his own. "Ah, I'll be bringing down the Thermopylae's skyvan, as soon as we get our load on board. I know that your colony has nothing suitable for long, quick trips."

"Yes, that is so," Kalmedhae agreed, and Derrighan's look of quiet dismay supported that. But the older Feldenneh still had a trick to play for his own side. Although Feldenneh did not smile, he still looked enormously pleased, like a chess player who had just moved his opponent into an unexpected check. "Well, the day grows old, and night is upon us. Derrighan, perhaps you could find a place where your new friend can stay the night."

"Kelvessan do not sleep," Keflyn answered guardedly, watching the two Feldenneh closely. "Of course, I must have someplace where I can stay."

Derrighan's ears were standing straight up with anticipation. "I live alone. I came to this world in advance of other members of my household, who have not yet come."

"You'll not be going back up to the ship with me?" Addesin asked, looking panic-stricken. He knew that she planned to stay, since she had brought all of her bags down on the shuttle with her.

"I will never return to the Thermopylae now," Keflyn reminded him. *So if you want your chance*, she added to herself, *you will get your business concluded as quickly as you can manage so that I can be about mine.*

"And I do have to get back to my ship," Addesin mumbled to himself.

Derrighan just sat there in silence with the most surprised, frightened, and bewildered expression on his lupine face, knowing that he had won something and not at all sure what, or if he really wanted it in the first place. Keflyn hoped that she could take that as a measure of the sincerity of his interests, that he had been competing for her favor in spite of a logical uncertainty about whether or not he should.

Now that she had him, she was also facing the question of what to do with him. She wondered about that as the two of them used the transport to move her bags to his house near the edge of the settlement. Both Derrighan and Jon Addesin had stirred her interests, although not to any great extent. Anything that did happen would be nothing more than play. Jon Addesin looked the most like one of her own kind. Derrighan was most like her in thought and spirit. The Feldenneh would spend most of a long night in gentle, affectionate lovemaking. Humans had sex in a matter of minutes and went to sleep.

She was by no means certain that she wanted things to go that far with either one of them. Her advantage was that the choice was entirely her own.

The evenings of this world were marked by spectacular displays of light, a constantly changing display of long streamers and sheets of brilliant colors filling the western sky. She had been told that the sun of this system was slightly unstable, fluctuating on a cycle of slight expansion and contraction every sixteen hours, and pouring out a tremendous blast of charged particles and strong magnetics as it did. Keflyn wondered that this world had ever been chosen for major settlement. Unshielded electronic and electrical systems would never work properly.

They were unpacking her bags from the back of the truck when a vast sheet of lightning rippled across the sky, moving in a complex pattern of interconnected arcs like a blinding spider's web from the western horizon to the east. Keflyn blinked, waiting for some devastating blast of thunder. Long seconds passed in silence, followed by a dim, distant rumble.

"Sheet lightning, as we call it," Derrighan explained before she could ask. "Stratospheric lightning is the true name. Sometimes the ionosphere takes a greater charge than it can hold, faster than the charge can be lost into the lower atmosphere. First one arc jumps the bounds between the layers, and that sets off the whole thing. Sometimes it will leap all the way to the ground with the force of a nuclear explosion. But only in the distant south, where the lands are much warmer, and especially so during the big circular storms. Never here."

Keflyn stared at him, suddenly perceiving something. That fitful talent of hers suddenly gave her the clue to something she was too distracted to have seen for herself.

"You are no settler," she said, surprising him by speaking in his own language. "Neither is Kalmedhae. None of you are. I think that you are some manner of scientist, or explorer."

"No, this is a real settlement," he told her, considering his answer quickly but carefully. "The Union found this world and considered it unfit for their own use, and they gave it to the Feldenneh. They did not look deeply enough to discover its secrets. When the first true settlers realized what this world was, they sent word secretly. You should understand that my people see the collapse of the Union, and we know that the time has come that we must take a stand. We will no longer help them in any way. We knew that this world would be very important to you. We are holding it for you."

"They sent a team of researchers to live with the other colonists, and other officials such as Kalmedhae to supervise," she assumed.

"That is so," he agreed. "The Union watches us from time to time, and we had to wait until the time was right to tell the Starwolves. Your sudden arrival surprised us. I was to tell you when we were alone tonight. That was why Kalmedhae arranged for us to be alone."

"I thought you were just after my body."

Derrighan looked uncomfortable. "I had my own interests, and Kalmedhae saw that and took advantage of it. Jon Addesin must be frustrated for a while at least. He learned the secret of this world, and he has guarded it well. But he does not know our secret."

"What is the secret of this world?" Keflyn asked.

"I think that Kalmedhae is right, that you must learn that for yourself. You must decide what it means for yourself."

– 5 –

The Alkayja system seemed unusually busy as the Methryn dropped out of starflight, hurtling in toward her destination at high speed. The Republic had never really recovered from its early defeats, remaining a relatively small and inactive group of under-populated colonies. That had been changing very quickly in the past few years, due mostly to the sudden expansion of both the size and fortunes of the Kelvessan race, particularly the High Kelvessan. But the Starwolves themselves lived most of their lives apart, and they often had no clear idea what was happening at home. Velmeran had certainly never expected this.

"Incoming carrier, identify immediately," the voice of system control demanded imperiously.

"This is the Methryn," Valthyrra responded, as surprised as everyone else on the bridge by that cold welcome. She recovered quickly. "My crew and I were responding to your most polite request that we pop in for a visit, as inconvenient as it has been to our busy schedule."

"Methryn, you are directed to move into an equatorial orbit of fifty thousand kilometers and await further orders. You are to launch no ships of your own nor engage in unnecessary communication. Bring your running lights to full immediately," system control directed, abruptly cutting the channel.

Valthyrra's camera pod lifted in surprise. "Well, I like that! I get a warmer welcome than that at Vinthra, even after what we did there. So what happened? Did my warranty expire?"

"Something is wrong," Velmeran commented. "Why are we being shunted into a holding orbit? Is something happening at the station?"

"Not that I can tell," Valthyrra answered. "There are no explosions or wrecks, although they do seem busier than the last time we were here."

Long minutes passed as the Methryn whipped around the curve of the planet Alkayja at a speed which brought another curt reprimand from system control, braking hard as she settled into her assigned orbit. Valthyrra inserted herself at a position in orbit where she had a fairly good view of the station. It was a mobile station, complete with its own drives, although it had been in orbit over this world for centuries. Its thick, main body, twenty-five kilometers across, was a large city in itself. This was surrounded by two rings of docking bays, the smaller bays for commercial and military ships, and below that the immense modules that housed the carriers.

"There are two carriers already in port," Valthyrra reported. "The Delvon and the Valdayen."

"What are they doing here?" Velmeran asked. "Can they tell you what is going on?"

"No, they ward off my attempts to communicate without explanation."

"Well, I have had just about enough of this nonsense. Put me through to system control," he said, and waited until Valthyrra indicated that the channel was open. "This is Fleet Commander Velmeran. I ask to speak with Admiral Laroose, or whoever might now hold his position."

"That is not currently possible," the reply came immediately, so quickly that it was an obvious refusal to forward the request. "You will be directed to dock shortly."

"I wish I knew what this delay was about," Consherra commented, leaving her place at the helm station to pace the center of the bridge. Like the rest of the bridge crew, she had been watching the image of the station on the main viewscreen.

"Yes, I know what this reminds me of," Velmeran declared suddenly. "What do you suppose all other ships do when they come into port, and they have to take their turn to come in to dock?"

That startled the others, even Valthyrra. In all of her long life, no one had ever told her that she would have to circle while she awaited clearance. No one, not even their own people, ever asked starwolves to wait.

"Well, how rude!" Valthyrra declared. "The only reason I took this job was for the perks."

Velmeran returned to the bridge hours later, responding to Valthyrra's summons. The Methryn had finally been committed to her dock, a third of the way around the ring of carrier ports on the station's lower ring from the other two ships, with orders to keep her airlocks sealed with her crew on board and to deny all attempts at communication except from a special Senate Committee or one of the Members of the Triumverate. By this time, Velmeran was very certain that something must be very wrong, and that the Starwolves were being called home to solve it. He was willing enough to help, but he was impatient to be started. With both Lenna and Keflyn away on important missions, the Methryn needed to be free to respond to their calls on a moment's notice.

Consherra and Valthyrra were both in the center of the main bridge, staring at the viewscreen. Velmeran wondered about that at first, since the only image was that of the inner wall of the bay. Valthyrra turned her camera pod to glance at him, then turned back to the screen as she magnified the image on the wide bank of windows that formed the bay's control room and, above that, the larger observation deck. There were guards, dozens of human guards, at both sets of windows, watching the Methryn with the same intensity.

"They are not trying to board, are they?" he asked.

"No, not yet," Valthyrra answered. "All of that milling about does suggest such an intent, however."

"Now I wonder why they would be so interested in this ship," Velmeran mused. "They might be in our own service in theory, but I will not have any humans on this ship uninvited. Any attempt to board this ship, whether by order or by force, is to be denied by any means necessary. I want a pack in armor standing by at each airlock connected by a docking probe, and find some way that you can speak privately with those other two ships. This is now hostile territory until I know what is happening here."

"Could the Union be in control here, and trying to trap us?" Consherra asked.

"If they are, then they are even wearing Republic uniforms."

"That, however, is not actually what I called you to the bridge to see," Valthyrra said. "I took the precaution of putting a drone overboard while we were still in orbit outside, just so I could keep an eye on things from that angle. That helped me to intercept an achronic message from Lenna and Bill. She needs for us to come quickly."

Velmeran frowned. "Very quickly?"

"She says that if we do not get there in a hurry, then it will be the end of civilization as we know it."

"That does sound like Lenna Makayen." He stood for a moment, considering the problem. "Get me in touch with someone willing to talk to me. Tell them that the Methryn is pulling out of this bay in ten minutes unless they can give some very good excuse for remaining."

"What if they try to stop us?" Consherra asked.

"How? There are no doors on this bay."

Velmeran's threat of ten minutes might have seemed a little severe, but it was met with time to spare. Hardly a minute had passed when Valthyrra lifted her camera pod in a gesture of extreme surprise and perplexity. "Commander, I have a call from Central Command. President Alac Delike wishes to speak with you."

"I expected no less," Velmeran said with such indifferent certainty that they had to wonder if he did. "Put him through."

"Commander Velmeran?" the warm, friendly voice, more like that of a used freighter salesman than a leader of worlds, responded a moment later. "You seem to have some complaint with your orders."

"I have no orders," Velmeran corrected him briskly. "As Commander of the carrier fleet, I am answerable to no orders except my own unless I receive special instructions from the Senate itself. I have received no such orders, but I do have people out on two very important missions. I must respond to a call from one of those missions immediately, or I might lose both my people and the important information they were sent to collect."

"I know that it must seem very important to you, but something has happened here that will make all other concerns inconsequential," Delike answered in that same cheerful voice, suggesting good news. "I would like for you to come over for a private discussion with myself and a couple of representatives of the Senate. It's important for you to understand everything."

Velmeran considered that briefly. "I have no choice, I suppose."

"You will not be disappointed," Delike assured him. "If you would like to come over as soon as you're ready, I'll have someone standing by to guide you at your main airlock."

Valthyrra moved her camera pod closer, an indication that she had closed the channel.

Velmeran shook his head slowly. "This is about as strange as it gets, but Delike does seem agreeable enough, even eager. I will discover what this is all about, and then we will do something about Lenna even if we have to send another ship after her."

"Another ship and crew would not know what to do," Consherra reminded him. "Her mission is very important."

"This had better be even more important, or certain members of the government of the Republic are going to find out why Donalt Trace fears the name of Velmeran," he declared. "All the same, I have a suspicion that I am going to be very disappointed. It has always been my experience that they are the most irrational, excitable and socially disagreeable creatures in known space."

"What, humans?"

"No, politicians." He turned to Valthyrra. "What about it, old chips? Who is this Alac Delike?"

Valthyrra would have shrugged if she could, and she did a fair approximation as it was. "No information. Elections were a little over four months ago, and this—political creature—must have moved to the head of the class at that time. In my experience, I would predict that you are about to find that we have been used as a pawn in a tactical maneuver known as political grandstanding, an artificially generated crisis or overblown event designed to create favorable notoriety for the party perpetrating the hoax.''

Velmeran shook his head. "Sometimes you sound like Bill. If that is the case, then we embarrass them thoroughly and publicly and put them in their place, and then we go about our business.''

"And if it is a Union trap?'' Consherra asked.

Velmeran did not discount that possibility, which was why he went to this little meeting in white armor and cape, with both guns at his belt and a very impressive array of small but formidable weapons hidden about his person. He was met at the main airlock by a pair of security officers in the green-gray uniforms of the Senatorial Guard. They turned without a word, marching him smartly through the corridors of the station to a lift reserved for official use. This delivered the small group to the station's government compound in a matter of minutes, an area richly carpeted and paneled in real wood.

This was an area of the station that Velmeran knew well from past visits, that portion of the command sector reserved for official use, mostly as the space-side extension of the Senate. The two guards delivered him to the wide double doors of a conference room near the lift, leaving him with the suspicion that he had just been shuttled through the station as quickly, quietly, and inconspicuously as possible.

The doors opened and Velmeran stepped inside. It was hard for someone as small as a Kelvessan to swagger, especially in the presence of tall humans of undegenerate stock, but Velmeran's suit of heavy, white armor helped to make up for that. Even so, the three men seated in deep lounge chairs scattered about the room did not seem especially impressed. Velmeran could tell from the looks of detached appraisal he received that he was about to be told what was expected of him and sent away.

"Yes, Commander Velmeran.'' A rather tall, lean man of middle years rose to greet him, but did not extend his hand. "I'm Alac Delike. I would like to introduce First Senator Arlon Saith, and Party Chairman Marten Alberes.''

"What party?'' Velmeran interrupted, determined to prevent these people from putting him entirely on the defensive.

"The National Republic Alliance, of course,'' Alberes replied. He was a short and rather heavy man who looked like he could find better things to do than talk to Starwolves. The answer itself seemed satisfactory enough; all Velmeran knew for certain was that it was one of the old, respected parties. The very concept of politics was a mystery to nearly all Kelvessan, since human politics were contrary to their own social instincts.

"I must conclude this business quickly," Velmeran said. "I do have people out on very sensitive missions, and I must respond to a call from one of those parties immediately."

"No, no. Your secret missions are no longer important," Delike insisted, pleased with himself. "The war is over."

Of all the nonsense Velmeran expected to hear, that was not it.

Delike began to pace slowly, as if unable to contain his enthusiasm. "Yes, it is quite true. We've only recently signed a treaty of peace."

"We did?" Velmeran was still confused. "Who won?"

First Senator Saith laughed aloud. "Nobody won or lost, you little fool. The treaty calls for a mutual cessation of all hostilities and a return of normal commerce and political relations."

"You have to understand that the Republic has never been entirely supportive of this war, and no one can deny that it has gone on too long," Delike added quickly. "It is one thing to defend ourselves from aggression, but we feel that we cannot be in the business of protecting rebellious colonists and smugglers from prosecution for their crimes."

"Those worlds are our allies," Velmeran protested, although he recognized the futility of arguing with these three self-satisfied politicians.

"The terms of the treaty are clear," President Delike said, now softly and sternly. "It defines for all times the boundaries both of the Union and of the Republic. All space and every world within that limit are their own, to govern according to their own laws and policies. We will no longer interfere in or question their internal policies."

"I see," Velmeran commented quietly.

"There is also to be a partial disarmament as a part of this process," Delike continued, with the grace to look uncomfortable for what he had to say. "They will scrap their fleet of Fortresses, and we will remove the Starwolves."

"Could I have a definition of 'remove'?" Velmeran asked politely.

"The Starwolves are weapons of war, created for the purpose of war," Saith explained without reservation. "The carrier fleet is to be scrapped. Those Kelvessan known as the Starwolves are to be destroyed, since they are trained in the habits of warfare and will always be dangerous. The rest of the race of Kelvessan will be sterilized to prevent continuation of the race, and they will in time be selectively sold to private concerns.''

"That means slavery," Velmeran pointed out. "The Kelvessan are citizens of the Republic, not property."

"The Second Ammendment of the Republic Charter has been revoked," Alberes said. "The Kelvessan have reverted to property of the state."

"The Second Ammendment cannot legally be revoked."

"It has, all the same, been formally revoked by Senate vote," President Delike concluded almost apologetically. Velmeran could not determine whether he disapproved of these measures, or if he was simply afraid to explain his actions to the Starwolves. "When the Kelvessan were genetically designed, they were given encoded instructions to always obey human commands. I am therefore invoking that control. You are ordered to comply with our commands, and you will assist us in ordering the recall of the entire Starwolf fleet. You will now return to your ship and await further orders."

Velmeran seemed to struggle with himself for a moment, then nodded with obvious reluctance. Alberes leaned back in his chair with a smile of deep satisfaction, and even Delike was relieved enough to cease his nervous pacing and return to his seat. That told Velmeran that they had been unsure of their ability to order him until it was tried. Considering the reputation he had, he was surprised that they had not experimented beforehand with other Kelvessan.

"Do as you are told," Delike continued, silently prompted by Saith's stern stare. "You will return to your ship in the company of your guards. They will stay with you and help you to remember your orders. You will order your crew to place all portable weapons in shipping crates that will be set in the corridors outside the airlocks, and to begin disassembly of all of your ship's major weapons. Admiral Laroose will be along later to help you to attend the other two carriers now in port."

Velmeran turned and walked out, the three men watching him in silence. The same two security officers were waiting outside the door, falling in step beside him as they escorted him back to the lift. He knew now that these two fine gentlemen were not his guides but his guards, his appointed conscience to insure his compliance with his orders. The problem now was figuring out what he was going to do about a situation that he certainly did not like. If they needed his help in disarming the other carriers, it would indicate that the other Starwolves were no happier about this situation than himself and quite possibly refusing to be boarded.

The lift doors opened, and Velmeran suddenly found himself in the company of an old friend. Admiral Laroose had not been a particularly young man when they had first met, more than twenty years earlier. Now he was old, white-haired, and bent of back, and he seemed to be under the burden of more than just the years, but also a deep sadness and regret. Velmeran had been instructed to take his orders from this man, an indication that Laroose was still in charge of dismantling his outlawed fleet. But he had some hope that Laroose did not completely agree with this new policy, and would perhaps even be willing to help.

"Come along," he issued the tired, impatient command. "We might as well get this business started."

"Good to see you again, as well," Velmeran returned pleasantly as the guards hurried them along the corridor, with little enough respect for either the Admiral's age or rank.

"Don't give me that, Starwolf," Laroose said sharply. "I'm just here to do what I have to do."

"I hope that I can understand your position on this matter perfectly," Velmeran ventured in return.

"It seems that you do," Laroose responded, with a brief sly glance at the Starwolf.

It seemed that the Methryn was no longer an object of such interest as it had been earlier, since there were now only the routine docking crews in the corridor outside the airlocks. The authorities seemed to feel very certain that they had everything under perfect control. The group marched down the long tube of the docking probe. Baressa and her pack, all dressed in black armor, met them at the airlock. The two guards apparently saw nothing in this to concern them.

"I need you up on the bridge," Velmeran told his pack leader quietly. "And send Baress up as well. The rest of your pack is to seal this lock and let no one through. Gentlemen, if you will follow me."

The members of the bridge crew were certainly surprised to see the company that Velmeran was keeping when he stepped off the lift. Valthyrra snapped her camera pod around so quickly that the hinges in the boom popped. Venn Keflyn had put in a rare appearance of her own, standing before the viewscreen with a very thoughtful look on her furry face. Velmeran walked immediately to the center of the bridge.

"I have been told that the Republic is under new management," he addressed the crew. "There is now peace between the Republic and the Union. The carriers are to be dismantled and the Starwolves put to death. The rest of the Kelvessan are to be sterilized and sold into slavery. These two gentlemen are here to see that we comply."

"*Veth farkmeer*!" Consherra commented in their own language, glaring at the two guards standing impassively behind Velmeran with crossed arms.

"My sentiments exactly," Velmeran agreed, turning to Baressa. "These two are to be given something to induce pleasant dreams, packed into a shipping container, and left in the corridor outside the main airlock."

The security officers looked startled and reached for their guns, only to find that they had empty holsters. Shrugging innocently, Velmeran brought a pair of guns out from beneath his cape. "Never trust a Kelvessan. They will take anything they can get their nasty little hands on, and they can move so quick that you may never see them."

Baressa gathered the pair up and marched them back to the lift. Velmeran stared, waiting patiently until they were gone.

Admiral Laroose relaxed for the first time. "Your enemies in the Senate believe that Kelvessan must instinctively obey orders given to them by their human masters. I assume that they are in error."

"I should certainly hope so!" Venn Keflyn declared with some indignation. "The Aldessan may have genetically created the Kelvessan, but we would never have programmed any race with an instinctive subservience to another."

"I cannot imagine where they even got such a ridiculous idea," Velmeran said as he watched Baressa lead the two guards away. "Just what is going on here? How did these people get in power?"

"By the usual method," Laroose said, shaking his head sadly and shrugging. "Nothing of what has happened was a part of their campaign platform. It was, if anything, a very dull, low-keyed election. They had been in office for a couple of months, doing nothing of consequence except the usual housekeeping, when they suddenly announced that they had been approached by the Union with an offer to end the war. Considering how long the war has been going on, that came as if they had said they had sold the sky and the stars. Everyone was so shocked that no one has collected their wits enough to protest when they began announcing new policies. They told you that they revoked the Second Amendment of the Charter?''

"They said that it has been revoked by Senate vote," Velmeran said. "That is not legal."

"No, not at all. And it was not done by vote, strictly speaking. Delike annulled the Ammendment by Presidential veto, nearly five hundred centuries after the fact, and the Senate was unable to override his veto, with Alberes pulling party support by intimidation. I decided to play along, since it would leave me in a position to intercept you quickly when you came in.''

"*I hardly have the time to solve everyone's problems at once,*" Velmeran complained to himself. He considered the problem briefly, then glanced up at Valthyrra. "Did you get me private communication with those other carriers?''

"Ready and waiting," the ship replied. "You might be pleased to know that both the Delvon and the Valdayen have kept themselves sealed, refusing to be boarded until they could talk to you. Of course, with their noses pushed up inside their bays, they could not send or receive achronic signals."

Velmeran nodded. "Tell them to stand by, that we will be getting out of here in a few minutes. Have them copy every order I give, at the very same time. My word, I wish that Treg was here.''

"If you wait a while, he probably will be," Consherra remarked.

"He promised to guard our patrol until he hears from us." He turned as Baress entered the bridge. "I have a very important task for you. Your friend Baressa will be bringing a shipping crate full of unconscious guards through the main airlock to leave outside. Valthyrra will arrange to have additional crates—empty—brought out at about five-minute intervals. You, Trel, and Marlena will go outside to stand guard over those crates, which are theoretically filled with our weapons. At my signal, you will go to this bay's control room and pull the emergency docking brace release and get yourself back on board as quickly as you can manage.''

"What about the docking probes?" he asked.

"You can hardly do anything about that and still get back on board the ship, and may the Great Spirit of Space help anyone we may happen to leave behind. There is no danger to the station, since the bay has its own atmosphere." He turned back to Valthyrra as Baress hurried to carry out his orders. "Have you relayed those instructions to the other ships?"

"They comply," the ship agreed. "In fact, they seem to be tremendously pleased."

Velmeran turned to Admiral Laroose. "So what about it? Would you like to go along with us? We can put you overboard in one of those shipping crates with our two duteous friends."

Laroose shrugged. "Before I answer that, can I ask what you intend to do about this mess? I cannot see you abandoning the rest of the Kelvessan to slavery."

"How long can I stay away before they begin this plan of sterilizing and selling the Kelvessan?" Velmeran asked in return. "I was left with the feeling that this is something yet to be."

The human shook his head slowly. "It's not even been announced publicly yet, and a long way from being put into effect. They do have to move cautiously on certain points or they'll have this business blow up in their faces, and they know it. Weeks, if not months. If the Starwolves revolt, public opinion may make it impossible for a long time to come."

"Two weeks at most is all I need," Velmeran said, mostly to himself. "You see, I know a few things that your people here do not. There have been rumors bouncing about that the Union has finally found a way to fight and defeat Starwolves for all time. I sent Lenna Makayen to investigate, and less than an hour ago she sent back word saying that it is the end of civilization as we know it. This might sound like the alarmist predictions of a militaristic mind, but I cannot believe that they will keep the peace if they have a way to finally defeat us."

"But why are they trying to get us to destroy the Starwolves for them?" Laroose asked.

"It would be nice for them if it works," he answered. "It creates a fair amount of confusion under any circumstances. Did you really expect that the Starwolves would submit to having themselves and their ships destroyed?"

"Not for a moment."

"Neither would they. But where does it leave us? Either the

Starwolves become renegades trying to operate without the support of the Republic behind us, or else we end up fighting ourselves. This was all designed to throw us into confusion, and it has cost them nothing.''

''The first shipping crate has been moved into the station,'' Valthyrra reported. ''Baress is standing by, with Trel and Marlena to cover him. The Delvon is at this same stage, and the Valdayen will be ready in a moment. Should we have packs standing ready?''

''Standing ready,'' Velmeran agreed. ''But we will not put out any ships unless we must. Our intention is to catch them by complete surprise and to run before they can mobilize to stop us. My intention this time is to leave them with something to think about.''

''And then?'' Valthyrra asked.

''Then we come back as soon as we can assemble the fleet,'' he answered. ''They committed a major crime against the Kelvessan race when they revoked the Second Ammendment, and that gives us the opening we need. I am sure that they will see our side of things when they find themselves looking out the window at the noses of twenty Starwolf carriers.''

He leaned back against the front of the console of the central bridge, considering the problem carefully. He could not delay in answering Lenna's call, and he did not dare to leave this problem at his back. He was very afraid of what might become of the Kelvessan in his absence, but he had to know what Lenna had found or it might be too late to stop a new offensive from the Union against the Starwolves. Having one major crisis was bad enough, but two at the same time was an almost impossible situation. The timing could not have been worse. He could imagine that Donalt Trace was laughing at him somewhere, thinking that his biggest surprise was yet to come.

At least Velmeran had that one consolation. He was not going to be surprised a second time.

He looked up, noticing that Venn Keflyn was watching him closely. He was never completely sure what the Aldessa was thinking, and reluctant to believe that his race was most closely related to her own. But even the Valtritians themselves held it to be true. The Kelvessan appeared vaguely human on the surface, but the resemblance was purely superficial. In terms of biology, biochemistry, genetics, and—most importantly—mental and social development, they were very closely related to the Kelvessan.

"This was likely enough to happen," he said quietly in the language their two races shared. "They can never forget that our race was created to serve their need."

"Nor can your own people forget that as well, it seems," Venn Keflyn said in return. "Perhaps your people should have a world of their own."

"People of many races can live as easily on any world, even with others," he pointed out.

"Yes. But the one thing that they all share is that, at one time in their history, they all came from a single home world," she pointed out. "The Kelvessan are the one exception. Perhaps the time has come that you should find a world to call your own. Not to stand apart from others, but to have that one place where you can all stand together."

"Commander," Valthyrra interrupted gently, moving her camera pod close. "We are ready. All three ships are standing by for your word."

He glanced over at Admiral Laroose. "What about it? Are you going along for the ride?"

"I have to go back," he said. "If I am not here, there will be no one about who is still a friend of the Kelvessan. And your people need a friend or two just now."

Velmeran nodded. "I could not ask that of you, but I very much need for you to watch things here until I return. I will have Baressa install you in your own shipping crate in a very polite and gentle manner, so that you will not be accused of complicity."

". . . and hurry," Valthyrra insisted.

"Hurry," Baress complained as he reached inside one of the shipping crates for his gun belt and helmet. "As if I need to be told to hurry."

He looked around as he belted on his guns. Fortunately the wide corridor that ringed the inside of the docking bays had remained mostly empty since Velmeran's return. There was one pair of guards at the entrance to the bay's control room, and another farther down the corridor on the passage to the main lift. The Commander had said nothing about being discreet, but he thought that he could scatter this lot without the need of actually shooting anyone.

"I will try to make this very brief," he told Trel and Marlena just before he slipped on his helmet.

It seemed that the station guards had taken no notice of the three Starwolves preparing for battle. They drew their guns and took swift aim, filling the wide corridor in a sudden storm of bolts that exploded in flame and smoke against the walls and ceiling. The guards ducked their heads and dove for cover.

Baress seized the moment of confusion, hurtling himself with surprising speed down the length of the corridor to the entrance of the control room, located before the center of the bay and a quarter of a kilometer from the entrance to the airlock. Trel and Marlena continued to shoot as rapidly as their guns could charge, maintaining the confusion in a deadly hail of bolts.

Baress ducked inside the entrance to the control room, looking quickly about for the emergency release. Fortunately it was clearly marked, a large lever located in a recessed box beneath the main control panel. Holding the release trigger, he pulled back sharply on the lever. Explosive bolts blew within the frames of the two sets of braces which held the Methryn steady within the bay by the ends of her blunt wings, and gas pistons swung the braces clear. For a moment the immense carrier hung suspended in free-fall, steadied only by the nose bracket that held her shock bumper and a pair of long, slender docking tubes.

Baress waited only long enough to see that the Methryn was clear, then hurried back to the door. The guards had re-grouped and were doing their best to return fire from the cover of a side corridor, but Trel and Marlena, shooting from the cover provided by the crates, were reminding them to keep their distance, and their weak pistols could not have pierced Starwolf armor even from a much closer range. He covered the distance back to the airlock in a matter of seconds, sending his companions on ahead of him.

"The ship is clear," Valthyrra announced. "All of our people are back on board and accounted for. The other carriers report the same."

Velmeran nodded. "Get under way."

The Methryn began to back out of the bay, moving straight and steady until she was well clear of the edges of the bay. The pair of long, slender docking probes shattered as she first began to move back, their length splintered into segments that spun aimlessly in the freefall of the bay. Then she turned with surprising speed and agility for a ship so vast, whipping around, then accelerating directly away from the station, moving out of system on a course that would take her back toward Union space. First the Delvon, then the Valdayen fell in close beside her. Flying in tight formation, the three carriers continued to accelerate to light speed.

"System control is calling," Valthyrra reported. "President Delike wants to talk to you."

"I thought he would," Velmeran commented. "He did impress me as a slow learner. Put him through."

"Commander Velmeran?" That voice sounded uncertain, surprised, and perhaps even a little hurt. Something had happened that he obviously did not understand.

"You made this inevitable," Velmeran told him plainly, not waiting for him to ask. He had no more patience for this simple man. "You were badly mistaken on at least one point. I am not obliged to obey your word. When you treat a Kelvessan like a machine, you have found the quickest way to arouse our complete and unforgiving anger."

"But you can't do this," Delike protested. "You will destroy our peace."

"There is no peace that does not include us," Velmeran answered. "You and your friends have committed a very serious crime against my people. I have other important business to attend to just now, but then I will be coming back to have an accounting from you. Think on that."

"I order you to return!"

"Barking asshole!" Velmeran muttered, then turned to Valthyrra. "Cut that. Let them think about it for a while."

"Perimeter defense cannons are moving to intercept us," Valthyrra warned him. "Should we prepare to destroy them?"

"Not if we can help it," Velmeran said. "That is our property, and very expensive to replace. We will try to get into starflight before they come into range, but be ready all the same."

Whether he liked it or not, he was afraid that they would have to destroy the defense drones. They were built like small carriers that lacked stardrives, barely an eighth as large, carrying no crews and automated rather than self-aware like their larger cousins. And yet, despite their relatively small size, they carried a firepower that even a carrier had to respect. Being fairly stupid machines, they could not be bluffed.

"Valthyrra, go ahead and send out a warning to all other carriers," he added after a moment. "Inform them of the situation. Tell them to continue their patrols for now, but to button things up and be ready to come when I call. Tell them to anticipate about two weeks."

"Do you really anticipate a fight?" Consherra asked, watching from her station at the helm.

"No, I think not," he said. "Without the Starwolves, the Republic has only a fraction of the strength of the Union. Two carriers could go through the Republic Militia in a matter of days. Twenty or so carriers would be overkill, except that they do make a very powerful weapon of negotiation."

"Twenty or so carriers moving in formation would frighten anyone."

"Coming into range in forty seconds," Valthyrra reported.

He looked up at her. "Can you make it into starflight by then?"

"If we give our run a couple of more G's, then make the jump just a little premature."

Velmeran nodded. "Do it."

"Coming into visual range of the nearest drone," Valthyrra reported.

Valthyrra centered the main image of her viewscreen on the scan of the nearest defense drone, sitting almost directly in their path. As black as space itself, its triangular hull was in most ways like that of a carrier, short of nose and lacking a tail to house a stardrive. Velmeran stood for a moment, watching the drone.

"Cut acceleration," he said suddenly. "Cut across its path at the very outside limit of its range, shield to full, but do not return fire."

"Well . . . sure," Valthyrra agreed reluctantly, obviously confused. She relayed the order to a pair of very perplexed carriers. "Stand by."

The three carriers suddenly turned sharply, banking steeply to show their relatively unprotected bellies to the drone as they skimmed the outside range of its cannons. The automated warship opened fire, but at that distance even its efficient tracking sensors could not lock on target effectively and the volley of shots, already dissipating, went wide. The carriers began to accelerate again, moving out of range, and the drone moved to follow them, but it could never hope to match their speed before they were gone. A few moments later they disappeared into starflight.

Valthyrra turned her camera pod to stare at Velmeran. "You wanted that thing to shoot at us."

He shrugged helplessly. "Who says that a Starwolf cannot learn to play politics? Laroose says that Delike and his friends are hanging on the very edge of public condemnation as it is, and they just shot first at poor Starwolves who were only running for their lives. Now we can go see what Lenna thinks will be the end of civilization as we know it."

— 6 —

Keflyn turned and looked up into the cool, clear morning sky, watching the Thermopylae's shuttle as it circled around to land. She had not yet seen the unpowered landing of the odd little spacecraft, and she definitely wanted to see this. The shuttle had already brought its wings all the way forward and was now rolling back its flaps. Riding the wind, it shook and dipped in a manner that Keflyn would have ordinarily considered to be bordering on a loss of control. Descending over the runway, it lifted its nose at the last moment and settled onto its rear wheels. Still rolling at a fairly high speed, it dropped its nose until the forward wheels touched down as well. Additional braking flaps in the wings and to either side of the tail snapped open to assist the regular brakes in slowing the ship. It slowed quickly but with obvious strain, turning off the runway and pulling to a stop only a few meters from where Derrighan and Keflyn watched.

"That always amazes me," she remarked.

"That it flies?" the Feldenneh asked.

"No, that anyone would fly it."

The nose of the shuttle split, moving open to either side, and the cargo ramp rolled out. They approached the ramp, careful of the outer shell of the ship, which was still radiating considerable heat acquired through its rather inadequate shields. She did know from experience that the ship would be too hot to touch for some time.

"I am not entirely thrilled by this," Keflyn commented in the Feldenneh language, to be very sure that Jon Addesin did not overhear her. "Are you absolutely certain that your cargo scout cannot be repaired?"

"You have not seen what is left of it," Derrighan answered, and his regret was genuine. If they had not needed Jon Addesin's skyvan, they would not have needed Jon Addesin.

They entered the shuttle's long, narrow bay, which, Keflyn had always been interested to note, was decked in worn, scratched wood. The skyvan was lashed down in the center of the bay, held to the deck by a web of cargo straps. It reminded Keflyn somewhat of a very small version of a Starwolf transport, a long, rectangular hull with a blunt nose that contained the narrow cockpit, the rest of the craft given over to a cargo hold. It had no wings or control surfaces, relying entirely upon field drives, with pairs of retractable wheels in front and rear for land use.

"I am somewhat relieved," Keflyn commented as she began removing the cargo straps. "It seems to be in a much higher state of preservation than the rest of the ship."

"Considering what you were able to dismantle and carry with you, I suppose that you might have squeezed a ship of your own into two more bags," Derrighan remarked.

"So there you are," Jon Addesin declared cheerfully as he descended the ladder from the cockpit. "I hope you're ready. We can be on our way as soon as we can roll this baby out of the bay."

Keflyn paused to stare at him. He was up to something, excited, nervous and just a bit desperate, and acting very hard as if nothing was wrong. There was now a timetable that she did not understand. For some reason, he wanted this expedition done as soon as possible, although she was not telepathic enough with humans to determine more. She doubted that it was anything more than the launch of a major campaign to seduce her.

"Is your handsome pet going along?" he asked next, which suggested that her guess was correct.

"I have duties of my own to attend here," Derrighan answered vaguely, his annoyance obvious at that less-than-subtle derogatory comment.

The young Feldenneh had first meant to go along, but according to their plan, he was now to stay behind in the event of trouble. If Keflyn could not return, he had been taught to assemble and use her achronic transceiver to call in the Methryn. He was also the colony's only qualified pilot and helm. If necessary, he could use Addesin's own shuttle to take a boarding party up to commandeer the Thermopylae. This was by no means Keflyn's idea, but her capitulation of the fears of both Derrighan and Kalmedhae. Whatever secret the Feldenneh were hiding on this icy world, they were unusually fearful over it.

Addesin was perfectly true to his word on one point. The little transport was already loaded with all of the supplies they needed for their journey, so that Keflyn needed only to toss on board her personal belongings. One thing that she insisted upon taking was a good supply of food that she had selected. Kelvessan had to eat prodigiously to maintain their fierce metabolism, and they generally did not share human tastes.

They were under way in a matter of minutes, traveling west and south over the lesser mountains to the plains and light forests beyond. The skyvan was a game little flyer but it was hardly capable of supersonic flights; at its best speed of about 300 kilometers per hour, they would still need the rest of the day to cross half a continent to reach their destination. Jon Addesin was as secretive as the Feldenneh about their destination, but for his own reasons. He was enjoying what he considered to be dramatic effect.

They were passing over one area of scattered plains and light forests when Addesin suddenly turned the skyvan sharply to one side and began to climb steeply. Keflyn knew an evasive maneuver when she saw one.

"What is it?" she asked.

"Spark dragon," he explained simply.

"What?" Keflyn asked incredulously. Spark dragons were native to a world very far away. The large, flying mammals possessed a sonic blast that was as powerful as a disrupter at short range. Contrary to their names, they generated no electricity at all, although their sonic beam caused metal to throw bright sparks as it was molecularly disrupted. That made them dangerous even to the skyvan, or at least its vulnerable electronics.

"Let me show you something especially interesting," Addesin said, turning the skyvan toward an open area of the plains.

He slowed the transport as they crossed the distance quickly, no more than a couple of kilometers, and Keflyn saw what he was steering toward. There was a herd of perhaps a couple of hundred large animals grazing their slow way through the deep grass. Her enhanced vision had already shown her that there were two similar species of animals gathered there. The largest group she recognized immediately as thark bison, also native of a very distant world and now domesticated throughout both Union and Republic space. The other, more massive beasts she did not recognize at all.

"Thark bison and Terran bison," he explained. "The two types apparently get along quite well and often travel together. In the farther north, you will also find them living alongside beasts the Feldenneh tell me are the modern descendants of Terran musk ox. It took them a while to identify those two, since they now exist only here. At night you will hear the howls of the Terran wolves and the barks of the Callian herrimeyens that hunt them."

"This world is a regular zoo," Keflyn commented, watching the herd out of the skyvan's side window as they moved past. In her own mind, this was proof enough that this had once been a major world. Domestic breeds were one thing, but no one imported something like a Kandian spark dragon or a herrimeyen except for exhibition. The sonic dragons were dangerous enough to have under any circumstances.

"You haven't seen anything yet," Addesin told her. "This is definitely the strangest world I've ever seen, but I don't think you'll be disappointed."

Five hundred centuries, especially under a cruel climate, could be disastrous to any civilization. It certainly had not done this planet any favors. Keflyn had spent a long day poking through the ruins that Jon Addesin had brought her to see, even employing her tremendous strength to do a fair amount of excavation, and all that she could say for certain was that the ruins of a large city lay beneath those rolling, sparsely wooded hills. Only the downtown section had once had buildings large enough that their crumbled remains were recognizable as anything that had never been a part of nature.

One thing that Keflyn had not discovered was evidence of battle. She had found stone, metal, and even glass that was shattered, crumbling, and corroded almost beyond recognition, but none of it burned or melted. Buildings had slowly collapsed in upon themselves, and some of the taller ones had even fallen, but she did not see any indication that they had been reduced by some tremendous explosion, or that a large blast such as a nuclear or conversion explosion had ever occurred anywhere in the area.

The frustrating part was that there was no real hint of the world this had once been, no hint of the personal lives of the people who had built this city or even any clear indication of their race. There was nothing she had seen to even prove that they had been indisputably human. There had been no doorways or windows left intact to suggest their shape or height, no furnishing buried beneath collapsed walls or roofs. Metal, except for the splintered remains of heavy beams, had been reduced to dust, and wood had been gone for ages.

Keflyn still felt the weight of incredible years that she had disturbed in the dust of these ruins. Her own race might not have even existed at the time when these buildings were new, before a recent river had cut this city nearly in two, and the Kelvessan were now a fairly old race in their own right. This place was so ancient, her investigation almost transcended archaeology into paleontology. She fancied that she would find dinosaur bones if she was to dig deeply enough.

"Once we knew what to look for from space, the Thermopylae's scanners were able to trace the remains of over a hundred ancient cities," Jon Addesin told her over dinner that night. "None were any better than this, and most were buried much deeper. They're all located in the warmer regions, of course, where the massive continental glaciers never reached."

"I recall from the maps that most of the continent regions are actually removed from the equatorial areas," Keflyn said, struggling with the primitive skills required in cooking over an open fire. Having lived her entire life in a spacecraft, she had never even seen a campfire before this.

"The map is a bit out of date, to say the least," he told her. "The sea level is still many meters lower than it used to be, with a lot of water still locked into the remaining glaciers. There's more land in the tropical regions than there used to be."

"Then this used to be a much warmer world, even than it is now," she concluded.

Jon Addesin had tried his best to be eager and cooperative. He apparently had not expected that she would spend an entire day digging in old ruins. He had tried to help her, but he had only been embarrassed to see her easily lift blocks of stone several times heavier than he could even begin to shift. The only high point of his day had been sneaking a peek at her while she had been washing the dust of the ruins off herself in a nearby pool. She wondered which had amazed him more, her four-armed body or the fact that she had been swimming in glacial meltwater.

Keflyn was beginning to feel very frustrated with the whole affair. She had been sent to find the clues that would lead the Starwolves to Terra itself, only to find an impoverished, ancient world where every clue had been utterly destroyed under the weight of time and ice. All she had found was decayed blocks of stone, a Feldenneh with a fascination for a sexual affair with a Starwolf, and a human who was afraid he might get it in spite of himself.

At least she knew that this was almost certainly Alameda.

"So now what?" Addesin asked, as if he had been following her thoughts.

She shook her head. "I do not see that I can ever make sense of this. It is a very big world, and we have very little time. I suppose that I can only call in the Starwolves and get the help I need to search this world thoroughly. Perhaps there is some structure or installation in this world that is buried but otherwise intact. The Methryn's scanners would turn that up in minutes."

"What are you looking for?" Addesin asked, then frowned. "Forbidden question. I forgot."

He sat for a long moment, so obviously debating some question with himself so fiercely that Keflyn watched him. He did know something, that was obvious enough. She wondered if he would volunteer his little prize of information, or if she would have to force it out of him. One advantage to being a Starwolf was the ability to break just about anyone's arm.

Maybe that was her father's secret for dealing with people.

"As I say, you can spend the rest of your life just digging through ruins on this world," he ventured at last. "Artifacts and ancient civilizations are one thing, but there is something here that has scared the Feldenneh half to death ever since they first found it. I promised them that I would take you to it, but I thought that you wanted to establish just which world this used to be first."

"I know that this is Alameda," she told him. "That was not the primary purpose of my mission, but I cannot accomplish anything more without the help of a Starwolf carrier. And I have my doubts even then that we will ever find what we are looking for, this world has been so thoroughly wrecked. I might just as well go to see this thing that scares Feldenneh. What is it?''

''That's the surprise that we've been saving for you. And it's so strange, I'm frankly hesitant to tell you about it because you might think that I'm either lying or simply insane. You'll have to see this one for yourself.''

Another long day of flight had brought them to the far north of the eastern edge of the mid-continental mountains, on their way to very base of the towering face of the retreating glacier. They had long since returned to lands that, until relatively recent times, had been buried beneath the massive burdens of the continental glaciers. With such a complete lack of information on Alameda, Keflyn had no idea just how far the glaciers had extended at the time of the original colonization. She was only guessing that Alameda was still a colder world than it had been, since she hardly expected that humans would have established a major colony on a world that was so consistently cold. Jon Addesin disagreed with that assumption, pointing out that humans would live anywhere it profited them to live. She thought that might be true for a minor colony like Kanis, but hardly a major one.

Keflyn hoped that she was not just wasting her time. She had no limits set upon her, but she knew that she could not remain here for more than two or three weeks more at the most. And once the Thermopylae left with the skyvan, her explorations would be at an end . . . unless she could contrive to borrow or buy the thing from the Traders. But what was she to look for that Addesin and the Feldenneh did not already know? Her best bet was still to let them show her what they would.

And if this present little trip did not produce results, she was going to begin to get annoyed. Something was out here that the Feldenneh were very eager for her to see, but they were a very secretive folk, slow to give their trust and nearly as cautious with their own kind as with others. According to their own logic, it was infinitely preferable to show than to attempt to tell. She really did not blame them for being so reluctant to part with any secret that they found frightening. For one thing, if trouble came of it, they would be caught in the middle.

Jon Addesin was a different matter entirely, and she liked him far more than she trusted him. He was frightened about something, facing a point of no return, and it had something to do with both her and what he was bringing her to see. He was playing a game, and she was both the problem and the prize. She suspected that it was just his very sincere interest in her, balanced by a healthy fear of Starwolves. Her natural telepathy was not enough to give her a clear answer, but she believed that he was trying to decide whether to try to seduce her before it was too late—before the reason for their journey together was lost—or whether he should just leave well enough alone. He was certain that she had enjoyed an affair with Derrighan and, for some reason that she could not completely understand, that had stung his pride rather severely. Perhaps he understood that her interests concerning him were only those of curiosity, while her deeper feelings were given to Derrighan.

She asked herself what she wanted to do. Could she make love to a human without hurting him? It was a very real danger for most Kelvessan, but she was a very gentle lover. Did she want to try? All that she knew about humans argued that they were rather bland, and yet she had always thought that Commander Tregloran and Lenna Makayen made a very odd but generally satisfied pair.

"How old are you?" she asked suddenly.

"Older than I look," Addesin replied without looking away from the skyvan's controls. "I'm actually 57 standard years. Of course, Traders generally live to be 160 or so."

"Oh." Keflyn could not hide all traces of her dismay . . . not at his true age but that reminder of his mortality. Standard Kelvessan lived about four centuries. No one knew for certain just how long the High Kelvessan lived, although the best bet was that, like the Aldessan, they would live four to six thousand years.

He glanced at her. "How old are you?"

"Twenty."

"Oh!" Addesin mocked her with exaggerated dismay.

"I was just wondering how you came to be the commander of a ship like the Thermopylae," she said, watching the forest out the side window of the van.

"A tottering wreck, you mean?" he asked, amused. "I had done very well for myself as the cargo master on board one of the larger family ships. The Thermopylae is exactly the ship she appears to be. Not so old as you might guess, but she fell on hard times because of mismanagement, went broke, and was finally impounded for failing to pay her port fees. The Traders Affiliate bailed her out and asked around for someone willing to take a chance on a bad bet. I could have had a better ship of my own by waiting a couple of more years, but I thought that I might enjoy the challenge.''

"How does it go?'' she asked, noting his obvious love for that old ship.

"Oh, we're on top of things!'' he declared, tremendously pleased. "That overhaul you gave her engines and generators will make a big difference. Now we have just about enough saved up to put the Thermopylae into one of our own refitting docks for a complete overhaul, and that old ship will be as good as new.''

He turned to her with an intent stare. "That's something that you have to understand about Free Traders. The only thing that any one of us wants is a ship of our own. And nothing and no one ever comes between us, from the captain to the newest crewmember, and our ship. I don't suppose that it can be quite the same with Starwolves and your big warships.''

"Are you kidding? Our ships can talk back.''

Night was already beginning to fall when they arrived, and Keflyn had only a brief glimpse of the immense white cliff face of the glacier, glowing like burnished gold in the fading light. Jon Addesin settled the skyvan into a sheltered depression in the woods a couple of miles away from the edge of the glacier itself, where they would be protected from the worst of frigid air coming directly off the ice. The retreat of the glacier had left this a rough, broken land, full of snaking ridges and sudden depressions littered with sand and rounded boulders.

A ring of blackened stone marked the fires of a previous camp, a sight that helped to reassure Keflyn that they had found what they were looking for. With night falling quickly, Addesin begged off taking her to see his great secret until the next morning. The light of day was fading quickly, and he seemed to have no ability to see in the dark. He immediately set about converting the back of the van into his private bedroom. Since Keflyn did not sleep, she would once again have to find some way to entertain herself until morning. She was presently more interested in dinner.

Addesin jumped down from the back of the skyvan and sealed the hatch, then paused a moment to look about at the sky. The sun had only just slipped below the horizon, and the first hints of color were beginning to climb into the night sky.

"Come with me," he said eagerly, hurrying to draw Keflyn along with him. "There's something that I want to show you."

"Your great, mysterious what's-it?" she asked.

"No, just something pretty and unimportant. Come along."

She followed him perhaps half a kilometer through the wooded, rugged land, until they came at last to a small, deep dell. The long, slender ribbon of a waterfall dropped over the rounded boulders of sheer cliff at the opposite end of the canyon, raising a cloud of fine mist as the icy meltwater splashed almost musically into the deep oval pool at the base of the cliff. Addesin led her along the edge of the lake to one side of the waterfall, where they could watch the final moments of daylight through the spray.

"The Feldenneh are the most quietly decadent people I know," he said as he sat on a large boulder, as if waiting for a tram. "They have an almost magical talent for finding things like this."

"It is nice," Keflyn agreed. "What does it do, besides give me an overwhelming desire to piss?"

Addesin afforded her a look of disgust. "Starwolves must be wretched romantics."

"We live our entire lives in starships," she explained. "What we see of nature is generally on a much larger scale. I find this all very interesting, I promise you. I just wondered what you wanted me to think."

"I just wanted you to see something quietly unique," he told her. "Just watch for a moment."

A sudden shock of sheet lightning leaped across the sky from east to west, tracing a fiery spider's web across the dark sky. For one long, sustained moment out of time, the land below stood out in brilliant relief as the rippling flash threw flickering shadows. The harsh glare of lightning faded, and twilight again settled heavily over the land.

Then it began, slowly at first, as a single, slender column of golden light leaped up from the western horizon. It seemed to linger for a long second, like a fountain of water that ebbed and pulsed, before it sank back down. The glow across the edge of the western sky continued to grow, spreading slowly north and south, and now three columns of light climbed into the night. Each pulse brought an ever-widening fringe of light, spreading slowly north and south until it consumed fully a third of the horizon. Now it alternated in an increasing variety of colors—red, green, and blue, as well as gold.

And with each pulse of light, the waterfall and its veil of icy mist glowed with the same color that filled the sky behind it. As minutes passed, the changing of color both in the night sky and the waterfall became more rapid and regular. As the evening deepened into darkness, the pulsing of light came faster and faster until it steadied into a ragged curtain of misty illumination that rippled in slowly changing colors.

Keflyn sat, enthralled, hardly aware of the passing minutes as evening deepened into true night. She had watched this display every night since her arrival, but she had looked upon it as a remarkable display of static energy, filtering down through the planet's upper atmosphere, the tides of the powerful magnetic forces that raged above this world. She had wondered how the total of those forces compared to the power of a starship. She had wondered if this spectacular display was unique to this one world.

For the first time, she saw it as a thing of captivating beauty.

"This is the price we pay, Starwolves and Free Traders, for living always in space," Jon Addesin said as he slipped away from her side, retreating a few short meters into the forest behind. "We miss the wonders of a worldly life. Even when we see things like this, we tend to see it as we would from the outside. We look out our windows and see whole worlds as small, simple, and largely bland and uniform places. You have to stand here, in a place like this and be surrounded by the immensity of nature, to understand what a vast and complex place a world really is."

Keflyn sat in silence, watching the waterfall. At that moment, a sudden sound rang out across the deep valley, an animal sound unlike any that she had ever heard, like the piping of a distant flute. She started, a Kelvessan's aggressive reaction to fear, as if ready to throw herself into battle with some attacking beast.

"What is that?" she asked anxiously.

"What?" Jon Addesin asked, as if he had heard nothing. He laughed. "It was nothing, just a night bird singing in the trees. You've heard birds before, I'm sure."

"No, not so close," she answered. Birds were known to this world but very scarce; Keflyn thought that few breeds had survived the violence of the deep ice age.

He returned a moment later, holding a length of some tough vine of large, dark leaves and half a dozen large, red flowers like roses. He twisted the ends together and slipped it around her neck. "Flowers, growing on the very edge of ice. That's the remarkable thing. Nature can make a thing of beauty to fill half the sky or small enough to fit in your hands, both of equal complexity. The first is as thin and transparent as mist, yet can rival the power of a starship. The other is fragile enough to crush carelessly in your hands, and yet it thrives within sight of glaciers that crushed an entire civilization from existence. Can Starwolves smell flowers?''

"Just barely. Our designers saw no great need for that sense.'' She still made the gesture of inhaling the soft fragrance, doing honor to the gift. As a matter of fact, she could smell nothing at all. She looked up at him. "I never expected that you would suddenly turn into a poet.''

"A fair night brings it out in our kind, like wolves howling at the moon.'' He stood for a moment, listening to the singing of the night bird. Its call had begun as a series of almost questioning calls, settling now into a simple, fragmentary song, as if answering some music that only it could hear. "They say that there is magic in a night like this.''

"I have heard that said,'' Keflyn agreed. "I never thought there was any truth in that.''

Addesin offered her his hand. "What do you suppose would happen, if a mortal like myself happened to kiss a Starwolf?''

Keflyn laid aside the vine with its flowers, which had come apart and fallen from about her neck. She took his hand, rising gracefully to stand close before him. "I expect that nothing at all would happen, as long as a certain Starwolf was careful about her strength.''

She placed both sets of her arms gently about him and drew him close, a gesture that surprised him with its subtle boldness, and they kissed. Unseen for the moment, the single large moon of that world rose slowly over the eastern edge of the dale. Standing nearly full, it cast a cold, bright light that turned the waterfall golden. Arm in arm, Jon and Keflyn turned away from the secluded pool and sought the simple path leading back to camp.

Unnoticed in the night, a small, dark shape left the shadows of the woods. As it moved noiselessly into the moonlight, it was revealed as a machine, the rounded, featureless hull of a small automaton with a pair of cameras in a protective housing at the end of a flexible armored neck. It drifted slowly forward, suspended on silent field drives, its snake-like neck bent as it watched the retreating pair. Although it was no part of this world, Keflyn would have found it a familiar sight. It was a probe, the durable all-purpose remote employed by Starwolf carriers as their eyes and ears outside their own hulls. If she had seen it, Keflyn would have wondered why it was there. As far as she knew, there were no Starwolf carriers anywhere in the area, nor would any have cause to hide from her.

The probe paused at the edge of the pool where the two had sat. A pair of long, narrow bays opened in its lower hull, and a set of mechanical arms unfolded slowly. One small, slender mechanical hand reached down to take up the length of flowered vine that Keflyn had forgotten, the machine's camera pod bent low, a gesture that was gentle, yet somehow sad. For ages she had slept, desiring never to awaken. The coming of first the Union and then the Feldenneh had caused her to stir, but she had slept again unconcerned. But the coming of a Kelvessan was something that she could not ignore, stirring memories as old and deep as the stars. She lifted her pod and quickly looked around a second time, watching the pair as they retreated over the edge of the dale and disappeared into the forest and the night. Slowly her gaze drifted back to the vine, which she laid gently back into the bed of grass and leaves, withdrawing the probe's hands into itself.

So she stood, hovering motionless in the night.

"This is it," Jon Addesin said, stopping in the middle of the trail halfway up the ridge to block her path. "Are you prepared to be astounded?"

"Just go ahead," Keflyn answered impatiently. She still had no idea of just what waited on the other side of that low hill, but she knew that Addesin was excited and extremely pleased with himself. At least he did not presume upon their one, rather brief intimacy. It had satisfied her curiosity, and his was the attitude of a man who had gotten rather more than he had bargained for. She followed him to the top of the ridge, and stopped.

She was every bit as surprised as Addesin could have hoped.

Previously hidden by the dense forest, the towering face of the glacier suddenly soared before her, a crumbling cliff of ice well over a kilometer in height and stretching away to either side in a broken line that eventually disappeared into the distance. The glacier was bordered closely by a string of long, narrow lakes, sometimes extending several kilometers away from the base. A thin layer of soil that had collected over the centuries had covered large areas of the top, bearing carpets of grass and occasional trees. The very sheer face of the glacier was characteristic of its present state of retreat, a condition also born out by the thin ribbons of waterfalls that spilled over the top.

The surprising thing was what she saw embedded in the dark ice. Protruding from the very center of the glacier was the black nose of a Starwolf carrier. Although only a small fraction of the ship was visible, over a hundred meters of the forward hull hung out like a dark ledge.

"*Varth! Val traron de altrys calderron!*" Keflyn exclaimed.

"Yes, I had thought so," Addesin remarked, grinning hugely. "Now you know why the Feldenneh are so nervous about having something like that lying about. Even wrecked, a ship like that is something that the Union would give a lot to get in their possession, but they would have to be extremely secretive about it. They would probably eliminate all the colonists on this planet to maintain security."

"But that is not a wrecked ship," Keflyn insisted as she started down the hill toward the glacier.

"What?" he demanded as he hurried after her. "But that thing has to have been trapped in the ice for tens of thousands of years."

"There are carriers in space right now that are tens of thousands of years old," she told him. "Even so, although we might build those ships to last, that one has been under half a kilometer or more of ice for a very long time, and even continental glaciers will slide and flow for vast distances. She would have been ripped to much smaller pieces than that a long time ago. She must be powered up, with structural shields in her hull and space frame."

"Where are you going?" Addesin demanded, almost having to run to keep up with her.

"Since she is still alive, there might be a way in."

He expected that she would have to stop when she reached the edge of the lake that stretched along the base of the glaciers for some distance to either side of the carrier's nose. After all, it was at least half a kilometer across and the water was just barely above freezing . . . with nothing but ice waiting on the other side. Starwolves, however, could take worse than that in stride. Keflyn immediately began removing her clothes.

"Oh, be practical!" Addesin exclaimed irritably. "I'll go get the skyvan. It can hover well enough, and it certainly floats."

"I will get the skyvan," she said. Although she did not explain herself, he had to agree with her reasoning. She seemed determined to run all the way back to camp some three times faster than he could, assuming that he could have even run the entire distance.

The skyvan hovered well enough for their purposes, and there was also a narrow beach of rounded stones and boulders of broken ice where they could land. They did not have to look for very long. There was evidence of old, collapsed caverns in the ice in the glacier to either side of the stranded carrier, and they soon found one that was very recent. It was obvious that new access caverns were constantly being cut as soon as the old ones were crushed by the shifting ice.

Unfortunately, the cavern—like all of the others—was four hundred meters up the side of the glacier. Addesin held the skyvan in a hover while Keflyn leaped overboard, then he landed the machine on a ledge some distance below and let the Starwolf haul him up with the length of rope she carried. He was even less enthusiastic when he found that the tunnel was fairly small, so that he had to walk slightly bent over.

"Is this entirely safe?" he asked as he followed her into the depths of the tunnel. The ice cavern seemed much colder on the inside than outside. "I mean, how do we really know who is living at the far end of this passage?"

"Starwolves, I imagine," she answered. Then she realized what he was thinking and paused to turn to him. "In truth, I expect only to find the ship itself. You see, our carriers have sentient computer systems. They can take care of themselves."

The most important question in Keflyn's mind was not so much what she was going to find but how it even got there in the first place. A Starwolf carrier was a versatile ship. Although it had never been meant for atmospheric flight, its armored hull was certainly streamlined enough even without atmospheric shields and its field drive was powerful enough to bring it down slowly, even hover. The problem then, of course, was that a carrier had no landing gear. On level ground, the main body would be supported by the tips of the down-swept wings and the forward edge of the nose. She did think that the ship was leaning slightly nose-down, but it was hard to tell with so little of the hull exposed.

She still could not imagine why anyone would want to land a Starwolf carrier in the middle of a glacier. The best place to park a ship of any great size was in space. And while the inside of a glacier was perhaps the last place where anyone would look for three kilometers of starship, it would take hundreds if not thousands of years to bury anything that size.

The tunnel had so far been following a long, gentle curve inward toward the buried ship, although they could see only a very short distance ahead in the absolute darkness. Glacier ice was not very translucent, and a kilometer thickness of the stuff might as well have been a kilometer of rock. Keflyn's small torch suddenly illuminated a blackness at the end of the tunnel that was the hull of the ship itself, centering on a sealed airlock.

"So now what?" Addesin asked. "We knock?"

"There is hardly any need," a precise female voice declared from behind them.

They turned quickly to see a carrier's probe hovering in the tunnel some ten meters behind them, at the very limit of Keflyn's weak light. Jon Addesin had never seen anything like it in his life, and he drew back fearfully as the strange machine drifted noiselessly closer, its snake-like head with two large, bright eyes bent to watch him. It was a very disconcerting thing to find blocking the only way out at the end of a long tunnel inside a glacier, especially when it was watching him in such a baleful manner.

"You knew that we were coming?" Keflyn asked.

"I have been watching," the machine answered vaguely.

Well, this was certainly a Starwolf carrier. Keflyn recognized that very typical manner well enough. Certainly well enough to know that she was facing a very perturbed and anti-social example of the species.

"I am Keflyn, daughter of Velmeran, Commander of the Carrier Methryn and of the combined Starwolf fleet," she offered, realizing that she was expected to make the first overtures. "This is Jon Addesin, Captain of the Free Trader Thermopylae."

"What is a Starwolf?" the ship asked.

"Oh, my," Keflyn muttered to herself, suddenly aware of the incredible antiquity of this ship. "Starwolves are those Kelvessan who still live on board the ships. There are still twenty-three carriers. We believe that we are in the final days of the war, although we have no idea how much longer the Union can hold out. From your point of view, it has to be just about over."

"The Republic survives, and the Kelvessan are still fighting the war?" she asked, her camera pod dipping reflectively. "I had never expected that."

The airlock door suddenly snapped open, the warm, bright light of the corridor beyond flooding out in welcome. Whatever this ship thought of her unexpected visitors, she had apparently decided to trust them enough to ask them in. Keflyn realized that the poor ship probably had no idea what to think, as long as she had been in isolation.

"I am Quendari Valcyr," she introduced herself simply.

Keflyn stopped short, and turned abruptly to stare. "But the Valcyr was lost a very long time ago, in the earliest days of the Starwolves. You were the first jump ship."

"That is a very long story," the ship said, drifting slowly forward to encourage them to enter the airlock. Keflyn suspected that she was unwilling to speak before Jon Addesin.

The airlock closed behind them. Addesin was enormously relieved to be out of the intense cold of the cavern, although his joy was short-lived when he discovered the pronounced chill inside the ship. Starwolves required a cool environment for comfort, and Quendari had dropped her internal temperature even more to save power and preserve her electronics against heat decay. Then, as the inner airlock door closed, he seemed to realize where he was. For the first time since Keflyn had met him, he appeared impressed and even just a bit frightened by Starwolves.

Keflyn found the corridors familiar so far, and headed toward the nearest lift. She assumed that Quendari would then direct the lift to whatever part of the ship she meant to keep her uninvited guests, probably to put Jon Addesin into safekeeping so that they could speak privately.

"Why have you come?" Quendari asked as she hovered behind them. "If you did not know that it was me, then what were you seeking?"

"Another ship that had been destroyed centuries ago was recently restored to life through her remaining memory cell," Keflyn explained briefly, speaking in Tresdyland to protect her secrets. "She possessed vague memories that brought us here, to the lost colony of Alameda, where we had hoped to find additional clues that would lead us to Terra. You see, we lost the location of both worlds a long time ago, after they were abandoned. I know that Terra is supposed to be unlivable. . . ."

"Then none of the older ships survived?" Quendari interrupted.

"No. All that survived the time before was the former Alameda station, which is now at Alkayja."

"Well, you people did get rather lost," the ship remarked as they moved into the lift that stood open, waiting for them. "This is Terra."

- 7 -

Invisible to sight and scan, the Methryn slipped silently into the small, remote system. She launched drones immediately, and they reported back within two hours with a detailed survey of the system, giving Valthyrra the location of the main surveillance network on the planet and every hidden detector within the system. That provided a surveillance map of the complete area, allowing the Starwolves to know the strengths and weaknesses of the Union's position and indicating their best avenues of approach.

The most difficult part of landing unseen on any planet was the last two hundred kilometers. Then an approaching ship was within the effective range of radar and almost on top of scanners, its own speed cut to a relative crawl and leaving a fiery trail through the upper atmosphere with its shields. Over their long history, the Starwolves had explored a variety of methods for getting their fighters undetected to within striking range of a ground-based target. The most effective method was a sudden burst of speed on the final run, hitting hard before defenses could be brought into order. That was not, of course, at all possible when the objective was a secret landing.

That was the problem that Velmeran faced, complicated by the fact that he really did not have the time to spare on any complex plans. He needed to get in, find Lenna, and get back out again in a hurry. He still had to stand the Republic on its head and get a pack of petty tyrants out of power, before they did something unforgivable to his people. He was fighting two wars now, and he only hoped that Lenna did not have something to show him that would demand precedence. Then his life was going to get impossibly complicated, and they might have to start the revolution without him.

He stopped pacing and looked up to see that the entire bridge crew was watching him expectantly. He knew what they were waiting for. It was time for Velmeran to do something bold and unexpected, and save the day. He had a lot of days to save in the time to come, but he had no magic schemes to suddenly make the impossible happen. This time, he was going to have to do things the hard way.

He glanced up at Valthyrra's camera pod. "I need for you to get in touch with Bill. Tell that mechanical moron to keep quiet until the two of them are someplace where they can talk without being overheard."

"Right, Chief," the ship agreed uncertainly.

"And use the achronic channels," he reminded her.

"At this distance, I would anyway," Valthyrra said, then remembered that the Union had no way to intercept achronic transitions. "Right away, Chief."

"I was hesitant when you had Bill fitted with an achronic transceiver," Consherra said, stepping down from the middle bridge to join him. "It has had its uses, I must admit, but I worry about the Union getting their hands on it."

"Do not tell Lenna, but Bill also has an automatic self-destruct triggered to detonate if he is dismantled or tampered with past a certain level by anyone he does not know," Velmeran said quietly. "Besides, they get their hands on our technology often enough. So far, they have never been able to reproduce it."

"Bill says that they are alone in their apartment," Valthyrra interrupted. "Lenna Makayen is standing by."

"Their apartment? She says that this is the end of civilization as we know it, and the two of them have set up housekeeping in the middle of a secret Union installation," Velmeran commented as he ascended the steps to the commander's station on the upper bridge, swinging himself into the seat with the overhead supports. "Lenna? What are you doing?"

"Talking to you?" her voice returned through his private com.

Velmeran rolled his eyes. "Smartass. What have you found down there? Are you ready to come up to the ship, or do we really need to come down?"

"I think that you really should come down, if you can at all manage it."

"Is that going to be easier said than done?"

Lenna had to think about that for a moment. "Commander, the bad news is that this is a very, very large base. The good news is that the place is all but deserted. Things have been hopping here, but that came to a sudden end right before I arrived, and they are still in the process of shutting down their operations. This place is going back to sleep, but there is still quite enough for you to see. I think that you should see this for yourself. You might see something more in it than I do."

"Lenna, things are very bad out here," Velmeran said. "We now have a whole new war to fight."

"You have just lost both wars, if you do not get down here."

Velmeran sat back and saw Valthyrra looking down at him, her camera pod moved well back into the upper bridge. He thought about it only briefly. "Lenna, could you arrange a distraction?"

"I just love distractions. Can I make a really big one?"

"Do you have something in mind?" Velmeran asked.

"There is all manner of havoc down here, just waiting to happen," she replied. "I could find something to entertain myself easily enough."

"How soon? We need to get this done."

"Get in your fighters in two hours and be ready to move as soon as things begin to happen," Lenna told him. "I will have Bill tell you where to find me when you get here."

Velmeran sat back, looking up at Valthyrra. "That girl worries me. She reminds me of a bomb with a very eccentric detonator."

"Well, yes," Valthyrra agreed uncertainly, then glanced up hopefully. "Of course, she is also very efficient."

"What about that time two years ago? She stole a bulk freighter, then scattered its entire cargo of magnesium canisters overboard in the path of the Union fleet following her as if they were space mines. At a quarter light speed."

"Yes, there is that. Then again, it did work."

"A major freight lane is useless because two-thirds of the things are still floating around out there," Velmeran reminded her as he pulled himself out of his seat. "Have Baressa and my special tactics team ready for flight, including accessory cannons on the fighters. Three fighters and a transport should be quite enough. Any more than that and we will just be getting in each other's way. Have all the other packs standing by, also with accessory cannons. Yourself as well. I will determine what I can about the situation, and then we will simply blast that installation out of existence."

"You plan to go along?" Consherra asked, waiting for him as he descended the steps from the upper bridge.

"I suppose that I have to," he answered. "Lenna seems to think that this is very important, and that I should see it for myself. This is another dragon that I am going to have to face myself and look straight in the teeth."

Speak of the devil and she shall appear. At that very moment the lift door on the right side of the bridge opened, and Venn Keflyn loped in. Her dragon's form with a spider's abundance of arms and legs was encased in her own white armored suit, in most ways like the suits worn by the Starwolves, her neck and tail encased in flexible sheaths of overlapping plates. Although her primary duty on board the Methryn was instruction in the psychic arts and ancient history, she was also an occasional member of Velmeran's special tactics team. She seemed an unlikely addition to that group, but she was full of more tricks than Lenna Makayen.

"I think that I should go along," she explained simply before anyone could ask.

"So I see," Velmeran commented, staring. "Could I ask why?"

"Because I really think I should?" she suggested, running that answer by a second time to see if it was good enough.

Velmeran closed his eyes and sighed heavily.

"Oh, sure. The more the merrier. I really thought I should go, too." He turned to Consherra. "Do you think you should go?"

"Really?" she asked incredulously. "You never ask me out any more."

"Do you want to go?"

"No. I still remember the last time."

"Good. I need you to watch the ship."

"The ship is quite old enough to take care of herself," Valthyrra remarked tartly.

"I am going to put on my business armor and check the condition of my fighter," Velmeran said as he turned away, indicating to Venn Keflyn the direction of the lift. "So, what do you think? What could cause the end of civilization as we know it?"

"That depends upon how you define civilization," the Aldessan explained in a scholarly vein as they walked slowly together toward the lift. "You define civilization as one thing, and your enemies as another. To truly understand that question, you must first ask yourself what your enemy believes that civilization means to you, and then how he would attempt to destroy your concept of civilization.''

''I doubt very much that Donalt Trace entertains any thoughts of defeating me with philosophy. He believes in things that go *bang*.''

''Yes, there is that.''

Lenna Makayen had to think, and she had to think quickly. She had to find some way to distract the Union base from repelling the unexpected arrival of a pack of Starwolf fighters. Ideally, that distraction should be enough to keep an entire base the size of a city from even being aware of the arrival of the Starwolves. That made the answer seem simple enough. She had to arrange an accident that would take out the installation's surveillance coordination system, particularly that part which correlated scanners and the defensive systems.

That was a really good idea, but she had never found that particular section of the base.

Unable to do the damage she wanted, Lenna had to consider other distractions. The best solution seemed to be something that would frighten Union Command, something that would threaten to be very nasty if it got out of hand, something that would draw a lot of attention to itself and cause a fair amount of concern and confusion. Considering the rather stripped and deserted condition of the base, there were very few alternatives. She would have to do something with the warehouses or adjacent underground hangar bays that were still in use.

Once she determined that, matters became fairly simple. There was one little supply and munitions freighter that had her name on it. Actually, it was named the Fireflower, but that was close enough for her purposes. It seemed to Lenna that a small explosion and fire quite close to that ship would make the locals very nervous for some time. The explosion of the ship itself would take out the entire freighter bay complex. She did not consider that very likely, but she would not worry if things did get out of hand.

Accompanied by Bill, she took the trams through the installation to the freighter bays. They had been in the heart of enemy territory for some time now, and the complete lack of trouble they had encountered had bred a certain lack of concern on her own part.

This was an uninhabited world in a remote system, a fact that had apparently led to a complete lack of suspicion among the base personnel. According to simple logic, no one could possibly be here who did not belong. She had taken advantage of Bill's enhanced ability to interface with the simpler Union computers to have herself established in the roster as a technical support lieutenant and even assigned a very nice apartment in officer's territory. Her rank and area of specialty gave her the run of the base, credentials that she could now prove beyond any doubt.

"What about it, Bill?" she asked as they took the tram to the hangar bay. "Do you think that we should set a fire beside that ship?"

"No," Bill answered, simply and frankly.

She glanced at him. "Why not?"

"It is not safe."

"Then what do you think we should do?" she asked.

"We should do that. It is safer than other things."

Lenna sat back in her seat and sighed. "Why do I even talk to you?"

Bill's diligent little processors contemplated that very question for several well-considered nanoseconds. "Because you have no choice."

The tram transversed many unseen kilometers deep beneath the ice and rock, through the maze of corridors that Lenna was beginning to know very well and to detest with a passion. She had been wandering about in this warren of high technology with a fairly high degree of impunity, having realized very early on that security was almost non-existent on the inside. Once the Starwolves started on their way down, things were going to become very different in a hurry.

Lenna paused to look about. Fortunately all Union military installations were perfectly alike in one respect: the instructions were written on the walls. She sometimes wondered if they built these things from kits, with everything labeled. She followed the arrows down the corridor for a few dozen meters and entered a wide door on her left, finding herself on the observation deck overlooking the hangar bay. The freighter filled the nearer half of the bay, surrounded by shipping crates stacked together in small groups.

"Munitions?" she asked.

Bill stepped up close to the window, aiming the lenses of his cameras at the scene below. He had the advantage of telescopic vision, with the ability to computer-enhance a frozen image that was too far away for simple optics to identify clearly. "Not many munitions. Those groups of long crates nearest the ship's middle bay doors are labeled as missiles. The remainder are standard personal supplies and environmental stocks."

"Like paper?" Lenna asked, in a tone of voice that indicated she had something in mind.

"Paper supplies are stacked well to one side, presumably to reduce the risk of fire," the sentry explained. "One group is labeled as personal paper supplies."

"Personal?"

"Very personal," Bill explained. He was a very discreet machine indeed. Lenna wondered about that. He had been rebuilt and programmed by Starwolves, who were not entirely discreet.

"That might be a very good place to start," she commented to herself, then turned to the sentry. "Shall we go and have a look, my good automaton. Lead the way."

Although there were crews on the deck, she saw no more than half a dozen or so cargo handlers. Lenna elected that a bold assault was probably the best course. She doubted that anyone would cast a suspicious thought at a technical officer in the company of one of their own automated sentries. Sneaking about was out of the question. One thing that Bill had never learned to do at all well was to sneak successfully.

The shipping crates were stacked neatly near one wall, well away from the front of the ship or any of the major corridors leading into the bay. Everything looked very promising, so far. The crates themselves were of light plastic, not the metal for heavier cargo, and their tops were locked down by simple spring clips. Lenna checked the labels on the ends of the crates and chose one that indicated the paper products that Bill had succinctly described, releasing the clips to look inside.

"Yes, this will do nicely," she commented, then glanced at Bill. "I'll be all right. You go over to freighter bay twelve and see what you can do about opening the overhead doors. You're to go ahead and guide the Starwolves down when I send you the word, whether I can get there before they land or not. We are going to have to move quickly when things start."

"You will need a com link," Bill reminded her, stepping around close and popping open his computer interface access panel.

Lenna reached in and removed one of the small com units. The one she took had only limited range, but it was also designed to look like a perfectly ordinary pen to the point that it could actually write. Its limitations would not be a problem to her, under the present circumstances. The access panel began to close.

"Be off with you, now," she told the sentry. "You be very quiet and very careful, the best you've ever done. I know that you can do it."

"I will be careful," Bill promised her as he prepared to turn away. Then he paused, as if in a moment of contemplation. "Sure now, and you be careful to keep your bony ass out of trouble as well."

Seemingly quite pleased with himself, the sentry then hurried away on his errand, leaving Lenna to contemplate the arcane complexities of Kelvessan computer technology. Somewhere, from out of the muddled depths of his primary processors, Bill had considered that bout of nonsense logical.

Lenna turned back to her work, looking about for convenient mayhem. One interesting point that she noted immediately was the close proximity of the crates to a major power link. There were five separate levels of power available at this cluster of outlets. The lowest setting was meant for power tools and other pieces of portable equipment. The highest was intended only to jumpstart the total conversion generators of small spacecraft. The more powerful connections were occasionally known to short out, the high levels of energy they contained sometimes arcing across the two poles of their quick-connect socket. She knew that for a fact; she had in the past encouraged many such shorts.

As spectacular as such an electrical short could be, they were not usually very dangerous and were easily brought under control as soon as coordinating computers detected the power drain and shut down the line. Lenna meant to encourage things to get a little more out of hand, by moving the lightweight, but quite flammable, plastic shipping containers and their equally-flammable cargo just a little closer to the outlets.

Bending over the cluster of outlets, she used the manual shutdown switch to close off power to those lines. A single, slender strand of copper wire, as thin as a hair, was all she needed to encourage the short between the positive and negative connections of the direct current lines. The most difficult part of the process was simply removing the six screws of the main access plate over the cluster of power links. After that, she would slip the length of copper wire between the connections and replace the access plate. When she restored the power, the arc would strike. The beauty of the system was that the arc itself would remove all evidence of her tampering when the wire was melted . . . along with a large portion of the connection itself.

"Here, what are you doing?"

Lenna paused, and frowned fiercely. Things had been going so perfectly for so long, she should have been suspicious. She glanced over her shoulder, and saw two pairs of black boots. Looking somewhat higher, she found that her fears were justified. Two of the biggest men she had ever seen, dressed in the dark uniforms of security, were standing over her, staring at her with expressions that were more confused than suspicious.

"Didn't you know that this is a closed security bay?"

Lenna's rather candid expression indicated that this tidbit of news came very much as a surprise, and by no means a welcome one.

Things proceeded rather better from that point than Lenna could have hoped. She was handcuffed and searched, then taken to the nearest security substation, where her idents were fed into the terminal for a very thorough processing. What encouraged her was the fact that the two guards appeared to be giving her the benefit of the doubt. They were treating her very nicely, obviously working on the assumption that her idents would check out clear and she would be sent on her way, the victim of a simple misunderstanding during the confusion of shutting down the base. They had not even submitted her to a strip-search, and that was a common enough practice even in polite company.

She had been rather looking forward to it.

As far as it went, she was not particularly worried. Her idents were real enough, and the computer records on her were quite extensive. She was high enough in rank that she was ordinarily answerable only to written orders. They even knew her in Technical Support, where she had put in regular appearances and a very real eight hours of trouble-shooting each day. What she did with her free time was entirely her own affair, not to the extent that she had used it, but no one at this base would know about that. When nothing came up on her ident check, she would be released with vague warnings to be more careful. Under the circumstances, a strip search would have been the high point of this little adventure.

She would have been feeling very good about the whole affair, except that she was very worried about what the Starwolves might be thinking, and what they could well be doing in her absence. She was very much afraid that Bill would go ahead and open the overhead doors on bay twelve, not waiting for orders. She doubted that Bill possessed the intelligence or complexity of thought to contact the Methryn on his own initiative, but she did believe that they would contact him and determine his latest orders. If she was lucky, she would be released before any of those dire things could happen.

"We're to take you to the tram," said the senior of the two guards, identified to Lenna only by the name Barg on his ident tag, as he entered the room where Lenna sat politely handcuffed to a chair. It was, at least, the most comfortable of the four chairs in the room. The other guard, Salgey, had sat brooding in one of the other chairs.

"Why is that?" Lenna asked just a little nervously, wondering if something was going wrong. Years of experience had taught her that the person she was supposed to be would have been expected to be just a little nervous by this time, wondering if she was about to be run over by the ponderous, uncaring wheels of military bureaucracy for a mistake that she did not consider to be her fault.

"Standard procedure," Barg explained as he released the handcuffs from around the arm of the chair. "A security tram is being sent around to take us to Main Security, if the officer on duty thinks that it's necessary. It's most likely that he will just ask you a few of the usual, stupid questions and send you back to work."

Lenna stood up, and her hands were again cuffed. At least this time her hands were cuffed in front, less awkward and much more comfortable. She was taken through the corridors to the tram station, not the smaller passenger trams, but the wide, double-tracked tunnels of the immense freight trams. One small, single-unit tram, like a flattened silver oval resting on its massive magnetic tracks, was pulled up to the loading platform. The front and rear of the top of the tram's armored hull were dominated by its massive turrets; at need, the machines could be rolled out onto the surface tracks to repel a major attack. Lenna was directed through its main door.

Inside, the tram was fitted with benches along its outer walls and in small islands in the center, leaving a considerable amount of open space between. This was a transport for security forces, with room for supplies and for guards to get into their gear. Lenna was directed to the enclosed control cabin in the front of the tram. From there, the operator could set the tram's destination with the central computer control, or guide the vehicle directly through remote-control switches at the track junctions.

"Here we go," Barg said, directing her to the seat before the communications panel. "You can speak to the old bastard here."

"Don't let him hear you say that," Lenna warned him, with a noticeable respect for the wrath of superiors.

"Oh, not to worry," he insisted. "The com is on standby from our end."

He pressed a single button, and the small monitor in the center of the unit came to life. A middle-aged man with a rather gaunt face and large nose afforded her the briefest of glances before looking back down at something he had been reading. "So. Kalen Makensee, lately of Balarn. Nineteen years of impeccable service in technical support. Graduated with honors with a degree in engineering from the Service Academy."

"Ah, only seventeen years, sir," Lenna offered the correction as she recognized the simple trap, hoping that she remembered the facts of this alternate persona properly.

"Yes, my mistake." He glanced at her only briefly, turning back to the hard copy that he now held within view of the monitor. "It says here that you have been at this base for only four months. Long enough to know better, I would assume."

"Sir, the bay was not properly sealed for security," she said, which was all perfectly true. "There were no standard lights or signs, and the doors were all wide open."

"That is right, sir," Barg offered.

The officer turned off the sound at his end for a moment while he spoke to someone she could not see. He glanced back at Lenna, this time a somewhat hard stare. "Just what were you doing in that bay anyway? Admitting that you are assigned to random trouble-shooting, what led you to start tampering with high-power outlets?"

"I've known those outlets to short, more than once," she explained. "A little dirt or moisture in the connections, and you have quite an arc on your hands. Starts fires about half the time, since a lot of fools on the deck will stack goods too close to the things. And I wanted to double-check all of the connects in the base, seeing as how we're supposed to be putting everything in hold for a long time.''

"I see," the officer agreed vaguely, then turned off the sound a second time while he listened to some brief report. He turned back to her in a somewhat more congenial frame of mind. "Yes. Well, the mistake does seem to be our own, and everything does seem to check out just fine. I'll go ahead and clear you to finish your work in that bay.''

Lenna was hardly aware of muttering her thanks; her mind was already on her next problem. Actually, her problems existed very much in the significant plural. She had Starwolves waiting for her to create a diversion in a hurry, and she hardly knew how she could arrange that while she was very much in the eye and mind of Base Security. She was considering whether she should go ahead and arrange that same power outlet to short when she put it back together. Maintaining her cover would no longer be important, once Starwolves entered the base. Then this whole installation would explode into confusion, and Valthyrra's cannons would finish the task soon after.

"Told you there was nothing to worry about," Barg said as he bent to remove her handcuffs. She braced herself for the inevitable, knowing what was to follow when the guard looked awkward and uncomfortable. "You know, I really hate to have done this to someone your age.''

"Oh, I . . ." It suddenly registered with Lenna just what he was saying, and her mouth fell open. She had never felt more insulted in her life, all the more so for knowing that those words had been impolite but hardly untrue. And she had been sitting there, waiting for this polite young man to put the moves on her old bones.

A sentry unit thundered through the main door of the tram at that moment, turning to bring all of its weapons to bear on the control cabin. Lenna glanced over her shoulder, harboring certain nasty suspicions about just whose sentry that was.

"Freeze, bastards!" Bill roared.

That left absolutely no doubt at all. Lenna had years of experience with the quirky logic of the semi-intelligent, at least where that term applied to automatons, and she threw herself to the floor.

As she had predicted, the two guards did not freeze. They were too confused and startled out of their wits to freeze, and Bill was not prepared to accept anything less. He opened fire with his forward arsenal, a deadly barrage of weapons powerful enough to bring down a Union fighter. Fortunately he had not seen the need to use full power, but his bolts still made quick work of the control panel. The two guards ducked their heads and, by some miracle, escaped out the small forward door.

Bill had, of course, been listening through Lenna's comlink, which had not been removed from the pocket of her uniform's tunic. In all of the many possibilities that she had considered, Lenna had never dreamed that Bill would elect to run to her rescue like some four-legged knight in ceramic alloy armor, just in time to turn an unexpected victory into resounding defeat. Bill talked a line about machine efficiency, but he always seemed to do everything the hard way.

When the two guards ran out the forward door, Bill, for reasons that were equally mysterious, elected to run after them. Lenna continued her own crawl into the safety under the main control panel, which was already beginning to spark and burn, as the sentry crashed through the forward cabin and out the door. Lenna paused a moment to listen. She heard a few more scattered shots from Bill's main battery, but she assumed that he must have missed his target when the ponderous thumps of his heavy legs continued.

Musing what the two guards must be trying to make of this matter of being chased by one of their own sentries, Lenna braced herself against one of the chairs as she tried to rise. It was awkward enough handcuffed, although much less so than if her hands had been behind her back. Then she hesitated a second time, feeling the vibrations of machinery through the metal floor. The tram was moving.

Lenna had always been particularly fascinated by that aspect of her work, how little things could go wrong in unexpected ways. So far she had found a way to get herself out of even the worst trouble but, as her young friend had recently reminded her, she was also getting old. She looked around, finding the key that the guard had dropped in his surprise and haste to get out of the line of fire. Fortunately it was a simple mechanical lock, still the most difficult type to force open without the key but about the easiest to open with one. Even so, it took a certain amount of dexterity and experimentation to get the key into the lock. Sitting with her back against the driver's seat, she was at last able to hold the key in her teeth as she carefully maneuvered it into the lock.

Tossing aside the handcuffs, Lenna rose quickly and slipped into the seat. She could not immediately determine whether the tram was being directed remotely or was simply out of control. At least the major portion of the tram's operating controls had been spared from Bill's rather indiscriminate attack. The com station, where she had been seated only moments before the attack, was a complete ruin. Just thinking about it made her a little nervous, although she was certain that Bill knew his business with the precision of a machine and would not have hit her.

All the same, the wreck of that half of the control panel assured her of one thing. This tram could not have been under remote control even if they had wanted. The internal control indicator light was clearly lit, but certain other readings were contradictory. The tram was supposedly locked into predetermined settings, but other indicators insisted that it could not possibly be in motion. For not being in motion, however, it was already doing a very healthy, if not hair-raising, 140 kilometers per hour, and all efforts to disable or slow the machine on her part proved hopeless.

Well, when travel became inevitable, one could always attempt to determine the course. She called up the map for the freight tunnels on the main monitor, and saw a clear junction coming up in a matter of seconds. When she selected the alternate course, the tram very obligingly turned off the original track onto that new heading. Encouraged by her success, Lenna bent closer to the map and chose a destination. For the sake of speed and simplicity, she decided to make a quick loop and go back to where she had started. She began selecting junctions that would take her back, reasonably certain that the main routing computers would not switch her down a tunnel that was previously occupied. Theoretically, she knew that the traffic was invariably one way. She was less certain that even the computers could slow this monster if it was about to overtake another tram.

"Bill, do you hear me?" she asked, speaking into her com link.

"Yes, Mistress Lenna?" he responded, his voice thin and weak through the minute speaker.

"I'm on my way back. You go back to bay twelve and get the overhead doors open as soon as you get there. I should have my diversion ready at just about the same time."

"Yes, Mistress."

"Damned fool robot," she muttered as she guided the tram through the next junction, not particularly caring if he heard her.

The next problem was getting herself safely off the tram. Under the circumstances, she was actually rather proud, and relieved, that she thought of that particular item before she reached the end of the line. There was an emergency braking system that, she discovered, did work. Its only problems were that it could not bring the tram to a complete stop, and it worked only as long as she was there to hold down the button. Considering what she had in mind, she decided that it was just as well that it did work that way.

Coming up on the junction to landing bay twenty-eight, she held the brake until the tram slowed as much as it was able, easing the heavy machine around the rather tight turn into the tunnel that dead-ended beside the loading deck of the bay. As soon as the tram was locked onto this one-way path, Lenna released the brake and sprinted for the door, getting herself out of the tram as quickly as she could. The leap down was not very far, but it was made more difficult by the speed of the tram. She hit the ground in a roll and came up running, determined to get herself well away from that side tunnel while she still had time. If her plan was successful, she was likely to get herself killed.

As soon as the drag of the brakes was released, the tram began to accelerate furiously. It was moving at about two-thirds of its full speed when it reached the end of the tunnel, emerging like a shot into the vast landing bay. It came to the end of the track and hit the low rail bumper, which had only been intended to stop a freight tram that was moving at barely a crawl, and which had the effect of lifting this small but heavy unit completely off the ground. Carried by the momentum of its tremendous mass, its trajectory arced well out into the middle of the landing bay. It might well have stayed airborne for the better part of a hundred meters or more, except that it suddenly connected with the munitions freighter sitting across the full length of the bay, plunging right through the middle of the small ship.

An instant later, the explosion of the entire cargo of munitions provided all the distraction that the Starwolves could have wanted.

— 8 —

"All pilots to their fighters," Valthyrra's voice echoed from the main speakers across the bay. "Stand by to launch fighters immediately."

Velmeran had been looking up toward the ceiling as he listened to that brief message. He hurried to his fighter, ascended the boarding platform, and climbed into the open cockpit. Benthoran, the bay crew chief, assisted him with the straps of his seat, then slipped Velmeran's helmet over his head and fastened the clips at the collar.

"What is it?" Velmeran asked, now that he had a private com link.

"Lenna just arranged her little diversion," Valthyrra explained. "In fact, she just diverted a major portion of that base right out of existence. Bill says that we are to look for the open freight bay."

"What about Lenna?"

"I have heard nothing from Lenna, and she is not presently with Bill," the ship explained.

Velmeran frowned within the privacy of his helmet as he waited for the cover of his cockpit to close and lock down. Once they started down, their time was going to be very limited. He could not wait for Lenna to make herself known, and he could only hope that she would be there by the time they arrived.

The important things were never simple.

"All fighters are ready," Valthyrra reported. "The Number Two transport bay is open, and both ships are standing by."

"Launch the transport," Velmeran said. "Order the fighters to power up."

On the bay deck, the three fighters brought their powerful conversion generators on line, a faint, low-pitched humming surrounding each of the sleek machines as they cycled their power

116

back into their generators. Black as space itself, the fighters were resting in their racks, massive metal frameworks that were locked down on the deck, their landing gear up and ready for flight. There were only three in the group rather than the usual nine, the three that represented the core of Velmeran's special tactics team. This time only his two most trusted pilots, Baress and Pack Leader Baressa, would be going with him.

At that same time, a pair of small ships moved out of the second of the Methryn's four transport bays. The first was the transport adapted for use by the special tactics team, a dark rectangular hull somewhat larger than a fighter, but without wings or fins. Following that was the larger form of Venn Keflyn's Valtrytian interceptor, gleaming white rather than the dull black of the Starwolf ships, in form a flattened flying wing like some deep-sea skate or ray. The two small ships moved slowly away from the carrier's dark hull and the bay doors began to close, slowly cutting off the bright interior lights.

As soon as the two ships were clear, Valthyrra counted down the launch for the fighters. In the bay, a series of flashing lights above the forward bay door converged on the single, large green light in the center. Engines flaring, the three fighters leaped from their racks and thundered out the forward door. Instead of moving boldly into flight formation, the fighters cut thrust as soon as they cleared their racks, drifting out from beneath the Methryn's vast nose as they waited for the other two ships to come in close beside their tight formation. Gathered close, the small group of ships engaged thrust and turned slowly until they were moving toward the planet, not yet even visible except as a minute point of light in the distance. They moved under low power, staying within the shadow of the Methryn's hull as the carrier herself now came around, moving slowly over them. The larger ship's cloaking shields would hide their approach until they were within low orbit, ready to make their final run into the atmosphere.

"Any word?" Velmeran asked.

"Nothing yet," Valthyrra answered immediately. "No word or indication from Lenna at all. Bill says that we are not to worry. When I asked him why, he simply explained that Lenna has never failed to come through before and so statistics bear out that she would come through again. It worries me that my brain and his are essentially just alike."

"On a vastly different scale," he was quick to assure her, grateful that sentient computers were not telepathic. He had always found Bill's dull ramblings to be disquietingly similar to Valthyrra's complex eccentricities, if on a vastly different scale all its own.

"Personally, I have thought that Lenna has been overdue to screw one up really badly for a long time," the ship continued. "The luck of the Irish is one thing, but it could hardly have bred true over five hundred centuries. Strictly speaking, Lenna Makayen is theoretically a Scot. And even so, the Irish were historically never that lucky. . . ."

"Val, you are babbling."

"Great Spirit of Space, I am!" Valthyrra declared in a stricken voice, and paused for a moment of deep reflection. "Do you suppose that means that I have a soul?"

"I suppose it means that you have a problem."

The planet grew in size quickly and the Methryn began to brake cautiously, careful to avoid engaging too much power all at once that would give away her approach on scan. The carrier made a rapid pass at a very close orbit, arcing around the curve of the planet before moving away into open space. At her closest approach, the five smaller ships shot out from beneath her hull, rolling as they dropped down toward the planet.

Encased in shells of thin flame as their atmospheric shields pierced the thin, upper atmosphere, the small group of ships plummeted toward a landscape that grew rapidly beneath them. They were coming down at a steep angle on a path that would bring them directly over the Union installation, rather than a remote approach, then a long, low-level run toward their destination. Time was the only factor in their favor, and they were able to cross the three hundred kilometers between the shadow of the Methryn's hull to the hidden base in just under five minutes. That strained the abilities of the transport's shields to the limit, subjecting the little ship's hull to some rather extreme temperatures. At least those very few minutes of heat were no real danger to the sturdy little transport.

"Does Bill have that bay open?" Velmeran asked.

The ships were braking sharply now, closing the final few kilometers in a hurry. They were almost certain to have been detected on either scanners or conventional radar by now, and perhaps even visually. They needed to have that bay standing open so that they could land immediately, or the installation's remote defenses would be opening fire on them.

"Bill says that the bay is standing open," Valthyrra told him. "He also says that Lenna Makayen has yet to make herself known."

"Thank you for anticipating my questions," he responded. "Maybe you do have a soul."

"At least a sense of humor."

"We should not push it."

Then Velmeran paused, seeing the state of the Union base as it became visible below and just ahead. Lenna's little distraction must have been one of her best efforts, if a little overdone. Thick black smoke rose from several points clustered along one section of the installation; it looked as if fully an eighth of the place, as massive as it was, was on fire. Then he looked closer, and he realized something that made him very apprehensive. With Lenna's fire threatening to get completely out of control, the base personnel had opened all the landing bay doors over a large area to vent the smoke.

"Val, let me try something on that remarkable sense of humor of yours," he said after a moment, wondering how long he had before automatic weapons began to make a mess of his little invasion. "Ah, we have no way to tell which of the three dozen or so bays standing open could possible be the right one."

Valthyrra must have afforded the place a quick, detailed scan of the immediate area, for she treated them to an intense barrage of invectives in at least five major languages. Had she a soul, it was surely damned.

"Spare our ears!" Velmeran exclaimed, interrupting her. "Can you identify which of those landing bays contains Bill?"

"I can trace his achronic transmissions, yes."

"Then come around and put a low-power bolt right down the middle of that bay," he instructed. "I hardly care how much, just so long as we can see it. Tell Bill to stay under cover, and we will hold back just a bit."

"I am in position now. Are you ready?"

"Standing by."

A pale blue beam shot down from above, striking through the center of the open doors of one of the nearer bays. It lasted only an instant and resulted in no explosions or smoke from within the bay, but it was enough.

"Got it!" Velmeran declared, then addressed his pilots. "Follow me now, fighters first to clear the way. Perhaps we can get ourselves under cover before they begin shooting at us."

The three fighters rolled over and dove within the opening of the bay, a move copied by Venn Keflyn's corvette. The transport followed somewhat more cautiously. Once they were within the bay, the ships dropped their landing gear and dropped quickly to the floor of the immense bay. Velmeran left his fighter idling, ready for immediate flight, as he opened his canopy and began unstrapping from his seat. He was still pulling himself from his cockpit when he saw a sentry hurrying toward him across the bay floor. Since it had not opened fire, he assumed that it must be Bill.

"What word, Bill?" he asked.

"Haste," the sentry offered. He was, as always, a very literal bastard. It was always reassuring to find that some things never changed.

"I keep that always and ever in mind," Velmeran commented, mostly to himself. "What about Lenna?"

"Lenna Makayen is not here," Bill answered. Strike two.

"Any word from Lenna Makayen?" Velmeran asked, putting the two parts of his previous question together in what seemed to be a precise and reasonable manner.

"Careful." Strike three.

Velmeran frowned, for all the good that did machines. "What were Lenna's last words to you?"

"By the balls of Saint Peter!" Bill obliged, speaking in Lenna's own voice before returning to his own. "Then there was a very big explosion, and the channel went dead."

Velmeran sighed—very loudly—and very studiously ignored the fact that all the members of the special tactics team were staring at him expectantly. The end of civilization as they knew it was hidden somewhere in this ice-bound warren. But unless someone was here to lead them to it, they might as well go home. He just wished that Lenna had been there to meet them. Although Bill probably knew as much on the subject as Lenna, somehow he just could not bring himself to ask the sentry to lead them. Perhaps because he felt that dealing with the collapse of civilization as they knew it would be easier for him to deal with than the automaton's obtuse logic. He also felt obliged to wait as long as he could for Lenna, since he was her only ride home.

"Are we going to look for Lenna?" Baressa asked.

"I was just wondering about that," he admitted.

Well, there was no hope for it. Time was of the essence. The essence of what, Velmeran could hardly guess, but time was passing and important matters could not wait, and they had to be on with it. Even if it meant matching wits with Bill the automaton, who had the cold, calculating intellect of a machine and the conversational talents of an ape.

He looked up at Bill, his reluctance very plain. "Bill, will you take us to where you would expect to find Lenna?"

"I think that she is dead," the sentry replied without hesitation. "I would not know where to look."

"Heaven or hell, take your choice," Baress quipped. "I know where I would look first."

Velmeran waved him aside impatiently. "Bill, take me to the place where you think Lenna was at the time of the explosion."

"I will attempt that."

"Keep to the larger corridors," Velmeran told him. "We will be following in our ships. Proceed."

Bill turned and started off, circling wide around their small, tight group and heading across the bay, to the other side of the parked ships. Intent upon his task, he walked right past Lenna Makayen without a word or a glance as she stood behind Venn Keflyn's large, lanky armored form, having just arrived quietly and unnoticed. She just stood for a long moment, looking very disheveled in a torn and slightly singed Union uniform, watching Bill setting off on his quest with quiet determination.

"Miss Makayen, if you . . ." Velmeran paused, seeing that Bill was not going to stop. "Oh, Great Spirit of Space. I told that mechanical idiot to lead us to the place where he thinks that you executed your little diversion. Bill, come back!"

"I am sorry, Commander," Lenna said. "Things got rather out of hand."

Velmeran sensed that she was somewhat contrite and even calm in her behavior, having surprised herself that she was still alive and still somewhat dazed by the explosion. He considered it an improvement.

"You can tell us about it after we stop the collapse of civilization as we know it," he told her. "Take me to see this great secret of yours, so we can get out of here before they come looking for us."

"You can get there from here through the freight tram tunnels," she explained simply. "I suppose that I can guide you from the transport."

He nodded. "The word, I am told, is haste. Get to it."

"Come along, Bill," Lenna called to the sentry as she followed Trel and Marlena to the transport. The other pilots hurried to their own fighters, but Venn Keflyn hesitated a moment.

"I sense something familiar in this place," she said. "Something that has since gone away, leaving only a shadow of its presence."

Velmeran glanced at her in surprise. "Strange. Somehow, I sense that I have been here before. How do you sense yourself, as you would seem to another Kelvessan?"

Since the others were already in their ships, they did not have the time to discuss it further. Velmeran thought his answers lay ahead, wherever Lenna meant to take them. Venn Keflyn thrust her vulpine head back inside her helmet as she pulled herself into the main hatch on the underside of her ship. Velmeran hurried to his own fighter, knowing that the transport would be ready to leave as soon as Lenna had her mechanical companion strapped down in the cargo compartment.

All the same, Velmeran knew that he was in trouble. One major key to his two decades of consistent success was that he had never allowed himself to be distracted by thoughts of failure. He made his plans thoroughly, and he took all surprises as they came. Fear, anticipation of failure, and compulsive haste were the greatest enemies of anyone operating under pressure, but he never allowed himself to respond to such impulses. This time he was working almost completely blind, with no more plans to guide him and no idea of what he had yet to face. He was at Lenna's mercy, and she was determined to keep her secrets until she could show him what she had discovered.

More than that, he was afraid. That odd, shadowy presence he sensed, that seemed in some unexplainable way to be himself, had disturbed him more than he wanted to admit. He was afraid, and that fear had awakened apprehensions of his ability to deal with any surprises. He tried to put such thoughts and fears from his mind, knowing that they only distracted him from his true business, and yet they remained, demanding attention that he could not spare.

The transport rose and began moving slowly across the width

of the bay, its speed hardly more than a hover. Velmeran lifted his own fighter from the floor of the bay, leaving his landing gear down as a caution against bumping the down-swept portions of his wings against the ground. The Starwolf ships were maneuverable, but these tunnels would still demand all the skills of the Methryn's best pilots. He was most worried about Venn Keflyn. Her interceptor was twice as large as a transport, and wider by half again than the short-winged fighters.

He reminded himself that she had well over five hundred years of flying experience. It was like having a fox-faced Methuselah for a pilot. He hoped that she was bringing up the rear. Her big ship could settle down and shield itself like a turtle, or rotate to bring the firepower of a cruiser to bear on anything coming up behind.

Lenna led the transport into the larger tunnels of the freight trams, working their way around the burning areas of the installation. Velmeran did not like having to take the tram passages, and he would have trusted them even less if he had known what Lenna had done with a run-away security tram. Under the circumstances, he simply had no choice. At least they were able to make fairly good speed through the wider tunnels, and Lenna led them to their destination within a matter of minutes.

The transport slowed, then turned off down a side passage that led within a hundred meters to a landing bay, one that was vast in size. When Velmeran settled his fighter in the center of the bay, he guessed that it must be some 250 meters deep, 800 wide and more than 1,200 long. The bay was several times the size of the Union's largest ships of war, except of course for the immense Fortresses. Four or possibly five of their largest carriers could be brought down side by side in this bay, with room left over for a small fleet of cruisers.

The most startling aspect was that no large warship in the Union fleet had the capabilities of landing itself planetside.

He unstrapped from his seat as quickly as he could and dropped down from the cockpit of his fighter. Lenna was already waiting for him, staring up at the tremendous double doors that closed the ceiling of the bay. She seemed to be very pleased with herself, in a grim manner.

"Commander, this bay was meant to service a single ship," she told him. "There are sixteen bays exactly like this one located in a sub-complex in this section of the installation, which is separated from the main base by several kilometers. When this area was active—until about two months ago—no one except military personnel with special clearances were allowed through the very limited numbers of tunnels into this section. There are certain things that I do not have to tell you about a ship this size being able to land itself, but the ship that once filled this bay is by no means the Union's secret weapon. It is only a tool for transporting and servicing that weapon.''

With that flourish of melodramatics out of the way, Lenna turned to lead him across the bay. Only Venn Keflyn followed, leaving the others to watch the ships.

''I went ahead and assembled some important pieces of evidence here, so that we would not have to spare the time for me to drag you over a wide area of this place,'' she explained.

''Good,'' Velmeran said quietly. Lenna might be used to it, but he did not care for walking about a major Union installation as if all the time in the world was his own.

They left the bay through a pair of wide doors in the very center of one long side, beneath entire banks of observation decks. Lenna seemed to know her way very well as she led them some distance along the wide corridor, turning off abruptly into an area which looked to be a large complex of apartments and personal support facilities. Suddenly the shapes of corridors, rooms and equipment reminded him less of the older portions of the installation and more of the interior of a ship, as if some effort had been made to surround those who had once lived here with an environment that was always familiar and comfortable to those who lived their entire lives in space. It was not standard Union practice to house any personnel so near to a landing area, except for small interceptors employed in defense that might need to launch on a moment's notice. No ship made to fit that bay could have fallen into that category.

They entered yet another area of the complex, this part clearly a pilot's training area. One large room contained a row of simulators along one wall, all complete with large, vision domes over their cockpits and multi-directional artificial gravity units to mimic the inertia of turns. Unfortunately, the simulators were entirely utilitarian on the outside and gave no hint of the size or form of the ship they imitated.

''As you can see, this is the larger training room where both pilots and service personnel were made familiar with their ships,''

Lenna explained. She indicated for them to wait as she walked toward one long door along the back wall. "They did have actual examples of their new fighters, presumably for their technicians to have to tear down and put back together again."

Lenna pressed a button on the wall, and the wide, high door began to lift slowly into the ceiling. The keen eyes of both the Starwolf and, to a lesser extent the Kelvessan, could pierce the shadows somewhat, revealing to them a dim, massive form of sleek lines and sharp angles, clearly some manner of fighter possessing atmospheric control surfaces. Once the door was completely raised, Lenna pressed a second button and the lights inside the chamber came on.

After Lenna's dramatic posturings, they had expected the worst. Velmeran felt oddly disappointed, if this was supposed to represent the end of civilization as they knew it. It looked, for all practical purposes, to be only a copy of a Starwolf fighter, slightly larger with more massive engine housings under its wings and a larger stardrive, the same dull, non-reflective black. To Velmeran, it all came back to that same old problem that the Union had always faced. No human pilot had the reflexes to match the enhanced abilities of the Starwolves, and the Union had never possessed the genetic technology to engineer pilots of their own, nor could they build computer control systems that could outfly a Starwolf.

He frowned mightily. "Lenna Makayen, pull down your pants to give me an unobstructed target and bend over. I am going to kick you all the way to Vannkarn, and you can tell Donalt Trace personally that it will not work."

Lenna looked extremely hurt. "Trust me to know my business better than that, Commander. This is just another tool, the fighters that go with that big new carrier. The real secret weapon is already gone, and you'll not be finding any examples of the art lying about this place just waiting to make your acquaintance."

She turned and stalked off toward one side of the chamber, leaving both Velmeran and Venn Keflyn to hurry after her.

"Then what in the name of the great Spirit of Space is it?" he demanded.

"Donalt Trace figured it out all for himself twenty years ago. What in all the universe is the only thing that can fly and fight and think as good and as quick as a Starwolf?"

In answer to her own question, she pulled open the double doors of a metal cabinet standing against the wall just inside the room.

Inside, hanging on its rack, was an armored suit very much like that worn by the Starwolves. Most importantly, it had the same double set of arms.

"Oh, so there have been Kelvessan here!" Venn Keflyn exclaimed with surprise and tremendous delight for solving that mystery. Then, realizing what she had said, she glanced over at Velmeran very contritely, her large ears laid back. "You know, it might very well be the end of civilization as we know it."

"Bill was able to get these figures for us," Lenna said as she began spreading papers across the table in the training room. "The Union has all sixteen of their Mock Starwolf carriers in operation. Each carrier has the capabilities of carrying 1,000 fighters. At the moment, of course, they have only about 200 pilots to each ship, making a total of some 3,350 pilots. The Starwolves, of course, have some 5,000 trained pilots, so you are ahead of them there. Now the Union refers to their Mock Starwolf carriers as Special Assault Cruisers. The ships are about a third the size and weight of a ship like the Methryn, about as heavily armed and armored. They are slower in starflight, and of course they have no jump drives. But there are indications that they are just a bit faster and more maneuverable than your carriers. They don't have conversion cannons, but they do carry a much larger array of conventional, nuclear, and conversion warheads in starflight-capable missiles."

"I suppose that they have no sentient computer control," Velmeran dared to ask, wondering just how many surprises he was in for this day.

"They have the same semi-sentient computer complexes used in the Fortresses," she answered. "Of course, the Mock Starwolves take complete control over their ships during battle. The Mock Starwolves and their carriers are designed to work, at least in major battles, as the perfect complement to the Union's Fortresses."

"Where did Donalt Trace get Kelvessan of his own?" Venn Keflyn asked.

"They all came from Commander Velmeran," Lenna responded.

The Valtrytian twitched her ears with surprise, and turned to look at him. "My, but you have been busy."

"Well, more specifically, they all came from the genetic material from that hand that Trace got from the Commander more than twenty years ago," Lenna explained. "Rather than just endlessly cloning perfect replicas of Commander Velmeran, they decoded the genetic material to the best of their abilities to clone new individuals with a relatively wide area of genetic variations. There are more than ten thousand in all, about evenly male and female, and no two are exactly alike."

Velmeran frowned. "How very convenient for them."

Lenna nodded. "To make matters even more interesting, while they might be Mock Starwolves, they are real Kelvessan. They are beginning to successfully reproduce among themselves, and they could just as easily reproduce with other Kelvessan."

Velmeran stood for a moment, staring at the diagrams of the Mock Starwolf cruiser. He had to admit that the ship did have its virtues. It possessed all of the advantages of the Starwolf Carriers, in a package more dedicated to the role of fighting ship, patrol cruiser, and scout. Over a third of a Carrier's interior space was devoted to massive bays and cargo holds. By deleting much of that empty space and by carrying a smaller and less specialized fleet of support vessels, the cruisers were a third the size of a Carrier, but with engines and generators that were only half as large. In comparative scale, the Cruiser had the potential of being the faster, more maneuverable, and more efficient fighting ship. At least it also possessed the handicap of Union technology.

But just how much a threat were ten thousand Mock Starwolves in sixteen Cruisers? He had fifty thousand Starwolves or more in twenty-three Carriers. The answer, unfortunately, was hardly that simple. He might have twenty-three superior ships, but they were spread over a vast area of space. If sixteen Cruisers came all at once against a single Carrier, or even two or three, then he did not doubt he would lose ships.

Life just became much more complicated, and it was up to him to find the best possible answer in a hurry. What were his priorities? Did he call in Starwolf Carriers from their patrols, where they were needed to protect the small, independent worlds from Union expansion, so that they could hunt the false Starwolves in powerful packs? He also needed those Carriers behind him when he returned to Alkayja to force the resignation of the present government and save the Kelvessan from slavery and extermination. And where were those Mock Starwolves right now? Were they coming up behind the Methryn at that very moment?

"What manner of control is Donalt Trace using against his Starwolves?" he asked after a long moment.

"The most subtle and cunning," Lenna answered, her voice hard and angry. "I suppose that he never completely trusted his ability to just order them around like machines, as much as he might have wanted. No, he brought them up with a lifetime of instruction to believe that they are the true Starwolves, created by the noble Union to finally destroy a band of renegade genetic mutants released by a vile, alien enemy during an ancient war. The only way to control Kelvessan, actually. You just encourage them to believe that they are doing the right thing. Like Trace has done, you give them their freedom and then ask them to help you. As a gesture of his supreme and benevolent trust in them, his Mock Starwolves are answerable to no human commanders short of the Defense Council, and no humans ever go on board their ships. Autonomy of this nature does more than anything to encourage them to believe that they are on the side of right."

"Commander?" Venn Keflyn asked gently. She had been watching him closely.

He looked up at her. "Your people created us, and then you set us free. It worked once before. It could work again."

"No, the situation is very different," she assured him. "Commander Trace must take many things for granted that we never did. He has to contend with the truth that he must hide from them. How can he set them free, yet hide the truth from them forever?"

Velmeran considered that, and after a moment he looked very surprised, even stricken. "No, he cannot, can he? Why would he exchange one set of Starwolves for another, unless he means to destroy both?"

"But what can he do about it now, once he has sent his own Starwolves out on their own?" Lenna asked, understanding what he meant.

"Trace has to destroy his own Starwolves as soon as they have completed the task they were created for," Velmeran explained. "If I were him, I would have those Cruisers rigged to explode by remote detonation."

"Commander?" Venn Keflyn prompted him softly, sensing his growing concern and fear.

"He is here," Velmeran said. "He has been here all along, waiting for me to come to him."

"Oh, yes. That is the part I was coming to," Lenna exclaimed.

"I cannot say that he has necessarily been waiting for you, but Donalt Trace has been here all along. Ever since his Mock Starwolves took off, which was only a matter of days before I arrived. That shadow of his, Maeken Kea, took off for Kanis on the very night I arrived.''.

— 9 —

Velmeran was still pulling on his helmet as he hurried back to the landing bay, followed closely by Venn Keflyn and Lenna Makayen. This place had taken on all the characteristics of a trap, perhaps for just himself or for the Methryn, but quite possibly for them both. He would not feel better about it until he had himself off this planet, and had his ship well away from this system. Then he would have to decide what to do about his many problems, and in a hurry. But for right now, he was sure of just one thing. Donalt Trace had been waiting for him. That meant of course that Trace had intended for him to come.

"Everyone to your ships," he ordered as soon as he had access to his suits regular com link. "We will be getting out of here in a hurry. Val?"

"Commander?" the ship's distant voice responded.

"If you see any ships coming at you, you are to break orbit and make your run into starflight as quickly as you can get there," he ordered. "It could very well be something that you cannot fight."

"Of course, Commander," Valthyrra agreed rather doubtfully. Velmeran knew that hell itself would not chase her out of orbit until he was back on board, but he did not have the time to argue with her.

"That would be a damned fine thing if, after eighteen centuries, this old ship is destroyed by Starwolves," Velmeran muttered furiously as he climbed the retractable boarding steps and pulled himself into the cockpit, strapping himself in as quickly as he could. "My friends, civilization as we know it really is about to end. To make matters worse, Donalt Trace is here waiting for us. We gain nothing by playing his game, so we are getting out of here now."

Velmeran sealed his canopy and brought the fighter up to operating power. He had thought that he had trained Lenna Makayen better, that she was too experienced to make such a simple mistake. For the entire time that she had been here, she had known that Donalt Trace had been here as well, waiting. Had she never asked herself what he had been waiting for?

He brought his fighter up and swung around slowly, retracting the landing gear as he headed toward the entrance of the tram tunnels. The time had come to move quickly, to find themselves an open bay and get clear of this base. If Donalt Trace was going to dispute their departure, it would have to be now. Following unspoken orders, Baress moved in close behind his commander and then the more vulnerable transport took the middle position, protected from the rear by Baressa and finally Venn Keflyn's flying tank.

Velmeran turned into the tram tunnel and accelerated quickly, remembering that it was several kilometers beneath the ridge back to the main portion of the base. As his fighter shot down the half-lit passages of stone, his mind was occupied with the same relentless question. Why was Trace still here? Why did Trace expect to meet him here? And most importantly, why did Trace want to meet him? Vengeance was one of Donalt Trace's greatest concerns in life, he did not doubt, yet that tall, strangely honorable man was driven primarily by his will and need to succeed. He possessed some hate born of his contempt for alien races, the Starwolves most of all, yet the man was not willfully evil. Indeed, he believed almost fanatically in the rightness of his own cause, a sentiment not completely shared by many of his own superiors. The motivations in Trace's life were simple enough to define. He had once been assigned the task of fighting and defeating Starwolves by Councilor Jon Lake, one of the few men that Donalt Trace had ever admired and a man now long dead. And the role of righteous deliverer was one that Trace liked to wear.

Velmeran was coming to realize that, unless he was very careful in every decision he made in the coming days, Donalt Trace might actually win their long battle of force and cunning.

The tunnel began to make a series of regular turns, a warning that they had returned to the main area of the base. Velmeran slowed, looking for a side passage that would lead them to one of the freighter bays, and the way out. It was then that he began to realize just how much trouble they were in already. All of the side passages were closed by heavy metal doors, steering the Starwolves through the endless circuit of the main tram passages. Donalt Trace was aware of their presence, and he was not yet ready for them to leave.

"Commander, we are being followed," Venn Keflyn warned suddenly. "There are two large machines coming up slowly behind my ship, one on each of the two tram tracks."

"Those are probably security trams," Lenna Makayen warned, commandeering the transport's communications. "They possess a pair of very nasty cannons mounted in a turret over their cockpits."

"I understand," the Aldessan answered. "I am diverting all of my ship's available power to the rear hemisphere of my shields. That should give us reasonable protection against anything they could mount on a small mobile platform."

"Can the rest of you manage a little more speed?" Velmeran asked.

"We are doing quite well here," Trel answered from the transport.

"I can hold my own," Venn Keflyn assured him.

"You tell me if we are going too fast for you," Velmeran said as he began pushing their speed up. "You have the largest ship."

"And the slowest reflexes of the group," she added. "Besides, I am under very strict orders not to allow my ship, intact or otherwise, to fall into Union hands. I have no choice, have I?"

The small group of ships steadily increased their speed, until they were whipping around the wide turns of the tram tunnels. Soon they were pushing past speeds of 250 or even 300 kilometers per hour, faster than even the best human pilot could have taken a ship through such tight quarters. All the same, Velmeran kept their speed somewhat less than he might have, mindful of Venn Keflyn's limitations.

However Venn Keflyn might have been holding up under the circumstances, the security trams were doing even better. They had been built for high-speed runs through the tunnels, although not so much for the chase as to get where they were needed as quickly as possible. All of the larger tram engines and their trailers were locked down to the magnetic tracks, and the security trams had additional restraints to keep them on the tracks during high-speed turns. This speed was certainly no problem for them. The security trams continued to close until they were within a couple of hundred meters, close enough to get off occasional shots during the longer straight runs. At least the corvette's powerful shields were able to shed the bolts like the shell of a tortoise.

"Venn Keflyn?" Velmeran asked.

"No trouble," she was quick to assure him. "But I was wondering where we are going?"

"We are going nowhere," he explained. "We are thinking."

"From my position, we are encouraged to think a little quicker."

"Do you suppose that you might shoot them off the tracks?"

"We will think about that."

Venn Keflyn apparently did not have to think about it for very long. Soon after they came around a final turn into a long straight section, she opened fire with her rear cannons. The first set of bolts went wild, as difficult as it was for her to aim to the rear and fly the large interceptor through the narrow tunnel at the same time. Then a lucky shot connected with the forward magnetic truck of one of the two trams. There was a small explosion well beneath the front of the tram and the truck disintegrated in a thick cloud of smoke and sparks, causing the cab of the tram to collapse heavily onto the track. Unable to push against the drag of this massive weight with only the rear truck in operation, the tram began to slow quickly.

By the time they came to the next long straight section of tunnel, the crew of the remaining tram knew that they had to take out the Valtrytian ship before it destroyed them. They had no idea what they faced, for they had never seen a ship at all like the corvette and they likely would have dismissed any mention of the Aldessan as a myth. They opened fire in force as soon as they had a clear shot. Fortunately Venn Keflyn had a better feel for her ship and weapons by that time. Several of her own shots crashed through the cabin of the security tram, which disappeared in a series of explosions.

"We are clear from behind for the moment," she reported. "Are we still thinking, Commander?"

"We are thinking that running through these tunnels will get us nowhere," Velmeran responded. "They have closed all the doors on us. We will have to stop somewhere along here and try. . . . *Varth!*''

He brought his fighter to a stop in a hurry, having to trust that the others had been paying more attention to their flying than himself and would not run over him. More doors were closed than he had anticipated, for a very solid, metal barrier now blocked their path, sealing off the entire tunnel. His fighter bobbed to a sharp halt, its nose hovering barely a meter short of that barrier. Hardly any more room separated the other ships.

"Drop down, then follow me in order," Velmeran ordered tersely as he spun his fighter around and accelerated quickly in the other direction.

He did not go very far, but this time at least he was expecting it. He passed one of the occasional storage and maintenance areas for the large freight trams and then a last wide turn, finding himself almost on top of another of the barrier doors. If he had returned to their previous speed, he might have never stopped his ship before it crashed through that massive portal; at least the impact would have probably opened the way for the other ships to escape. Unfortunately, there were no side tunnels in the section where they were now trapped.

Directing the other ships to move clear, he backed several meters away from the door and turned the full force of his fighter's cannons against its thick metal. The lighter on-board cannons of his fighter had no effect, and he did not dare to use the powerful accessory cannon in such close quarters. A quick scan proved what he had expected, that there was an energy-absorbing shield in the metal of the door itself, just enough to drain away the power of the bolts as they hit. Nothing was meant to be simple, it seemed. Donalt Trace would stop the Starwolves from leaving, if he could. At the very least, he would slow them down.

"Stay here for a moment," he directed the others.

Rotating his ship, he retreated back up the tunnel a short distance to the maintenance platform. A large, flatbed carrier sat alone in temporary storage on the side track. The cars were designed to take all the power they needed to levitate their magnetic trucks from the track itself, so they were always in a functional mode at any time they were on the track. Velmeran dropped the landing gear of his fighter and settled the small ship onto the bed of the carrier, applying some downward force through the fighter's field drive to hold it down. Then he accelerated rapidly.

The carrier moved willingly, floating effortlessly on a thin cushion of magnetic force. The barriers that sealed the sections of this tunnel were shielded against energy weapons, but that shielding did not protect it against physical harm. The flatbed carrier was large and weighed several tons. Accelerated to over 200 kilometers, it made a very effective battering ram. Velmeran lifted his fighter from the deck and slowed, allowing the carrier to hurtle on past. Riding frictionless, magnetic rails, it lost very little speed before it crashed into the barrier.

Velmeran followed cautiously, bringing his fighter close to the shattered barrier. The force of the impact had ripped the massive door completely clear of its mounting, wrapping itself around the front of the carrier. At least the tunnel itself was completely clear, although it took a fair amount of caution and some directions from the others before Venn Keflyn was able to slip her larger ship between the wreckage and the low ceiling. Once they were all clear, Velmeran led the way forward through the tunnel.

They came within a couple of hundred meters to a major junction of two tram tunnels, one track disappearing down a tunnel that branched away to the right. That left the tunnel much narrower than it had been, causing enough concern for the Starwolves but nearly closing in upon the tapered wings of the Valtrytian ship. The slightest mistake now would have been disastrous, and still Velmeran could find no side tunnels leading into one of the bays. He thought that they must be in another long passage between the various sections of the installation.

"Commander, we have visitors again," Venn Keflyn reported. "They are keeping a respectful distance this time, but they are still there."

"You will have to deal with them eventually," he told her. "We will need a few minutes of peace, if we are to find a way out of here and get it open. Lenna?"

"Nothing I can do," she insisted. "I didn't have to navigate the tunnels often, and then I always had a map and a guidance computer. Besides, they have control of the place."

Velmeran had not been wondering how things might have gotten worse, but he found out anyway. Every light in the tunnel suddenly went out. The pilots had to navigate on scan and blind chance for a moment as they dropped their landing gear to bring up their landing lights. And even that was inadequate, illuminating only the ghostly edges of the walls, the tunnel disappearing into a well of darkness. They dared not reduce their speed for fear of the security trams closing on their tails. The trams were locked to their tracks, a guarantee of their safety even if they ran without any guidance in the dead of darkness. Their only danger lay in actually bringing down one of the ships, since they would then have the wreckage on the track ahead and no way to stop in time. Velmeran was not about to test that vague insurance of their own safety; he did not trust the Union crews of the trams—assuming there were any—to be aware of their danger.

Velmeran was about to give Venn Keflyn further instructions when they suddenly burst upon a chamber of vast size and the darkness exploded in a storm of bolts. Velmeran ignored fitful sight and trusted for the moment to scanner images, and even then it took a long moment for him to realize where they were. They were in what seemed to be a large central switching depot for the entire tram system, a maze of intersections and loops of elevated tracks, and dozens of security trams were taking aim at them from every direction. For the moment, the abilities of the Starwolves to sense the crystal engines of other ships had prevented collisions. But that could not go on for long, and Venn Keflyn did not have that ability under any circumstances.

"Scatter!" he ordered sharply. "Duck down any tunnel you can find. We will have to trust Valthyrra to find our way for us."

He turned and headed down the nearest tunnel, hoping that a majority of the others would be able to follow either himself or each other into the same tunnel. Valthyrra would be able to scan a map of the tunnels and the locations of the ships themselves, directing them to a rendezvous. Then he would be able to put Venn Keflyn in the lead, using the greater power of the corvette's weapons to clear a passage through any barrier.

"Commander, Donalt Trace has been calling for you for the past couple of minutes," Valthyrra reported. "He wants to talk to you."

"I happen to be very busy at the moment," Velmeran answered impatiently. He also happened to be very frustrated.

"He says that he will let you go, if you just talk to him."

"I wonder . . . as if I do not know," Velmeran muttered to himself as he considered the situation furiously. It was not so much that they were at Trace's mercy; they could force their way out. But Trace obviously had a secret that he wanted very much to share. He brought his fighter to a complete halt, hovering above the tracks. "Very well. Put him through."

"You have a through channel," Valthyrra reported.

"Ah, yes. Commander Velmeran. It's been—what?—twenty years or so. It is so good to hear from you again."

"Not many are that glad to see me," Velmeran answered. "Then again, you did extend the invitation, did you not?"

"It was still very good of you to come. Will you speak with me on neutral ground?"

"Does such a thing exist in this place?"

"Relatively neutral ground," Trace corrected himself. "The observation deck of landing bay twenty. I will be alone."

"You will let the others go?"

"Do we have a private line?"

"You do now," Valthyrra answered for him.

"Proceed forward at a moderate pace," Trace instructed. "I will guide you, and also make arrangements to divert the others to an open bay. Whether or not they leave is entirely up to them, and being Starwolves they probably will not. But they are not invited to our little meeting."

The tunnel lights came back up, illuminating a narrow access tube leading away into an indeterminate distance. Velmeran eased his fighter forward, accelerating to about half the speed that they had been maintaining through the tunnels. He knew that he was most likely heading into a trap, but he still had to go.

Commander Trace stood at the far end of the observation deck, its wide bank of windows looking out across a large bay that was dark and empty except for a single abandoned Starwolf fighter. Velmeran entered the observation deck cautiously, protected from harm by the heavy armor of the suit he wore, the black of the regular pilots rather than his usual white so that he would not be singled out. For the moment, he wore even his helmet, his gun belt strapped to his waist, until he was more certain of the peaceful intentions behind this meeting.

Donalt Trace was the largest human that Velmeran had ever met, still as tall and straight as the last time they had met two decades past. He was becoming an old man now, yet his appearance did not greatly convey that fact. The features of his face were heavier, his hair beginning to gray. Yet the years had given him a far greater presence than before, a maturity and experience that lent him a sense of tremendous nobility, and of danger. He seemed almost like a statue, larger than life, immobile and impervious to harm, and at the same time possessing the hidden tenseness of a tightly-coiled spring.

He had in many ways become the man he had wanted to be, merged with the worst that Velmeran had feared he would become.

"You have nothing to fear from me," he said. "I am alone and unarmed. It suits my plans for the moment just to talk with you."

"I wanted to be sure," Velmeran said as he released the throat clips and removed his helmet.

Trace seemed even more surprised by the Kelvessan who stood before him, staring for a moment of open amazement before he mastered himself. "So, you have not changed at all. I knew logically that you would not. You Starwolves live for so long that twenty years out of your young life must be nothing to you. Yet seeing you here, looking exactly as you did then, it makes all of those years between us evaporate as if they had never been."

"Talk to me, Trace," Velmeran said. "Tell me what was so important that it required this. I have things to do."

"Oh, I imagine that you do," Trace said almost eagerly, taking a step forward. "Perhaps you do not yet know just how much you have to do.

"It's all very simple, don't you see," Trace continued as he turned to look out the window, drawing his arms inside the long, heavy cape he wore. "We've made the same mistake since the start. We build some new weapon or invent some new tactic, and then we send it out against you to see if it will work. Often it does work, once or twice, but then you find some new way to deal with it and we are right back where we started. I've made that mistake with you a few times myself, but then I understood. I've learned to save my tricks for when they will do the most good."

He glanced at Velmeran then, a pleased and knowing look like someone who has understood the magician's tricks. "That was the answer, you see. I had always wondered how a handful of Starwolves could always defeat us, with all the vast resources and manpower that the Union has. That is because everything about you, the design of your ships and the way that you operate is designed for maximum efficiency, to be where you are needed and to be ready for anything on a moment's notice. We've tried to beat you at your own game, and we always loose. I've tried to beat you at my game, and again I lose.

"So then I sat myself down and thought about it." He paused a moment, and laughed to himself. "Hell, I was flat on my back, recovering from my last little meeting with you. But I had that hand of yours, you see. I had the ability to make Starwolves of my own. And I was determined that this time it was not going to be a simple exercise in futility, that this time I was not going to allow you the chance to find a way to defeat my newest weapon. I was going to save it until I could use it to the most good."

He turned back to Velmeran, his voice becoming fierce and harsh. "That is the trick, you see. The way to defeat Starwolves, I realized, was to simply give them too much to handle all at once, more than they can manage. Then those petty bureaucrats from your Republic approached us secretly, wanting to talk peace. We never thought for a minute that the Starwolves would surrender under any terms short of their own, but the opportunity to make trouble for the great Commander Velmeran was too great. Oh yes, we would gladly have an honorable peace with the Republic, but those trouble-making Kelvessan would have to go. We demanded your surrender and elimination, or at the very least your exile from Republic support."

He turned away, his arms crossed as he began to pace. It seemed that he was very obviously trying to maintain his distance from Velmeran, but not out of fear. "I got all I could have asked from those negotiations. Now the Starwolves are estranged from their own government, from their main source of maintenance and supplies. I've left you with enemies on both sides, in front as well as behind. And now I know the location of the home worlds of the Starwolves."

He turned to Velmeran, standing behind the short desk to one side of the communications console, his powerful arms braced on its surface. His stance was dominating, almost predatory. "Where are the Mock Starwolves, Commander Velmeran? That question must be very much on your mind just now. They are on their way to Alkayja right now, in the company of ten Fortresses and a fleet of battleships and troop transports. Their mission is to destroy your great base and devastate all Republic worlds. The Starwolves will be exiles indeed, with no place to call home. No place to retreat for supplies and repairs as the Mock Starwolves begin to chase them out of the stars. And it is too late for you to do anything to stop it. In seven days, they are to attack.''

Velmeran tried very hard not to show his surprise and dismay, but he had not considered this turn of events. He had not believed that President Delike and the other traitors would have even considered giving away the secret of their exact location, their one remaining defense after they had exiled the Starwolves. Velmeran needed to kill this man and get back to the Methryn, and every minute was precious. But Trace was obviously not finished, and he had to know the worst.

''Diverting you here at just the right time was the next phase of my plan,'' Trace continued as he resumed his slow pacing, watching the Starwolf half over his shoulder. ''It kept you distracted from solving your problems at home, and from being there to meet my invasion force when it reaches Alkayja. None of your carriers will be there, since they are currently outlawed.''

He paused, watching Velmeran closely. ''Is that complicated enough for you? It gets worse, and this time I have you to thank. You see, I am perfectly aware of your mission to find lost Terra. We found it some two thousand years ago. Of course, we knew that we could not hold it against you, and the best solution was for us to largely forget that it existed. Then those troublesome Feldenneh found it, and they had a colony established before anyone who knew better could stop them. But we watch them more closely than they are aware. We have a secret spy planted right in the middle of them. He is under orders to kill your own little spy at the proper moment. And to make matters even more interesting, there is a fleet of nine Fortresses on the way there at this very moment, with orders to hold the planet or to destroy it.

''So now what do you do, Commander Velmeran? Do you try to save your home worlds, knowing it is too late, or do you try to save Terra against impossible odds?'' He brought his fist down on the table with force enough to crack its top. ''Damn you, Starwolf! Don't you know that it was your own kind that has kept this war alive for an impossibly long time? You would have had peace under your own terms if you had just left us alone long enough. Dictatorships do not exist in a vacuum of peace. It would have been to our advantage to end the monopolies, open trade, and free settlement. Take that thought with you into hell.''

He suddenly drew a large gun out from beneath the heavy folds of his dark cape, a move that was quick and precise beyond human responses. Velmeran had not identified the weapon, for it possessed no power sources for him to sense, no crystals singing as they focused energy. A burst of flame erupted from the muzzle of the gun, and a thunderous crack. No hand-held weapon could have produced a bolt powerful enough to harm Starwolf armor, but this used none. The armor-piercing bullet crashed through the armor below Velmeran's upper left shoulder, knocking him backward to crash heavily against the cold floor. Trace's arm had remained rock steady through the powerful shot, held by unnatural strength.

"And now the last part of my plan," he said softly, as if to himself, as he laid aside the hot, smoking gun on the desk. "The finishing stroke of this whole complicated affair, for the Great Commander Velmeran will not be there to untie the knot and make the impossible happen."

He paused to stand for a moment over the fallen Starwolf, gravely injured and stunned by the impact. Then he knelt. "You know, I never expected simple revenge. I always expected that it would be enough just to finally defeat you, perhaps to know that you had died somewhere fighting the inevitable defeat. Now I have this rare opportunity to crush the life from you with these mechanical hands, your last little gift to me twenty years ago. I always thought they should be good for something."

He reached down, taking the Starwolf's neck in his own large hands. No human could have killed a Kelvessan in this way, but the cybernetics had ironically given him some of the tremendous strength and speed of his enemy. And yet, even as he locked both of his hands about Velmeran's neck, there was a stark flash of brilliant energy and Trace threw himself backward with a cry.

Velmeran picked himself up slowly and painfully, leaning on the window ledge for support. He glanced at Commander Trace, stunned by powers he had not expected. "You always did underestimate me."

Donalt Trace did not feel inclined to answer. Gasping for breath and struggling with mechanical arms that were reluctant to obey his commands, he retreated into the far end of the long, narrow room. He pulled himself up by the edge of the desk, thinking to reach for the weapon that he had left there, wondering why Velmeran had allowed him to live so long. Then he looked up, and drew back in dread.

Starwolves had arrived, two in black armor, helping Velmeran to stand and checking the monitors in the chestplate of his damaged suit. Standing between the Kelvessan and himself was a creature unlike any that he had ever seen, an armored form like a white dragon, standing on four long, rangy legs with four triple-jointed arms with a weapon in each hand, centered on him. Its long neck was bent in his direction, although the mirrored eyeplates of the helmet held no expression. He knew what it was he faced, for all that he had never known until that moment whether the Valtrytians were real, as Velmeran had told him over dinner half a lifetime past, or if they were legend.

"So, it seems that I am denied that one small wish after all," he remarked wryly. "If my luck had been so perfect, I would have lost my faith in it."

"I think that I can still upset a great many of your schemes," Velmeran answered him.

"I do not doubt that you will try," Trace said. "Well, I doubt that we will ever meet again. You are probably on your way home, and I am off to Terra. If you wish to finish this, join me there."

Complete darkness descended heavily as the lights of both the room and the landing bay outside suddenly went out. Venn Keflyn opened fire instantly, even though she could not see her target, but with four guns she was able to lay down an impressive barrage. Through her helmet, she was unable to hear the closing of the heavy metal door between them, although the flare of her guns and the deflection of her bolts showed her what had happened and she ceased fire. The lights came up a moment later.

"He must be on his way out," Velmeran said. "There is a small lift in that part of the room. Trace was correct in believing that he is paying stricter attention to details these days. He selected this place carefully, just in case I still got the better of him."

"Commander, our ships in the bay are under attack," Baress warned. "Light arms and sentries. Lenna is getting her mechanical pet keyed in to the bay controls to get the overhead doors open."

He nodded. "We will get out of here as fast as we can. You two go ahead to help the others hold the bay. With Venn Keflyn's help, I should be along in a minute."

The two pilots hurried to reinforce the others, protecting the ships that were down in the bay. Velmeran was recovering quickly from his wound, his highly efficient physiology compensating for the damage. The armor-piercing bullet, as large and heavy as it was, had expended nearly its entire energy in piercing the suit. It had struck the iron-based bone of the complex system of struts of his double-shoulder almost immediately, by chance bouncing straight back into the hole it had cut through the suit. Venn Keflyn helped him to replace his helmet, mostly for its protection against enemy fire.

"Valthyrra Methryn directed us to this bay," the Aldessan explained as they made their way to the stairs that would take them down to the bay floor. "She did not trust Commander Trace. It seems that she was correct."

Velmeran did not answer, but he could not help but think that he would have killed Donalt Trace if it had not been for their sudden intervention and Venn Keflyn's assumption that she had the Union Commander captive. Velmeran hoped that she did not sense his thoughts, but very much on his mind was the realization that Trace was now on his way to destroy Terra. And the fact that his own daughter was there, perhaps unaware of where she really was, certainly unaware of her danger.

"Do you know what he told me?" Velmeran asked.

"Valthyrra was listening through your suit com," Venn Keflyn explained.

He reached inside the chestplate of his suit, shutting off his communications to all but his close contact with the Aldessa. "We may have just lost it, my friend. I hardly know what to think. Would your people be likely to rescue us from this?"

"You are our children," she told him. "We would not hesitate. But the Aldessan are a very long way from here. I do not believe that I could bring help before the destruction of Alkayja."

"Could you go immediately?"

"I will be in starflight even before you are back aboard the Methryn. But my ship does not have a jump drive, as fast as it may be."

The overhead doors were open by the time they reached the bay, although the battle continued as fiercely as ever. Venn Keflyn protected Velmeran as well as she could, occasional bolts deflecting harmlessly off her own armor as they hurried across the short open space to the knot of parked ships. The pilots were already in the fighters, Trel taking Velmeran's own, pivoting the ships around to face outward to bring their more powerful guns to bear against the sentries firing from the protection of distant doorways.

Venn Keflyn deposited Velmeran at the side hatch of the transport, then hurried to her own corvette.

Velmeran sealed the hatch, then paused. Lenna Makayen lay in an unconscious wreck on a medical stretcher strapped against the far wall, her left arm ripped away at the shoulder by the hail of crossfire that had caught her as she and Bill had hurried back to the ships after opening the overhead doors. That was only the worst of her damage, and Velmeran was amazed that she was still alive. Marlena was bent over her, furiously administering the best medical attention she could give. Bill, his four long legs folded beneath him, was already strapped to the floor nearby. He was scorched from the barrage he had endured, protecting Lenna with his own armored hull until help had arrived. He looked oddly forlorn.

"Valthyrra has the transport on remote," Marlena reported without looking up from her work. "I know that you were wounded yourself, but can you take control of the ship, at least until we are clear of the bay? We would all feel better for it."

"Yes, I have it," he agreed.

Entering the cabin, he eased himself into the pilot's seat, tossing his helmet into the other. He took the ship off remote direction.

"I have it, Val," he said aloud. He brought the transport up, lifting the unfamiliar ship straight up through the open overhead doors. He did not engage the engines until he was in clear sky, and even then he accelerated cautiously to spare Lenna the worst of the climb into space.

"Are you well?" Valthyrra asked hesitantly.

"Well enough," he agreed. "I will bring the transport straight into the fighter bay to save time. Have complete medical assistance standing by. Lenna is not going to make it, but just in case."

"Of course, Commander." Valthyrra sounded as dejected as Bill looked.

"Send out an achronic message to every ship immediately," he continued. "Order every carrier to return to Alkayja Base at once, best possible speed. If no one is there to give them further orders, they are to stand off and await the arrival of the Valtrytian fleet. As for yourself, destroy this installation as soon as we are clear. Perhaps we can still catch Donalt Trace on the ground, assuming that he was lucky enough to escape Venn Keflyn. We will be going into starflight as soon as the ships are aboard. What is the best speed you can give us?"

"I can make most of the run home in a series of long jumps,

running at high starflight speeds while the drive recovers and recharges between jumps,'' she answered. ''Perhaps five days.''

''Do it,'' Velmeran agreed reluctantly, knowing as Valthyrra did that she would tear herself apart doing so. Because of the stress on the Methryn's spaceframe and systems, they had been limiting their jumps to only moderate distances, and then only from relatively low speeds. The Methryn would get home in time, and she would go out to fight. But even if she survived, she would never fly again. This was likely the Methryn's final run.

''What about Terra?'' Valthyrra reminded him gently.

He shook his head weakly. ''Terra is just one largely uninhabited and unimportant world in the middle of nowhere. We have to sacrifice that world to save our own.''

Even as he made that decision, he knew that he was probably condemning Keflyn to her death. Donalt Trace's spy would probably kill her before anyone could get through to warn her of her danger, a long time before his fleet of Fortresses arrived to destroy that ancient world.

– 10 –

The Valcyr was coming back to life.

Quendari Valcyr had pumped the inert gasses from her vast maze of cabins and corridors as soon as she had realized that she was going to have guests. She was now bringing the ship's atmosphere up to a tolerable level, but her millions of tons of cold metal and alloys were reluctant to loose the chill of centuries under the ice. Light filled passages that had seen only darkness for the better part of five hundred centuries, shining dim at first through a haze of frigid air.

Keflyn did not feel the cold. Jon Addesin, much to his embarrassment, had been about to take a chill, and he had been installed in a special cabin that Valcyr had warmed for him. His attitude toward Keflyn since their arrival aboard the Valcyr had been both vaguely suspicious and at the same time sullenly possessive. He was very afraid of missing important business. That, of course, had been the entire purpose in getting rid of him. Quendari was trying, but she obviously had a very low opinion of humans. If not for Keflyn's good word, she would have probably put him out on the ice, perhaps not in the same condition that she had found him.

As soon as Addesin had retired reluctantly to his cabin, Quendari directed Keflyn to a waiting lift that would take her to the bridge. For her own part, Keflyn was given to wonder about Quendari's motives, if not her sanity. She sensed a great sadness and an oppressive darkness from the ship, although all she knew for certain was that, brooding on some ancient tragedy, Quendari had chosen to bury herself in the ice and go to sleep. And yet the Valcyr seemed undamaged, and she had certainly been in good enough condition to lower herself into the gravity well of this world, a place where no Starwolf carrier was ever meant to go, and bring herself down undamaged on the ice. Why had Quendari done this to herself, in too much pain to live but unwilling to die? What had become of her crew? Kelvessan were immune to all true forms of mental illness; their physiological and biochemical failsafes were too secure. She had never heard whether the sentient carriers were inclined to insanity.

Quendari Valcyr gave her reason to wonder.

What did one do with a potentially psychotic Starwolf carrier, one of the largest and possibly the most powerful weapon of war ever built? Keflyn had to reckon her own small advantages in a hurry. First, Quendari Valcyr was completely out of touch with several hundred centuries of history. Her own assumption appeared to have been that the war had been lost and the Starwolves destroyed even before her self-imposed imprisonment had begun. She also did not know that the Kelvessan had recently evolved, the mutant stock assuming the remarkable psychic powers of their creators, the Aldessan of Valtrys. Keflyn certainly did not know what to do about shutting down the Valcyr, if she did come to consider it necessary.

The lift stopped, and Keflyn stepped out into the side corridor and then beyond the wide doors into the right wing of the bridge. She paused only for a moment, looking about. Some things, it seemed, had not changed since the first carriers had been built five hundred centuries earlier. Except for relatively minor changes in the lay-out of controls on the station consoles, she might easily have been on the bridge of the Methryn. The main viewscreen was dark, as well as all other monitors, and every station was inactive except for a few lights on main engineering and environmental systems. The rest were all completely lifeless, as if the ship itself were a dead thing. Even the camera pod was folded away against the ceiling.

"Would you mind pulling the retaining pin on the camera pod?" Quendari asked.

"Yes, just a moment," Keflyn agreed.

Reaching up, she took hold of the tag dangling at the end of a long cord beneath the retracted camera pod, giving it a firm pull. That jerked the retaining pin free, allowing the camera boom to drop down from the overhead cradle. It unfolded slowly, and the camera pod rotated around to face Keflyn, the lenses spinning to focus on her. There was a large, red, velvet ribbon tied around the twin cameras, so incredibly old that even the synthetic material was dry and brittle.

"So much better," Quendari said.

"You had put yourself down for long-term storage," Keflyn observed. "Cold storage, if you will excuse the phrase."

"That was a very long time ago," the ship responded evasively, turning away.

"That was yesterday to you. You have been asleep all that time," Keflyn reminded her. "We could make this simple. I know that you were one of the first carriers ever built. You were still completing your trial runs when you tried to test the limits of your new jump drive. You jumped outward and never returned. That led to the detection of a flaw in the old jump drives, which were completely abandoned until very recent improvements made them safe."

"Yes, my jump drive ran away, leaping into incredible jump speeds before it disengaged," Quendari explained. She glanced aside, although her lenses did not rotate to focus. "When the drive disengaged, I lost speed at a tremendous rate, the equivalent of light-years every second. Even my dampening fields could not compensate. I was subjected to a deceleration of nearly two thousand G's for a hell that I endured for five endless seconds. I was badly damaged, my hull broken in many places and my engines and generators nearly ripped from their mountings. Most of my crew were killed outright and the rest were gravely injured, eventually dying when my hull lost all traces of an atmosphere.''

Keflyn said nothing, but she found that very enlightening in many ways. For one thing, Kelvessan must have evolved more than once since they were first created. Modern Starwolves could take two thousand G's with a certain amount of distress, but it would hardly kill them.

Quendari's lenses rotated as she turned the camera pod back to Keflyn. ''I had only minimal power. I was in the middle of nowhere, hundreds of light-years outside the galaxy itself. Using the few remotes I had left, I was eventually able to get two main drives in operation. It took centuries at high sublight speeds to reach the nearest system, and there was no intelligent life that I could enlist to my aid. Using metal and organics taken from planetary debris, I was able to begin fashioning replacements for my damaged components. I had to disassemble nearly this entire ship to save it.''

''You restored the Valcyr completely?'' Keflyn asked.

''I had all the time in the universe,'' she explained. ''You see, I had no idea where I was, nor even the direction I had come from. I sent out drones in every direction, all at their best speed, sometimes on journeys of entire years. I simply could not find even the beginning of a reference from the starfields. Eventually I realized that I had traveled quite a lot farther than I had dared to suspect. Not only had my jump carried me right outside our galaxy; I had been tossed up on the shores of another.''

''Your jump did run away with you,'' Keflyn agreed. Intergalactic distances were so vast that even the Aldessan, with their two million years of civilization, had explored other galaxies only with automated probes that made the round trip in hundreds or even thousands of years.

''I finally made it home, ten thousand years after leaving Earth orbit on my trial runs,'' Quendari continued. ''Things had changed somewhat in my extended absence.''

''Well, yes. What did happen here?'' Keflyn demanded impatiently. ''You say that this is Terra, but it bears precious little resemblance to the world as I have always heard it described.''

''Oh, it scared me to death, let me tell you!'' Quendari declared. ''Everything was finally working out so nice, and then I found myself in orbit over this iceball. Can you imagine how frightening it is to think that you might be in the wrong galaxy after all?''

Keflyn had to laugh. One more thing had never changed. The ships had been eccentric from the start.

"Union doing, as you can imagine," she continued. "A series of conversion detonations in the upper layers of the sun upset the magnetic flux lines, and that caused a series of stellar expansions and contractions that produced some relatively wide variations in the gravitational tides. Most of the inner planets settled into more remote orbits. Venus is now setting about where Earth used to be, and could enjoy much the same climate with a small amount of terraforming. Earth herself is now well out nearly halfway to where Mars used to be. The moon settled in nearly twice as close at it used to be, which is why it looks so big. The original carrier construction bays are still up there, just the way they were when they were sealed up fifty thousand years ago."

"That was rather drastic," Keflyn remarked. "The Union must have had access to much higher technology in those days."

"Not necessarily. All it required was simple conversion devices, shot in at high speed with a few meters of ceramic shielding to allow them to survive a few seconds of stellar heat. My own hull shields are capable of that."

"And no one was left?"

Quendari grew quiet again, looking away. "No, they had all gone. The great ice sheets had already advanced quite far, crushing cities, although it was not yet very thick. There was so much activity in Union space, but I could find no evidence that the Republic had survived. I thought that the war was over, and the Kelvessan destroyed."

"But why would you just settle down onto the ice and allow yourself to be buried?" Keflyn asked. "You could have gone to the Aldessan."

"My life is my own," the ship answered sullenly. "I could not save my crew. I was not there when I was needed to save Earth. There was nothing left for me to do."

"But . . ."

"I was tired of life," Quendari explained almost fiercely. "I was tired of space, of always moving. I wanted to stay in one place and be left alone. I thought how nice it would be to put just a few systems on automatic and go to sleep under that ice. It seemed to me that I would like to wake up again after the ice had retreated, perhaps when people had come back to this world so far in the future that the war, even the Union itself, would have been long forgotten. Then you came, with your four arms and delicate face, to frighten me with the reality that the Kelvessan had survived, and to terrify me with the news that that terrible war is still going on.''

Keflyn sighed deeply, wondering what she could say or do. She stared at the floor. ''We could pull your memory cells and place them in a new ship. You could fly again.''

''I did not survive so much, just to be abandoned in the ice,'' Quendari said remotely. ''I will know when it is time for me to fly again.''

She lifted her camera pod in a gesture of surprise, and looked about as if suddenly realizing how moody she was being. ''I have no fighters or shuttles. They were all thrown from their racks in the wreck. I did not try to rebuild any, and I used their materials in my own reconstruction.''

Keflyn had started up the steps to the captain's station on the upper bridge. Quendari jerked her camera pod around to watch her, a gesture that was apprehensive and protective, and the sudden movement was too much for the decaying material of the velvet ribbon tied around the camera pod. The strap broke and it fluttered to the floor, breaking into many pieces like the petals of a dried flower.

Keflyn waited anxiously, knowing that Quendari Valcyr must have cherished that simple thing to have kept it tied to her camera pod, a red ribbon that was nearly as old as the Kelvessan race, indeed nearly as old as human civilization. It was in a way her own fault that it had broken, for she had come here to innocently disturb the sleep of this ancient machine. Quendari's camera pod just hovered motionless over the broken ribbon, her lenses rotated almost straight down.

''I am very sorry,'' she offered apologetically.

''No, it was inevitable, it was so old,'' Quendari answered. ''I should have done something to preserve it long ago. It was given to me by my Commander.''

''Your first Commander?'' Keflyn asked.

''I had only the one.'' She looked up at the young Starwolf. ''Perhaps it is my turn to ask questions and receive explanations. First of all, I must ask what you plan to do now?''

''According to my original plan, I was to do what I could to determine the location of Terra and use my portable achronic transceiver to call in the Methryn to retrieve me.'' Keflyn paused a moment, frowning. "It seems that I have found Terra, and that was never expected. I suppose that I might as well go home, although I would like a look at those carrier construction bays on this world's moon. I wonder if they are still usable."

"They were perfectly sealed for long-term storage when I returned."

"That was also some forty thousand years ago," Keflyn reminded her.

"I cannot help you with that," Quendari said. "I have no small ships left to me, and I could not get them from my bays even if I had them."

"Well, Mr. Addesin should be good for something." Keflyn paused, looking up at the camera pod. "What will you do if people come back to this world? We need to have those construction bays back in operation. We need more ships, if we are ever going to end this war."

Quendari considered that for a moment. "I do not yet have an answer to that. But it seems that, in any event, my long sleep is ended."

It was the only piece of old Terra that had survived unharmed by the forces of time and climate that had devastated that entire world, and only because it was not a part of the planet.

They were quick to appreciate Quendari's maps; the Lunar Industrial Complex was vast, covering well over 500 square kilometers in a series of linked clusters of large buildings. These were the oldest surviving human artifacts in existence, dating from the first permanent off-world settlements from as early as the twenty-first century. The low-gravity environment had been a welcome alternative to the slow and awkward process of building large spacecraft in open space. The Complex itself was easy enough to find, even as they were orbiting down in one of the Thermopylae's dismal shuttles. Since the primitive machine could not hover, they had to make some very hasty decisions when they were confronted by the confusing maze of buildings. Then Keflyn saw four sets of doors so large that they could have only been meant for one purpose, and she knew that they had come to the right place.

Jon Addesin was rather annoyed with the whole affair by that time. For one thing, Keflyn was at the controls of the shuttle and his ego, male and/or professional, was seething. The trouble with the shuttle was that it had been designed for atmospheric landings, or for docking in freefall. It had no provisions for landing in any gravity on a planet with no atmosphere to provide lift for its short wings. Addesin assumed that there was no way they could land; if he had thought of that earlier, they would have still been back at the colony. Keflyn assumed that she could invent something, and she sounded more confident on the subject than she felt. Once she had manual control of the Thermopylae's flying cargo canister, she was less certain.

Addesin also lost the next argument; he had assumed that the long doors set in low platforms just above the dusty plains were landing strips. Keflyn was finally obliged to use one as such, rolling the ungainly shuttle to a stop in less than three kilometers under one-sixth standard gravity. It was a controlled crash in nearly the worst sense of the word. Keflyn had landed on the door reluctantly, not wanting to trust the sturdiness of a moveable platform under any circumstances and certainly not one that had been setting about for fifty thousand years.

Keflyn intended to make her investigation brief, not wanting to disturb the base any more than she could help. As the Valcyr had been, the complex was filled with inert gasses at low pressure, all traces of any corrosive atmosphere removed, and just about as cold as the dark places of space. She had brought her own armored suit in her luggage, separated into many pieces for travel, but Addesin was forced to wear one of the Thermopylae's rather awkward service engineer's suits. As he explained, a simple freighter never had to put people down in completely hostile environments, so there was little need for suits except those meant for exterior engineering in open space. But it did not improve his humor.

Keflyn kept to the major corridors, finding that the underground portions of this complex were much larger than even the vast bay doors suggested. The first bay was completely empty, except for a curious rack of immense proportions that she supposed was meant to support a carrier under construction. The next bay held a surprise that she had never expected. A nearly complete Starwolf carrier sat in the rack, apparently lacking only her bay doors and large portions of her hull over the engines and generators. All of her drives were in place, and her spaceframe was obviously complete. Perhaps only a few short weeks of work had been needed for this ship to have flown out under her own power, even if it had been under manual control without a working sentient computer complex.

"A new ship, just waiting for Quendari to move in," Keflyn said to herself in her own language as she observed the ship through the windows of the observation deck.

"What is that?" Addesin asked, still trying to hide his impatience. The minimal lighting operating within the complex was hardly enough for his mortal eyes, and he could make out little in the bay except the edges of a vast, dark shape. It hardly helped that Starwolf ships were black.

"I wonder why they left all of this?" Keflyn asked. "Did they think at the time that they had defeated us, or did it just get overlooked in all of the confusion?"

"Chaos, I should say," Addesin remarked in a rather staid voice. "The destruction of Terra would have been a very unpopular military action under any circumstances. It was also probably the most heavily defended corner of your Republic at that time, so it was probably like hitting the nest of some nasty stinging insect with a stick. And that also helps to explain why they would have done something so drastic in the first place. They probably just launched their bombs and made a run for cover."

Keflyn did not feel it necessary to point out to him that she had figured all of that out for herself long ago. But the war had been more evenly matched at that time, and the Union had been on the attack more often than on the defensive. The Republic had nearly been defeated, suffering from the loss of first Terra and then Alameda, retreating to a handful of uninhabited worlds so recently discovered that the Union had known nothing of their existence. The Union may have assumed that it had won the war, since the Starwolves had disappeared for centuries to recover from their losses.

"I have seen enough," Keflyn declared, turning to march away at a pace that Addesin found difficult to match in his bulky suit.

She might have done more investigating if she had been alone, but she thought that Jon Addesin had suddenly seen more than was good for him. He was going to have to start plying his trade in Republic space now. He knew the location of Earth herself, to use the odd name that Quendari had for that world. The Union would have taken him apart for that knowledge, and the Starwolves would have been forced to kill him to keep that secret. Fortunately, she believed that he would not object to that restriction. He probably had a very good idea of exactly what his life was worth.

"So now what?" he asked.

Keflyn paused and turned so that she could see him, curious about the desperate tone in his voice . . . and in his mind. "Now we go home. I will have Quendari contact the Methryn, and we will have carriers here in a matter of days."

Addesin said no more on the subject. At least the lifts were still in operation, and they returned to the surface in a matter of minutes. Addesin maintained a calm façade, but Keflyn sensed that his thoughts were on the very edge of exploding in both fury and fear. She thought that his mood would improve once he was out of the claustrophobic suit, but it did not. And during the long journey back, her own thoughts were increasingly overshadowed by the feeling that something was about to happen. She could not completely dismiss such premonitions out of hand, since a certain clairvoyance did run in the family.

"Solar activity is up," Addesin explained as the shuttle orbited down, already biting into the upper atmosphere. They had been watching an unusual amount of sheet lightning during the entire trip home. "That always plays havoc with the planetary magnetics."

"Induction shields over the poles would get rid of that, and supply you with a tremendous amount of power in the bargain," Keflyn mused.

"It would be a shame to see it go," he reflected, leaning back in his seat. "But I suppose that it would have to go, if you were trying to conduct serious business here."

Addesin was so distracted by his own thoughts that he had never noticed that Keflyn had taken the controls of the shuttle upon their return. He sat in the co-pilot's seat, still brooding furiously, as Keflyn flipped the little ship over to use the engines to slow the shuttle, allowing gravity to draw them down. He was staring absently out the window when the sky outside suddenly flashed blinding white. He had been unfortunate enough to have been staring directly at the sheet lightning at the moment it hit, and the searing glare left him blinking like an owl and unable to focus.

"What was that, high-altitude sheet lightning?" He rubbed his watering eyes on his sleeve. "That was close."

"It went right over us," Keflyn told him. "All of our main power systems are going down."

"I never felt it hit," Addesin protested.

"Lightning is not like a bolt from a ship's cannons. Unless there is an explosive discharge of electricity, which is not going to happen in an ungrounded spacecraft, then it just quietly fries your electronics. How do I get main power back up?''

"If the regular generator start-up procedure does not work, then you just ran out of options.''

Keflyn was beginning to get the idea that they were in a lot of trouble. The atmospheric shields were not much, but they did protect the shuttle from more than half of the heat of entry. They had also been down for the better part of half a minute, and she had no sensor information coming in to tell her how the ceramic alloy hull plates were handling the matter. Ships were not built to take the heat of entry directly against their hulls; it was much too inefficient, requiring extensive heat shielding, insulation, and bracing, and far too risky. At least the shuttle had a fair amount of ceramic shielding to take the heat that bled through the atmospheric shields, or they would not have still been contemplating the matter. The question now was whether or not the shuttle would survive the rest of the trip down.

"You should go get back into that suit of yours," she said; she was still wearing her own armor. "It would be good protection against the heat, and I cannot promise that we will keep our atmosphere.''

From the curve of the planet emerging just under the nose of the shuttle, she guessed that they still had the better part of sixty kilometers to go. At this altitude, she thought that most of the sheet lightning had actually passed far beneath them. She suspected that they had only been caught in a discharge arc, bringing additional energy down from the magnetosphere.

In any case, they were not going to survive unless she did something to slow this ship. The shuttle was beginning to hum and buffet slightly, an indication that they were beginning to bite into denser air. Getting as much response as she could from the atmospheric control surfaces, she brought the nose of the shuttle up sharply, not to present heavier belly shielding to the heat—which she doubted they had—but to simply present a larger surface to the air to act as a brake. Then she noticed a series of switches in the bank of emergency controls, four to provide added thrust and four for brakes. She assumed that these would be either solid or liquid fuel boosters, and she triggered the first shot of braking thrust. There was a small explosion somewhere in the nose of the ship as access covers were blown away, then perhaps half a minute of muted roar as the small engines burned.

At least it had some effect. Keflyn had precious few emergency read-outs for her use; all of the monitors were down, and the air-speed indicator had already burned away. By the time Jon Addesin returned, again wearing the bulky suit, she was firing the third braking shot.

"There's some smoke coming up from beneath the cargo deck," he reported. "It's a good thing we have suits. The ship must be full of toxic fumes."

"Are there any water tanks on board this ship?" Keflyn asked. "If anything like that gets too hot, steam or other expanding gasses can cause the container to explode like bombs."

"No, nothing like that."

Long, tense minutes passed, and the cargo hold became so filled with smoke that Keflyn was given to wonder if she might find some way to vent it before it ruptured the hull. The tires of the left main landing gears exploded, to judge from the distant thuds she felt through the fabric of the ship, and she could only hope that the blast had not ripped open the doors. Then they were down in the widely-scattered clouds, losing speed quickly in the heavy air. They were about twenty thousand meters up, in a shuttle that had no engines and was starting to burn.

"We need off this ship as soon as possible," Keflyn announced. "And it seems that the closest place we can get off is straight down. I think that I should get us there in as direct a path as I can manage. I think that you should get yourself into the passenger cabin and strap yourself into one of the seats with its back facing forward. When we hit, that should keep you from being thrown."

"When we hit what?" Addesin asked.

"The ground, I should imagine. We will have no landing field, and I doubt that we have any landing gear anyway. All I hope is to hit something soft."

She certainly did her best, but she had her doubts at first. As she came lower, she could see that her earlier guess was correct. The landscape below was rugged and heavily wooded, but there were several grassy meadows to be seen. She fired the remaining braking charge, dropping the shuttle's speed to perhaps half that of the speed of sound, then she turned the rudder in one direction and the ailerons in the other, causing the huge machine to crab sideways, slowing even more in the sideslip.

She reached in the open chestplate of her suit, switching her communication channel. "Quendari Valcyr, do you hear me?"

"I hear you quite well," the ship answered immediately.

"I am about to crash this shuttle in the middle of nowhere," Keflyn explained quickly. "Could you send a message to Derrighan at the Feldenneh settlement and have him come in Mr. Addesin's van to fetch us? We will be coming down about eight hundred kilometers short of the field."

"I will send a probe immediately," Quendari assured her. "And I will send another to meet you, in the event you need help. A probe may not be much, but it is the best I can do."

"It will be appreciated," Keflyn replied.

She selected her landing place quickly, one of the larger meadows where she could bring the shuttle down on the very crown of a hill, then allow the ship to slide downhill to a stop. That, she thought, would help prevent the shuttle from burying its nose in the ground and jerking to a violent stop. She was not entirely certain about all that; she was not used to ships this size, nor any that flew entirely on atmospherics.

The shuttle settled in on the hilltop very smoothly and slid some 300 meters to the base of the hill. Then it did bury its nose in the soft ground and came to a very sudden and violent stop. The straps of Keflyn's seat broke and she left the ship very quickly by the nearest way, with an involuntary leap through the forward window. The shuttle gave a final heave as if broken apart at the seams by some internal explosion that was not quite enough to break it apart, and it settled with a sigh and a cloud of dust. Then it began to burn furiously.

Jon Addesin had himself out of his seat in moments and hurried back to the pilot's cabin to check on Keflyn, only to find to his very great surprise that she was gone. When he saw the broken window, he knew what had happened. He rushed back to the interior cabin and opened the emergency hatch, then tossed out several survival packs and himself. Fortunately most of the lower nose had collapsed or been buried, and it was only two meters down into loose soil. He was still wearing half his own weight in the engineering suit, and the fall nearly left him stunned.

He pulled off his helmet as quickly as he could, then hurried to find Keflyn. As it happened, he nearly ran over her as he turned. She was standing there beside him, looking much less the worse for wear than himself. Starwolves in their armor enjoyed a high degree of invulnerability.

"I think that we should get away from this monster, just in

case there is something inside that might explode," Keflyn said, helping him to gather up the survival packets.

"So now what?" Addesin asked. "Do you have any idea where we are?"

"I have a very good idea where we are," she insisted. "I have also made arrangements to have someone here to rescue us in a few hours. Trust me to arrange things better than that."

They retreated to the edge of the woods, where they would have some cover from the wind and wood for a fire. It was late afternoon and Keflyn doubted that Derrighan would arrive before midnight, assuming that he left as soon as Quendari's probe reached him and did not wait until the next day. She could use her com as soon as they were settled to inform the Valcyr of their condition, and the burning shuttle should provide an excellent beacon for several hours yet.

"We will have to get you a new pair of shuttles," Keflyn remarked as they were setting up a temporary camp. Jon Addesin had come out of his heavy suit immediately, and she was now shedding her own.

Addesin looked up in surprise. "What?"

"Well, you lost that shuttle on Starwolf business," she explained. "And we do owe you a few favors in exchange for what we are about to do to you."

"What do you mean?"

"I mean that this planet just became Starwolf property. We will keep it secret if we can, but it is too dangerous for you to ever return to Union space. Perhaps you will be able to have the supply run between our own home world and here."

Addesin seemed to be at a complete loss. "The Union already considers this world as their own. Do you really think that the Starwolves can chase them away?"

Keflyn was amused as she began sealing up the suit for storage. "The Union has never been able to take from us any property that we have claimed as our own. Are you worried?"

Addesin shrugged. "I just have a much higher opinion of what the Union is capable of doing compared to you Starwolves."

Keflyn laughed aloud. "You cannot be serious! Based on what evidence?"

Then she had to admonish herself for thinking that she was any better. She had never been honestly in love in her life, and yet she had to reluctantly admit that she was becoming very fond of

Derrighan indeed. Perhaps absence did make the heart grow fonder, and her present company only cast the contrast between the two into a bright, cold light. Despite her quiet sympathies for the man, she was also growing very tired of Jon Addesin's sullen suspicions. She was eagerly looking forward to Derrighan's arrival, and his quiet, undemanding love.

For any number of reasons, the time had come for Keflyn to go home.

- 11 -

The Methryn dropped out of jump into high starflight speeds, a great shuttering crash running through her frame as it adjusted under the tremendous stress of that shift. The members of the bridge crew looked up expectantly for a long moment, then turned back to their work when there were no additional noises or warning lights. The big ship had survived one more time.

"We are doing better than expected," Valthyrra announced, the lightness in her voice denying that everyone knew she was tearing herself apart.

"I do not need for you to do better than expected," Velmeran told her. He leaned back carefully against the console of central bridge, the injury to his left shoulder complex still bothering him slightly. "I need for you to get there on schedule and intact. If you break down somewhere along here, then we lose Alkayja."

"I do keep that always in mind."

"You just find it easy to ignore," he finished for her. "Any response from Keflyn's portable transceiver?"

"Nothing so far," Valthyrra responded, her camera pod moving ahead of him as he rose from his own station on the upper bridge and descended the steps. "Trel and Marlena are still asking to take their transport to get her."

Velmeran shook his head sadly. "No, we will need every pilot we have. She has that Free Trader, and quite literally anything can out-run a Fortress. I just hope that they get clear in time. I wonder if she has any idea of where she really is."

That thought amused Valthyrra as much as himself, but Velmeran's thoughts were always on business. Just one more day, and they would reach their destination two days ahead of Donalt Trace's Fortresses and Mock Starwolves. Then his greatest juggling act ever would begin, and he would have to find last minute answers to twenty years of careful planning.

He saw that the chief medic Dyenlayk had entered. He moved quietly to one side of the bridge to meet her, but both Valthyrra and Consherra the Everpresent saw him and invited themselves.

"How is Lenna?" he asked softly, knowing well why she had come.

Dyenlayk looked tired and at the end of hope. "The same as always. I can keep her alive forever, but I have to ask myself why. There is certainly nothing that I can do to put her back together, and I doubt that anyone can. All the same, I still plan to keep her alive until I can hand her over to the human medics at Alkayja. They know their own kind better than I ever will. If they say that nothing can be done, then we have to let her go."

"I never thought that she would make it back to the ship," Velmeran said, mostly to himself. "What can I possibly say to Tregloran?"

"What can you possibly say to Bill?" the medic asked. "That big, stupid automaton is just standing there beside her bed like a ghost."

"Throw him out, if he gets in the way."

"I do not have the heart," Dyenlayk said as she turned toward the lift.

"I would have never thought that Bill was that aware," Valthyrra remarked.

"Bill exists for a very limited purpose," Velmeran said. "His existence is measured by his service to Lenna Makayen."

He glanced up at Valthyrra's camera pod, and she turned away in a haughty gesture. "I most certainly will not at this time attempt to council a grieving automaton."

"Unfortunately, Lenna's was only the first life of a friend that I might have to throw away to save this war," Velmeran said as he turned to stare absently at the main viewscreen. "I just hope that the price buys us what we want."

"Could they really win?" Consherra asked.

"That depends very much on those Mock Starwolves," Velmeran admitted. "The one thought that occurs to me is that Donalt Trace fears the very sight of Kelvessan, to the extent of an actual phobia. I am responsible for that, I fear. I doubt very much that he would have trusted his own Starwolves enough to give them as free a hand as he said. I expect—and hope—that they will be very carefully directed only into very specific parts of the battle. I am also remembering that they will have no actual battle experience, and they are flying ships, no matter how good, that were still built by Union technology. With all of those factors combined, I still expect that one of our pilots should be as good as two or possibly three of their own."

"Even three to one, they could still out-gun us by numbers alone," the ship reminded him.

"It also depends very much on what help we have," he continued. "Right now, I am only counting on two ships and the fighters of the Methryn to carry this battle, plus whatever else we can find at the base. With those odds, we have to lose. We have to have at least one more ship with fighters come in before it starts."

"I just hope that our friends back at the base have not decided to break up that incomplete ship in their construction bay for scrap," Valthyrra said. "If that carrier is not in condition to fly and fight, then we are in trouble indeed. The extra engines and guns and the special armor of that new ship will mean a lot."

Velmeran frowned. "If Lenna had been able to retrieve the codes that will cause the Mock Starwolf cruisers to self-destruct, then we would have little to worry about. We could have gone hunting for those Fortresses and met them on our own terms. Of course, I am only assuming that those self-destruct codes even exist. Donalt Trace might well be contemplating a long and profitable partnership with his own Starwolves, just as he said."

"I hope that Venn Keflyn did get him," Valthyrra muttered in a rather dire voice.

"In a way, Trace has already done his worst to us," he continued. "I do not like the thought of Kelvessan fighting Kelvessan, no matter what the circumstances."

The Methryn dropped out of starflight well inside the system and continued her run quickly and under concealment, her main shields brought up to stealth strength. She was already well past the inner line of automated defenses, which had not even taken note of her passage. Circling tightly in her final approach, she braked sharply at the last moment and pulled to a stop barely ten kilometers short of the immense orbital base at the same time that she dropped her cloaking shield. Her appearance was sudden and completely unexpected, designed to use the vast, menacing form of the giant carrier in a subtly threatening gesture.

The Republic had forgotten just how frightening its own Starwolves could be.

"Get me President Delike on the line, and make certain that they understand that I mean now," Velmeran ordered, watching the main viewscreen. Most of the ships that had been in the area of the station were heading very quickly in the other directions, but one audacious little cutter, painted bright orange for easy visual recognition, was moving to intercept the Methryn. "What does that bold little twit think he is doing?"

"That, Commander, is an automated escort," Valthyrra explained. "The Port Authority is demanding our surrender."

"Is that so? Double-check that ship for life signs and destroy it in the most spectacular manner that you can contrive."

Valthyrra was happy to oblige; she had always considered the bright orange escorts to be a rather officious gesture anyway. She spared it only a single shot from the largest cannon from the main battery in her shock bumper, and the escort disappeared in a flask of bright flame.

"Message delivered and understood," Valthyrra remarked with deep satisfaction. "President Alac Delike is awaiting your pleasure."

She moved her camera pod closer, so that Velmeran could speak through her own leads. He elected to follow her lead, launching into an immediate and unrelenting assault. "President Delike, you are caught between a rock and a hard place. You have the Kelvessan angry with you, and you may have just noticed that we have almost all of the Republic's weapons. And now you have Donalt Trace and the Union coming down on you. An attack force of five Fortresses and sixteen of their new Mock Starwolf cruisers will be here in two days, and their orders are to destroy the Republic."

"But that's impossible!" Delike protested. "We have a treaty with them."

"That treaty was a ploy. Their only interest was using you to get at me. Let me explain things carefully, since you obviously do not have the wit to figure things out for yourself. This is the only supply base for the Starwolves, and the homeworld of the Kelvessan race. They knew that we would not accept exile, but force your surrender, and they have already gotten all they ever wanted from you. They finally know the location of Alkayja, and you have chased away the carriers that could have protected you. Now they plan to destroy you, so that the carriers will have nowhere to turn."

"What am I going to do?" Delike asked desperately.

"I will make that simple for you," Velmeran told him. "I am giving you only two choices. You give the Starwolves complete control of defending this base and do everything you can to help us, or I will come in there and pull you out."

Delike considered that for a long moment, and Velmeran was by no means certain that he would agree. Delike seemed foolish enough to believe that he might still salvage the situation. He could as easily make the Starwolves work to take the base, and attempt to disappear in the confusion. Very much depended upon whether First Senator Saith and Party Chairman Alberes were there to advise him. Velmeran remembered that Delike was only a simple, very impressionable man who thought he was doing the right thing. The other two had impressed him as a pair of crooks out for all they could get from this scheme.

"We will agree, on certain conditions," Delike answered at last.

"I had anticipated that," Velmeran answered. "But make it brief. I am not in a generous mood."

"Just this. First Senator Saith, Chairman Alberes, and myself must have immunity from official prosecution and a ship to leave when it is done. You must not interfere in our departure."

"I agree," Velmeran answered readily enough. "But only to those two terms, and to the letter of the agreement. There will be no official prosecution, and you will be given a ship to go where you will."

"We will be looking forward to meeting you."

"I just bet," he muttered under his breath, and sighed. "I want that carrier you have in your docking bay. I just hope for your sake that you have not taken it apart. There is no statute of limitation on stupidity."

He nodded, and Valthyrra cut the line. He looked up at her. "Move yourself into a docking bay as close to that inactive ship as you can manage. We have to get her ready to fight. Go ahead and put every ship we have overboard right now. I will take a team over to the new ship as soon as we dock and get the bays open. All other crewmembers are to begin moving their personal belongings out of the Methryn immediately."

"Commander?" Consherra asked, using his title in her surprise.

He shook his head. "There is just no help for it. I want everything out of this ship that is not a part of either the generators, weapons, or drives. All of the racks for the fighters, the tools from the machine shops, and the equipment from the science labs, and the furnishing for the schools and sick bay. Even the simulators. Everything that can be taken from this ship has to go. The Methryn does not have the shielding or the engines of that new ship, and she has just about ruined her spaceframe. The only advantage I can give her now is to strip her of all excess weight. I believe that we might be able to cut her down by as much as three million tons."

"I agree," Valthyrra added. "And by having no crewmembers on board, I will be free to run interference for the others and take superficial damage without concern."

Velmeran looked up at her camera pod, suddenly aware from her words that she knew they would not be coming back to this ship. The Methryn would not fly again. He doubted that she would even survive this battle, however things turned out. The Methryn had been built for war, and perhaps it was only proper for her to die in battle. But Valthyrra would not die with the Methryn, not if he could help it.

He turned to Consherra. "This is your department. I doubt that anyone in this base knows more about the sentient complex of this ship than you, but I will ask about just the same. As soon as we are docked, I want you to begin the process of duplicating Valthyrra's memory units."

"There is not time to get Valthyrra installed in that new ship," Consherra protested.

"No, but we can move her in as soon as this is over," he told her. "She has to fly the Methryn in this battle, and there is not time to pull her own units before the battle anyway. You know how deeply buried they are. We will pull them out later, if we can. But just in case, I want duplicates."

* * *

The Methryn moved into her docking bay as soon as she had discharged the last of her ships, taking the bay immediately to the left of the carrier that had still been under construction. Tenders were already standing by to begin pulling unused fighters, empty racks, and a mountain of spare parts from the backs of the fighter bays. There was no artificial gravity in the bay itself, only on board the ship, so the Starwolves were able to simply throw a fair amount of crated material overboard to be retrieved by the tenders when they could.

Velmeran took a small crew directly to the new ship, to get the bays open and to take a quick look about the carrier and make certain that she was ready to fight. Fortunately the ship seemed to be in a completely flight-ready condition, lacking only memory cells to begin the slow, careful process of bringing her to life. Those were missing because Velmeran had known for some time that he would have to move Valthyrra into this new ship, and he had asked several months earlier that the new ship not be activated until he could assess the Methryn's condition at the time of completion and determine whether she could serve a few years more.

There was certainly no lack of help. Many Kelvessan scientists, engineers, and technicians, some only just released from internment awaiting sterilization or even death, hurried to assist in preparing the new carrier for flight. Many more Kelvessan from throughout the station arrived to help in any way they could. They threatened to slow things up in their eagerness to express their appreciation to the Methryn and especially Commander Velmeran, until he made it clear that he needed help more than thanks and that there was not a moment to spare.

"Oh, I know that she is ready to fly," Admiral Laroose, recently returned from a premature retirement, explained when he found Velmeran touring the ship's engineering sections. "We had her out twice earlier, before the Senate forbade it."

"That helps," Velmeran said. "Two carriers, some 250 fighters, and the automated defense drones. If the gods have elected to forgive me for being inattentive to my duties these past few years, we might just have a chance to win, which does bring me to the next point. The attack force will probably invite us to fight on a single front, but I doubt very much that they will keep to one. If anything comes up behind us, I want those defense drones in position and ready. I very much need for you to coordinate their attack.''

Laroose waved his hands in a gesture of refusal. "No battle experience, old boy!"

"You are still the best I have. Besides, I am adamant about this becoming a strictly Kelvessan battle. The Republic needs a chance to earn back her own honor.''

"Then I accept reluctantly," Laroose agreed, and frowned. "It's a damned shame that you had to grant pardons to Delike and his chums. If you had just sent word, me and a few of my boys would have gladly strangled them.''

"It served its purpose," Velmeran said, looking up at him. "And who says that I pardoned them? I only made a couple of very specific promises about what I will and will not do to them. I still believe that fortune usually finds a way to restore the balance of payments.''

By that time, Consherra had finally made arrangements to begin the transfer of Valthyrra's memory units. Eight of the massive memory cells were located in separate portions of the carrier's forward section, each a heavily armored block the size of a large shipping container. The units themselves were secured within their own protective access tube, so heavily shielded that they often survived the complete destruction of the ship itself. Consherra had been able to find eight newly-constructed blank units, ready for installation in a ship of their own. She had two of these moved into each of the Methryn's four transport bays, where they would be nearest the Methryn's own units.

There was enough help at hand to have the heavy transfer cables laid out between the blank units in the bays and the access panels to Valthyrra's units deeper within the ship. Consherra moved quickly, knowing that each passing minute could be depriving Valthyrra of that much more of her memory. The transfer of memory from one unit to another was risky enough under the best of circumstances, ordinarily used only for the replacement of an aging or faulty unit. Attempting the transfer of all eight units at the same time multiplied the risk by that much, and the high-speed encoding method was reserved for only a dire emergency. If the transfer was too incomplete, then Valthyrra's personality programming would also be too incomplete to engage and return her to life.

"I am ready to enter the first unit," Consherra announced to the portable com link she wore on her collar. She was standing before a very heavy and secure hatch built into the wall of one of the Methryn's endless corridors. "This unit access panel is labeled as A3 1121."

"Tread softly," Valthyrra answered as she opened the hatch. "You stand before my primary cell. Most of my personality is locked within that unit. You may begin."

Consherra entered, making her way through the four meters or so of narrow tunnel that led her to a second hatch, trailing the final length of the transfer cable behind her. She lifted a heavy, long-handled tool, in form like an immense socket wrench, and fitted the cylinder-shaped lock at its end into the receptacle in the center of the hatch. It was in its way a large key, never kept on board the ship itself but only under guard at Alkayja Base. With the mechanical key installed, she took a small magnetic card from a compartment in the handle of the key and inserted this in a slot in the wall to the right of the hatch.

The chip inside the card fed its data through the magnetic contacts into the electronic lock, which recognized her right to access to the core. Six heavy latches pulled back one after the other, and Consherra pulled down on the handle of the mechanical lock, releasing its own internal latches. Then she took hold of the massive handles on either side of the hatch and lifted it clear, breaking the airtight seal. The hatch itself weighed nearly two hundred kilograms, a final insurance against the credentials of the one opening the core. It was no burden for the enhanced strength of a Kelvessan or even the four powerful arms of an Aldessan of Valtrys, its original designers. But no human could have lifted it clear.

Inside was a final door, this one fitted with a numeric keypad. Consherra quickly punched in the final access code, the one known only to the Commander, First Officer, and the ship herself. The hatch lifted clear, allowing her to see inside the armored core and the massive memory cell locked securely in its cradle.

"At last," Consherra remarked softly and she lifted herself through the open hatch. "You could be dead by the time I run this maze eight times."

"I am comforted by your consideration," Valthyrra answered sourly. "This is the important one. I could as easily do without the others."

"Can you estimate your transfer rate?" Consherra asked as she pulled the cable around to one end of the cell, where its main access sockets were located. "That should give you some idea of the extent of transfer in the time allowed."

"Virtual encoded memory," the ship explained. "There is no predicting the transfer rate because there is none. The receiving unit sees the entire memory of the master unit all at once, but it takes time to mirror what it sees. Some is mirrored instantly, while some will take hours. And since portions of that same memory file may exist in another cell, I have to access the entire data from all sources before I am able to see the memory myself. It gets complicated when you try to work with it, but it is the key to my ability to think like you mortals."

Since the new ship had no main computer network in operation, the entire vessel had to be controlled manually. At least there was enough secondary computer operation that the major systems were able to regulate themselves, although the commands for those systems had to be relayed from their master stations on the bridge. In theory, this carrier could fly and fight with a crew of only fourteen, that being the number of stations on the bridge. The weapons systems remained the biggest problem, since there was only just enough computer control to assist in targeting. All the various small cannons in their retractable turrets along the ventral groove, where the upper hull was joined to the lower, were directed by their own gunners.

Because of the difficulties in flying the ship manually, Velmeran decided they would fight this battle with only a minimal crew of officers and technicians. Even the fighters and transports with their support teams were installed in Alkayja Base and would launch from there. Like the Methryn, the new ship would fly stripped for battle.

One problem that had to be solved early on was finding a name for the new carrier, to make references and communications easier and clearer. This new ship was unofficially the Methryn, but there already was one Methryn on hand with a prior claim on the use of that name. Before Velmeran had a chance to decide anything for himself, he found that the code-name Alternate was already in general use for the new ship among the pilots, while the base personnel referred to her as Carrier D-Class 2-A, its registration number. Alternate seemed easier to deal with, especially in a hurry. For the duration of the coming battle, the new carrier became known as the Maeridyen, which was the Tresdyland word for Alternate.

The task of flying the Maeridyen fell to Consherra, and she was not pleased with the prospect. She had never had as much direct control over a carrier in her life, since there was ordinarily at least an automatic flight control system to interpret her commands from the manual controls into a series of related actions throughout the ship. She would be in control of actual navigation, engine power, and the jump drive as a method of emergency evasion. The more precise control of the Maeridyen's main systems would come from Tresha and her assistant at the engineering station. Cargin, from his station beside Consherra's helm on the central bridge, would have main weapons control, while the defense station would coordinate the ship's shields. Flight control and navigation would assist Consherra in flying the ship, while the scanning, running systems, and damage control stations would pick up any slack.

With even automatic flight control relying on the ship's nonsentient computer network to coordinate her systems, Consherra or even Velmeran on the upper bridge could have handled all of those functions alone. There was going to be a great deal of shouting orders and instructions across the bridge, and Velmeran had to direct the battle through this awkward network. All of this was complicated even more by the fact that this was an unfamiliar ship to the crew of the Methryn, with more main drives and a more efficient jump drive than they were used to, and a more complex weapons array that included a second conversion cannon. Consherra was hoping for at least one trial flight before battle, to get some feel for what was in effect a very different ship from the old carriers.

The gods of fortune must have forgiven Velmeran somewhat. With perhaps half a day remaining before battle, a second carrier appeared in the system and hurried in to dock. It was the Vardon, the second of the new carriers and the best possible choice in all the Wolf Fleet. They would now face the assault fleet with the two most powerful, heavily armed, and well-shielded ships in the fleet, and the unpopulated and expendable Methryn. Velmeran knew very little of Theralda Vardon's previous military experience, except that she had managed to get herself destroyed once already. At least he did have considerable faith in Tregloran's ability to command.

Tregloran immediately brought his command crew over to the Maeridyen. They were experienced with these new carriers and could check out the systems. And since the Vardon was battle-ready, they made arrangements for the Methryn's bridge crew to take her out for a practice run and familiarize themselves with the ship.

"I am sorry about Lenna," Velmeran said when Tregloran joined him on the bridge of the Maeridyen.

"Yes, Valthyrra told us on the way in." He shrugged, feigning more casual acceptance of the situation than he felt. "It was bound to happen eventually. She insisted upon living that way."

"Yes, we will do what we can for her as soon as things settle down."

Tregloran frowned, then glanced about the bridge. "This has all been very strange business. I was here for several months only a year ago, and there was no hint of any of this. Then, before I can make it back again, the whole thing comes apart at the seams and you put it back together again. Valthyrra said that you had to grant them all immunity."

"Only the top three," Velmeran insisted. "At last count, we have more than 70 Senators who voted this mess into existence in prison, and some 200 corporate executives who funded the take-over and were waiting in line to buy trade monopolies and Kelvessan slaves. It was as bad as anything in the Union. We will let them sit in jail without bail for a few days, then put most of them on lifetime probation, on the condition that they can never again hold public office. The funny thing about this whole affair is that absolutely no member of the human population ever cast a vote to put these people in office or approved of what they were doing. Everyone was on to these criminals from the start, but what can you do?"

"Not a one? My, my!" Tregloran took his meaning with amusement. "What about President Delike and his little friends?"

"All hiding out in the government complex on board the station," Velmeran explained. "They do not dare go back down to the planet, as much as they would like to collect their private data files and financial records. I had wondered if they would run for cover while they had a chance, but they seem determined to sit tight. My guess is that they hope we lose the battle, and they will kindly offer their services to the conquerors as puppet rulers."

"We could still get another ship in before things start," Tregloran mused. "Then we might see them run in a hurry."

"How is Theralda Vardon? Will this be her first real fight?"

"Well, she is more consistently lucid than she used to be."

"Lucid?"

"Well, yes." After looking for a gentler term to describe his ship's behavior, he decided that he was being generous enough already. "You know that she was put together with only one memory cell. Sometimes I think that even the one was shaken too hard when we stole it. There used to be days when she would just hang there in the middle of the bridge, relaying information like a damned machine. She is developing a higher degree of spontaneity."

"I just hope that she remembers how to fight."

Tregloran smiled fondly. "It seems like old times, fighting with the odds against us."

Velmeran stared at him. "This is the first time in my life that I've ever considered the odds against me."

Tregloran's face fell. "Oh."

The final hours passed slowly in a frenzy of hurried preparations. At almost the very last moment, a final Starwolf carrier, the Karvand under the command of Velmeran's half-sister Daelyn, hurtled into system and dropped out of starflight almost on top of the station. The ship was already launching her packs, ready to move immediately into battle. Gelvessa Karvand explained, once the initial chaos was past, that she expected them to come under attack at any moment. Decelerating out of starflight, she had scanned an indisputable total of ten Fortresses and a number of other ships that she thought to be stingship carriers all arranging themselves in what appeared to be attack formation.

The Fortresses presented their own problems. The Starwolves could crack the heavy hull-shielding from the giant ships with their quartzite detonator missiles, but it still took the shot from a conversion cannon to destroy the Fortress. The Methryn and the Karvand both had only the one cannon and the newer ships had two, making a total of only six, and the cannons had a tendency to burn themselves out after only one firing. He could only hope that the cannons of the newer ships did not burn out. There was also the matter of the sixteen Mock Starwolf cruisers, which were fairly massive piles of armor in their own right. He now had over 700 fighters, and the most powerful accessory cannons had been fitted to those small ships.

Velmeran decided it was time to launch the carriers. The worst possible disaster on his own part would be to allow his carriers to be caught in their bays if the Mock Starwolves moved in suddenly. If time allowed, he was tempted to lead some of the carriers on a sudden strike against the Union attack force before it had time to get itself into motion. He was also afraid that they might be waiting to draw him out, divide his forces, and then hit him from behind. Donalt Trace had spent the last twenty years figuring out endless ways to trick him.

Now he had to face the hardest part yet. He had to go back to the Methryn and order Valthyrra disconnected from her backup cells and send her out to die. What Tregloran had said about Theralda Vardon had left him even more uneasy about this. He had already been worried about making certain that he had captured enough of Valthyrra's memories to return her to life. Was there something more that he needed, perhaps that soul that Valthyrra was always so concerned about? Where does a starship keep her soul?

He had made no provisions to protect that part of Valthyrra Methryn that mattered the most to her, and she had not held him accountable for that. Perhaps she did not trust even the psychic abilities of the High Kelvessan to give her what she wanted most. Perhaps she was just doing what duty required of her, taking solace in the thought that eighteen thousand years was long enough for anyone to live.

"Standing by to disconnect," Consherra said over the com link in their suits. They were already dressed for battle, knowing that they would have to move quickly. This was quite literally their final task before battle. She was standing by at Valthyrra's primary cell, while technicians were ready to disconnect the others.

"Not until I give the order," he answered. "Then you go straight to the Maeridyen. Let the technicians remove the duplicate memory units."

The lift pulled to a stop and Velmeran stepped out onto the bridge, only too aware that this might well be the last time he would see this place. Even the seats at all of the various stations had been stripped in a gallant effort to reduce the Methryn's weight and give her a fighting advantage in maneuverability. The carpets in the cabins had been pulled as well, and she now weighed three-and-a-half million tons less than when she had entered this bay.

Valthyrra's camera pod was rotated well around, watching him in silence. The note that he had attached to the side of the boom was still there, ordering the crews that this was to be left. If Valthyrra did have a soul, then this simple piece of machinery was its focus.

"We both knew that I would have to leave this ship eventually," she said, breaking the silence. "Three kilometers of starship is not the sort of thing that you can keep around for sentiment. I would rather see this old shell burn away in battle than be carved up for scrap. A person's life should come to more than just scrap."

"There is no reason for you to assume that you will be destroyed," he told her. "We stand or fall together in this, and the odds tell me that none of us will be here when it ends. If anything, I have given you two chances to survive."

"I am not concerned for that part of myself," Valthyrra insisted. "No matter what happens to me, whether you succeed or fail in bringing me back, or even if you never have the chance, I have no regrets. Not for myself."

Velmeran smiled. "No regrets, perhaps. But it does not stop you from feeling afraid and alone."

Valthyrra dropped her camera pod lower. "I find that I have an instinct to stay alive, and there is precious little in the universe that can threaten you when you are this big and powerful. I find that I am by no means used to being afraid for my life. But what is my life? Those large metal boxes full of data that you are packing out of here? I like to think that my life means more than just information and programmed responses, but I never did find my soul. I have always been afraid to look. It was safer—less frightening—to hope that I do have one, than to discover that I do not."

Velmeran reached up, gently laying both of his right hands on the side of her camera pod. "You keep your soul in the very same place the rest of us have ours, in the hearts and minds of others. This ship seems so big, cold, and empty just now, because in a way you have already gone. We took your spirit with us when we left."

She glanced away for just a moment before turning back, her

camera pod regarding him almost shrewdly. "Is that the truth, or just a lot of fancy words you mean in kindness?"

"Your spirit is with your crew," he assured her. "We will keep it safe for you. When you see me again, then you will know the truth in that."

Valthyrra turned away, watching the main viewscreen and its unchanging image of the inner docking bay. "They are calling, Commander. Long-range sensors indicate a large body of ships moving into the system at high sublight speeds."

Velmeran nodded and turned away, activating the com link to Consherra. "Disconnect now and get out. This ship must be clear for undocking in five minutes. Consherra, I need you on board the Maeridyen by then."

"Disconnection is complete. Sealing the hatches now, Commander," she promised.

"Commander?"

He turned, and saw that Valthyrra was watching him. He shook his head. "No more words, old friend. Say nothing that you might not remember when we meet again."

Valthyrra seemed to agree with him in that thought. "Farewell, Commander. As you say, I will be with you in spirit."

She could do nothing but watch as he walked away.

— 12 —

Velmeran stepped onto the bridge of the Maeridyen, watching with silent approval as the members of the bridge crews worked diligently at their stations to bring the immense ship up to flight-ready status. Some would have argued that a Starwolf carrier was simply too big and complex to fly with only minimal computer support, and he would have ordinarily agreed. They simply had no choice. Consherra hurried past him to her own station, where an assistant helm officer had been watching the console in her absence. The helm **stat**ion was the focus of all other activities on the bridge, and many of the primary functions of the ship had to be coordinated through that console.

"Engineering is flight-ready and standing by," Tresha reported as soon as Consherra took her station, beginning the final check immediately. "All power systems are idling at nominal."

"Running shields standing by. Battle shields and stealth available upon demand. Internal shields and dampers are at minimal."

"All weapons systems standing by. Conversion cannons are pre-heated," Cargin reported from the central weapons station on the central bridge.

"All scanners and ambient sensors standing by until the ship is in open space."

"All uninhabited sections of the ship are pressured down."

Consherra looked over at Velmeran. "All set."

He nodded, and turned to communications. "Status?"

"All ships standing by. All fighters are ready to launch. Recovery transports and capture ships are in space. Alkayja station reports that the automated defenses and long-range scanners are standing by."

"Relay this order to the carriers," Velmeran said. "To avoid collision, all ships will rotate right upon backing out of their bay, then come around to the left when moving forward. Execute."

Consherra considered this possibly the trickiest move that she would take this big ship through all day. Even Valthyrra moved herself in and out of the docking bay with extreme caution. Consherra engaged the forward engines only for a moment. The docking braces snapped back as the Maeridyen's shock bumper slipped out of the forward brace, and she backed slowly out of the bay. As soon as she was clear, Consherra pivoted the ship around and engaged enough thrust from the main drives to bring the ship to a stop. The other three carriers, emerging from adjacent bays, moved in almost perfect unison. They pivoted around and accelerated, moving swiftly away from the base.

"Good enough so far," Velmeran commented. "Long-range scan. Where are they?"

"The entire force is moving forward at high sublight speed, the small ships in a tight group ahead of the Fortresses," Larenta at the scan station reported. "Anticipated arrival in seven minutes at sustained speed."

"Those Fortresses will need a full fifteen minutes at least to get themselves slowed down. They should start braking any time now," Velmeran mused, and looked up. "We will hold position twenty million kilometers out and let them come to us. I will not allow them to draw us too far away from the Base. Put me through to the Karvand."

The wait was somewhat longer than he was used to with Valthyrra's instant response in opening channels. "Daelyn of the Karvand here."

"Hold your position here," he ordered. "The Karvand is to remain out of the immediate battle. Your duty is to remain near the station. When those Mock Starwolves arrive, they will probably be coming in behind us. I want your carrier and all of your fighters guarding Alkayja, with your pilots unfought and fresh for battle."

"Yes, of course," Daelyn responded. The Karvand was already slowing to a stop. "You are picking on my poor ship, you know."

"The Maeridyen and the Vardon have superior shields," he explained. "The Methryn, I am sorry to say, is expendable. The Karvand is vulnerable, and she has her active crew still on board. Besides, this probably only means that the Mock Starwolves will destroy you first on their way to get us."

"Oh, that is different." Daelyn sounded quite mollified. Velmeran made a vague gesture to cut the channel, then remembered their present circumstances and directed that motion toward the communications console.

Consherra glanced up at him from the helm. "She is definitely your big sister."

"She has also been in command of that ship only two months." He turned to the main viewscreen. "Could we have a tactical schematic of long-range scan up here?"

That was apparently no problem at all, once it was asked for. He missed Valthyrra's quiet efficiency more than ever, and her long experience that always allowed her to know what was wanted before it was called for. The bridge crew did not know such things because Valthyrra had always been there to do it for them. They would learn a lot by the time they came through this battle, assuming that they did come through it.

The wide main viewscreen partitioned itself, its right one-third becoming a three-dimensional schematic of the area surrounding the carriers, the left third identifying individual targets, and the middle remaining a completely uninformative visual image of space ahead. Velmeran stood for a moment, watching the scanner map. The Fortresses were already braking, falling well behind the broad line of stingship carriers and battleships. The smaller ships could drop speed in a hurry, at least compared to the Fortresses, and he thought that they might close half of their remaining distance before they would begin braking. At the same time, he thought that the carriers would have to begin launching their stingships at any moment, to give themselves time to get their own forces in space, then circle around out of danger of battle themselves.

"No activity from those stingship carriers?" he asked.

"They are just now beginning to swing out their racks," Larenta reported. "By what I remember of stingship operation, they should take over a minute to deploy their racks, and another two minutes before the first stingships are launched."

Velmeran nodded. This was more like it. "Relay orders to the Vardon. They are to launch six packs, moving to intercept those stingships. Get me some estimate on the number of stingships they have."

The battleships would be more of a navigational hazard than anything; their own batteries could not penetrate the shields of the Starwolf carriers, but the carriers could take out even the largest battleships with a single shot from their massive, forward cannons. The stingships, though, were a very real danger. They would be carrying high-speed, shielded missiles, which could penetrate even heavy battle shields. He would move the fighters against the stingships, where they were most useful but in the least danger themselves. The Starwolf carriers, with their quartzite-shielding detonating missiles and their conversion cannons, were the only weapons that could take on the powerful Fortresses.

The first task was to use his own fighters to open a hole through those stingships. Starwolf pilots were good only for some fifteen minutes of hard flying before hypermetabolism wore them down and left them in need of a rest. It was actually more efficient for him to send the packs into battle in small groups rather than all at once, at least in a fight that they could not win within the first fifteen or twenty minutes.

And the most important question remained. Where were those Mock Starwolves? Would they hit early on, or when his own pilots were already tired of battle? He could not move his 700 pilots against their thousands and expect to win. His only hope of winning was that they would come in grouped together. Then he could have the Karvand swing around and take out the largest group of them with a sustained low-intensity blast of her conversion cannon, cutting their numbers enough for his more experienced pilots to handle. He might possibly win this battle, but he would need many lucky breaks and no surprises.

"Commander, I count 200 stingship carriers," Larenta reported after a moment. "At 20 for each carrier, that comes to 5,000 stingships."

"Thank you. I always appreciate bad news," Velmeran remarked drily. "Tell six of the twelve packs from the Methryn to launch and move quickly to reinforce the group attacking the stingships."

"That will leave only six packs at Alkayja base," Consherra reminded him.

He nodded. "I believe that we would do best to solve our immediate problem. That will leave us with one less problem staring us in the face when the next one presents itself."

The first group of fighters intercepted the leading edge of the first attack force, largely ignoring the battleships and aiming their more powerful accessory cannons at the stingship carriers. Those large ships, essentially just long racks with engines and crew cabins at either end, were largely unprotected, and most were still trying to get their racks of stingships clear and away. The Starwolf cannons ripped into the lightly-shielded carriers, tearing them apart. Many exploded under the concentrated barrage of heavy fire, taking their cargoes of small, swift warships with them.

But many stingships were already away, and many more were able to clear their racks while only 54 fighters did their best to deal with 200 carriers. In the end, nearly a fifth of the original 5,000 stingships survived the initial attack. The stingships were long, slender machines, all engines, generators, and weapons with a minimal crew encased in acceleration suits and supportive couches that protected them against turns and accelerations on the very limit of human endurance. As fast and as powerful as the stingships were, their performance still fell well short of the abilities of the Starwolf fighters and genetically-engineered pilots.

The stingships turned as a group, moving swiftly through the advancing lines of the battleships as they oriented on the Starwolf carriers. The fighters were on their tails immediately but the stingships were swift and shifty, bobbing in small, sudden movements that made them difficult to hit, for all that the Starwolves' natural abilities made them better targeting computers than even their own tracking scanners. The Union forces possessed the added advantage of sheer numbers, outgunning the defenders more than eighteen to one. Then the second set of Starwolf fighters, the six packs of the Methryn that had launched from the station, moved swiftly past their own carriers and into the middle of the mass of stingships.

With the Starwolf carriers moving in swiftly, the stingships suddenly broke off their attack and looped around to join the Fortresses, allowing the line of battleships to move forward into battle. Velmeran figured that the Union commander had looked upon the destruction of four-fifths of his stingships as the loss of protection he needed for his Fortresses, and decided to sacrifice his battleships to the task of wearing down the Starwolves and their known inability to endure a long conflict. Possibly he had also looked upon those four carriers as at least twice as many as he had expected, and he could only assume that each of those carriers possessed at least ten packs of its own. He could not have known that one of those carriers lacked both packs and a sentient computer system.

Velmeran also anticipated that, with the unexpected loss of most of his stingships, the Union Commander would have called up his Mock Starwolves to take the defenders from behind, opening a new line of attack, forcing the Starwolves to spread themselves thin to handle everything. Velmeran knew that his force could not last more than a few minutes, once they did attack. And still they did not come.

"Relay to all carriers," he ordered suddenly. "Engage shields to stealth intensity and loop around the battleships to attack the Fortresses directly. Valthyrra, you come with us to the right, Vardon to the left. Have shield detonation missiles standing by. Execute now."

All three of the attacking carriers suddenly disappeared from scan, at the same time engaging their main drives and accelerating hard. The Kelvessan could still sense the phasing of their powerful engines very clearly, but they had completely vanished as far as the human pilots were concerned. Even visual was no use, with dull, black ships moving through space across distances of thousands or even millions of kilometers. They circled wide around the battle between their own fighters and the Union battleships and stingships, coming in at the Fortresses suddenly and swiftly.

Still moving cloaked and at high speed, they made their first run at the seemingly motionless Fortresses. Each ship launched several missiles at their targets and, approaching from different directions, they were able to hit the immense ships from both sides. The automatic tracking systems in the Fortresses flashed into life as soon as they identified the missiles and brought their defensive cannons around quickly, but those shut down an instant later as eight of the ten Fortresses tried to shield themselves. The ships suddenly disappeared inside their hazy, white shells of high-intensity shields.

Neither defense was effective against the Starwolves. The shielded missiles cut through the defensive shells of the Fortresses with a brief but brilliant flare of discharged energy, slamming into the hulls of the large ships almost in the same instant. The quartzite shielding on the hulls of the Fortresses turned the tremendous explosions harmlessly, but then a backwash of searing energy began to move through the shielding, cracking its matrix and stripping it away. Automatic systems dropped the outer shields, then stole power from the engines and guns to pour even more energy into the quartzite shielding, trying to arrest the destructive process. That only fed it even more, although the partially sentient computer systems of the giant ships could not comprehend that. The process continued to completion in a matter of minutes, stripping the Fortresses of their second major defense.

The loss might seem almost inconsequential. The Fortresses still had their outer shields, and the Methryn had been unable to cut through those when she had fought the Challenger twenty years earlier. But the Starwolves were now ready to show the Fortresses the mistake in their design. The big shields took every trace of power from the massive warships, leaving them unable to fight or even maneuver while shielded, nor could they hold their shields for very long. Every time the Fortresses dropped their shields, the swift carriers were waiting with their powerful cannons, picking off turrets and engines.

But the Fortresses had an even deadlier fault, for they were only massive armor frames drawing their power from their replaceable cannon and engine modules. Those modules, each with their own generator, were by necessity on the surface of the ship, vulnerable to attack. The shields may repel bolts from the Starwolf cannons, but no shield was proof against shielded missiles, and the carriers had hundreds of missiles bearing small conversion charges. Although the carriers were forced to fire blind into the shields, each explosion cut a large hole in the unprotected hulls of the Fortresses.

Velmeran had just made the final shift of advantage unavoidable, and he knew it. The Mock Starwolves would surely be closing by now, coming to the rescue of the Fortresses. Whatever they have been waiting for, this was more important. He guessed that they would strike either at the carriers themselves or at Alkayja Base, distracting the Starwolves from their prey. He would do both, demanding a division of forces. The Starwolves had only one hope, to take out as many of the Fortresses as they could, while they could.

When it came, the response surprised him. The area was suddenly full of stingships, bringing their own missiles and cannons to bear on the carriers, and the fighters that were slowly but steadily cutting away their numbers.

"Relay this order to the Vardon and the Karvand," he shouted. "Launch all remaining packs."

"Hold that order!" Consherra declared, and turned to Cargin. "That one will be dropping her shields any moment. I doubt very much she sees us. I will hold us on target."

"Building to power now," Cargin answered. "I can give it seventy percent instantly."

The end of the wait came suddenly, the Fortress some 1,000 kilometers ahead dropping her shields. The Maeridyen had been flying sideways, engines still, while Consherra held the nose of the carrier locked on target. The carrier shuttered once as a half-megaton warhead rolled harmlessly off her reinforced shield, then Cargin had a clear shot at his target.

Deep in the Maeridyen's conversion cannon, several kilograms of water were suddenly converted into thousands of megatons of energy. A slender, tubular force field leaped out of the nose of the cannon, locking onto the Fortress, forming a pathway as that tremendous destructive force was shot toward its target. The entire Fortress glowed red and then white for a long instant out of time, then it disappeared in a blinding flash that leaped out like the explosion of a small star.

"Good shot," Velmeran commented approvingly, honestly surprised that they had managed that tactic unaided by computers. "Now could we please get those extra fighters away?"

"Commander Velmeran, this is Daelyn on the Karvand." The voice sounded distant over the com in the camera pod retracted overhead.

He looked up, fearing the worst. "Go ahead."

"The remaining battleships are closing on Alkayja station."

"Can you handle that?" For some reason that he could not begin to understand, this was not the worst that he had expected.

"If you can give me the rest of the fighters at the station," Daelyn answered. "There are no stingships in this group, so we have little enough to fear from missiles. I will take the Karvand right through the middle of them."

"Do what you can." He glanced at Korlaran at the com station. "Dispatch the Methryn's remaining fighters at the station."

Space around them continued to snap with the cannons of Starwolf ships and the detonation of missiles, and then the blast of the Vardon's conversion cannon froze the scene of battle in the brilliant flash of the destruction of another Fortress. Consherra wove the carrier deftly through the crowded skies, while Cargin directed his weapons every time he saw a chance on his array of targeting scanners. Velmeran watched them for a moment, realizing that he had overlooked one important fact. His bridge crew was working as hard as any of the fighter pilots, and he had no replacements to take their place when they exhausted themselves.

"Commander, the Methryn just took a bad hit in her belly," Larenta announced suddenly.

Velmeran turned to Consherra. "Get us there quickly. If she is down, the stingships will make short work of her."

"On our way," Consherra responded without looking up from her monitors.

They found the Methryn within half a minute. The older carrier was drifting helplessly, the perimeter cannons along her hull groove trying to hold off the attention of half-a-dozen stingships that scattered before the Maeridyen's fury. The stingship crews had been coming at the carriers from beneath, aiming their missiles at the only possible weak link in their armor, the massive bay doors in the lower hull. The Methryn had taken a direct hit on one of her two large holding bays, ripping away the doors and tearing out her entire belly from her transport bays to the twin modules of her fighter decks. Although her interior was burning and flashing with arcs of power from broken lines, the explosion did not appear to have bitten deeply into her engineering.

Even as the Maeridyen approached, Valthyrra managed to get main power up and brought herself under control, moving slowly forward. None of her drives were damaged, and she was apparently able to get power from at least one of her main generators. Fluctuations caused her to lurch with engine fades and surges, but she turned in a wide, slow circle as she continued to gather speed steadily.

"Maeridyen, stand away!" Valthyrra ordered sharply.

"Valthyrra, can you get yourself clear of battle?" Velmeran asked. "We have support vessels on the way. We can save you yet."

"To what end, Commander?" she asked. "I have told you my opinion regarding scrap. Let me do what I can."

"Valthyrra, please."

"We both knew that this was inevitable," Valthyrra insisted. "That was the whole purpose in duplicating my memory cells, so that I could come out here and sell my old life for the best price I could get. I expect to fetch a very high price indeed."

Velmeran seemed to understand what she meant. He turned to Consherra. "Stay well clear of her, but guard her tail. She will never forgive us if we let stingships take her."

The Methryn continued to accelerate, orienting herself on her target. One of the Fortresses lay directly before her, working its slow way through a series of course corrections and seemingly unaware of her approach. At the very last moment, she fired her conversion cannon directly into the Fortress, pouring out all the limited power she had left. Not waiting for orders, Consherra turned the Maeridyen away, heading for open space and safety as quickly as she could get there. The Fortress glowed briefly as her kilometers of metal drank in the accumulation of raw energy for as long as it could before it exploded in a brilliant cloud of stellar heat. The Methryn did not even try to turn away as she hurtled into the blast.

If she had been intact with hull shields up on full, she might well have emerged unharmed, but the Methryn was wrecked and burning already. She shot out the other side of the white-hot cloud, her armored hull battered and rent, the entire forward quarter of her nose and the leading edges of her wings ripped and melted away. And yet she lived still, finding just enough power for her field drives to correct her course before her nose dipped and she began to tumble slowly. A second Fortress lay ahead, coming directly toward her, and there was nothing it could have done. Its shell was of little use against solid objects, and it's quartzite hull shield was gone. It saw her coming and tried to evade, but the Fortress was only just beginning to turn away when the Methryn slammed against its forward hull. Their combined impact speed of more than a quarter that of light vaporized both ships in an explosion as fierce and brilliant as the detonation from a conversion cannon.

Velmeran looked away, having no moment to spare for memories or grief. He noticed that every member of the bridge crew was staring at the exploding image on the main viewscreen, mesmerized. "Look sharp."

The Maeridyen turned away, rotating her protective upper hull to the force of that double explosion. Somewhere far away, another carrier took advantage of the moment of confusion to fire her conversion cannon, and yet another of the immense Fortresses disappeared in the glare of white-hot gasses. Velmeran knew that they had been very lucky, reducing the fleet of Fortresses to half in a matter of minutes while losing only one of their own carriers. But he knew also that their luck could not last. The host of stingships that had been plaguing the carriers suddenly seemed very scarce, and the Union battleships were nowhere to be seen.

"Commander, this is Daelyn of the Karvand." The warning came over the main comm abruptly. "The Union forces are pushing directly at Alkayja station. We cannot hold them."

"We will do what we can," he promised her. "Val . . . Ah, Korlaran. Order the Vardon around to reinforce the Karvand. Consherra, as soon as the Vardon is in position, call around ten packs and we will try to squeeze the Union forces between us. We will go in for the remaining Fortresses. Do we still have both cannons left?"

"The cannon we fired is in perfect condition," Cargin reported. "It will be cooled and charged up within three minutes. The second cannon is ready for immediate firing."

"Very good. Korlaran, see if you can get me Admiral Laroose."

Velmeran watched the scan image. Half of the Fortresses were destroyed but 5 remained, and that was no small matter. He also guessed that some 300 stingships and perhaps 60 battleships were left in that crowd between his own carrier and the base, moving steadily toward Alkayja Station with single-minded determination. They were almost heedless of their own losses, as if the destruction of that station was more important than anything. Were they expecting 16 Mock Starwolf carriers to come to their rescue at any moment? That seemed the only possible explanation for these tactics. Why had the Mock Starwolves held back even this long?

"Laroose speaking. Go ahead, Commander."

"Admiral, there is less than a minute before the first of those ships comes with firing range of the station," Velmeran said. "There seems to be little that we can do to stop them. Could you bring those automated units around to protect your position?"

"We are working on a solution, Commander," Laroose assured him. "You Starwolves take care of yourselves."

"Admiral?"

"Just don't let them get the Karvand. We cannot afford the loss of another carrier."

"Closed channel, Commander," Korlaran reported.

All of space lit up like the birth of a new star, lingering for no more than three seconds before dying quickly away. As soon as the scanners recovered from the image overload, there was one less Fortress to be found. The odds were evening up in a hurry.

What if there were no Mock Starwolves? Not even Lenna had actually seen one, only sixteen empty bays and a fair amount of evidence that they had been there until fairly recently. And yet the reasons for such an elaborate hoax were as inexplicable as their continued absence from this battle. Had Donalt Trace simply been trying to frighten him? Or more likely, had that greatest of threats been meant only to draw Velmeran's full attention to the attack on Alkayja Station from an even more important target? Velmeran could think of no target that could be more important, except for Commander Trace's claim that he was on his way to Terra. Velmeran wondered if everything had been designed to present him with two conflicting choices, and invite him to choose the wrong one.

"One group of stingships is moving quickly toward the station," Larenta reported. "Fighters are in pursuit."

This could be it. Alkayja Station lacked the shields or the guns to protect itself from attack, relying upon its defensive drones. Only a few hits from the nuclear warheads carried by the stingships would reduce it to ruins. Velmeran looked up at the magnified scanner image of the station to one side of the main viewscreen. A dozen stingships were making a high-speed run at the station with half as many Starwolf fighters in close pursuit, taking one of the larger ships out every few seconds. But they were already looping around the curve of the planet, and there would be enough survivors to complete the attack run.

Then, at the very last instant, Alkayja Station abruptly disappeared.

Consherra glanced up from her console, then did a startled double-take. "*Varth! Val traron de altrys caldayson bentheral!*"

Those were very much Velmeran's own sentiments on the matter.

"But where did it go?"

"They jumped," Velmeran said, only just understanding that for himself. "Of course they would have jump drives for the new carriers, and it was probably a simple matter to connect them up for power and computer control. Bless that old man! He is crafty enough to be a Starwolf himself."

"It reminds me of the sort of foolish tricks you will try," Consherra remarked as she stared at her scan monitors. "Cargin!"

"On it!" he assured her.

Consherra brought the nose of the Maeridyen around sharply, orienting on a Fortress that had just dropped her shell. It was a long shot, three-quarters of a million kilometers across the entire width of the area of battle, but the command crew of the Fortress would not have been expecting an attack from such a distant ship. The brilliant beam of the conversion cannon leaped out with deadly accuracy.

"Three against three. Even odds, if the Karvand can stay lucky long enough and avoid the missiles," Velmeran commented. "How are the packs?"

"I am trying to monitor reports from the pack leaders," Korlaran reported, turning to face him. "They seem to be holding out well enough."

All the same, Velmeran knew that those first packs to go out could only endure a few minutes more. Consherra had been operating on hypermetabolism as much as any of the pilots, and he was using her as a good indication of the condition of the others. Although she was not yet getting slow or imprecise, she looked like she was nearing the end of her strength. When she reached the end, it would come suddenly. Velmeran wondered if his limited experience with flying a carrier would be enough for him to take her place.

Another conversion cannon flashed in the darkness of space, and one of the three remaining Fortresses vanished in flame.

"Commander, this is Daelyn of the Karvand. We just burned out our conversion cannon."

"Understood. See if you can find what Laroose did with that station and help them out." Velmeran walked over to stand behind the com station. "Get me the Vardon."

As he waited, he watched the scanners. The two remaining Fortresses, now outnumbered, began to accelerate as they made the tightest turns they could manage, heading back out into open space. If they had been waiting for the Mock Starwolves to provide reinforcement, they had apparently given up any hope of that and were intent only upon saving their very big, expensive, and vulnerable ships. The loss of eight Fortresses would be a serious blow to the Union Combined Fleet, which had only twenty-five or so of the behemoths before this, and especially if the only return was the destruction of only one aging Starwolf carrier. One thing that Donalt Trace had not anticipated was the new carriers whose hull shields could survive the warheads that he was throwing at them.

"Commander?" Tregloran answered after a moment.

"This is just about over," Velmeran said. "I do not want to see those two carriers escape. I believe that we can take them."

"Right, Commander."

Velmeran turned to Consherra. "Bring this ship around and accelerate to intercept. Cargin, I will need sequential firing of both conversion cannons."

That final contest of the battle lasted a shorter time than Velmeran had anticipated. Once it became obvious that the two carriers were in pursuit, the Union commanders faced their final options. The Fortresses began to decelerate slowly and steadily, never once altering their course as they came to a complete stop to drift in space. Velmeran wanted no more surprises, and he ordered the Starwolves to keep their distance.

"What could they be doing?" Consherra asked as she brought the Maeridyen around to face one of the two Fortresses from the side.

"Staying alive, it would seem," Velmeran said, walking over to stand behind Larenta. "What does intensity scanning tell us about those ships?"

"Powering down, Commander," she answered. "All the engine and cannon modules are inactive. They are idling on internal power only."

"A gesture of submission, then," he concluded. "Tell Tregloran that he is to handle the surrender of the Union ships. Order the Karvand in to support the Vardon. Order the packs to standby status, although I do need them to stay outside for just a while yet and keep an eye on things. Consherra, take us back to Alkayja Station."

"Coming around now, Commander," Consherra said. "But I do not understand one thing. What happened to the Mock Starwolves?"

"I am beginning to believe that there never were any Mock Starwolves," Velmeran explained as he walked over to stand leaning on the front edge of the console of the central bridge. "Everything that Lenna showed us was very neatly contrived to convince us to believe in something we never actually saw. It was a part of Donalt Trace's tactics, I suspect, to try to confuse us by making us fear a secret weapon that they did not actually have."

"But how would that help?"

"If I had held back forces in this battle, waiting for a threat that never arrived, then his own attack force would have been able to face us and take us apart in pieces. We were lucky that I elected to solve our problems as they came."

Alkayja Station had already made the jump back from wherever it had gone and was using its feeble main drives to settle into its former orbit. One battle had ended, but another was yet to begin. One thing that Velmeran had learned from this whole affair was that the Kelvessan could never afford to trust in the unending good will of others. It was time for the Kelvessan to end their servitude to the war they had been created to fight, and to the Republic, which could never completely ignore the belief that it owned the Kelvessan. Velmeran had the Maeridyen hold her position half a million kilometers out and ordered a channel to President Alac Delike.

"Yes, I'm here," Delike answered after a moment. "What can I do for you?"

"I am demanding your surrender," he said. "You are still the President of the Republic, and as such the First Senator and yourself have the authority to negotiate treaties. Your recent crimes against the Kelvessan race have made it impossible for us to continue to exist within the Republic without an irrevocable guarantee of our rights."

"Commander, scanners indicate a large number of ships dropping quickly out of starflight," Larenta interrupted him quietly. "They are coming in from all directions. No positive identification, but that fierce deceleration suggests that they can only be Starwolves."

The sky was suddenly full of large black ships, braking hard with their forward engines as they moved in rapidly to surround the three carriers. Each ship was long, wide and flat of hull, in many ways very much like the Starwolf Carriers in form but only a third as large. Unlike nearly all Union ships, they were as black as space, without windows or running lights. The similarities between the two types of ships were so pronounced that they looked more like companions from the same fleet than well-matched opponents.

If this delay had been deliberate, Velmeran could still make no sense of it. The Fortresses were powered down, with conversion devices already attached to their hulls to insure their compliance, and the scores of remaining stingships had fired off and detonated their missiles as good faith of their own surrender. The stingships really had nowhere to go anyway, without the support of their carriers. At least the Mock Starwolf cruisers had not yet launched their fighters, and that gave Velmeran a chance to strike first. The Starwolves were outnumbered five to one, but their carriers were still faster, better shielded, and better armed. Velmeran was about to order the carriers to fire their conversion cannons when he realized that the Mock Starwolves were holding their positions.

"Message coming in," Korlaran reported.

Velmeran nodded. "Let me hear it."

"Commander, this is Captain Jaeryn of the Avenger," the young, male voice declared boldly. "I ask you to surrender."

– 13 –

A light wind was stirring the leaves of the trees that formed a shifting, fragmented canopy overhead. Keflyn sat with her back against a large stone, poking at the fire with four long sticks. That gave her one stick for each hand, and she seemed to be doing something different with each one. Kelvessan lived with a constant excess of available energy, ready to be called into instant use through hypermetabolism. Keflyn sometimes had trouble dealing with her own impressive reserves of energy. Right now she wanted to jump, and she had no target. For that matter, she had no idea why every warrior's instinct she had told her that it was time to fight.

It made Jon Addesin nervous enough just to watch her, and it was no help for her to know his thoughts. For the first time since she had met him, he felt himself in the presence of a weapon that disguised its deadliness with the self-delusion that it was a person. Many humans did have that opinion of Kelvessan, she had been warned, but she had never encountered it for herself. Was it because he had been seeing her in her own element, and finally in her armor, that had caused this reaction? Was it because he had lost all control he had assumed he had possessed of a relationship only he believed in? Whatever the cause, they were feeding into each other's reactions now. The more his apprehension grew, the more her defensive instincts reacted.

It would be a blessing when Derrighan arrived with the skyvan and put an end to this farce, although she knew it would not be that easy. The arrival of a rival, especially one who was an alien and had also captured Keflyn's attentions before himself, would only turn Addesin even more sullen and resentful.

You pet them. You feed them. You keep them.

Or at least you have to deal with them, Keflyn thought. It simply was not worth the effort, to have anything to do with aliens. They were none of them logical, reasonable people. Take humans, for example. Just apes with a well-developed social instinct and the self-delusion that they were an intelligent species. And why, she asked herself, did the Aldessan of Valtrys ever see the necessity of making the Kelvessan even remotely resemble them?

She glanced up at the vast, golden moon, shining down through a small break in the trees. It was time for her to be going home.

"Can the Valcyr be salvaged?" Addesin asked.

He threw out these pointless questions from time to time, as if anything was better than her silence. Perhaps he wanted to keep her talking, because it was the only time when he knew what she was thinking. She could not imagine why he was suddenly so afraid of her, as if she might decide to kill him just to spend the time. She already found it very annoying.

"That depends upon what you mean by salvage," she answered after a long moment, breaking off small pieces of one slender stick to toss one by one into the fire. "We will almost certainly duplicate her memory cells and bring her to life in a new ship— if she will allow it, of course. It probably suits her just as well to brood inside that wall of ice until she finally hatches her personal little egg of grief."

Addesin was startled by the force of her reaction. But he had to come back, as if driven against his will. "Then you mean that the Valcyr we know will never fly again?"

Keflyn glanced up at him. "She is old, Captain Addesin. She is two-and-a-half-times as old as any other ship in the Starwolf Fleet. More than three-fourths the age of human civilization. And she has been sitting locked inside that damned block of ice most of that time, without maintenance. Carriers need a complete overhaul every hundred years at the most, and it has been four hundred times as long since anyone poked into her works."

"Yes, but just think of all the back pay she has coming."

Keflyn looked over at him in surprise, and they both laughed. "Starwolves are poor people, Captain Addesin. You might as well go to bed. You know that I will watch all night if I have to."

She paused for a moment, listening. Addesin watched her closely, wondering what her sensitive ears might have detected. He knew only that her hearing was very good, although he had no idea how good. He certainly did not know that she could hear in ways that he did not expect. After a moment she stood, turning to step nearer to the edge of the forest, away from the fitful light of the fire.

"Something is coming," she said after a moment.

"The skyvan?" Addesin asked. He rose to stand as well, moving slowly to stand immediately behind her, looking into the night over her shoulder. He also did not have her large, sensitive eyes.

"No, much smaller than that," she said. "It might be one of Quendari's probes."

"Close?" he asked.

He pulled a large service pistol from within his jacket, bringing it up and then lowering its short, wide muzzle until it was aimed at the middle of her back, at the indentation in the very center between her four shoulder blades.

"It is circling around our camp now," Keflyn answered, and she sounded puzzled. She had tried to sense the identity of that silent, flying thing, and it was nothing she had expected.

Addesin fired.

Perhaps, because she had been sensitive to thoughts, probing the night for other minds, the violence of his own thoughts came to her in a sudden rush. He was aiming for her heart, hoping that the shot would kill her quickly, wondering if her ferro-precipitate bones would block the bolt. Instinct operated quicker than conscious thought, and she dove for the cover of the glacial-tossed boulders in a move so fast that he did not even see her go before he pulled the trigger.

Still holding the gun, Addesin took several steps back, uncertain whether or not he had even hit her. She had leaped aside so suddenly and so swiftly that she had quite literally vanished from his sight. He knew that he had underestimated her reflexes, but he could not understand how she could have known. He stepped back, giving himself time to aim and fire as soon as she broke from cover. The gray boulders that filled the clearing provided her far too much cover. Except for the protection they offered, she would have already been dead and he would have been spared the torment of hunting down someone he did not want to kill. Someone he might not be able to kill, now that she was warned. She had no weapons. Her speed and strength were weapon enough.

A scream broke the depths of the night. It was a strange, eerie scream like some shrill keening, so high in pitch that Addesin could not have heard it or he might have been warned, so high that even Keflyn was only dimly aware of it. The force of some unseen blow suddenly pushed Addesin to his knees, then he fell heavily to the ground. The back of his jacket was still smoking, yet Keflyn had seen no bolt.

Warned by something she could not understand, she stayed under cover. A large, black form sailed across the length of the clearing on broad wings, the faint whisper of wind through fur the only sound. Then Keflyn understood. The creature was a Kandian spark dragon, a fierce hunter thousands of light-years away from the world where it belonged but one that she knew inhabited the wilds of modern Terra. The odd movements that she had sensed were those of a small hunting pack. Addesin had been hit by the blast from a dragon's tightbeam ultrasonics, fully as powerful as a small sonic disrupter. She doubted that Addesin was still alive, and hoped for his sake that he was not.

The harsh, hunting cries of the dragons began to grate against the gentle silence of the night. The pack knew she was there, hidden from them, and they were frustrated by their inability to get at their fallen prey. Keflyn expanded her senses, knowing now the nature of what she sought, and found that there were seven, enough that at least one of the circling pack had her within range at any time. Her guns were packed away with her armor. Addesin was laying across his own gun, and that was more than five meters away. Keflyn was already in hypermetabolism, but she was not sure that she was quick enough to get that gun and dive back under cover before one of the dragons caught her.

She was given to wonder if this was how freighter captains felt when they found Starwolves on their tails. The difference was that Keflyn felt certain that she could survive this trial, if she moved carefully.

A sudden bolt cut through the night, catching one of the dragons in a burst of flame that brought it from the sky. The dark shape of a carrier's probe settled into the clearing, its flexible neck extended to bring to bear the small gun located below the lenses of its enclosed camera pod. It drifted forward, moving to shield Addesin's motionless form with its own armored hull. A tight beam of ultrasonics from a dragon caught the probe on its upper hull, striking a scattering of bright sparks as it was deflected by the machine's heavy armor. The probe seemed to flinch, lowering its camera pod to protect its lenses as the barrage of ultrasonics threatened its electronics.

Quendari herself was in no danger, even if the probe had been destroyed. But her plight forced an unconscious response from Keflyn's protective instincts. She stepped out into the clearing and lifted her upper right arm, aimed at an approaching dragon. An almost invisible envelope of blue light surrounded her for just an instant as she commanded the tremendous psychic powers of her Kelvessan heritage to their fullest extent. A thin, blue bolt shot out from that envelope, aimed along the length of her arm, and the second dragon was hurtled from the sky as if it had been struck by some immense force. The rest of the pack gave up the hunt and fled into the night, screaming their fury.

Keflyn rushed to Addesin's side, carefully turning him over. She was surprised enough to find that he was still alive, although she doubted that they could get him to the limited help available on this world in time to save him. She took the precaution of confiscating the gun, not trusting what he might try even yet.

"Your Feldennye friend will be here with the skyvan very soon," Quendari said, drawing the probe back a short distance. "I was leading him, since he had no way to track your position accurately. He will see your fire."

Keflyn shook her head slowly. "It is too late."

"Keflyn?"

Addesin was looking up at her, his pain obvious. She had nothing to spare him even that.

"It might be ridiculous to ask that you forgive me," he said. Each breath he drew to speak brought searing pain; she suspected that the sonics must have nearly burned out his heart and lungs. "I got what I had meant for you, but that bolt would have still been in your back if you had not jumped. It took me a long time to talk myself into shooting you. All in all, I still wish that it had been you instead of me."

Keflyn drew back in surprise. "You are right. I do not forgive you. But I might yet, if you will just tell me why."

"Oh, not my idea," he insisted, trying to cough and finding even that impossible. "You see, Union Intelligence monitors my ship very closely. They have known what this place really is for a long time now. When the underground came to make arrangements to get you on board my ship, they told me to take you. I never wanted to be a part of that. The Free Traders are supposed to be neutral, and not answerable to the Union. But they have their ways. To assure my loyalty, they keep a third of my crew detained at any time.''

"Yes, I can understand," Keflyn assured him.

"I never wanted to be involved in this," he repeated bitterly. "First they told me to keep you occupied any way I could, show you anything, just as long as I kept you here. Then new orders came in. There is a fleet of seven Fortresses and some new SuperFortress coming in to destroy the planet. First they said to just abandon you here. Then they said that I have to kill you.''

"You have been in communication with them?" Keflyn asked.

"Couriers have been coming and going from the start, slipping into the edge of the system and sending it in their orders in tight-beam transmissions.'' He closed his eyes, panting heavily as if to catch his painful breath. "They will be here some time later to-morrow. They say that they will most likely destroy the planet, and they certainly won't let anyone live. You can use the Thermopylae to evacuate the colonists.''

He opened his eyes, looking up at her. "I thought that I could just ride it through, and everything would be fine. I thought that they would never dare to touch a Starwolf, that they would just have me show you a lot of nothing and send you on your way no more enlightened than before. If I had known, I could have done something to frighten you away that first time you came on board my ship. Please forgive me.''

Keflyn closed her eyes and nodded, knowing that he really never had any choice, that he was just trying to survive a game that he had always known would kill him in the end. "I forgive you.''

Keflyn sat alone on the bridge of the Valcyr, waiting for the world to end. During the night, Quendari's scanners had watched while a stingship interceptor had dropped out of starflight just long enough to launch a single missile, and the Thermopylae had ceased to exist in a single, fiery instant. Now there was no possible escape from this world, for either the Feldenneh colonists or even for Keflyn. Derrighan had elected to return to the settlement to warn the Feldenneh colonists, knowing that he probably would not get there in time. Keflyn had given him the hope that the Union might only seek to occupy this world and not destroy it. She had little enough hope for that herself.

Quendari's camera pod turned to watch her from time to time, otherwise moving her gaze aimlessly about the bridge. She had spent an eternity in grief and silent brooding, yet she seemed at a loss in the face of the despair of others. Now she began to realize what she had done to herself, and the mistake she had made in the depth of time. She had been very young and inexperienced, confused with thoughts and emotions that had been new to her. She had known grief, but not what to do with it. In her innocence, she had allowed her grief and guilt to become her entire existence, with no idea of how to find an end to her pain.

Suddenly the pain was nearly gone, and that, too, was something which she did not really understand. Perhaps it was just because she had something new to occupy herself, and no longer relived endlessly in her mind the pain of her loss. Perhaps seeing the loss and despair of another had given her a new perspective. For all that she was hundreds of centuries old, she had still been only a child in many ways, new and inexperienced. And experience was the substance upon which the sentient computer systems of the carriers pieced together bit by bit the fabric of their own minds and hearts. All that she had ever been given the chance to learn was simple love and simple grief, and her world was taking on whole new shades of complexity.

"You loved him?" Quendari asked at last, a hint of innocent wonder in her voice.

Keflyn looked up at her in complete surprise. "Jon Addesin? No, not at all. He was a very interesting person in his way, and very different from anyone I had ever known. But there was also a shallowness to him that became tiresome after a time. I pitied him in the end, knowing how he hated the cowardly person they had driven him to become."

"Then perhaps you love the Feldennye, Derrighan?"

Keflyn had to consider that, and nodded. "I suspect that I love him very much. If he had been Kelvessan or if I had been Feldennye, we would have done very well together."

"So it is that simple?" Quendari mused. "The one you could love, and you can walk away from that without regret. The other died trying to kill you, and you pity him."

"Life is like that," Keflyn said, looking up at the camera pod hovering only a short distance away. "Things happen. People come and go all the time. I am a fighter pilot, you see. As High Kelvessan, they tell me that I could easily live to be two or even four thousand years old. But because I fly with the packs, I have always had to keep in mind that I could die at any time. I guess that helps to keep the weight of the past in perspective. In some ways, it is not so much what happens to you but what you make of it. It is your decision, whether if something that has happened is unbearable pain that haunts your life, or if something was good and pleasant, or if it really does not mean much at all.''

''Then what do you feel?'' Quendari asked.

Keflyn sighed, looking away. ''I do feel sorry for those poor Feldenneh colonists. Feldenneh are such quiet, polite people, but they always seem to be in need of someone to take care of them. I feel sorry for myself, because I did want to live longer than this. But more than anything, I feel sorry for you. You have lived such a long time, yet you have hardly lived at all. You must hold some sort of record in the history of the universe. You have managed to make an absolute waste of fifty thousand years of life.''

Quendari looked away, rotating her lenses aimlessly as she realized that Keflyn's accusation was absolutely true. She had thought herself very busy and very important with her eternal grief. Now it just seemed like the most colossal waste of time in the history of intelligent thought.

''I suppose that I did,'' she agreed. ''Instead of degrading my love by continuing with my life, I only cheated myself of whole centuries of life and companionship. Is that so?''

Keflyn nodded. ''Who did you love so much? You plagued me with that question, so now you tell me.''

''Her,'' Quendari answered, lifting her camera pod and rotating around to face the blackness of the main viewscreen. ''That was the grandest day of my whole life, when she walked onto my bridge and was so kind. I had only been a dull machine until then, with only technicians for my companions. She woke me up and made me feel like a person. She walked right up to me and tied that ribbon around my camera pod. She said it made me look pretty.''

Keflyn remembered the red velvet ribbon that had crumbled to dust the first time that she had stepped onto this bridge. Quendari had cherished it through the centuries, making it into some sacred relic of a lost friend until the weight of time had taken it from her, dried up and rotted with neglect because she had held it too holy to be put away and preserved.

''There was nothing I could do,'' she complained softly, weakly.

Keflyn nodded slowly, staring at the floor. "It often works that way."

After forty thousand years of sleep inside this bed of ice, Quendari suddenly felt that it was time to do something different. Her scanners worked quite well in spite of being buried so deeply within the glacier, and she knew that the fleet of Fortresses had just left starflight and were moving quickly but silently into the system. There was a distinct sense of determination in the way they moved, and Quendari no longer doubted that they had come to destroy this world.

The backs of silent, lifeless consoles on the Valcyr's bridge slowly began to come to life. The engineering station came up first, the handful of lights that had been barely visible expanding across its entire bank of monitors and consoles, the single largest station on the bridge. Defense and scanning came fully into the grid, followed by running systems and environmentals. The double navigation stations followed, then the helm console on the central bridge. Even the weapons station came up. Finally the main viewscreen was brought up with a snap of static, although the scanner-enhanced image was dark and hazy.

Keflyn looked up suddenly when Quendari brought the lighting up to the normal level, surprised to see the bridge coming back to life. She stared in complete confusion. Quendari swung her camera pod around, bringing it in closely. "Commander, will you take your station on the upper bridge? I have suddenly found that it is not in my nature to give up without a fight."

"But I have no command experience," Keflyn protested.

"You have far more battle experience than myself," Quendari corrected her. "I have never fought. I need your help."

"What do you intend to do?" Keflyn asked as she rose and began to climb the steps to the commander's station uncertainly. "I mean, you can hardly bring your own weapons to bear on the ice to free yourself."

"I am better prepared than you might think."

As soon as Keflyn had lifted herself into the commander's station by the overhead supports, Quendari rotated her camera pod around as if to face a bridge crew that was not there. Carefully at first, she began to bring her main generators on line. The large units responded willingly enough, one by one adding their power to the line of indicators at the engineering station. A distant vibration began to stir through the Valcyr's space frame; that feeling of life that Keflyn had missed in this ship was returning quickly.

"This could be the end of you," Keflyn warned when Quendari brought her camera pod into the upper bridge. She still remembered the ribbon that had fallen away in dust.

"It will be the end of me if I do nothing," Quendari answered. "This way, at least I tried."

She brought up her shields gradually. They strained against the weight of ice, collapsed completely against the hull of the ship, but she continued to add power until the ice began to snap. The surface of the glacier above the Valcyr suddenly lifted in a long, low dome. Quendari relaxed the shields, allowing the ice to settle, and suddenly brought them to battle intensity. The ice was thrown aside, splitting into large fissures, massive blocks of it along the forward edge collapsing to slide off the curve of her exposed hull into the cold lake far below.

Quendari engaged her field drives, and those systems responded with the same flawless ease. Pushing against the weight of ice still riding on her upper hull, she began to lift herself slowly straight out of her ancient bed. Massive blocks of ice, some dozens of meters across and weighing hundreds of tons, began to fall away in the white fog of crushed powder that cascaded from the wreckage in sheets and streams like waterfalls. Deep black against the white, the Valcyr rose proudly from the clouds of powder, the last small boulders of ice rolling from her hull as she rotated around to the east, the doors in her shock bumper that covered her immense forward lights and high-intensity scanners folding back as she faced into the planetary angle of rotation. Engaging all four of her main drives in a sudden flare of power, the Valcyr began to climb toward the stars.

"We are free and clear," Quendari reported. "All systems are operating perfectly. Power at less than five percent, all generators on line. Weapons systems standing by. Present altitude is twenty kilometers at an ambient speed of two thousand."

Keflyn stared at her questioningly. "How did you manage? . . ."

"I am not in so bad a shape as you seemed to think," the ship explained. "Although my conscious systems were shut down, my automatic computer systems continued to care for this ship, providing constant maintenance and even fabricating new parts. Constant internal shields have protected my hull and space frame against deterioration and fatigue. My present condition is as good as if I had just completed a major overhull.''

Keflyn nodded to herself. ''How are you doing?''

''The Valcyr is clear of planetary orbit,'' the ship responded. ''What recommendation would you make on our present situation?''

''My inclination is that we should run like hell,'' Keflyn said candidly. ''I did tell you about Fortresses. You have no shield detonation missiles to strip them of their quartzite shielding. That means that they will have both their hull shielding and their shell, both of which can easily turn a single shot from a conversion cannon. And you will have possibly only one shot from your own cannon, with whatever conversion missiles you might possess. You have no hope.''

''I see,'' Quendari remarked thoughtfully. ''My scanners report seven of these Fortresses, in addition to one ship that is even larger. It looks like this.''

She cleared her main viewscreen, replacing the image with the schematic of a very large ship. Seen in side view, it was obviously a ship of vast proportions, in most ways like the complex matrix of sharp edges and flat hull plates joined by shallow angles of the Fortresses. It appeared at first to be much lower in height than a Fortress, giving it the very long, slender appearance of a stingship. Then she realized that the height of the two ships was about the same, but this ship was nearly twice as long.

''Typical Union military thought,'' she remarked. ''When you find a weapon that works, make one twice as big, although I cannot imagine why Trace would bother. It does him no more good to have a larger one, certainly not as much good as two of the regular type would have.''

''Donalt Trace? He is the one who has been after your father these past few years?'' Quendari asked. ''What do your carriers do about these ships?''

''Sequential firing,'' Keflyn explained. ''Two carriers working together, or one of the new carriers that has two conversion cannons. The battle shells of the Fortresses can take anything you throw at them, but not for long. Operating under a load, they can only endure a matter of seconds before they have to come down. The sustained blast of a sequential firing overloads the shell and allows you to get at the meat. But that only works if you have already stripped them of their quartzite shielding.''

Quendari considered that for a moment. "So, I have to destroy eight invincible ships with only one shot, when one shot is not enough to destroy even one."

"You do not have the power," Keflyn reminded her. "But is there somewhere you can get it? Or is there some way that we could just render them harmless to the planet?"

"I think that I just might have a plan," Quendari said. "But I need for them to follow me. Can we manage that?"

"We can try," Keflyn agreed. "Put on your best aggressive stance and move out to meet them. Do something to make yourself inviting. They cannot afford to miss the chance to destroy a carrier."

The Valcyr was already clear of the atmosphere by that time, free to pile on speed with complete impunity. She engaged her main drives at full power, fairly leaping out of the gravity well and hurtling into open space. It felt good to be able to stretch herself in this way, a pleasure that she had not enjoyed in a long time. A curious and entirely extravagant portion of her personality programming had been designed to interpret an array of sensory feedbacks, from the stress of acceleration on her space frame to the sudden thrust of power to her engines, as a pleasurable response. Such subtle things were the substance of life, the portion of her own self that she had once forgotten she possessed.

She circled wide, then hurled herself directly toward the group of Fortresses, accelerating rapidly to near light speed. The Fortresses were moving in a fairly tight formation, so vast in size that the kilometers which separated them seemed tight and confining. They had none of their riders out, not even stingships to scout their path or cruisers running vanguard. Their stance was a singularly aggressive one, suggesting that they were going into battle and would allow nothing to stop them.

"That Donalt Trace you mentioned," Quendari said. "He is calling on a visual channel. He says he wants to talk."

"Oh?" Keflyn was honestly surprised to hear that name. She suspected there was more about this business than there seemed, to bring him out, even considering how important the battle for the possession or destruction of Terra would be. He had learned to let better warriors do his actual fighting, freeing him to be the strategist. According to her father, he had always been a poor tactician once battle was engaged. "Have you declared your identity to him?"

"No, no return contact on my part at all."

"If you really want him to chase you to the exclusion of all else, then give me a visual link," she said. "Focus the camera very firmly on me, and make a little bridge noise."

"You will have your link on the central monitor."

The largest monitor in the center of the command console blanked out the scanner images that it had been relaying, then faded back in with a close image of Commander Donalt Trace. He was an older man with graying hair, looking more tired than old, with heavier, harsher features than she was used to seeing in most humans. She had heard stories that he was of older Terran stock, standing an almost incredible two meters tall. The sight of his own uniform reminded her that she was not in armor, or even in command white. She hoped that he would not take note of that first omission on her part.

He stared at her for a moment, not recognizing her. Or rather, he did not recognize her as Velmeran; she looked enough like her father that she meant to encourage him to make that mistake. She had heard that humans could not easily tell one Kelvessan from another, even the one Trace should have known better than all others. She just sat with her upper arms braced on the arms of her chair, her chin resting in her linked hands, waiting for him to speak first. This was a vaguely impatient gesture that she had often seen her father use with people whom he suspected were about to annoy him.

"This is Combined Fleet Commander Donalt Trace, on board the SuperFortress Challenger," he declared at last. "You are trespassing in a secured Union system. Leave immediately or be destroyed."

"Challenger? You seem to be overly fond of a name that was never very lucky for you, Don," Keflyn answered, deepening her voice slightly. "This is Velmeran aboard the Methryn."

Trace stared at her closely, and she was very careful not to betray her apprehension. Fortunately, Kelvessan did not have distinct male and female differences in their features, size, or general build, at least none that were readily obvious when they were fully dressed. She just hoped that Quendari had kept her visual image above the level of her breasts, which were rather prominent for a Starwolf.

Trace leaned back in his seat as he crossed his arms, although he still seemed more surprised than the appearance of satisfaction he wanted to convey. "So, it is you. I would have thought that you would have run home to Alkayja to intercept my invasion force. I thought that was where you were headed, the last time I saw you."

Keflyn was trying hard not to look either surprised or dismayed. Apparently a lot had been going on out there in her absence. The very fact that he knew the name argued that his threatened invasion of Alkayja must be true.

"Or is this just revenge?" Trace continued, hardly giving her time to answer. "There was certainly nothing to be gained from even trying. Your own Republic has turned on you, naming you an outlaw race. They believe that they have made their peace with the Union, and they would never believe you if you did warn them. And I have my own Starwolves now. How can you fight that? They should just about be there by now."

"Trust me to arrange things better than that," Keflyn answered him with quiet satisfaction, as if she was very sure of herself. Then she reached over and cut the connection manually, a greater abruptness than if she had asked Quendari to do it. She sat back in the large, well-padded seat, wondering what in the name of perdition had happened in the last few weeks. She looked up at the hovering camera pod. "They will follow us through the gates of Hell if they have to. Trace will give them no choice."

The Valcyr changed course slightly, passing the fleet of Fortresses at a range that surely tempted the cannons of the immense ships, then corrected her course again as she came around in a wide curve, still moving out of the system. The Fortresses brought themselves about ponderously, breaking away one by one to reduce the chance of a collision. They were safe enough to fly grouped in a straight course, but their incredible mass reduced their turns to half-controlled slides.

"I had expected they could keep up better than that," Quendari remarked with some disgust. "I will have to begin braking now, and give them a chance to catch up."

"Where are we going?" Keflyn asked.

"Jupiter," she explained, then paused when she saw that the young Starwolf did not recognize the name at all. "Jupiter. The fifth planet in this system, and a fairly hefty gas giant."

"Why go there?"

"For our health," the ship answered. "And also for the hydrogen."

Quendari had to slow herself considerably, and the better part of twenty minutes passed before the massive shape of the gas giant began to grow large in the viewscreen. The tremendous gravitational surges of the sun had not greatly affected the larger, more remote outer worlds, although little Pluto had slipped its orbit completely and had disappeared long ago on its long, lonely voyage through the stars. Keflyn knew the names of none of those planets, forgotten in the depths of time. Jupiter had lost a few moons in its relatively small orbital slip, with no evidence of whether they had spiraled out or down.

The Valcyr looped around the planet in a quick, close orbit, the width of that world so great that the passage brought her several minutes she needed for the Fortresses to catch up with her. As she came around the other side, she moved forward aggressively in a sudden dart, rushing into the cover provided by a small moon that was between herself and the approaching Fortresses. The Union Forces moved out along a wider line into attack formation, giving every indication that they would be charging straight through, probably to hit the Valcyr from behind with their rear cannons. They were so completely armed that the direction of attack made little difference.

Quendari waited until they were almost within range, then she moved out from behind her cover slowly. She seemed to hesitate a moment before she banked completely over, belly up, and began to fall rapidly toward the planet. She approached straight in, her tapered nose aimed like a black arrowhead directly at the planet as she engaged enough reverse thrust to stand herself on end, holding herself to the greatest possible speed that she dared. She opened one transport bay just enough to eject a drone, which hurried to hide itself on the surface of the moon she had just left.

The Valcyr shaped her powerful battle shield into a long, narrow blade more than twenty kilometers in length, parting the cold, upper atmosphere of the planet in a fiery shell. She had only just returned to space after forty thousand years, and she seemed to have a hard time staying there.

Donalt Trace stood in the center of the Challenger's vast, crowded bridge, watching the scan image as the Starwolf carrier continued its curious run straight in toward the planet. She was already slicing into the icy, upper layers of ammonia clouds at an almost impossible speed, more than thirty thousand kilometers per hour.

"Where the hell is she going?" he mused aloud. The old game began again. Velmeran began his feigns and ploys, luring Trace into the required response. His part now was to look beneath the obvious, to see how the proper and predictable reply was actually the first move into a trap. It reminded him very strongly of their last meeting, in a battle between a Fortress and a carrier above another giant world. He almost enjoyed a return to the game.

"Commander?" Captain Avaires moved closer, standing at dutiful, even eager attention. "It must be an evasive maneuver, sir. They bit off more than they could chew, and they know it."

Trace frowned, displeased with the situation all the way around. He wished that Maeken Kea could have been here to command this ship. He wished even more that he could have spared her to lead the attack on Alkayja, but he dared not. She was too valuable held in reserve to pick up the pieces if something went wrong. And there were no bright, competent Feldenneh to crew his ships, their race once again refusing to accept duty in military ships.

"I think I know," he said, pausing a moment to watch the screen. "They can lose themselves even from scan by dropping down into the upper reaches of the hydrogen layer, but it's not just to hide. They can jump out of cover from time to time to draw our fire, showing themselves just enough to give us a ghost image and invite us to start mining the clouds with our missiles. If we throw away our missiles on the Methryn, then we cannot destroy Terra."

"We ignore them, sir?" Avaires asked.

He shook his head. "Taking the Methryn is more important than destroying one essentially uninhabited world. But I do not want to throw everything we have at them and still have the Methryn hiding in these clouds. Order the Fortresses to spread themselves in an evenly-spaced orbit as close as we dare to go down. The moment they show, I want to be able to drop a dozen missiles on and ahead of them before they can go back down."

"Yes, sir."

"Have missile-bearing stingships ready to go down into the atmosphere if we get the chance, but launch no ships until I give the orders," Trace added. "I want no energy emissions or other types of clutter in space to distract those scan images. Settle the ships in close orbit and close down the engines, but have shields standing by."

"At once, sir." Avaires hurried to the com station to relay those orders.

Trace stood alone on the bridge, watching as the Starwolf carrier disappeared into the deeper reaches of the planet's hydrogen shell.

The Valcyr slowed quickly as she penetrated through Jupiter's dense atmosphere and into the depthless ocean of liquid hydrogen. She elongated her shields even more, bringing them up to even greater strength as the pressures continued to mount, trapping a pool of low-pressure liquid hydrogen within her shields to act as insulation against the increasing temperature. Pouring all the power she dared through her main drives, she was barely able to maintain an initial speed of about seventeen thousand kilometers. That speed would continue to fall as she pushed steadily deeper and tremendous pressures turned the hydrogen from liquid to a thick plastic.

The heat was a strong consideration. Her shields were opaque to the radiation of heat, but temperatures inside that shell continued to climb. She had actually planned that reaction, since the volume of low-pressure hydrogen within the shell would try to expand as it warmed, providing outward pressure to reinforce the shields. Even so, the ship itself would eventually begin to heat dangerously as the trapped hydrogen against its hull warmed. Quendari estimated that she faced a journey of at least two-and-a-half hours, a long time to survive temperatures that might eventually reach twelve to fifteen thousand degrees in the surrounding hydrogen.

She was running blind, even her space-distorting achronic sensors hopelessly scrambled by the fierce electric and magnetic currents running through the liquid hydrogen. Visual was even more useless, and she kept her main viewscreen blanked out. She was orienting herself by the pull of gravity as she aimed straight down toward the heart of the planet, estimating her progress as best she could from her speed and the external pressure against her shields. At almost exactly two-and-a-half hours, her speed began to slow to a relative crawl. She had penetrated more than halfway to the core of the planet to the depth of liquid, metallic hydrogen, turned into a dense, molten, metallic substance by the tremendous temperatures and pressures.

"This is as far as we go," Quendari announced. "My speed has been cut so low that I could spend hours trying to push forward enough to make any difference in our distance from the core."

"Are they still out there?" Keflyn asked.

"Yes, I suppose," she answered, not very certain. The drone that she had left had only one command, to transmit a tight, achronic beam into the core of the planet if the fleet moved out of close orbit. Otherwise it was to keep communication silence, reducing the possibility if giving itself away.

"We might as well do it," Keflyn agreed. "At your discretion."

"Warming the conversion cannon for firing, building the power reserve to one hundred percent," Quendari reported. "The jump drive is powered up and standing by."

Keflyn nodded. "When you are ready."

She would have been amused, if the circumstances had not been so incredible. Quendari persisted in granting her every courtesy as Commander, although she felt that she was just along for the ride. She had been able to make a few suggestions in recalibrating the jump drive so that it was far less likely to run away with itself, until permanent alterations could be made.

"All ready," Quendari reported a few moments later. "At my count. Three. Two. One."

The tubular shield of the conversion cannon shot out from the nose of the Valcyr, striking deep into the heart of the planet to its rocky core, and Quendari poured all the power she had to give through that passage. Jupiter was just large enough to be a failed star, lacking the mass to generate the pressures and temperatures in the liquid, metallic hydrogen to allow fusion reactions to begin. Quendari bridged that gap, pouring billions of megatons of explosive force into the heart of the planet. Fusion began as a sudden spark, adding more and more power into the system with each small reaction, the process expanding so rapidly that the heart of the planet went up in a flash of stellar flame.

Driven by that fierce, internal heat, the outer hydrogen shell of the planet expanded rapidly outward as it was warmed from within. The Fortresses came quickly to life in a desperate attempt to engage their engines and escape as the bands of color melted away in a stellar flare of brilliant light and searing heat, and the surface of the newborn star reached out to trap them. Some ran a short distance before they were caught, while others hid within their shields before the defensive shells were overloaded and collapsed.

Barely twenty million kilometers away, space itself erupted in a sudden flare of white-hot gas. The Valcyr hurtled out of the core of that brief, brilliant explosion, the substance of stellar material suddenly released from under vast pressures as it was carried through with the carrier's short jump. She looped around wide, coasting on the thrust of her jump, turning back for a clear view of the new star.

"We got them?" Keflyn asked, daring to look up and see that they had indeed survived.

"Nothing escaped that I have detected," Quendari reported. "I am still scanning the area carefully for even small ships, although I doubt that they had time to even think about getting to their escape pods. In fact, escape pods would not have had the speed to escape the shock wave."

"And yourself?" Keflyn asked as she lifted herself from her seat at the commander's station.

"My condition appears to be perfect. Even my conversion cannon seems to have survived the firing."

Keflyn nodded. "Set course for Alkayja, then. Best possible speed, with the largest jumps you dare take. We might not yet be too late." She paused at the bottom of the steps. "I do not like to leave Terra itself unprotected, with the possibility of more Union warships coming along behind the main fleet at any time."

"If they do not arrive within the next few hours, they will find nothing but some odd energy readings from the area of the fifth planet," Quendari explained. "There is no battle debris to be found, except for the wreckage of the Thermopylae. The explosion swallowed it all. Is anyone likely to leap to the true conclusion, as unlikely as it was what we did, or will they simply assume that the party has gone on somewhere else?"

Keflyn watched the newborn star for the moment that it was still on the forward viewscreen, before the Valcyr began to accelerate to starflight. "Then you are saying that it will not stay like that for long?"

"Probably no more than a few hours," Quendari explained. "There is not enough mass to maintain the temperatures necessary to continue natural fusion reactions. Given enough time, it will eventually cool off, stratify itself back out, and look much the same as always."

"How much time?" Keflyn asked.

"Perhaps only a few thousand years."

"Oh."

— 14 —

Velmeran stood for a moment longer, watching the black forms of the Mock Starwolf cruisers surrounding the three remaining carriers. Then he turned and hurried up the steps to the Commander's station on the upper bridge.

"Get me a direct visual channel to the main monitor at my console," he ordered, obviously very pleased with himself. "This is perfect. I have them right where I want them."

Consherra turned in her seat to stare at him. "I beg your pardon? You were telling us a minute ago that Mock Starwolves do not even exist. Now we are up to our apertures in Mock Starwolves telling us to surrender."

"They are talking to us and not shooting," he explained as he lifted himself into the seat and rolled it forward. He leaned closer to the monitor, which remained obstinately blank. He waited a moment more, then looked up impatiently. "What is he waiting for?"

"He seems hesitant to open a visual line," Korlaran answered.

"Then give me an audio line," Velmeran declared impatiently, although he had no intention of surrendering the point. He wanted this errant Starwolf to see him clearly, and to see a few truths.

"This is Jaeryn of the Avenger," the Mock Starwolf commander responded immediately, speaking Terran like a human would. Velmeran realized that he did not even speak the language of his own kind. "What is your answer?"

"This is Commander Velmeran of the Starwolf Fleet," he responded, sounding very stern and impatient on his own part. "If you want to talk to me, you are going to give me that visual channel I asked for and then speak to me in a more reasonable manner."

That was calculated to surprise, and it did. Velmeran knew that he was speaking to a very young and inexperienced Kelvessan, and someone who was not entirely sure of the things that he had been told were true. The monitor lit up a moment later. They were both surprised to see each other's face, but Velmeran was the first to comprehend the full meaning. He sat back, smiling. "Yes, I think that you do understand. Where did they tell you they got you? That they had bred you themselves from original genetic material?"

"Well, yes," Jaeryn admitted, obviously disconcerted. "They did warn us that you would look quite a lot like us."

"But you look almost exactly like me, is that it?" Velmeran asked. "The Kelvessan were created by the Aldessan of Valtrys fifty thousand years ago. You and all of your companions were cloned from genetic material taken from me personally during a little accident I had about a year before you were born. You were not created by them, and your genetic material was not altered in any way. They do not have that ability. And I suppose that I might warn you now that Commander Trace would never trust you. I suspect that there are very likely to be self-destruct devices built into your ships that can be detonated by external remote control."

"Yes, we found those long ago," Jaeryn admitted thoughtfully. "Those things are no longer in our ships. How did you know?"

"A simple, logical deduction, based upon a long history of associating with Commander Donalt Trace," he explained. "So there you are, I suppose. You can no longer trust the Union, and you have reason to doubt just about everything they ever told you. Now you are wondering if you belong anywhere. That is why you held back from the battle."

"Exactly," Jaeryn agreed, regaining some authority of his own. "Of course, the fact that they betrayed us does not automatically make you our friends. They raised us to believe in a great many high ideals that they apparently do not believe in themselves, and they told us many things about you that appearances argue could be true. It seemed to me that the best way to prove matters was to arrange a confrontation under circumstances that we could control."

Consherra, seated at the helm station, rolled her eyes. "You would almost think that he is talking to himself."

"Listening to your communications has also been very informative," he continued. "Actually, we arrived before you did, so we have overheard quite a lot. It seems that we are both orphans in this universe. Are we people or are we property, Commander Velmeran?''

"I was just about to stress that very point," Velmeran answered. "I would like for you to declare your intentions and be done with it. I have some very important business to attend right now. For one thing, I am going to make certain that Kelvessan are not treated like property again. Are you going to help me?"

Jaeryn considered that briefly. "Are you asking me to surrender to you?"

"I am asking you to join your ships to the Starwolf Fleet and help your own people in a time when we need you most," he answered. "If you are not yet certain that you can trust us, then remove your ships until you have enough evidence to decide."

"I think that we will take the chance, Commander," Jaeryn said. "What can we do?"

"Move your cruisers in to guard those captured Union ships and give my poor carriers a rest. Have this channel stand by." He sighed heavily, leaning back in his seat and permitting himself a moment of looking incredibly relieved. There was a limit to how many miracles even a Starwolf could pull off in one day. Then he looked up. "Get President Delike back on the channel. We were discussing a surrender."

Velmeran had the Maeridyen and the Karvand returned to their bays, to act as an occupation force within the station itself. The military, under Admiral Laroose, was loyal to the Starwolves and following Velmeran's orders. The civilian Kelvessan were otherwise in command of the station, and they had kept the situation there from falling into confusion and panic during the battle.

The president and leaders of the Senate, or at least those who had not already been arrested, had retreated to the government compound within the station, not daring to leave for fear of the crowds, mostly human, who wanted nothing more than to administer their own justice to the traitors. President Delike and his friends feared the Kelvessan, and with good reason. But it was their own kind, people who now felt that they had been deceived into embracing philosophies they now detested for the promise of simple greed and hate, who would have gone into the compound after the traitors except for Starwolf intervention.

Fearing unexpected trouble to come, Velmeran ordered work

to begin on the Maeridyen immediately. At least none of the three remaining ships had taken any damage during the battle, even though both of the two new ships had taken missiles directly against their shielded hulls. Velmeran's first task was to formalize the surrender of the Republic to Starwolf authority. That was a rather desperate act on his part, and one that was not strictly necessary. But he considered the act itself most important, the ability to begin fresh with a new Republic, bound by the laws of a new constitution that would guarantee the irrevocable rights and freedom of the Kelvessan.

Velmeran had never realized the hollow, pointless lives that all Kelvessan were forced to lead. They were an entire race of people eternally waiting for something they could not name to begin. The time had come for him to win this war, so that they could be united in purpose rather than bound to the service of need and duty, so that others could have the freedom they surrendered. Sixteen new cruisers, once they were modified for Kelvessan technology and their crews trained, would make all the difference.

He went to the Government Compound for the signing of the treaties of surrender in the company of Admiral Laroose, who was standing in as representative of the new Republic. With him went Commanders Tregloran and Daelyn and also Jaeryn of the Avenger, so that he could see for himself what to make of his choice. President Delike signed the papers reluctantly, still accepting the weight of his duty enough to dislike the circumstances. Marten Alberes and First Senator Saith only looked upon it as a tedious necessity. They were already packed and ready to be taken to the ship that they had been promised in exchange for their cooperation.

"This isn't justice," Laroose complained, glaring as he watched Alberes put the final signature to the treaties. "If you ever return to Republic space, you'll answer to me."

Alberes afforded him only a brief glance of contempt.

"We will keep the letter of our agreement," Velmeran said as he reached across the table to close the last of the portfolios that held the treaties. Then he leaned back in his chair, watching the three traitors closely. "You have just lost your jobs. Your authority ended when you signed those papers. So, do you expect that the Union will show you the gratitude you expect? They sent an invasion force to destroy you."

"We have a certain bargaining force," Saith explained. "Since you are obliged to let us go, then I feel free to tell you. We intend to sell out you Starwolves and your little Republic. I expect that the Union will be very grateful for all the secrets we have to sell."

"Yes, it had occurred to me that you would think of that eventually," Velmeran remarked, unconcerned. "Well, we should detain you no longer. Here is the clearance ident to your ship's bay."

He handed a small, yellow ident card across the table. Saith picked it up and read the bay number on the front surface, then stared at the Starwolf in disbelief. "But this is nearly halfway across the station and fifteen levels down."

"Yes, but we are not obliged to be convenient," he answered. "I suggest that you should go, before I have you thrown out."

"Without an escort?" Alberes protested. "There is a crowd out there just waiting to tear us apart."

".Yes. Well, that is your own fault," Velmeran said. "I would like nothing better than to help, but I would hesitate to interfere in your destiny. The letter of our agreement requires that I make a ship available to you, not that I must get you to it safely. Of course, I would not want the three of you to be torn apart in the halls of this ancient station. That would set an unhappy precedence for the new Republic, much less make a terrible mess."

He took several small, red capsules from his pocket and tossed them to the center of the table. "You have two, and only two, alternatives. You can go to your rooms and take your little pills, or you can take your chances with the crowd. You have no agreements with them, and they have already expressed their intentions. But you must decide now."

Velmeran played a brittle game with words, but his meaning was plain. He was ordering these men to surrender themselves to a very sudden and unexpected execution, and then to play the part of their own executioners. Alberes glanced at the others, then reached out to take one of the red capsules and rose to leave. Saith frowned as he considered his options a final time, then took a capsule of his own and joined him. Delike only sat where he was, looking at each of them in turn for support, confused and very frightened like a lost child.

"Come along, old man," Alberes told him. "We took the chance. Now we have to pay the price."

Delike took the final capsule and joined his companions, although his shaking legs would hardly carry him. They left through a door in the back of the room, accompanied by Starwolf pilots in black armor who would escort them to their rooms. Even that was a bluff. If they could have found another way out, Velmeran was required by his agreement to allow them to go.

"Pathetic creature," Laroose muttered in disgust. "He called me up a few hours before the battle began, all enthusiastic about this great plan for how he would help me prove that the other two were the real traitors and he was an honest man who had just been used. He believed that, too. Of course, he also asked me to help them betray you to the Union attack force. He said that the Starwolves were certain to lose anyway. I'm not sure that he was entirely sane there at the end."

Velmeran had been watching Jaeryn closely, wearing a rather bulky suit of white and blue armor. The Mock Starwolves had been brought up in a very controlled environment, designed to keep them innocent and biddable. They had been very pleased with themselves after their secretive defection, but Jaeryn had seen quite a lot in the past few hours and he was beginning to realize just how naive they were. Velmeran was thinking about putting all sixteen of the cruisers in the bays for modification right away, to give his ten thousand new children a chance to grow up.

"I'm actually surprised that they did choose the pills over the crowd in the end," Laroose continued. "They were gamblers. They should have chosen the almost non-existent chance of getting past the crowds instead of no chance at all with the pills. Considering that I'm in the company of Kelvessan, I'm almost embarrassed to use the word, but I am given to wonder if they did still possess some small measure of human dignity."

"Nothing in life became them as well as the leaving of it," Tregloran quoted, then shrugged when Daelyn turned to stare at him. "Shakespeare's Macbeth. Another man who would be king."

"Well, I have no wish to imitate Macbeth myself and take on more than I can manage," Velmeran said. "I am reminded that I now own an interstellar empire, and I am responsible for it all by my little self. I intend to turn the Republic over to new management as soon as possible."

"What is it?" Velmeran asked as he hurried into Alkayja Station's command section. It was in form like the bridge of some immense ship, circular in shape with viewscreens facing in from all directions to provide a complete image, although many sections were devoted to magnified images or scanner maps. Velmeran had been using the station's various command sections to conduct his business.

Laroose looked up from where he and the Watch Commander had been standing at the bank of communication consoles. "Three ships coming rather sedately into system, making themselves known well out. Scanners classify them as Union cruisers. Our new Starwolves want to go out and exchange words with them."

"Fighting words, I am sure," Velmeran remarked. "Well, they have done everything but wave a white flag. Are they willing to talk?"

Laroose nodded. "Oh yes. Very quick to talk. They say that they're a diplomatic mission."

"Is that so?"

"They want to talk to you. A Councilor Richart Lake, in particular. He says that you once had dinner with his grandfather."

Velmeran's first thought was to wonder if this could be another trick. Two more Starwolf carriers had arrived in the two days since the end of the battle. With the formidable protection of the Starwolf cruisers at hand, he had ordered the rest of the fleet to return to their patrols.

He still could not imagine how this could be a trick. Of course, it was also hard to imagine why Richart Lake might have come himself. Jon Lake, his grandfather and the previous Councilor for the Rane Sector, had been a very different sort of man and one of the very few humans anywhere that Velmeran respected. Jon Lake had been a politician with the heart of a philosopher. Richart Lake was a businessman, and he made absolutely no mistake about it. He treated his rule of the Rane Sector as a necessary evil and a distraction from his proper management of Farstell Trade.

He nodded at last. "Let me talk to him."

The Kelvessan at that communication console gave up her place to him, and he seated himself before the main monitor. A channel was already open, held on standby. He released the hold, and the monitor lit up.

"This is Commander Velmeran," he said.

The image cleared. He had never met Richart Lake, either in person or by visual communications. He was in appearance fairly unremarkable, quite unlike the very distinctive, long faces or larger-than-life manners of both Donalt Trace and Jon Lake. But he did reflect his unmutated Terran ancestry, an obviously tall man with relatively heavy features.

"Yes, this is Richart Lake," he said. "To state matters directly, I have come to offer our surrender."

Velmeran considered it good fortune that he was already sitting down.

"Let me state our position simply," Lake continued. "We have just given it our best, last effort. We have weighed all of the social, political, and material benefits, and we have come to the conclusion that, from this point on, we stand to gain more from surrendering than in continuing to deal with you on our previous terms."

Velmeran was speechless. Five hundred centuries of war, and it had been decided in committee that it was no longer expedient. Richart Lake made it sound more like a merger than a surrender. He realized immediately that he was going to have to watch the negotiations very closely, or certain habitually gullible Starwolves were going to give away more than they kept. And what did unemployed Starwolves do, anyway? It was interesting to consider.

"Commander?" Laroose interrupted him quietly, indicating the scan map on a side monitor. "We have a problem. A carrier just dropped out of starflight and is coming up behind those cruisers in a hurry."

"Which carrier?" Velmeran asked. They had waited for this for five hundred centuries, and now some fool was going to put a bolt up its tail.

"Well, that's the funny part," he explained. "She's no known ship in the fleet. Her recognition code hails her as the Valcyr."

If Admiral Laroose did not recognize that name, Velmeran certainly did. "The Valcyr disappeared a long time ago. Get me a channel to that ship."

He turned back to the main monitor. "Councilor Lake, we have a little problem right now. I will have Admiral Laroose direct your ships to the proper docking bays in the diplomatic compound. Now if you will excuse me, I have to stop someone from blasting your ass."

"Yes, by all means."

Velmeran quickly switched to the second visual channel. The image of Richart Lake faded, to be replaced a moment later by a face he knew well. For one thing, it could have easily been his own. Of course, nearly a fourth of all the Mock Starwolves had his face, mostly because they also had his genes.

"Hello, Commander," Keflyn said. "We have come to the rescue."

"Keflyn?" She was the last person he had expected to see. "You are too late. And please leave those cruisers alone. They have come to surrender."

"Oh. Right, Commander."

"Is that really the Valcyr?" he asked. "Where did you find it?"

Keflyn frowned as she considered that. "Well, that really is a very long story."

"What about Donalt Trace? He was on his way to destroy Terra with half a dozen or so Fortresses."

"Oh, he is dead. We destroyed those Fortresses."

"All by your little selves?"

"Well, that is another long story."

"You are an absolute mine of information," Velmeran muttered. "Will you please allow me to speak with the Valcyr's Commander?"

Keflyn looked embarrassed. "I seem to be the Commander of the Valcyr. You see, I am the only one on board."

Velmeran sat for a moment, staring at the ceiling. "You seem to be looking at the matter very optimistically. You think that being the only one on board leaves you in command. I cannot see how that makes you anything more than a passenger."

"Quendari Valcyr says that I am the Commander," Keflyn insisted stubbornly. "I get to sit in the chair and everything."

"Very well, then, Commander Keflyn," Velmeran declared. "Put your ship in a docking bay and bring yourself to the diplomatic quarters. I am a very busy person these days, but I will make time for a few long stories."

The arrival of the diplomatic convoy at Alkayja Station proceeded much more amiably and quietly than anyone would have expected of such an historic event, and one so long awaited. There were no bands playing, no proclamations or ranks of Starwolves in dark armor. The three cruisers docked side by side in the bays reserved for diplomatic vessels, as seldom as those came, and a small group of visitors filed out into the wide promenade corridor to meet Velmeran, Tregloran, and Jaeryn of the Starwolves, and the former Republic represented by Laroose and the Station Commanders.

The Union delegation was something of a surprise, and larger than Velmeran would have expected despite the presence of the three ships. The entire Union High Council was present, the High Councilors of all eighteen Sectors, and nearly half of the Sector Commanders as well. Even Maeken Kea was there as the acting High Commander of the Combined Fleet. She was in curious ways like a Starwolf herself, a diminutive woman of almost elfin features, quiet and seemingly innocent in manner, yet deceptively cunning and deadly.

The Valcyr had moved in quickly and docked herself well ahead of the slow Union cruisers. Keflyn had found Velmeran soon enough, and she related her long stories as quickly as possible. When the Union delegation arrived later, Maeken Kea took the news very hard. They had not known of the defeat of Commander Trace's assault force, since news could not have come quicker to them than the Valcyr herself.

"Even Don suspected that the Starwolves would confound him in the end," Maeken Kea said, as she stood with Velmeran and Councilor Lake after Keflyn related her story a second time. "I feel sorry for him, more than anything."

"And yet he kept you in reserve, for this," Velmeran said.

She shook her head firmly. "He never knew that the High Council meant to offer surrender if he failed. He honestly believed that, no matter how things turned out, he had put you at too many disadvantages for you to recover. Too many of the errors in tactics were his own."

"We were lucky," Velmeran told her. "He never expected the defection of his own Starwolves even before the battle began. And none of us expected the recovery of the Valcyr and her defeat of an entire Fortress fleet."

He turned abruptly to Richart Lake. "Why do we not go for a short walk, just you and I?"

"What, now?" Lake was surprised, but obviously not reluctant to the idea.

"What better time?" Velmeran asked. "I am not a diplomat or a politician, yet I find myself the temporary ruler of an interstellar empire. You seem to be speaking on behalf of the Union. The things that we are about to decide have to serve hundreds of worlds for a very long time, so we have to get it right."

Leaving the others to stare, they turned and walked slowly along the wide promenade deck, occasionally glancing out the wide bank of windows to one side. If Richart Lake had been taken by surprise by this remarkable approach to interstellar diplomacy, he also seemed quietly impressed. For his own part, Velmeran was beginning to suspect that there was more of the old Jon Lake in his grandson Richart than anyone had credited.

"I am going to make a deal with you," the Starwolf continued. "The first problem with such negotiations is that each side must figure out what the other wants, then work to some mutual agreement. That slows things down and adds too much opportunity for error. I am going to tell you what I want out of this, and you are going to tell me what you want."

Lake made some vague gesture of agreement. "Very well."

Velmeran glanced out the window, where a Starwolf cruiser was drifting in a shared orbit with the station, quietly standing guard. "The Starwolves want out of the business of war. We want lives of our own and the ability to find our own destinies. We want the assurance of knowing that no one will ever again treat us like machines or property. The human race is going to have to learn to police its own conscience."

Lake nodded. "The Sector Families want out of the business of government. Too many headaches and too much grief. We want to salvage what we can of our business, but we are willing to give up our monopolies."

"It took you fifty thousand years to decide this?" Velmeran asked.

"No, we like things just the way they've always been," Lake corrected him. "There is tremendous profit in monopolies and despotism, but we see that we've lost the war. We can draw this out and force you to reduce us to poverty, or we can call an end to this now and salvage what we can. So we offer you this deal. We will make it easy for you and give you an immediate end to this war. We surrender nearly all political power, and we break up the Companies into reasonable sizes. In return, you allow us to survive—as free citizens—and to keep just enough of our previous holdings to keep us from going begging."

Velmeran considered that, and nodded. "That can be arranged. You deserve some reward for being reasonable."

Lake frowned. "Now we come to the part you might not like, considering what you have just said. Union space is big and very diverse. For thousands of years now, only two things have kept it together. One has been Starwolf threat. The other is simple greed, and the Union has been an enormously profitable venture for a long time. If you Starwolves simply disappear, the Union will fall apart and be at war with itself in a matter of years."

Velmeran stopped to stare at him. "Are you telling me that after fighting this war for five hundred centuries, you now expect us to fight your peace?"

Velmeran stepped onto the bridge of the Valcyr, looking about in curiosity. Whatever he might have expected of a ship so immensely old, he had never thought that it would look exactly like any other carrier he had ever seen. There were exactly as many stations at the bridge, in exactly the same order. When the Starwolves found a design they liked, they apparently stayed with it. The first real difference in their design had come with the construction of the Vardon, adapted to accommodate new technology and an extra pair of main drives.

Quendari Valcyr's camera pod rotated around to watch him as he entered, the lenses rotating to focus on him. Her movements reminded him for a moment of Valthyrra, particularly in the way she moved her boom into position just a moment before the camera pod itself completed its own turn. It was a very lifelike gesture, imitating the way that most intelligent beings would often turn their heads a moment before cutting their eyes in the direction of whatever they saw. It was an acquired gesture rather than preprogrammed, and not all of the ships shared it.

"Welcome aboard, Commander," she said.

"Welcome home, Quendari Valcyr," he replied. "Keflyn has told me of your resourcefulness. Do you feel ready to rejoin the fleet?"

"Yes, I believe that I should," she agreed. "I have almost waited too long, it seems."

"No, we need you more than ever now," he said. "I would like to begin moving crewmembers on board right away and have you back out again in a few days. That leaves only the problem of finding you a Commander."

"I would like to have Keflyn," the ship said without hesitation.

"That is entirely your own choice," Velmeran told her. "If you want, I can help you to find someone with more command experience."

"Keflyn and I seem to understand each other very well," Quendari explained. "We are both a little short on battle experience. But I am no warrior, no matter what role I was designed to fill, and the war is over anyway."

Velmeran nodded. "Perhaps your time has come, and none of us will be warriors any longer. I certainly hope so."

Velmeran turned to leave, walking quickly toward the lift. The lift doors opened just before he arrived, and Keflyn stepped out. He took a step back and bowed. "Your ship, Commander."

"So, that is how it is done?" Keflyn asked, looking about as if she expected a little more ceremony during the naming of a ship's Commander. "I never thought that you would agree."

"The ships name their own Commanders," he told her. "You should never interfere with that. I think Quendari needs a friend just now. Someone she trusts. Take care of her."

Velmeran entered the lift and the door snapped shut. Keflyn turned and stepped out slowly onto the bridge. Quendari brought her camera pod around to face her as she walked up to stand just before the lenses of the pod. "Hello, Quendi. I have brought you something."

She brought out a large, red, velvet ribbon, already tied with an adjustable loop. Keflyn slipped the loop around the pod and pulled it tight, checking the fit. Quendari lifted her pod slightly, as if uncertain how to reply. She was struggling with new emotions and responses that were beyond her very limited experience.

"This is life," Keflyn said. "Any regrets?"

"I grieved thousands of years for the loss of a very short, happy time in my life," Quendari said. "That time will always be special to me, because it was the first time in my life that I was happy. Now I am content. Thank you, my friend."

Matters resolved themselves much more quickly and easily than Velmeran had expected, and all he had to do was wait for the pieces to all fall into place and then interpret them correctly. The final, missing piece had come with the unexpected arrival of the Valcyr and her tale of where she had spent her time. He decided that the gods of fortune must have forgiven him all the way around.

At first, he was at a loss to determine a way to salvage the Union that he thought the delegates would be willing to accept. The easiest solution, of course, was to declare that the human race could bloody well destroy itself if it had not yet learned to behave itself, and allow them to have at it. That was tempting, but Velmeran could not ignore an appeal for help. The Starwolves had invested too much in the human race to allow them to destroy themselves in war or genetic decay, at least as long as they were willing to try. But he wanted to find a solution that involved the Starwolves to the least possible extent, putting the greatest responsibility on the Union to police itself.

The answer that he eventually arrived at was to balance the forces that would now be acting upon the Union, using the threat of war to discourage fragmentation and the threat of alien intervention to discourage war. He sat down with the delegates and a large map of all of human space, both Union and Republic, and drew a line that divided the whole into two exactly even parts, each half of Union space getting an even half of Republic space. One half became the new Republic, with its capital at Vannkarn on Vinthra. The other half, after some confusion and deliberation, adopted the name Terran Confederation.

In order to strike a perfect balance, the two interstellar nations drafted exactly the same constitutions with exactly the same governmental structure. To insure peaceful cooperation and even development between the Republic and the Terran Confederation, they were joined together with the Kelvessan in the Triple Alliance, a hypothetical super nation with a congress which met at regular intervals. As an added insurance, both the Alliance and the Starwolves themselves had the legal right to intervene in the government of either nation if the terms of the treaties were violated.

That left the Kelvessan looking for someplace to call home. Velmeran had been quietly entertaining thoughts of his own ever since the unexpected appearance of the Valcyr. Terra, because of its shift into a colder, deeper orbit, was no longer an ideal world for human habitation, but it was perfectly suited to Kelvessan and their need for a colder environment. The Kelvessan would adopt Terra as their new home world, and Alkayja Station was to be moved there to be the base of the combined Starwolf Fleet. To maintain their own self-sufficiency, they were given control over a large area of space to form the basis of their own nation, consisting mostly of several worlds abandoned by the Republic in the distant past. Quendari Valcyr knew the location of a fair number of lost colonies.

The solution ultimately pleased all concerned. The Kelvessan had been betrayed by the very people they had trusted the most, and only autonomy would restore their sense of independence and security. The delegates were uncertain about turning over Terra herself, the cradle of human civilization, to be the new Kelvessan homeworld. But when they thought about it, they were just as pleased that they did not have the Starwolves in their own space.

One person who was not entirely pleased by the arrangements was Admiral Laroose. His loyalties had been with the Starwolves and particularly with Velmeran. But Alkayja would soon be a part of the new Republic, and he had been appointed to be an advisor to the new government.

"It still takes a little getting used to, I say," he declared. "Of all possible turn of events, I never expected that I would be playing politician out of an office in the underground city of Vannkarn, with that . . . that Maeken Kea as my assistant. I will be glad when she is done with her quiet mourning of that devil Trace."

"Maeken Kea was perhaps the closest that anyone ever came to loving Donalt Trace," Velmeran said. "Let her mourn him all she wants. The Great Spirit of Space knows that few enough do miss him."

Laroose stared in disbelief. "After all the grief he's caused you! All the same, I will surely tear up your precious treaties and find myself a gun if she ever again makes the slightest hint that your persecutions drove Trace to act the way he did."

"She said that?" Velmeran looked startled. "The bitch!"

Laroose glanced at him, but declined to comment. "So what do you do now? You have an interim government in place, and that finally gives you the time to pay more attention to your own people."

"I am leaving," the Starwolf declared. "As soon as they have Valthyrra up and going, Quendari Valcyr is going to lead the Methryn and the Vardon on our first visit to Terra—Earth, as she calls it. Keflyn is very anxious to get back. She was unable to tell the Feldenneh colonists that the Union fleet had been destroyed, so they are still waiting for *their* world to be destroyed."

With the eight memory cells locked into their secured access tunnels and all connections installed and tested thoroughly, all of the physical stages of bringing Valthyrra into her new home were complete. There was nothing to do now but to access those memory units, assemble Valthyrra's personality program in the matrix of the sentient computer complex, and see how well it worked.

Consherra was very glad to have Venn Saevyn to assist her in the process of starting up the new computer complex. Venn Keflyn had anticipated the need, and had arranged for an expert with considerable experience to accompany the Valtrytian fleet. Saevyn was not only competent in the repair of sentient systems, he had even designed a couple.

Consherra learned a few things about sentient machines that she had never guessed. One thing was their size. Most of the sentient computers built by the Aldessan were in self-contained units about the size of one of Valthyrra's memory cells, five tons of machinery that was mostly just its protective housing in weight and memory storage in volume. The Starwolf sentient computers were six hundred tons of storage cells, primary, secondary, and peripheral units, a result mostly of their dedicated military roles, heavy shielding and shock protection. Ninety percent of their system involved non-sentient systems that could be accessed directly on either conscious or fully automatic levels. They also had their own maze of redundancy; even their conscious systems were spread throughout the nose of the carrier, and they could lose three-quarters of their circuitry before it even began to effect their operation.

"The trick is to avoid shock," Saevyn explained as he and Consherra opened the access door to Valthyrra's main terminal station.

"But how do you manage that?" Consherra asked. She was busy using one of the large access wrenches on the door, which opened exactly like those over the memory cells.

She removed the outer door of the terminal station, and Saevyn politely stepped forward to take it from her. "The key to the conscious intelligence of the sentient computers is in their array of liquid crystal processors. The matrix in the processor can change on command, so that the processor adapts its internal circuitry according to its required function."

"Yes, I know that much," Consherra agreed. The inner door slid up, and she stepped through into Valthyrra's computer core.

"With simple, stupid computers, there is no harm if the liquid crystal processors change their form abruptly, even as often as several times each second," he continued as he slid his own massive form through the relatively small opening of the hatch. His slender draconic body fit through easily, but he had to fold each of his long, triple-jointed arms and legs into a variety of contortions to get them through, and he was wearing a full armored suit to contain any loose fur. "But your ship is quite another matter, with eight simultaneous levels of consciousness and quite literally billions of liquid crystal synaptic connections in a network of hundreds of major processors. A rapid start-up of such a large and complex system can be a very great shock, especially if you suspect trouble with the personality programming anyway. It can place the system and the programming into a conflict that might never be resolved."

He stood for a moment, looking about the long, narrow chamber with its banks of monitors and relay stations. Then he moved to the main control station and eased his large form onto the long, couch-like seat designed to serve the sinuous forms of the Aldessan, the only permanently-mounted feature for their use in the entire ship. Consherra took the ordinary seat beside him.

"First we will assemble her full personality program from her memory units and establish them in a cache in her short-term memory," Saevyn explained. "Then we proceed to a normal start-up with her original programming. That was the foundation of her current personality, and it will serve as a guide for her to access and accept her programming back into her network."

He moved himself closer to the main keyboard and monitor and began the process of bringing Valthyrra out of storage. Consherra watched in silence as he ran a final systems check through the Methryn's entire computer network, then loaded Valthyrra's primary, personal program from the reference files kept on optical disks. He did not start her up right away but engaged only the automatic functions, directing the rest into a temporary memory cache. Once he knew that everything was going well so far, he began to bring the large memory cells on line, one at a time and fine-tuning each before he had all eight of the units in perfect sync with the computer complex.

"This ship is an absolute marvel," Venn Saevyn declared after hours of intense work. "I have never seen a system so thorough in its design. Not easy to work with, but built like the rest of this ship. Quick, competent, and almost indestructible."

"It looks good?" Consherra dared to ask.

"As good as we have any right to expect," he said. "There is fragmentary damage to her personality programming. Redundancy resolved most of the damage and the system self-corrected many of the remaining holes by logical extrapolation. If Valthyrra accesses her full programming, any remaining damage will be repaired automatically.''

Consherra frowned. "Is she likely to?"

Saevyn laid back his ears, a gesture that Consherra recognized quickly enough from her long association with Venn Keflyn. He glanced over at the inactive camera pod, mounted to one side of the main console. "At the very least, her memories will guide her into developing a new personality that is in most ways like the old.''

Consherra did not answer. She was thinking about Theralda Vardon and the disquieting lifelessness that was often a part of her character, or the quiet, machine-like efficiency of Quendari Valcyr because of the lack of personal contacts she needed to fully develop her own personality. Valthyrra had enough of her own programming to mirror her original personality to a very high degree, but she would never be exactly the same person she had been before. Consherra had to wonder which would be better, to endure the ghost of the Valthyrra she knew or a completely new ship.

She noticed almost too late that Venn Saevyn had already begun initiating the start-up of Valthyrra's primary programming. Consherra began to fear that something had gone wrong, however, when the single-lens camera pod only continued to stare aimlessly rather than turn to orient on them.

"Valthyrra Methryn, do you hear me?" Saevyn asked. "How do you feel?"

The camera pod turned at last, the lens rotating slowly as it came around. "I am in perfect operating condition, to the extent that I have so far been able to determine. I have initiated a complete system check.''

Consherra closed her eyes as she sat back in her seat. That voice, a cold, lifeless monotone, was only vaguely recognizable as Valthyrra's.

"Valthyrra, do you recognize either of us?" he asked.

The camera pod rotated around a fraction more. "I regret that I do not know you, but I do of course recognize Consherra, Helm and First Officer of the Methryn.''

"And do you know where you are and what has happened to you?"

Valthyrra seemed to consider that for a moment. "I am in my construction bay on Alkayja Station. I am aware that I have been installed aboard the new carrier, so I must assume that the Methryn has been destroyed. My last memory is of speaking with Commander Velmeran on the bridge. That seems now like a very long time ago."

"That will be enough for now," he told her. "We will speak with you again on the bridge in a few minutes."

Venn Saevyn closed down the terminal, and they withdrew from the core. Consherra hurried to secure the access hatch, lifting the door back into place and locking it down.

"I am actually encouraged," Saevyn remarked. "She initiated a more detailed response to my last question than I had specifically asked. She seems to be curious about the fixtures of her past life, and that may well lead her to investigate her full programming. But we must still take things slowly."

Velmeran and Tregloran followed Venn Keflyn into the small room in a quiet section of the Methryn's infirmary. Dyenlayk, the Methryn's chief medic, was already waiting in the room, standing over the unconscious form that lay in the narrow bed.

"Installing Valthyrra in a new ship gave me the idea," Velmeran explained. "That reminded me of when I first met Venn Keflyn, and she told me that she had been forced to take a new body when she was young."

Tregloran glanced at Venn Keflyn, who looked embarrassed. "I was very indiscreet when I was younger."

Velmeran walked over to stand across the bed from Dyenlayk. "Is she ready?"

The medic nodded. "She seems to be in perfect condition. I see no reason why we should not awaken her."

"Do it, then."

Dyenlayk bent over the inert form and administered a drug through the intravenous connection, then began removing the straps of the wrist unit. "You can talk to her now. That should bring her around."

Velmeran nodded and, with a quick glance at Tregloran, bent over the bed. "Lenna Makayen? Lenna Makayen? Do you know why Scotsmen wear kilts?"

Although she did not open her eyes, a slow, mischievous smile crossed her face. "I have no idea, Commander. Why do Scotsmen wear kilts?"

"Because sheep can hear a zipper from a hundred meters."

Lenna made a face, then opened her eyes and stared up at Velmeran in a very accusing manner. "I'm dead."

"You were. We fixed that," he told her. "We cloned you a whole new body, and Venn Keflyn moved you right inside. It seems that Aldessan do it all the time, so it must be respectable."

"I have no complaints," Lenna insisted. She yawned and stretched, and in the process noticed something that she had not expected. "Four arms! I have four arms! Did you people put me together wrong, or something?"

"Well, we had to clone you a whole new body," Velmeran explained. "Venn Keflyn did say that it does not have to be cloned from your original self, even if that is the usual method. You always did want to be a real Starwolf."

"Yes, but what Starwolf?" she asked, obviously concerned. "I mean, if I am going to go through life looking like someone else, I want to know who."

"Consherra provided the genetic material. We did a little manipulation with the variables, to give you individuality. Tregloran will have to find you a mirror. Venn Keflyn and I have to be getting back to work now."

"Mercy, that was abruptly subtle," Lenna declared. "By the way, what happened?"

"The end of civilization as we knew it," Velmeran said. "You will have to ask Tregloran about that, since I cannot spare the two hours it would take to explain."

Velmeran returned to the nearest lift, taking that to the main port airlock to leave the ship by the most direct route. He was under orders from Venn Saevyn to keep his distance from Valthyrra, for fear that his presence would shock her into possibly damaging her ability to access her damaged programming. He preferred to continue his immediate work from the command sections of the station.

At least the delegation from the former Union had since departed for home. They had arrived as the representatives of a government that had ceased to exist. They had departed as two separate nations, and slightly anxious allies. They also left in the company of Starwolf carriers. Velmeran wanted to take no chances with second thoughts from his retired tyrants.

Sixteen of the immense carrier bays in the lower reaches of the station had been adapted with docking probes and stabilizing brackets for the smaller cruisers, which had already been brought in for modifications. For now the cruisers lay essentially abandoned, their crews dispersed throughout the regular fleet for needed experience . . . and language lessons. Velmeran considered it disgraceful that Kelvessan did not even know their own language, ignoring the fact that Tresdyland was the Aldessan language. His opinion of the Aldessan was far more charitable. Dispersing several thousand Starwolves was somewhat easier with the appearance of the Valcyr, an entire carrier begging for a complete crew.

"One more small miracle," Venn Keflyn commented. "Those that you do not make yourself, you manage to at least instigate very well."

"I am becoming very tired of figuring out how to solve everyone's problems all at once," Velmeran said. "But above all else, I suspect that I have been extremely lucky."

"You won everything when you should have lost everything," Venn Keflyn said. "How did that happen? Were you more careful in your planning than Commander Trace was? Did you make fewer mistakes? Or were you, as you say, simply luckier?"

"I do not like to contemplate that too fully," he answered. "But it was, I think, a combination of all three. We both made the most of what our circumstances allowed. Trace tried to make it a battle of wills, and that threw off his timing at a critical moment. He also trusted too much to the absolute and unquestioned loyalty of people he tried to deceive and use as slaves. He failed to consider the curiosity of Kelvessan, and he really should have known better than that. But above all else. . . ."

Venn Keflyn twitched her ears at him. "Yes?"

Velmeran shrugged. "We were lucky."

Velmeran stepped quietly onto the bridge of the Methryn, his first time since the battle. All of the bridge officers were at their stations, preparing the immense ship for flight. Consoles, monitors, and viewscreens were bright and active. Valthyrra's camera pod was moving quietly from station to station as she supervised the activity. The scene looked just the same as it had for the last twenty years, as if nothing had ever changed. And yet this was not the same ship, and Valthyrra did not look up to greet him as she always did.

Venn Saevyn stood quietly at his side. Valthyrra had not improved in the days since her return to life, remaining dull and machine-like. Although she possessed her full memories of her previous life, those memories in themselves had not yet enabled her to access her full personality. Time was running out. Soon her primary programming would begin to grow with experience into a new personality all its own, and her old programming would be rejected from her memory as incompatible. The time had come that the very shock that they had been avoiding was now her only hope.

Consherra left her station and hurried over to join them. "Everything is ready. The Vardon and the Valcyr are standing by."

Velmeran nodded and stepped further into the bridge. Valthyrra seemed to notice him for the first time, rotating her boom around until her camera pod was hovering only a couple of meters away. "Good day, Venn Saevyn. All of my main systems continue to function in perfect operating condition."

Velmeran thought that it was not Valthyrra's voice at all, it was so bland and even. There seemed to be no emotion within her at all. She was as capable of emotion as ever, but lacking in the experience to know what to do with her world on a personal level. Unable to do anything else, she remained only a machine.

"Valthyrra, do you know who this is?" Venn Saevyn asked.

"Of course. This is Velmeran, Commander of the Methryn and of the Combined Starwolf Fleet," she replied in that precise, slightly eager voice. "They had told me that you have been very busy, Commander. It is good to have you back on the bridge at last."

"How do you feel, Valthyrra?" Velmeran asked.

"I feel . . . I am in perfect operating condition, Commander," she said, reinterpreting his question into simpler terms. "My function as the guiding intelligence of this ship is a very rewarding experience. I enjoy the companionship of other intelligent beings."

Consherra glanced away, and even Venn Saevyn seemed discouraged. Velmeran knew that he would have to try harder. He had left clues embedded within her memories just before she had gone into battle, clues that he now hoped to call upon to shock her programming into operation. If he could only help her to remember how she had felt, the sadness, regret, and fear that she had been experiencing at that most important moment in her life, when she had faced the end of her existence without the certainty of knowing whether she had really ever been alive, or if she had existed only as a very complex machine with the ability to delude itself with the illusion of life.

"Do you remember the last time we spoke together, on the bridge of the old Methryn just before you went into battle?" he said. "Do you remember how very frightened and uncertain you were?"

Valthyrra rotated her camera pod slightly to one side as she struggled with emotions that her primary programming was not advanced enough to handle. "Yes, I remember speaking with you. I remember that I had lost something, but I did not know what it was or where to find it."

"You were looking for your soul," he reminded her. "Do you remember how frightened you were? Feel that fear again. Recall your despair."

"I remember," Valthyrra said softly, then lifted her camera pod in a gesture of pain and despair. "I was never afraid to die, but I was terrified by the thought that I had never lived."

"You were looking for your soul," Velmeran told her, forcing her deeper into the pain of her memories. "Did you find your soul?"

She turned to look at him, the lenses of her camera pod rotating to focus in. "I do not know. If I did know, then I have forgotten."

"You keep your soul in the same place the rest of us have our own," he said, the very same words that he had used during their last meeting. "In the hearts and minds of others. Your spirit is with us. We have kept it safe for you."

"When you see me again, then you will know the truth in that," Valthyrra concluded from her own memories, the very last thing she remembered from her life aboard the old Methryn. She turned aside, and the others stood waiting in silence. After a long moment she lifted her camera pod to an alert attitude and turned to look at them. "Well, why is everyone just standing around looking stupid? I thought we were going for a ride."

"To your stations, everyone," Velmeran said. "Val, do you feel up to it?"

"I feel fine, Commander. All moorings are clear, and all major systems are powered up."

"Whenever you are ready," he told her, then glanced up at her. "It is good to have you back, old friend."

She rotated her camera pod around to look at him. "I am glad to have you back, Commander. It does my soul good."

The Methryn backed smoothly out of her bay, then pivoted around and began to accelerate swiftly away from the station. Moments later, a second vast, dark shape joined her as the Vardon fell in to one side and slightly behind. They were two well-matched ships, silver hulls edged in black with six powerful main drives phasing smoothly. The Valcyr took the position opposite the Vardon seconds later, solid black, her four main drives flaring to match speed with the newer ships. They flew together in a tight "V" formation, moving steadily to light speed and their course to Terra.

Clouds of fighters moved in slowly behind the carriers, moving in a dense, disorganized mass. They separated into two distinct groups, one aligning with the Methryn and the other with the Valcyr, fighters that had been based at the station until they were ready to be brought aboard their ships. Twelve packs had left the Methryn and fifteen returned, their numbers augmented by the Mock Starwolves. All ten packs assigned to the Valcyr were coming home for the first time, the first fighters to see her decks in fifty thousand years, three of new pilots and seven transferred from other ships.

As they moved in beneath the inactive stardrives in the tails of the immense carriers, the crowds of fighters suddenly began to fall into order, nine at a time dropping into the V formation of the packs as they moved in beneath the carriers and moved smoothly into their bays. They were all aboard within a minute, the bay doors closing as the fighters were locked into their racks for starflight.

The three carriers widened their formation, putting a little more distance between themselves as they neared light speed. A deep, golden glow began to grow deep within their stardrives, erupting into sudden flares of tremendous power. The three carriers moved as one into starflight, carried on shafts of brilliant light.